The
BLOOD
THIEF

VOL. 1

The Short Happy Life of Alex Rose

Charles L. Close III

The Blood Thief, Vol. 1: The Short Happy Life of Alex Rose
Published by Blue Crown Bunny
San Diego, CA

First Edition
ISBN (print): 979-8-9993293-0-1
ISBN (e-book): 979-8-9993293-1-8
FICTION / Occult & Supernatural
FICTION / Coming of Age

Publishing management by KLR Literary Management. Cover and interior design by Victoria Wolf, wolfdesignandmarketing.com. All copyrights owned by Charles L. Close III.

QUANTITY PURCHASES: Schools, companies, professional groups, clubs, and other organizations may qualify for special terms when ordering quantities of this title. For information, email chazclosebiz@gmail.com.

This book is dedicated with love to The Great Creator of Being, and all of their Muses. Whatever form they take, and however much light they shed or darkness they conceal with, I am happy and eternally grateful for their inspiration.

And to the memory of the queen, Anne Rice! Thank you for inspiring my fantasies as a kid and making me proud to be LGBT by giving me voices I could relate to. I will treasure the lessons learned from you forever.

ACKNOWLEDGMENTS

TO MY WONDERFUL FAMILY, the Closes, Howards, Wiers, Haworths, Moells, and all the other branches. Your continued support has been a blessing.

Special thanks to my pop, Charlie Close, not only for your financing, but for always supporting my outrageous endeavors and always being my number one fan since I was a kid. Any similarities to your spelling abilities within are lovingly inspired.

To my brother, Collin Close, and Lizzy Ritti, for always being there when I needed some extra love and support.

To Connor Close and Betsy Kelley for your encouragement. Y'all were the first ones I read any part of this book to, and your enthusiasm for it made me feel like I actually might have something going on here.

To Micki Ireland and Jess Haley. Your inspiration while I was writing was a gift, and I wouldn't have had some of my best ideas without you both.

And an extra special thanks to Francisco Mena. Your gift of the rhetoric book all those years ago was a delight, and it helped me to become a better writer. Thank you for always being a true friend.

And to my literary manager, Kirsten "Kiki" Ringer, and editor, Nadara "Nay" Merrill, I am in awe of your knowledge of the industry and your ability to polish up a work of art. Thank you so much for helping me shine. And thank you, Kitty Coy, for bringing us all together.

To all my Funky Monkey, Not Not Down, and More Than Apples and various other loved ones and communities too numerous to mention, you all have been an amazing part of the wonderful story that is life, and I love you to the moon and back for your help along the way.

PROLOGUE

THE FIRSTBORN OF DEATH IS DEAD as a doornail.
Scattered to the wind. If something as supernaturally powerful and
immense as the Firstborn of Death can truly die, that is. I helped
stop it from unleashing death on a catastrophic scale, but I had more
than a hand in what it did, unwittingly or not. That's why I want to
set the record straight. Get my confession out like a good Catholic
boy and hopefully feel absolved in the matter.

I believe the Great Creator of Being—or the Universe, or whatever quantum explanation we have for why anything happens the
way it does—doesn't judge. Because why would you condemn the
things you took the time to create and hopefully have some kind of
love for? I think of my father just before he died and the love that
was written across every inch of his face in that moment, and the
look in his eye that said *I'm here for you no matter what*, and I hope
the way the world truly works reflects that.

The biggest part of it all is forgiving yourself, even if you know you weren't entirely to blame. It's tough for me not to feel guilty about things I was wrapped up in, even when they were perpetuated by abusers and killers who wanted so badly to draw me into their little petty worlds, which they thought were so grand and complex. I wanted to be the good thief! I wanted so badly to come clean and fly straight. I wanted to do the right thing!

So I'm telling this story to shed a little light on events that may seem a little full of gray areas. And I won't lie, the gray areas are where I have always lived. I never had the best moral compass. Or maybe I had a moral compass that always pointed towards what was right, but the waters were so rough in the world that the way I navigated them left people wondering exactly why the master of his fate and captain of his soul would have ever continued along in those seas. All I can say is I was making the best of what I was given.

To tell the whole tale, set the record straight, and clear my good name of Alex Rose, I will have to start from the very beginning to show you how this all was some long, crazy road I was set upon by ghosts and monsters and things that go bump in the night, and how these events were so wound up in my being that it seemed like threads were woven all around me and I could never really see the design on the tapestry until it was all finished and spread out.

I am still trying to do no harm, even though it seems like my life is inextricably geared towards harming others. I want to find atonement and be at one with myself like we are all meant to be, instead of at odds with everything and always fighting, always striving on and on, even though the cause was not always on the side of the angels and the way was full of enough twists and turns to make me lose the path even before I set my feet on it.

So hear me out, as any genuinely guilty person will say to you, because I have a tale to tell you that'll maybe make you have a more sympathetic view of me, even though my reputation in the public's eye isn't what was tarnished. No, this one is more for those I loved and hurt along the way—because those are the ones who really matter to us in the end and who we probably hurt the most with our actions when they aren't as noble as we aspire to be.

For them, I dedicate this telling of my truth, and I hope there is love enough in the world to forgive everyone for what they do. Because a good man once told me it's never too late to turn your life around and do something good with it. And so I write this with that in mind . . .

1.

"WHICH DO YOU PREFER, POP?" I asked my father, A.J., short for Alex Rose Jr., as he drove his tiny little Cayman-green, typical nineties car, Ford Festiva around a tight corner which opened up to the sprawling sapphire-blue horizon of La Jolla Bay, with its glittery diamond sparkles flickering throughout the waters and golden sandy shores. "Good guys or bad guys?"

"What do you mean, Allie Boy?"

"Don't call me Allie!" I groaned. "I'm Alex. Allie is a girl's name."

"Not if you're my Allie *Boy!*" He laughed.

"Quit it," I whined and lightly punched him in the arm. "Girl's name!"

"Hey, no messing with the driver," A.J. said playfully with a smirk. He swerved the car like he was going to go off the road and then whipped it right back on its course down that steep pair of hairpins of a route that was La Jolla Shores Drive. The eucalyptus trees provided dappled shade that made the hot summer day seem almost tolerable in that no-AC-equipped little box of a vehicle. "Hmm . . . good guys."

"Good guys should always win," I stated matter-of-factly with all the hard-earned knowledge that my nine years on that little corner of the world had provided. "But bad guys are more fun to pretend to be."

"But good guys save the day. They protect people. They fight for truth, justice, and the American Way, all the good things."

"But they're so *boring!*"

"As your pop," A.J. said like he was feigning an oath, "I am honor bound to tell you that good guys are the way to go. But . . ." He paused and smiled mischievously at me. "Even grown-ups like to be a little naughty sometimes."

I gazed at all the rich people's houses along the way. I was envious of them but pretended I hated them. The kids from those grand modern palaces always showed off in ways that probably seemed harmless to them and their parents but caused deep scars of shame in me for knowing my father was not cut from the same cloth as their banker fathers and lawyer mothers.

It was the two of us, father and son, against the world, and we didn't even know enough about what our cause was to form a suitable battle cry for it. We lived in the spare bedrooms of a little hippie lady's house who legally changed her name to Windsong. She let A.J. do random work on the place and take care of her when she had had a bit too much to drink and needed a ride for a pack of Capri Slims or a bottle of peach brandy. She was always making the most dazzlingly beautiful signs in her ornate calligraphy script or decking out a bottle in a rainbow of puffy paint that turned a piece of trash into a work of art.

Our neighborhood was full of houses that each repeated a mold—same architecture, different colors of paint. There was a canyon down the road that I was certain was full of dangerous creatures and people bent on murder. It had tons of appliances strewn about the entrance that looked like they had been chewed up by much bigger appliances and left to bleach their bones in the sun. I didn't dare go in there, it seemed more haunted than a graveyard.

We were on our way to our random, sometimes annually, sometimes monthly church excursion. We had our boards strapped to the roof so we could get some surfing in after we did whatever soul-healing that compelled my old man to go into that beautiful jewel of a town called La Jolla and her church down by the beach.

I never liked going there as a kid. The first time I could recall going was on some dreary morning, and all the stained-glass images of martyrdom had been a shock to my five-year-old mind. And then I had to stay still through an hour of songs I didn't know and stand up and sit down at random intervals, in a place so boring it was like I was in school on a weekend. I didn't have a toy to play with and was forced to try to read the few words I knew out of a hymnal, and every time I asked my pop how to pronounce a word, he told me to be quiet.

It was all a little penitential for someone who didn't quite get the concept of penance.

I learned to make the most of my time there though. I could have spent the hour sitting and staring into space, but I had been reading bits of the Bible ever since I could string a couple of letters together. I went to catechism classes every once in a while, enough to get the major sacraments in like Communion and confession, but mostly our religious experiences depended on a whim of A.J.'s when he randomly felt we needed to go. So that day, we were cutting across the fancy town to save our souls before we hit the waves.

He pulled out the dog-eared and dinnerware-stained packet of papers from between the car seat and the parking brake.

"Okay, practice time! Spell blubbery."

"Aww," I whined. "Not the spelling bee! C'mon, it's the weekend!"

"You wanna win it this year, right?"

"Yeah."

"Well, you don't win it without practice. You almost had it last year. Let's go for it this year! Don't settle for second if you know you can bring home the gold!"

I knew he was right. But there were a million things I would rather be doing.

My teacher had a policy where she would let whoever got one hundred percent on the spelling test skip taking the test the following week. And they got to give the test to their classmates. Great incentive, right? Except the student had to take the tests home and grade them on Friday. So I always had the added work on the weekend, and friends who were terrible at spelling would ask me to cut them a little slack, which I knew I couldn't do to the extent they wanted. Maybe a little feigning not being able to decipher their handwriting, but spelling "carpet" with an obvious *k* couldn't be overlooked.

So after all those wasted weekends, spelling was not my idea of a good way to kill time, even if there was nothing better to do in the car than say it, spell it, say it again. I was tired, T-I-R-E-D, tired of spelling.

"C'mon . . ." he coaxed. "We can go get bubble gum ice cream later. Or have Pizza Hut for dinner."

"Personal pan pepperoni? No weird sausage like you eat?"

"Personal pan!" he promised.

"With pepperoni?"

"How could you forget the pepperoni?"

"And money for the arcade games!"

"Let's see you bring home the bacon."

"Humph," I protested, crossing my little arms.

"All right, some money for the arcade," he finally caved. "But *study!*"

"Okay, bring it on!"

The already warm morning sun was heating the car up to a slightly uncomfortable level. I waved my arm out the window to feel the cool breeze on my fingertips, trying to reach out as far as I could, which usually drew a reproach from him, even though we both knew I wouldn't get within a dangerous distance of another car.

"Blubbery," A.J. said, glancing at the word sheet.

I laughed. "Easy as pie."

"So spell it," he said, swerving around a car driving at a crawl.

It was easy to see how the older man driving that slow convertible would have wanted to cruise in Sunday driver fashion. The day was a magical one where the sea felt like it was carrying in new sensations of happiness on the breeze. All that moisture that had collected from every corner of the world by way of the currents was making its way onto our shores and was evaporated into the air in a salty feeling that spread out among those big houses and shops.

There was an underlying current of violence to my mood though. Not a threat of danger from a random crime; this was probably one of the safer neighborhoods in all of San Diego. This was a violence of structures and settings.

Maybe it was the heat, or the restlessness in my soul that even then threatened to come out in random ways that took things from a sulk to a frustrated lashing out. But there was something about being an outsider in places that promised belonging, like this fancy neighborhood was letting us know that the American dream was really a lie and we were fighting our neighbors to see who could collect the most scraps from the bigger tables. That want was instilled in me at that young age and it was pervasive, making even a trip to a beautiful neighborhood by the sea seem like a trial by fire.

All I wanted was to be free from that want.

I felt a twinge of jealousy thinking about how those people were able to feel so good all the time and we only felt the heat and the weariness of stale routine in our neighborhood. We were only up the hill from them and closer to the freeway, with those little houses from an era when someone decided that every new home in Southern California should mimic the rest of the ones in the U.S., in a vastly unoriginal picket fence and ranch-style crowd. I wanted to see all the places they told us about in school books or the ones that blazed larger than life on the screen from the VHS tapes that we picked out from the video store once a week.

But just like that video store, it all had that one beaded curtain room that everyone seemed to say I wasn't allowed to go into even though I could see alluring things calling out from the other side. I knew we weren't supposed to be in those clean and manicured streets of La Jolla, with their bougainvillea and their geometric hedges, just as I wasn't allowed in that back room.

"Blubbery, B-L-U-B-B-E-R-Y, blubbery. Boom," I said.

"Eyaannnnttt!" he squawked, mimicking a game show buzzer for a wrong answer. "Wrong-o!"

"What?! You're kidding."

"Nope."

"Spell it."

"B-L-U-E-B-E-R-R-Y." He smirked proudly.

I sighed. "Pop, that's blueberry."

"No, it's ..." He glanced at the sheet, then back to the road, and then to the sheet again. "Huh."

"Yeah. Blue. Berry. Blueberry. Crazy how the two come together and make one big word. We call those compound words."

"Smart-ass," he said with a smile and a shrug.

I liked that about A.J., nothing really fazed him. I probably would have blushed shades of red that would have made blood from a rose seem pale for making a mistake like that, and he simply grinned and drove on. Even a little smarty-pants kid telling him what's what was nothing to ruin even one second of his day.

"That's what I love about you, son number one," he said. "You're so smart. I know you don't get that from me."

"I'm your only son."

"And that's why you're number one." He elbowed me and then wrapped an arm tight around my neck. I tried to give him a few weak punches to loosen his hold, but he swerved again and said, "No hitting the driver! But seriously, that's what I love about having you for a son. You always find ways to teach me something. And that's why we study. So you can do something good with that wisdom."

"I thought only old people have wisdom," I said, staring up at him in admiration. I loved hearing the compliments, even if they were for something I didn't like doing, like knowing how to spell a word. I was a sucker for that feel-good emotion of getting praise for my meager little triumphs.

"Naw," he dismissed the notion. "You're wiser than yer old man."

"Yeah, but that's not hard," I teased.

We liked to riff off of each other. Windsong said we were two silly boys together, all locker room humor and fart jokes and dead-arms like it was a fraternity of two, only he was supposed to be a patriarch, not a brother. But something about the way we got along was borderline chummy, like we were old pals. We were an island of our own in the turbulent sea that was the world. Everything we did together was our own calm little chaos while the rest swirled and flowed by around us.

He laughed. "All right, don't start getting a little big for yer britches, tryna tell me what's what. But serious, you're one sharp cookie, and I want you to do something that I never did. Go ta college one day, make something of yourself. You can be and do anything you want. I never could. That's why I want that for you. I promised yer ma before she went to Heaven that I would do that, and I'm a man 'a my word."

At the mention of my mom, I had a flash of my last memory of her, one of the only ones I had before she passed away. I must have been a little older than two, no more than three. I was trying to see her in a big hospital bed, and people wouldn't let me in. I cried and cried, reaching out my hands, but an adult I can't recall more than the strong arms of wouldn't let me go any farther. A.J. was right next to her. Someone kept shouting to get me away, and I ran towards her, but they caught me and their grip was too strong.

I was way too young to appreciate the sentiment of A.J.'s words at the time, that noble calling of trying to leave the world a better place and give your children something they can carry on long after you're gone. I was too busy with my own little cares. I felt my mother had abandoned us, even though she had no say in the matter.

There was always a resentment I carried in my heart at the world that could do such cruel things to people, and because of that, I think I didn't fully, properly appreciate that little love that A.J. and I had. I didn't appreciate his plans for me. I didn't want college, and I didn't want things mapped out for me. I wanted an ultimate and thrilling experience to break up the monotony, a brilliant moment to make everything feel real and not full of dull pain and sadness that would turn into frustration at the drop of a hat.

We cruised up to the church playing Nirvana from the local radio station, 91X, at full blast, and everyone in the church parking lot shot sideways glares at us until A.J. sheepishly turned down the wailing chorus of Kurt Cobain belting out lyrics that were completely unintelligible to me but spoke to something primal and resonant that I clicked with.

Our church was called Mary, Star of the Sea, and the name of it sounded very glamorous to me. The building was a little mission-style gem with big murals all over the frontward facade. The painting looked like a Hollywood premier was taking place in it, with angels on either side of the serene little Mother of Our Lord as she hovered above rippling stylized waves in a mythological body of water that existed only in the most intimate of dreams and on that wall.

That art was the one thing I grew to love about the church. The whole building was filled with symbols to be discovered everywhere you looked. I saw them as a comic book display of stories and hieroglyphs that begged me to figure out what they meant.

There were hints of blood on the figures on the walls, enough to elicit my morbid curiosity without scaring me too much. These figures were of people who knew how to suffer and had the strangest, most indecipherable expressions on their faces while they did it. I would have been wailing in horror with those nails in my hands and feet, but Jesus was patient and had a look about him like he could not be moved to be concerned with such a trifling matter.

We were about five minutes late as we hurried into the crowded building, but I saw the old woman again on my way in. Not a regular old woman, but a dead one. She was crying and asking for people to pray for her. She was pale like the people in the washed-out color photos I saw in a dust-covered book from Windsong's shelf, where the shades were distinct, but they weren't matching what I knew they should be if they were anything real and under the sun. She had on a shawl covering her hair up like she was going for a ride in a convertible in an old 1950s movie.

I tried not to stare, because when I stared too long, they oftentimes took it as an invitation to try and talk to me, and I definitely did not want her coming up to me and yakking away. It was hard to pretend to be normal under the best of circumstances, and I certainly didn't want some aggrieved spirit moaning in my ear and driving me mad.

"Why won't anyone pray for me?" she wailed in a voice that only I could hear. "I only had one mass in my name, and that's all it would take is a few prayers. Just say the rosary for me. Not even my own family would do that, and where are they now? No one knows, but they should have come around by now. I don't know where they are. I thought I raised them better . . ."

I caught one last glance at her as we entered through the big doors and slipped into a pew at the end. She pleaded with a random passerby who simply walked right through her. He shuddered involuntarily, without realizing why he did so. A.J. caught me staring and narrowed his eyes at me as if he was suspicious of something, but then he only smiled and tousled my hair.

We went through the mass, solemn as good little Catholics could be, but we added our own little smart-ass flair to it. The priest went into a strange tangent in his sermon, mentioning the church's fundraising initiative where they were asking for people to contribute more than their usual amount.

"I know there have been rumors about this being used for the legal funds for a priest who has been disciplined for inappropriate behavior," he said. "I want to make sure you know that is *not* what the funds are for. They are for the diocese, not legal funds for a priest. Despite what gossip you might have heard, this is for the community, *not* a priest."

"Kinda makes ya wonder . . ." A.J. snickered.

"Dare me to go up to him after mass and say 'Father, ya know, between you 'n me . . . maybe just a little for the priest's legal troubles, knowwut I'm sayin'?'" I said, giving a little theatrical wink.

"Do it! I dare ya."

We both erupted into muffled peals of laughter, and the people around us shushed us and darted little glares in our direction. That only made us laugh harder until we were red in the face and had to take a breath and let it out.

"Don't actually do it," A.J. said, knowing that I might seriously be inclined to take things a bit far. He faked a stern look, and we giggled a bit more.

We finally resumed our solemn expressions and got back to our proper motions and worship. I think we both reasoned that the Lord doth have a sense of humor and we were his opening act in his stand-up routine.

Once we were out of church, we loosened up our collars and rolled up our sleeves.

"Surfing?" A.J. asked.

"We surf," I concurred.

We rolled out to our favorite spot at La Jolla Shores. Big enough waves to have fun on, but not so huge that A.J. would get knocked off his old man board, a big yellow monstrosity we called the Short Bus that he bought off of his friend Tommy.

The early afternoon sun was pouring down hard on us, but the constant batter of cool blue water that washed over our skin and left us covered in a misty spray when we paddled over each wave made it feel like the ocean was a perfect womblike kind of stasis that kept us between the extremes in temperature in perfect chaotic comfort.

Even when we weren't catching a great ride on in, I loved it out there. Just sitting on the board swaying to the rhythm and flow of the water, my California tan coming in in a shade of golden brown. I swore I could sense the ripples starting all the way somewhere over in Japan as they swelled up and tore our way, eventually pounding on our little shores of San Diego. I smiled, listening to the crashing sounds of that energy making contact with soft sands.

"So I was talking to Father Sheslo the other day," A.J. began.

Father Sheslo was one of the two priests who said mass on a regular basis at our church. He was a tall older man with thick white hair and a severe-set expression that could change into a beaming smile or a chuckle when he pleased. I felt you had to work for those, but that's how you knew he loved you.

"You know what he said? That Catholic means 'universal.' And I said, 'Well if that's so, how come everyone isn't Catholic, why are there Jews and Protestants and all the others?'"

I had the vaguest impression of what that meant. We'd cele-brated Hanukkah once with a Jewish family in kindergarten, and

I got into it with a little punk-ass kid in my class that mouthed off to me when I told him I was Catholic. I didn't feel the need to justify the Church and its teachings, but he pointedly said he was a Christian, and so I pointed out that Catholics were Christians too, and he insisted that they were not.

I wound up tussling with him on the playground mostly because I didn't appreciate being called a liar by someone with more illusions of superiority than he had original thoughts. He got a few good hits in that made my braces cut into my cheek, so I threw sand in his eyes and kicked him in the shins before running off.

I knew it wasn't a fair way to fight, but fair fights always got my ass kicked.

"Because that's how their families were raised?" I ventured.

"Nope. Father Sheslo said that even though not everyone's Catholic, Jesus's message is for everyone. Anyone can hear those words that he said and find something that hits home with them. Because he was all about love and peace and all that good stuff."

I was barely paying attention to him. A wave had formed, and a handful of other surfers were trying to paddle as hard as they could to catch it, but it was too soon for them to make it. I knew I would be in that sweet spot if I could start paddling, so I swung my board around.

"Whoops, go for it! Get it!" A.J. hollered after me.

I took off and dug into the water with my hands and then swung them behind me, as fiercely as if I was trying to tear out a hole in the earth, but it was only shapeless reforming water. A.J. cheered and clapped as I matched the wave's momentum. He caught about half as many waves as I did, but he was more excited about seeing me have fun out there than he was to try and display any athletic prowess.

I hopped up onto my board in one quick dance move of a motion. One second I was lying down on it, and the next, I kicked knees under and popped onto my feet like I was walking on the surface of a thundering storm cloud of salt water and energy. My board was an extension of my determined little boy will and strength that I rode all the way in to shore, where I hopped off and ran alongside it until I came to a stop with my toes in the muddy dark grains of sand.

I picked up my board and immediately paddled back out to A.J.

"Did you see me?" I asked when I reached him. My arms were exhausted, but they felt powerful in the way straining muscles makes you aware of how close you can take yourself to your limits and come back from the brink.

"Sure did. Gonna start calling you Duke out there!"

"I sometimes fall off my board trying to stand up. I go over the falls and then get too far in the front, but that time I was on a perfect ride and I stood right up and I rode it all the way to the shore. Didja see it!?"

"Sure did! It's because you practice. Toldya it pays off."

"And I'm getting stronger!"

"From practicing."

He gave me a high five, and we turned back to face the horizon, scoping out more waves. We sat on our boards and kept our eyes on the tiny ripples forming in the water that might turn into something promising.

"Thank you for coming to church with me," A.J. said. "I know it's not your favorite thing to do on the weekend. But I need it from time to time, and I'm glad to have you with me."

"I'm happy to make you glad," I said.

"What's your favorite story in the Bible?"

I thought about it for a second, staring at the vast and radiant blue sea for a shred of unexpected inspiration. I glanced at my board and the answer occurred to me. "I always liked Noah's ark. When I was a kindergartener, I used to read the book with the pictures of it in the doctor's office. I liked how he saved all the animals. He knew something bad was going to happen to them, so he did what he could to save them."

"You always did love animals. You were even smart as a little kid. You were practically a baby and you knew all about animals I never even knew existed. I hadta look a coupla them up, ta see if you weren't making them up. And you never did. It was all facts right outta your brain."

"I have a good memory."

"*Good* memory?" He laughed. "You're like a little computer. I gotta watch my language and all around ya, make sure you don't pick up bad words, because I always knew you'd repeat them if you heard 'em outta me."

I smiled at his praise and soaked it all in same as I did that sunshine. I might as well have been a happy microscopic plant in that ocean, photosynthesizing that praise of his and growing from it, feeding off of it.

"My favorite story in the Bible is the one about the good thief, the one who Jesus saves on the cross by letting him into Paradise. Now, I don't know how it all goes when we push up daisies, but promise me one thing, that at my funeral you'll play 'You Can't Always Get What You Want' by the Stones, like they do in *The Big Chill*."

I wasn't familiar at all with his old movie but was vaguely familiar with the Bible story. Three people were crucified up there that day, two on either side of the Lord. And one thief mocked Jesus, but the good thief rebuked him for doing so. It was one of the few stories that made a certain kind of sense to me without them having to explain it.

It seemed like a dick move to be teasing someone who was in the same predicament as you were and who didn't really deserve to be up there anyways. I didn't think thieving deserved execution either though. Maybe a few hours of community service, but they probably didn't have good parole officers back in the day.

"Father Sheslo was talking to me about it, and you know what he said?" A.J. asked.

"Huh-uh," I shrugged.

"He said that story tells you there isn't anyone out there that can't be redeemed." He sighed and gazed off into the sea, probably as relaxed by the continuous motion of the water as I was. "I asked Father Sheslo, 'Even Hitler?' And he said, 'Even Hitler.' That means there isn't anything so bad that we can't be forgiven for it. That it's never too late to turn your life around and do something good with it."

"It's never too late to turn your life around and do something good with it," I repeated.

I liked the sound of that. I always carried a feeling of guilt with me, and not simply in a Catholic way. Like maybe if I had loved my mother harder, she would still be around. Or if I had tried to be a better person to the other kids at school, things would be easier for A.J. and me.

No more scrambling for money, no more being teased by the kids at school for eating PB&J on a hotdog bun because it was the only bread we had. Those magical thoughts children have that can still be haunting later on when they become a part of their being and have to sort out what they can and can't control.

Because at a certain point, hanging onto all that shame and self-punishment becomes too much, and we have to realize it's not our fault. All we know is that something broke the Edenic bliss we enjoyed at one point and we don't know how it all happened, but something was wrong after and the world was slightly darker than before.

I would have made any promise out there on my tiny board floating in that great big ocean, under that scorching sun, to God and all the angels and saints out there for a shot to turn it all around and do something good with it.

I suddenly started feeling anxious. It had all been such a perfect day with A.J., and I didn't want my good mood to go away and be replaced by worries. I searched around for a sign that everything would be okay, hoping the sun sparkles on the water would be blazing crosses, some vision of Constantine telling me "In this sign thou shalt conquer" or even a few simple words of encouragement. "It's all gonna be okay" would have sufficed. And all I wanted was to conquer my fear and self-doubt, not an empire. That wasn't too much to ask.

I looked up and saw three other surfers trying to get in on the same wave, all paddling out furiously, neck and neck, until one fell back and the other two caught it. I imagined the two who were riding it were Jesus and the good thief, gliding off into sweet salvation. I took it as a minor sign of the fearful symmetry of the universe that could be so full of joy and dread that it left me a little confused and scared so often.

A.J. seemed to sense my frustration and put a soothing hand on my shoulder. "You're already doing something good. All the time. I love all the amazing things you can do, kiddo."

He gazed at me with his big soulful dark brown eyes. Mine were a shade of blue in the center with a hazel ring around them that appeared green under most circumstances but could look grayish blue under the right light or if I wore the right color shirt. They were probably blazingly blue in that water. I thought that green eyes were my coolest, most unique feature, besides the white streak I had in my bangs.

"I love you too, Pop," I said.

"You wanna go get that pizza, then maybe an ice cream?" he asked.

"What about the studying?"

"Call it a down payment on future studying endeavors." He smiled as bright as that sunshine, or so it seemed in my eager childhood-optimistic eyes, anyways.

2.

I DON'T KNOW IF I BELIEVE IN ANYTHING like fate, or that premonitions are valid, but that presentiment of dread seemed to have been not without merit.

The next weekend, A.J. had his friend Blackboard Tommy over, and I was never pleased when those two got together. They would get to drinking, which A.J. usually didn't do around me, and "talk shop," as they called it. It was all part of the work my old man did that he was always so cagey about and not willing to give up any concrete details on.

I would always ask him what he did for a living, and his reply would be "fart around." He did a couple of random odd jobs helping remodel houses here and there, but even as a kid, I knew it wasn't enough to be any kind of gainful, regular employment.

I asked Windsong about it once, and she said, "He does enough to get by for you both and get you what you need. It might not be an honest day's work, but your dad is an honest man who would get you the world if he could."

I still wasn't satisfied. I was like Bluebeard's wife, longing to see what the keyholes in the house would open.

One time, I asked him to come in to my class for the take-your-parent-to-class-day, where everyone brought in their parents and bragged about the cool things that they did. The few kids I did hang out with came with parents in hand and talked about how awesome it was to have a father who was a computer programmer or a mother who was a stock broker. I didn't want to be left out. I didn't even care that I didn't know what A.J. did. I only wanted to say that he was my pop and he's a great friend, and such a funny and fun guy, and I was lucky to have him.

I got chewed out for my troubles, with A.J. saying, "I don't want to come all the way down to your school to rub elbows with a bunch of rich tycoon motherfuckers."

I didn't know it at the time, but he must have been more than a little ashamed of our situation. We lived on a friend's good graces when he wanted to be the breadwinner he always dreamed of being. He could tell I didn't like living in a poor situation while being surrounded by affluence. He wanted that good life. He just didn't know he was a good person and so he did questionable things.

He came to all my plays and all the spelling bees, but he was always way in the back and wanted to skedaddle right after every time. He was uncomfortable around normal people, even though he was incredibly outgoing and funny. Ms. Petri, my teacher, might have even had a bit of a crush on him. She always talked about how she loved it when he came by.

It stung, though, not knowing why my dad didn't want to let me in on parts of his life.

It felt that he had this great side that was opened up to the world, a guy who could chat up any bank teller, cashier, and waitress that we ever happened upon. This guy could make people feel like they were his best friend since elementary school and have them smiling at his every compliment that he knew exactly how to deliver to make them feel as if they were the number one person in the room.

But he wouldn't let me in, and it made me believe that all those strangers and random people were real to him and I wasn't.

So, on the night that Blackboard Tommy came over, I snuck out of my bedroom to see what they were up to. Some random power had given me Pandora's box, and I was determined to see what was inside of it. My curiosity was enough to kill me, and I had every intention of living at least until I could drive a car.

I left the volume up on *Batman: The Movie*, with Michael Keaton and Jack Nicholson, loud enough so it would hide any footsteps and then I pretended to fall asleep. Windsong was already in bed, crashed out after drinking a bottle of her favorite brandy. I tiptoed down the hallway, lay down next to the stairway, and peered through the spindles lining the steps that led to the living room.

A.J. and Blackboard were sitting on the couch, drinking whiskey shots and chasing them with beers. A bunch of peanut shells had been eaten and were being used for a scale model they had made out of Big Mac boxes and drink cups, as they gestured at them and talked heatedly together.

"Just think, A," Blackboard said, "you do this one job with me, you'll be set for a long time! No more livin' in a clapped-out place with the old broad."

"Hey, be nice. Windsong's not some old broad. She's nice enough to take me 'n little Alex in, and we haven't had it so easy since 'is mom passed on."

I was glad A.J. stood up for Windsong, and I wanted to cheer him on for doing so because she was nothing if not the sweetest. But I covered my mouth to remember to keep quiet.

"I'm just sayin', you two'll be able to strike out on yer own."

"I've got big plans of my own," A.J. proudly said.

He stared off wistfully, and I wondered what those plans could possibly be. I wondered if we were going to move, and if we were, where we were going.

"You wanna share 'em?" Blackboard asked.

"Nope." My pop smiled. "They're for me and my boy."

"Whatever. The point is you'll be able to live like a fuckin' king!"

"All right, let's go over this again. We want to make sure this goes exactly as planned."

At that point, Blackboard swigged the last of his beer. When he glanced up, he happened to look in my direction. He might not have even seen me, as I sat motionless, but I panicked and darted back to my room.

"Yo, A.J.," I heard him say as I tried to conceal my scrambling footsteps on the hardwood floor that sounded like they must be louder than beating drums as they betrayed my position and movements.

I didn't know it at the time, but that was one of those pivotal moments, some little event that everything else hinged on, where it could have slid the gears of fate working in one way, or they could have gone on working in another. If I could go back and say to my young deer-in-a-headlight self, "Be still!" things might have worked out differently for me.

I hid under the covers and scrunched my eyes shut tight.

It was definitely not as good an Olivier-level command performance as when I played a reindeer in the Christmas play, because when A.J. came up, he stared at me for a few seconds by the light of the nightlight I still desperately needed to keep the fear of the dark from keeping me awake at night.

I was always afraid of the dark, but I didn't want to admit it. I would lie awake at night thinking that any dusky space in the room could be something malevolent waiting in the shadows with claws of sharpened steel that never dulled after a million and one kills. Every corner held a killer that never slept but managed to find a hiding place away from the light of day before dawn.

After the third night in a row of me keeping A.J. up telling him about the horrible things in my mind that wouldn't let me sleep, he got me the light and put it in my room before I went to sleep without even saying a word about it.

Now, A.J. sat down on the mattress at my feet, the blue frame with its many flecks of paint that I had peeled off creaking under his weight. He gave my leg a squeeze. "What'd you hear, Sport?" he asked, his voice a mixture of sadness and severity.

He hadn't called me that since I was a kid and had insisted on the first day of kindergarten that my name was Alex and I was too old for baby names like that. I think he was trying to keep me a little child in his mind to remember not to be too hard on me. I knew he had a temper and sometimes could fly off the handle when he was upset, but he was always quick to calm down and apologize for his yelling.

This was a time where he was opting for care and consideration, and I wasn't quite sure why, but I knew it was some serious shit. I kept my eyes tightly shut.

"C'mon, buddy," he coaxed. "I know you're awake. You can't kid a kidder."

After realizing he wouldn't leave without talking, I slowly opened my eyes. I tried to stare at my X-Men poster on the wall instead of his sad and penetrating stare. I knew I was going to cry, and I hated it. I believed I was supposed to be stronger or smarter or more mature, and I had failed at those things. He wouldn't say anything about it, I knew that much, and it would ultimately be okay in his eyes, but I wanted to be the young hero who was clever and strong enough to be a part of what my dad was up to. Like if I somehow learned the magic password like "Open sesame," it would open up everything to him, and he would invite me into that strange and enchanted world the adults were all a part of.

I tried with all my too rapidly racing heart to be strong and brave and instead just cried and broke down.

"What do you do out there with Blackboard?" I sobbed. "I know you guys are doing something you shouldn't. That's why you want me to go to bed early when you guys are conspiring." I didn't know if it was conspiring; I had heard the word in a story and it sounded good. I wanted to use a brilliant phrase that would make him know I was worthy of being paid attention to. "You only drink when people like him are around. And then we go to church afterwards every time. Is that why we go?"

He tried to pat me on the back, but I squirmed away. I didn't want comforting gestures like I was some kind of baby. I wanted him to talk to me like a grown-up. I knew I was being taken for someone that wasn't capable of understanding, but I probably could if he would only tell me.

He sighed and stared down at the toy-covered hardwood floor, with its piles of clothes and comics dispersed in random intervals of controlled chaos. "I take you to church because my father and my mother took me to church. I want to teach you right from wrong, but I don't know if I'm good enough at that first part of the equation. Can definitely do wrong though ..."

He gazed off, trying to search for the right words. He was a good talker, but sometimes he wasn't a man of very many words with me. I would try to get him to speak about something serious, and he would trail off and tell a joke or a story.

A lot of his stories were the same old ones, but I loved them the way people love an old classic movie even though they've seen it a thousand times. And I would laugh every time, even though it was always the same few words.

There was something so comfortable about him to me. I could talk about everything or nothing, but I always knew he was listening to whatever dumb things I had to ramble on about. But this time, he didn't have an old joke to tell or a story about his buddies.

"I can teach you all kinds of wrong, but I need a little help with teaching the right," he finally managed to breathe out.

My eyes welled up with tears again, obscuring my vision in a blur of crystalline and reflecting moisture. "So you *are* a bad person?" I almost wasn't able to get that out because of a sob welling up in my throat.

He held me close in a big hug that I attempted to get out of but surrendered to. My tears were making a damp spot on the rolled-up sleeve of his plaid dress shirt.

"I'm a good person," he reassured me. "I wouldn't be anything else for you. It's just that sometimes good people make big mistakes. I'm doing what I can to fix those mistakes."

I had no idea what he meant. It still seemed like some riddle or half-truth. I knew there was something at the center of everything that was going on that was shut out, a labyrinth, but filled with doors that only led to other parts of the outside instead of passages to the center.

"These things I do with Blackboard," he continued, "they are all for something good. You'll see one day. I'll make it up to you, and you'll see that there's a reason why I did what I did."

That wasn't enough though. I had worries and fears piling up faster than any monsters under my bed. Even the ghosts I saw around cemeteries and in certain spots didn't scare me. They were usually little chittering or sobbing things that either pleaded with the living to see them or went about pretending they were still alive and didn't know they had passed on until they saw some car that wasn't from their time, or people talking on phones in the streets, things that didn't square with the world they last knew and confused them into an existential crisis.

But with A.J., each new fear was there on the periphery, snatching at my racing mind with claws that, once sunk in, would not let go, elongated fingers gripping with the strengths of all the unknown.

What if he went to jail? I knew there was no way they would let me stay with Windsong, and I would probably wind up in some foster home with some drooling bully for a bunkmate. I was used to me and A.J., in our little band of brothers, even if we were father and son.

"But why can't you tell me?" I pleaded. "I could help you!"

"No!" he shot back a little too roughly, startling me.

I darted back with eyes wide open in alarm and started crying again. He held me close, his arms feeling bigger than tree trunks to me even though he was a pretty slim man.

In a gentler tone, he said, "No. You're a smart kid, and you need to keep learning so you can be a better man than your old man. I know you're gonna be some kind of brainiac like a CEO or a doctor, *something*, and you'll do me proud. So let me do all the hard work so you can do the good work with your brains."

"Okay," I said. But it wasn't okay. I knew there was something terribly wrong. I had been sensing that nameless thing for a while, and his denials only confirmed all my suspicions.

There's something about when a kid can see a grown-up is afraid and can't quite hide it. It makes the child feel so utterly floored, because they know if this is something that can make the world feel so big and unforgiving to an adult who is there to protect you, then you're basically fucked if it should ever decide to come after you as well.

"Everything all right in there, A?" Blackboard hollered up the stairs.

"I'm gonna get back to Blackboard," he said. "You get to sleep. For real this time, no TV."

"No!" I almost choked in my sobs. "Please don't leave me!"

"I've got to do some business with him. It's important stuff."

"But aren't I important to you?" I demanded, gripping his sleeve.

He grabbed me tightly by the wrist and gently loosened my fingers. "Don't you forget it," he said. "You'll see. One day I'll show you why I do what I do, and it'll all make sense to you. You'll have a life I couldn't have but always wanted. Just wait and see."

After he left my room to me and my nightlight, I cried until I didn't have any energy left, hugging my toy rabbit Fifi. Jose, my swim instructor, kindly gave him to me in Boy Scout camp at Hual-Cu-Cuish when I cried there nonstop. Jose let me sleep with Fifi because that fluffy toy calmed me, and he said that his friend couldn't have a better home with anyone else.

I hated that it took childish things to calm me down because I thought that was the reason why A.J. didn't want to include me in what he was working on. That I was an immature and weak baby who needed toys and cried all night when he should have been a braver version of his little self who never made mistakes and always was as useful as anyone who needed a helping hand could ask for.

I threw Fifi across the room but got sad when I saw his cute, smiling stuffed animal face and wondered how I could ever be so cruel to something so loving. So I picked him up, caressed him, and hugged his broad chest and petted his silky soft rabbit ears.

I don't know when sleep overtook me, but I soon drifted into a restless one filled with strange dreams.

3.

I DREAMT MY POP WAS HIDDEN somewhere in a house like ours, but it wasn't ours.

It was the same style of house, only it had a massive eucalyptus tree—one of those giants that grows everywhere in California but isn't from there—reaching up through the center of it like a huge treehouse. The house was in a terrible state of disrepair, with the moldings falling off in chunks and doors hanging off of their hinges. Big flecks of paint, the size of a Nerf football, were peeling off in geometric shaped patches.

I was flying up over the house as easy as Peter Pan did, but my thoughts were anything but happy; they were full of anxiety.

I was searching for something but couldn't figure out what it was, and that caused me terrible pain. Every window I peeked in was to a room full of nothing but furniture and cluttered things. Every room had no one in it, none of the love I was used to, and despite the disorder was an empty space with no meaning to it.

Flying through every room in the house wasn't helping me get what I wanted; I couldn't find A.J. anywhere. At first, I didn't know he was the one I was looking for, but when it became apparent that he wasn't helping me out with what I needed to find, I realized it was him I was frantically seeking all along.

I flew down to the basement. Our house didn't have one, but this one did.

A basement would have been such an essential part of a normal house, at least according to TV, and I always thought I wanted one, but this one was frightening. It smelled old and damp, the scent of things that had been decaying underneath it longer than houses had been around, in a prehistoric stratum of life feeding on death.

The great tree was growing up out of it, its roots sunk into the dirty, teeming ground. Squeezing the life out of all the dirty, crawling things that squirmed about. Twining throughout an entire dirti-er-than-dirt substrate.

I refused to alight on that ground, because I knew it could drag me down into it.

My voice broke as I tried to call out for A.J., and a group of people who weren't people were all waiting inside the corridors of the house. I knew if I drew their attention, it would mean danger, maybe even death. The People Who Weren't People weren't even visible, but I somehow knew they all had pale skin and blue eyes that could see through walls and ears that could hear a mouse scurrying about. They could even hear the light and noiseless gestures I made as I glided about on the wind.

Each and every one of them slowly came crawling throughout the house, sliding around corners and curving their bodies around doorframes as if the bones in their slender forms could bend in the frightening and hypnotic ways that reptiles do as they search for prey. They scratched along the walls as they traveled, not because they were habitually noisy, but because they wanted to proudly announce that they were the things in the night to be feared and that they would indeed get you and there was nothing you could do about it.

They all had the rapt attention to their quarry that a fairytale monster had on its way to devour the hero of a story. And I was that hero, the child in that story, only I had no breadcrumb trails to follow back, and it was long past midnight and all the fairy godmothers had long since gone to bed, leaving pumpkins galore in their wake and me crying eyes out but not daring to make a sound.

Fee, fi, fo, fum, I smell the blood of an Englishman . . .

An involuntary shudder coursed through my bones at the horrible sounds they made as they came laughing and chittering down the halls, always downward, in a continuous spiral, as fluid as water flowing down a drain. Bloodshot whites surrounded their pale blue eyes, giving them a tired appearance, even though their predatory movements were always alert, always searching.

The first one was knocking at the door to the basement, scratching with claws of an unimaginably compact density.

I wanted to shout out, scream, so someone, anyone, would come to my rescue. But even my breaths, held in with a hand over my mouth, were enough to send them into frenzied motions that I could tell were taking place on the other side of the door and throughout the walls. The tension was mounting and I wanted to hide, but the ground would drag me down into it if I didn't stay afloat.

More and more came.

My invisible tormentors became a flood on the other side of the door. It barely held them back, as it comically bulged on its dream-material hinges in a bow shape, curving to an impossible cartoon parabola of strain, only there was nothing hilarious about it, only jaws and claws, and glowing eyes.

"Allie!" they called, using the name I hated in a chorus that sounded mocking but strangely familiar, like they knew everything about me and were waiting for me to join them in their ghastly invitations to some strange fellowship of terror and fear.

And oddly enough, I was tempted, tantalizingly curious as to what exactly they had to offer. On the other side of that door were taboos broken and permissions granted. Limits lifted and dark lessons that only true citizens of the night could teach.

I almost shouted out "Here I am!" Almost gave in to their pleas and their offers.

Almost.

And then I woke up and sat up in my bed.

4.

IT WAS VERY MUCH PAST MIDNIGHT, well into the witching hour moments of the darkest parts of the nocturnal cycle, when shadows take on new hidden meanings in a well of emotions and only those with strange business are up and about. I decided I was going to do something brave. I was going to go down to the one place that scared me more than anywhere else on Earth and prove I was a force to be reckoned with, or so I thought.

I was going to go down to the canyons at night.

I can't say what compelled me to do it, because even now I feel that there was something otherworldly that drew me to such a mad idea that night. It was as if I was pulled by some unnatural thread of destiny that was attached to some ends I couldn't see, with frightening deities tugging at the frayed bits as they were deciding where and when to cut it.

From the feel of the house, I knew that no one was stirring; the usual murmurs of activity weren't present. Only the television downstairs was making its noisy efforts at entertainment, but somehow

I knew that its intended audience, my pop and Blackboard, was crashed out on the couches.

Slowly, I lifted my feet out of the covers and lowered them onto the wood floor, cold lacquered surface connecting to the pads of my feet and making shivers go down the rest of me.

What compelled me to do what I did that night, I can't rightly say.

Maybe I had the need to get the hell out of that house. Maybe I wanted to prove that I was as brave as I hoped I could be. Maybe there was something at work in my soul that I just couldn't explain.

I pulled my jeans up off the floor and put them on over my pajama bottoms, and then opened up my window. I sat up on the sill and dangled my feet out of the room. Glancing back towards my stuffed animals and toys, I imagined I could see beyond that into the rest of the house to the deeply sleeping Windsong and A.J., my troublesome but troubled pop, and gave them all the slightest of nods.

And then after saying goodbye to all my childhood loves and cares, I hopped out into that cold night.

I moved slow as the moon crossing the night sky traveled her rounds. Each step was carefully applied to make it not sound like there was any new creaking pressure on the overhang that covered the porch beneath my window as I crawled along that rooftop, all crouching low like a spider, because I thought from movies that that's the best way to slink about.

After making it to the edge, I slid over it and hooked my feet onto the metal latticework with its vines of Mexican blood-flower twining around it. The vines tangled around my toes and I had to shake my feet out of them, making the ruckus I was hoping to avoid. Nature wasn't about to betray me, though, and I wound my way through the plants, gripping the metal through their snarling embraces.

The climb was a success in quiet maneuvering, and I hopped off at the bottom and glanced around. Not a creature was stirring inside the house, like in the Christmas poem. I tried to think of times like that, happier ones of holidays and family togetherness to ease me and my troubled thoughts.

I quietly scampered around coiled up hoses and avoided strewn about gardening tools. Most of the pitfalls of the yard I knew from playing about in it afternoon after afternoon, and the full moon illuminated all the rest. The big test was the massive scraping wooden gate.

The past summer, I had finally grown to a height where I could easily reach up and pop the latch, but that was usually accompanied by a clunk that could wake the dog of my neighbor, Mr. Wagner, and set him to barking. I gave myself the boost I needed off the trim of the wood gate and pushed at the latch. It was stuck. I tried again, and finally popped it up with a jarring screech.

My heart was racing; I could feel it in my ears. I paused and waited, seeing if anyone came outside. No barks were heard, and no screen doors were sliding open.

Luckily, the dog was in a deep sleep, chasing rabbits or whatever his mind went to, probably dreams of him being a yappy grouch, same as he was all day long.

Eeeeekkkk, went the gate slowly as it dragged along, scraping in protest to my plans of escape. I was running on solid willpower and determination to get away from that place and face the unknown, even though the unknown was terrifying enough to make me run back up that floral latticework with its tangles of vines that snag things in their grasp and into a house where I knew trouble and bad things were hatching that I wanted no part of.

After carefully pushing the door back enough so it wouldn't be wide open, I walked off down that moonlit road. I kept off the sidewalks and stuck mostly to lawns, hoping not to be seen by anyone. I was old enough to know that not too many people would be awake at this hour, but anyone who saw me would probably immediately call the cops. All it would take was a nosy old lady peeking out or some man going to the bathroom in the middle of the night to give the game away.

The full moon was half covered by stray clouds, all flat on the bottom but billowing up like dark midair mountains. They sailed about through the night, painting it through with a sense of the extraordinary and the dreadful.

A car came cruising down the street, and I ran behind some trash cans out on a driveway and squatted down to avoid being seen peering up over the edge of the plastic Rubbermaid lids.

I passed by Alicia Jeffrey's house, our neighbor who used to give me candy corn from a crystal dish every time I visited. Her home was also the former and current dwelling of Orville and Mary Smith, unbeknownst to her. Ms. Jeffrey bought the house after they both passed away. They had been married for over sixty years and died in their eighties. They loved each other so much that it only seemed natural one wasn't far behind the other in enjoying the afterlife.

Those ghosts liked to chatter on and on about the weather and how perfect it always was, which was all rather pedestrian behavior for ghosts. But every so often, they would let some really fascinating historical detail slip in their conversations. She told me how Orville was stationed as a cook in the navy in Pearl Harbor when the Japanese bombed it, and he barely escaped drowning aboard the Arizona. He couldn't save his friend Billy, who was Mary's little brother, and that's how they met, when he attended Billy's funeral. Or they would talk about how they remembered hearing about the Titanic sinking in the papers when they were kids.

The Smiths were sitting in their usual spots on the lounge on the front porch as I walked past their house with the red door. "Where ya goin', pumpkin?" Mary asked. I gave her the gesture of quiet with a finger over my lips and the sternest expression, letting them know precisely how serious I was. Nobody could hear her besides me anyways, but I wasn't about to holler back at her.

She looked as if she was about to say something in protest about a young boy walking alone out at night but thought better of it.

As I made it to the end of the block where the houses turned into empty lots, I felt safer from the eyes of the neighbors, but became afraid of the eyes of what was in the dark. The road dead-ended up a ways and dropped down into a creek bed that almost never had any water in it, but enough of a forest cover to make it a dense place where night was never darker, and anything could be lurking about, ready to carry me away if I dared to set foot in it after sunset.

Every worry I ever had about being kidnapped, killed, or torn apart originated from this place. I knew that animals of all kinds, and people who never slept but had beds all the same, could be in wait. All I had to do was stumble upon them and they would swarm about.

A.J. took me to see the life-size tyrannosaurus rex at the natural history museum when I was a preschooler, and I screamed the whole time because I knew that beasts such as that were made to kill and I knew they were real. And this place I was walking towards had seen them all, ancient and recent, right by my own home, hiding the dark things in the daytime until it was their time to ascend and rule the night.

I knew that Nature had made things that murdered long before Cain came about and killed his own brother. Her hands were bloody way before man ever had the chance to invent tools of his own to make blood flow with greater ease.

Ghosts didn't scare me; they were only after attention and maybe could make some harmless mischief. The animals and humans that stalked about down here could harm your body, and that was pain I never wanted to endure. They were out to take something so innocent as a child and make his precious dreams end in one night with a flick of a wrist or a snap of a jaw. They were after innocence, which made them go wild with desire, and hungry for blood.

The entire place scared the shit out of me, but I was determined to be independent. I was venturing out; I was brave. I was somebody who was strong enough to help others, and maybe my father too, if he'd only let me.

The path leading down into the canyon was the real test. Here was the heart-pounding chill of terra incognita. Off the map of civilization. Here be dragons. Beware the call of the sirens. The dirt path down was a silver thread in the moonlight, winding into a maze of oaks and cottonwoods that grew up around creek beds and left cover where there ordinarily wouldn't be any in the dry Mediterranean climate of San Diego. Short and broken branches shot out like amputated limbs, reaching with fingerless hands for their other bits and pieces. Garbage surrounded an old couch plopped in front of the entrance to the canyon like a giant turtle, immobile and timeless. The place was a cauldron of anxiety and unknown, and I was determined to walk straight into it.

I stepped onto the slippery crunch of the crumbling dirt and sliding gravel. My bare feet were tough and calloused enough from years of roaming around shoeless like some feral changeling of a wild child, but I stepped on a patch of goat heads, those little caltrop stickers that grew rampantly about in our fields and were strong enough to pop a bike tire.

Jumping up, startled and in pain all over, I tried to assess what was happening. I brought my weight down on that foot again, sending the thorns deeper, and then lost my footing and fell to my knees. The plant was huge, and falling on it drove several more of the pointy little devil stickers into my knees and the palms of my hands. I lay there for a second, a whimpering, blubbering mess, not letting a single tear drop from my eyes out of pure spite against the world, not letting it bow me down. I then began the excruciating process of pulling the thorns out.

"Fuck!" I howled and almost covered my mouth as if in shame, but then I realized no adults were around, and I said it all the more. "Fuck! Fuck! Oooooohhhh fuck!" I went as I pulled all the little bastards out.

The way was already trying to tell me not to go into it, and I was still determined to soldier on. I tried to hold back the tears, embarrassed and wondering what I was doing pretending to be a grown-up.

The moon sparkled its beams from behind the clouds to lend a little light to my task of pulling each one out. I could see drops of blood trickling out of the holes they left behind even in the dark.

"I see you!" I called to the moon. I smiled at her despite the pain and bared my white teeth to match her brilliance. I wanted to be like Peter Pan must have been, with no rules of the day and the freedom of the night as my guide. I knew there were dangerous things out there, but I could bring the danger too, because nothing is more dangerous than being young and acting as if nothing can hold you back. You're a hurricane and a half of natural disaster fury, taking everything pent up and letting it out in waves of emotion.

After I pulled out the last one, I gingerly stepped on the ground, feeling for any more painful bits of enemy vegetation and walked on.

I tried to hum a song, but then thought I would draw the attention of something I was afraid of. I loved to make up little rhymes and songs as I went about anything I did. Insane amounts of noisy and overpowering thoughts were always racing through my young mind, and I had no control over them. But if I worked words into the shape I wanted them to be in my mind, it convinced me that the world made slightly more sense. My heart was beating too fast to try to keep a tune up, and the thoughts were all racing about wildly.

As I rounded a corner, I realized by the light of the moon glinting off of a huge pair of eyes that I was face-to-face with a coyote. I froze and stared into the eyes of what I had imagined was to be the cause of my death on so many nights. We had lost cat after cat to these savage creatures, with only hair patches around the yard or a single solitary bone licked completely clean of all flesh to tell the tale. I had lain awake at night several times, listening to their squawking laughter as they communicated with each other and roamed the streets.

Instead of screaming at him like I desperately wanted, I stared in mute fascination, cocking my head and taking in his silk-in-the-moonlight shaggy fur as his big ears perked up and he stared right back. He seemed to be questioning me with his gaze, as if wondering if I was slightly mad for being out here in his world.

And maybe I was, because something about that creature made me want to reach out and touch it, scratch him right underneath those terrible jaws of his, where the tongue was hanging out at the moment but the teeth could turn to razors in a heartbeat. I knew

I shouldn't, but I wanted to so badly. And so I just stared at him, trickster death of that canyon, and kindred spirit.

I looked death in the eye and said, "Not today." And then he walked off, scampering into the bushes and blending right back in with the rest of the dark and hidden things.

Feeling much braver than before, I wandered down into a clearing at the bottom of the canyon near some old railroad tracks with big darkly rusted beams. Random bits of old furniture and appliances were scattered about, the detritus of a society that wastes a lot and wants to conserve not, torn apart by tramps and kids.

The grass moved in waves of bluish silver under the moonlight that whistled and rippled in a steady, calming susurration as the wind blew through it. The night was alive in ways that the daytime could never quite match, with every inch of terrain I bounded over having hidden facets to it that wanted to twist my ankles or send a snake out to bite.

Scanning the area, I picked up a rock, tossed it, and watched as it flew off into the dark. Instead of a light thump, I heard a loud and heavy thud that sounded like something much bigger than my rock had fallen from a great height. It was followed by an angry scream, shriller than a harpy who had found its lover with another in bed and wanted to tear them both apart. I froze and wondered if it was my coyote finding something small and helpless to eat.

Even though my fear was gripping my heart and my legs were threatening to stop working, I went to see what it was.

In the distance were two dark forms lying next to each other on the ground. I froze, silent and alert. Panicked thoughts went through my mind, but I was strangely, calmly processing them without flying to any hasty conclusions.

Some instinct told me I should turn tail and run, but I wasn't about to back down. I had come this far, and I couldn't turn from a challenge even if my courage was threatening to drop right out of the soles of my feet and run screaming all the way back home. I was trapped between two strong, pulling forces like Odysseus between Scylla and Charybdis. I had a strong urge to see what the forms on the ground were, and that glimmer of curiosity pulled me one way. The other pull was fear, weighing me down and threatening to drag me back the other way.

That tension was threatening to consume me, in something as brutal as a physical pain but shouting with a strange and foreign voice in my head that was clamoring to be heard over my own thoughts even though it wasn't making a lick of sense. Just a scream in my mind that I was afraid of letting out into the world, because I knew if I did, I would never stop that throat lashing yell, which would eventually drown out all other sound, every pleasant melody or delightful utterance, until I couldn't hear or speak anymore.

If I looked closely into that moonlit field, I swore I could almost see a barrier, a line drawn in the sand. On one side was me facing my fears and being brave at all costs, and on the other was the shame of not being able to look danger in the eye and tell it I wasn't going to flinch a muscle. But it was more than that; I realized a real voice that only I could hear was commanding me to come to it. Some presence without words, that demanded I come and see to it that it wasn't left alone, see that it was taken care of. Some desperate need was calling to me and I found it hard to resist.

I took a step forward and then one more, each harder to manage than the last. Each footstep was harder to take than if I was walking up to the doors of the castle where the giant lived, knowing he had teeth that ground up bones and arms that could rip a child in half as easily as I could tear off bits of construction paper for an art project.

Fee, fi, fo, fum.

The path into that clearing seemed so long that it could very well have been the one leading to the center of the world, the one I always tried to dig to in the sand at the beach when I was younger. Except those steps were tiny and led to nowhere but sand. These steps were towards a nameless, shapeless feeling of dread that was deeper than any hole I could dig.

As I got closer, the clouds gathered and darkened the night sky, making it even harder to see the scene before me.

Being interested in the occult and the supernatural because I was hoping for answers to everything about the ghosts I saw, I had read a little bit of Dante in a book from the library. The book didn't have any practical advice, only beautiful poetry and the engravings of Gustave Dore, with their dramatic darks and lights contrasting in wonderfully imagined scenes of dread and torture that were enough to leave me reading at the library until the kind librarian told me it was time to check out my books and go home.

That gate to Hell and those lines—"Abandon all hope, ye who enter here"—were enough to make me afraid for my poor soul in a very Catholic way that left me wondering if sin actually existed, something that could seep out into the world and infect what it touches, damning people as it went along.

Those worries were very real to me as I walked up to that clearing under the starry sky. I was certain I would be tainted by a miasma that once unleashed could damn a child even at a young age, where reason was newly forming and making sense of the world was a struggle. Barely time to have done anything wrong, but still damned by chance and actions. It was such a horrid thought to tell children that kind of thing—I knew it even at that age—but that didn't mean I didn't have a sneaking suspicion that it could happen if I wasn't careful.

As I finally got close enough, I saw one of the shapes was a man lying on the ground. I say man because he had on a torn leather jacket over his heavyset frame and big black boots, but maybe the most part of a man is more accurate, because as I stared at him under that full moonlight, I could see his head was gone.

Something had ripped it off, and a gaping stump, all slashed and torn with bits of bone sticking out sharp as jagged spurs stared at me. Dark blood pooled around the neck wound, a wide puddle, mixing with the dirt and coating random stalks of the dried grass. His tattered clothing revealed a mass of open wounds. I was pretty sure, even at that young age, that many of them would have been enough to kill a person before the decapitation was necessary. I almost turned around to run, but the voice in my mind urgently begged me to stay. I noticed a motion out of the corner of my eye— the man's hands were writhing.

His fingers reflexively grasped like they were reaching for something, but they only scratched in the dirt. The hand was as shivery as mine would be on a freezing winter day, even though it was probably no cooler than sixty degrees out on that spring night. The leg was moving too, the way my pop's legs did when he fell asleep on the couch and had one of his muscle spasms in his sleep. The corpse's leg kicked about but couldn't stretch all the way out.

The body then did the strangest thing and started to crumble and dissolve the way a wasp's nest does when trampled on the ground. Parts of it blew away on the breeze, and the clothes began to deflate like a bounce house when the air isn't circulating and one part begins to topple before the others.

The other form was a person as well, but smaller of frame and with long, dark hair, in lovely curls matted with dirt and bits of grass. They had on a wool jacket that looked expensive, but it was ripped and tattered, as if someone had cut holes all over it.

The second form lay there, curled up as if in sleep.

Glancing about from side to side, I made sure something wasn't waiting to do whatever it did to them to me. Nothing was stirring in the chaparral bushes that lined the canyon, but that didn't mean it wasn't in the dark, licking the blood from its lips and sharpening its claws.

I finally decided it was time to run and get help from a grown-up, when the lovely-haired form rolled over and stared at me with deep violet eyes that almost glowed in the moonlight.

It was a woman, with an aquiline nose and sharp cheekbones. Her skin had a sheen to it, like frost on a cold morning. Her eyes flashed bright and big for a second before she winced in pain and clutched her stomach as her insides gushed out like crushed grapes. She held her hand to them.

I almost ran to her but was worried I might step on one of her formally internal, now external organs and that would be the end of her. I knew only a little bit about first aid from my Boy Scout training on the subject, but I was pretty sure she should not have been alive with the damage she had to her. I caught a flash in the light and saw the weapon that had presumably torn her apart, glinting more dangerously than the teeth of a shark in the depths of the ocean. It was a deadly little blade, about six inches long and curved in the shape of the crescent of a waxing moon and covered in blood except for a small spot near the guard.

She weakly reached out a hand.

A loud gasp escaped my lips when I saw her wound begin to heal right in front of me. The edges of each of her cuts pulled themselves together and joined where they had been ripped apart. I thought it was a trick of the light, but she removed her hand, and her organs were no longer in danger of spilling out and she was able to stretch out a bit.

"Please," she murmured. "Help. The blood wasn't enough . . . Need more . . . Firstborn of Death . . ."

Firstborn of Death. Such a strange phrase, and it sent chills through my body.

Her eyes were the picture of helplessness, so afraid and alone. The urge to run was overpowering; I knew I should run and get help, but something was begging me to stay in a thundering command echoing throughout my mind. The rest of the world, along with every experience I'd ever had before, was all a hazy dream to me, because at that moment, she and I were the only souls on Earth, and I was the only one who could give her what she needed to get well.

"Let me run and get help," I protested weakly, but I might as well have been making up a lie that I knew no one would believe in a million years.

A memory suddenly flooded to the forefront of my consciousness, blocking out all other thought, even the voice. It was of a traumatic core moment of my life. I was hardly older than a toddler when it happened, and so young that everything was a blur of emotions and strong images leaving imprints that lasted through the years, resounding into all the development stages I later experienced. The images were hazy, a carbon copy of a copy, but solid and full of all kinds of other sense memories in light and sound.

We were in a brightly lit room—it had to be the hospital because my mother was lying on a bed, connected to machines that hung down from hooks and metal poles like vines from jungle plants, but in clear plastic. A.J. was there, and he was crying, but he didn't want me to see him in his distress.

"Get him out of here," he said. "Don't let him see her like this."

"No!" I screamed. "I want to be with her, I can help her! Let me give her kisses!"

I thought whatever was wrong could be kissed all better exactly as she used to do for any scrape on my knee.

"Get him out of here, now, please," he said through clenched teeth, so loud it scared me and I started to cry.

Someone was trying to drag me back, and I kicked and scratched at them harder than I had ever raged before, with all my might and mien. They dropped me, and I ran straight back to my parents, but A.J. intercepted me and picked me up in his strong arms and whisked me out of there.

The last thing I ever recalled of her, and maybe one of the only clear impressions I have of her, was her staring up with eyes that I knew were full of pain right before they shut the door and left her among the things that were. They sealed her off into nothing but memories with a resounding thud.

There wasn't a day that went by for many a long year that I didn't think I could have saved her if I'd have been strong enough to get to her before they carried me away.

I stared into the eyes of this woman lying on the ground in the dark and thought of my own mother on that bed in the harsh light. I thought I could maybe actually help this one. Maybe I could make things right in a way I never could before.

"You need a doctor," I whispered to her.

Her only reply was a hand out in a gesture of beckoning. The urge to go to her that felt like another screaming being inside my mind was her, I was sure of it. Her emotions were somehow reaching me, and I was terrified that I would be overcome by them and lose myself in them if I didn't do what they asked of me.

I reached out to her and was instantly pulled into an embrace I could not get out of, not knowing which way was up or which was down. I knew only that this was stronger than those hands keeping me from my mother, but made out of a grip of iron and powered by a will that was stronger than any metal on Earth.

Something sharp bit into my neck in a brief explosion of pain, followed by an intense rush of pleasure that was full of more elation than anything I had ever experienced before.

It was as dizzying as spinning on a tire swing so that you go so fast you think you're about to fly right off, but you hold on and pull yourself in tight and spin even faster, and later on that night you'll still feel the vertigo in your bed as you try to fall asleep. It was as sweet as eating all the candy to the point where you know you ordinarily can't take it anymore but not being sick. It was more exciting than falling asleep in the car and waking up at Disneyland. It was a rush of confused excitement that should have been a dream because it wasn't ordinary. This sort of thing didn't ever happen, but there I was, stuck in the middle of it.

"What are you do—" I tried to protest, but it came out as a helpless squeak, carried off by the night.

I shut my eyes and saw her face, that woman who was on the ground, but she couldn't be her, because we weren't on the ground; we were flying, weren't we? We had to be, because there was no ground beneath us and we were moving so fast. Her face then turned into a million golden and silvery glowing crystals that glistened brighter than the twinkling fireworks from the Fourth of July with A.J., where I tried to sing "Proud to Be an American," and "Born in the U.S.A.," even though I didn't know all the words. Then those golden great crystals bounced and scattered until they reformed and turned into a face I was sure was my mother's even though I only remembered my mother as impressions of sensations and those sorrowful eyes.

Those eyes.

They were the last thing I saw before she went to Heaven, so that's where I must be. *But I don't deserve that,* I thought. I hadn't done anything good enough to go there. And as if sensing my despair and my lack of confidence in my ability to accept salvation, the vision changed, and blood began to pour down everywhere. It filled the limits of my vision with skulls and moving shapes of living bone, coming out and twisting amongst themselves with the terrible grace of serpents and worms. Great writhing dragons covered in gore filled the horizon of my mind, and I wanted to scream so bad, but still no sound came out.

And then everything went completely black in my mind.

Velvety cold silence.

Nothing.

5.

I WOKE UP NEXT WITH A LIGHT so blindingly bright that it hurt to open my eyes and no recollection of where I was or even really who I was. The world was one bright glare in the field of my vision and a body full of all manner of aches and pains.

My head was a pounding mass of throbbing veins in my temples and pressure all over, like someone had decided to press down on me, from every direction at once. Everything hurt so bad I wanted to thrash about, but I was so weak I couldn't even move my hands properly. I looked down and was shocked to see a needle sticking out of me. When I was a younger kid, I thought that I was a trooper for getting my shots and not crying when I felt the little pinch, but this was so disturbing to me that I wanted to rip it right out.

I tried to do just that, and that's when I heard a voice speak. "He's awake!"

I glanced over, slowly as a shadow crossing a sundial, because that's how slow my aching muscles would permit me to move. It was A.J., and he had the look of supreme joy on his face of a man who had lost the most precious thing there is on the earth to him and just got it back in the most unlikely place ever.

I forgot about how mad at him I was for a second and tried to smile weakly. A large middle-aged man in a white coat came in. He had dark hair with flecks of gray around the temples and big hairy knuckles that reminded me of a gorilla. "He's going to be okay, but it's best not to get him too agitated," he said, placing a hand on A.J.'s shoulder.

Fuck you, I thought, *my pop is happy to see me. And that means I wasn't kicked out of Heaven. That means maybe everything was a dream.*

But then I realized where I was. I was in a hospital, and hospitals were where people went to die. Panic sunk in and I frantically pleaded with them, "You *have* to get me out of here! I don't want to die!"

"You're not gonna die, my little man," A.J. replied. "I'm right here, and I'll stay here as long as it takes you to get better."

His words were the most heartfelt I had ever heard from his mouth, but I couldn't shake the terror of being in that place. The white walls brightened up waiting rooms that led to death, sterile places that prepared people to accept that they were going to burn out like a candle wick in a cold room.

I started crying, and once I did, the tears wouldn't stop. The doctor said I needed my rest and motioned for A.J. to step aside, but that only made my panic worse, and I cried harder. The fool still tried to get my father to leave, even though A.J. tried to come to my side.

That man made an enemy out of me for that. His droopy eyelids and cold stare made me want to yell at him for taking the one person I wanted to see in the world away.

I wanted to try and get up, but I was extremely exhausted. Not merely sleepy, but some dazed dreamy state where everything would almost come into focus and then scatter about in a flock of frightened crows taking off as I tried to get near. Their feathery wings would creep into my periphery, threatening to block out all the light. I tried to resist it, thinking it was wings that would take me straight down to death, but eventually the darkness won and I was back in a profoundly deep and dreamless sleep.

For a good long while, I drifted in and out like that. I can't say how long it was. Days, a week. Sometimes it would be nighttime, sometimes daytime. Sometimes it was that strange, not fully lit sky that could be either twilight or dawn, and it gave me this eerie impression that time was not working anymore and nothing was as it used to be.

A.J. never left my side. He would often be right at the bed, whispering things to me. "You're gonna be able to get up and about soon." Or "Windsong came by while you were asleep. We're gonna have everything ready for you when you get back. All the pizza rolls you can stand to eat. Maybe you and I can beat our best times at two-player Mario Brothers."

Sometimes he read my favorite books to me. He read my book about a colobus monkey in the rainforests of Africa named Silky. I once tried to bring it to a Padres game we were going to, and A.J. let me know that people might think I was a nerd if I brought a book to a baseball game, but I said that I needed it in case the game got boring.

"I'll read whatever you want," he told me.

The book stayed by my bedside, and I felt comforted by the tranquil primate on the cover, staring out among those brilliant oranges and pinks. He had the calm demeanor of a creature that never had a care in the world. I found that mostly reassuring, but other times I found it unbearably dreadful, because I was among the things that knew the deep fear of being certain they would die. I did have cares. I wanted to be free to roam about and live like that little creature. It was unfair that the world ever placed cares on poor suffering people in any way, shape, or form. I had tasted death, and its bitter flavor wouldn't leave my mouth.

A.J. brought in *Where the Wild Things Are* and read it.

Every time the doctor came in, I cringed at the best times, cried during the worst. He said something about anemia and ran tests to see if I had sickle cell even though Pop swore it had already been done when I was a baby. They had no idea how I had got in the state I was in. They said a woman who must have been in an accident brought me into the hospital and dropped me off. And when they tried to ask her what had happened, she was gone. I told them that was her—the Haunting Woman, I called her because I didn't know what else to call her.

They had to call a man and a woman, both wearing dark suits and saying they were from the courts to make sure no child abuse was involved since I had disappeared from my home in the middle of the night. I told the authorities about the man without a head who crumbled apart and the woman with the dark violet eyes that could draw you in to her in the night, but nobody believed me. They checked the canyon and nothing was there. I informed them of the exact spot, and they said there was a patch of scorched grass around from some homeless people making a fire, but no sign of a body.

"There wasn't a fire pit there!" I practically shouted at them. "You went to the wrong spot."

But they insisted that they went exactly where I said.

"I've seen it myself," A.J. said. "Son, there's nothing out there like you're saying."

"You believe me, don't you?" I insisted. "I'm not lying! You believe me, don't you?"

He paused for a minute, weighing his words before answering.

"I believe you saw something out there," he said, putting a hand on my shoulder. "And I don't think you're lying. We just didn't see anything like you're talking about." He glanced up at the doorway as if making sure there was no one around. "Maybe it got cleaned up."

"And what is the Firstborn of Death?" I asked.

"Where did you hear that?" A.J. whispered with urgency.

"From *her*!"

"Okay, okay, shh . . ."

The doctor mentioned delusions and even hallucinations.

I remained firm and let them know in no uncertain terms that I saw exactly what I saw. I didn't tell them about the ghosts on the way. Having learned from a young age that other people didn't see them, I knew it was best not to bring them up. I didn't even mention anything to A.J. of them. But these things I had seen were real. They made the grass move and the dust come up when they shuffled.

They bled on the ground.

There was no blood anywhere, they said.

When no one believed me, I went silent for a good little while. I had seen something profound and frightening out there. Circe was back on her island, and I had mysteriously survived her advances and washed up to shore somewhere else, more experienced in death and the workings of fear but weaker and without anyone around who could have proved what I had seen or who would believe me.

When Pop talked to me, I merely stared at him. I wanted to say something several times, was about to move to speak, but was afraid he would start to think I was crazy too. So I thought it better to not say anything at all.

They released me from the hospital when I regained enough strength and they had run enough tests to figure out I wasn't still in any danger of succumbing to an as of yet undefined illness.

I wasn't ready for school again yet, but I read books all throughout the day. A.J. went back to working one of the odd jobs he had in place of a real one. He did a random bit of handyman work here and there. Did some landscaping jobs. Any kind of day labor, but still nothing of the steady variety.

A psychologist came and visited me, and I nodded yes or shook my head no for his questions here and there, but didn't speak unless I had to.

"I'm worried about him," I heard A.J. confiding in Windsong once.

"He'll come back around when he's good and ready," she confidently replied. Her logic seemed a little too hippie for A.J. sometimes.

"I sure hope so," he sighed.

The days turned into weeks. I went back to school but cried so much they had to call A.J. to come over from work and come pick me up. It was the end of the school year anyways. A part of me was sad I was missing the summer fun, trips to the public pool and class parties, but another part was tired of little kid stuff even though I didn't know how to handle all the adult stuff.

The house we squatted in with Windsong wasn't a home anymore, but a horrible movie set where people spoke badly scripted lines and dangerous emotions were spilling out backstage, affecting the entire performance.

A.J. kept talking around me when he wasn't talking to me. It wasn't his fault. He was a man's man, never showing his emotions and always trying to be quick with a joke when things went pear shaped.

"Did I ever tell you about the time I had too much to drink back when I was a young man in PA?" he asked, sitting down on the bed next to me one day while I read a National Geographic special on rain forests. He was talking about Pennsylvania, where he grew up.

"I had a bottle of aspirin, and I popped a few before gettin' inta work. Well, the bus comes up, and I get on, still feelin' ridden hard and put away wet, know what I'm sayin'?" He was smiling as he reached the crescendo of his story.

Despite my best attempts at trying to ignore him, I couldn't resist his charm, even when he was pissing me off.

"I check my pockets and whattaya know, no aspirin. I look back, and there they are, right there on the bench where I left 'em. So I shout out ta the driver, I say ta him, 'Driver, pull over, my aspirins, my aspirins!' 'Aaaaawwwww, stick it out tha window!' he says back."

My studying and sulking fell apart for a second and I smiled at him.

"See?" He smiled back at me. "I know my little guy is in there somewhere. You'll come back soon, when you're good and ready. Maybe that ol' broad Windsong is right after all."

It wasn't until one early July day that I finally did. Pop was off on a job, and Windsong was off playing bridge at her women's club. I was left alone at home, and the assumption was I would be fine left to my own devices. I came and went as I pleased, knew where the key under the rock on the front porch plant was. My injuries notwithstanding, they still trusted me not to burn the house down and to stay on the straight and narrow.

So I took my rusty white mountain bike out and cruised down the road. I was still a little weaker than I thought but got back into the rhythm of being active again once the wheels really started spinning. My bike was no longer simply a pedal powered toy for kids. It was the Batcycle, and I was out on patrol. I was Terminator, from movies Pop told me weren't supposed to be for kids but he watched with me anyways, doing our best Schwarzenegger impressions as we laughed together.

The canyon was still on my mind, and I made sure to stay away from it as if it was radioactive. I wasn't ready to face anything down there again, maybe ever if I could help it. So I made it towards the beach, the cool sea air feeling like an old friend giving me a hug after we had been separated for too long. The sun was intense in the spots where the eucalyptus trees didn't cover the streets. The downhill grade was going to be murder getting back up on the way home, but I didn't care. It felt great to be free again. I believed that maybe if I was on the move, I could shuffle off the cares of the world. I stood up on the pedals and flew down the roads.

"Wooooooohooooo!" I called out to the cars on the streets, daring their flashing colors that whirred by to chase after me.

I rode up around the cove and into the town of La Jolla, beautiful buildings lining the ocean as lovely to behold as palaces from a book. The whole town was a work of art built into the environment with contrasts all about—land and sea, white columns and green palm trees, sand on the feet and salt in the air. I stopped at the church.

Mary, Star of the Sea, with her mission facade and her statues and stained glass, was comforting despite my ambivalence to the religion of my forefathers. She was a place where I could come to feel safe when everything else was scary and clouded with uncertainty.

The old woman was out front again, crying out to no one in particular.

Instead of ignoring her as per usual, I looked her straight in her sorrowful eyes, with her tearstained gray cheeks that looked like they were made of dry paper-mache.

"Can you tell my family to come see me?" she asked.

I held up one hand and shook it, jazz hands fashion. I did it with the other hand.

She laughed.

Doing a little twirl, I moved all about in the toppling comic spins of a loveable tramp from a black and white movie. I tilted in one direction, then the other. I made a couple of somewhat vulgar little shakes of my rear end. Then I spun around and threw up my hands in a complete expression of joy.

It didn't strike me to care if anyone saw how ridiculous I looked; I only wanted to make this poor spirit happy.

She broke out in soundless applause, cheering me on.

We both started laughing and didn't stop until the muscles in my cheeks hurt, and she sighed a breathless sigh.

Before, I had seen her as an annoyance at best but also a dreadful reminder at worst. She was this constant presence about the door to the church reminding me that one day, Pop, Windsong, my teachers, my few friends, and everyone else would die. They would wither and grow as old as that ghost had been when she passed, or be taken away sooner. They could have their minds go to mush and die and still be some addle-minded spirit that searched for its probably also long-dead relatives that had been pushing daisies a long time.

And even if they went to church every Sunday, said the right prayers, did all the things, they could be stuck out in the cold for a good while.

I reached out for her hand and she reached for mine, and the strangest thing happened—I was actually able to feel her grip. And when I did, a torrent of memories blasted through me. Memories of a woman who worked hard in life and felt underappreciated for it by husband, children, and friends. I saw visions of a farm in South Dakota, where she had to ride carriages even though cars were invented by then. I saw it all, a lifetime in a second. Some memories lingered on longer than others. Some bright moments shone forth more than others.

"Your family isn't here," I gently informed her. "But they'll come for you soon." I thought about A.J. and Windsong and how they nursed me back to health. "That's what families do. They're there for each other when you need them most. Wait for them."

She gave me a big hug and then released me and stepped back. Her color became less gray and more vibrant, her form more distinct and not so blurry around the edges. As she stepped back once more, like a loving sigh, she just vanished. The last thing I saw of her were her eyes filled with tears of joy instead of sorrow.

She never told me her name, I realized. She wasn't merely some thing anymore, and I thought it appropriate to give her one, at least in my mind. I decided to call her Mrs. Beakley, since she reminded me of the cartoon character from *Duck Tales*.

Rest in peace wherever you are, Mrs. Beakley, even if it is nowhere at all, or everywhere at once.

The setting sun made the shadows longer and the dark places darker as I rode my bike back on those long roads. I rushed home to get where it was warm and the lights were always on to ward off the dark. Pop and Windsong were relieved to see me when I rode my bike into the driveway and hopped off it.

I raced up to them and gave them both big hugs. I had rarely done that since the accident, and didn't realize how much I missed it until I felt their warm embraces. I held on for as long as I could, even though I knew that a hug should end sooner than I was letting it linger.

"Hey, guys," I said. "I missed you."

"Glad to have you back," A.J. said.

6.

GARY HAD BEEN DEAD SINCE AROUND the grunge era, but he became one of my best friends in the whole wide world.

I met him on my first day of high school. Most of the other kids were in their own respective clicks, and I'd no inclination to join their pubescent cults of conformity, so I sidled up to Gary at lunch break.

He had freckles across his nose and cheeks, and ashy brown hair that was trimmed very short, just long enough so he could part it. He sat there with a pair of Chuck Taylors on and blue jeans, with a black Cure T-shirt, and I knew he was one of my people, even if he was no longer people, but ghost.

"What's your story?" I asked him, sitting down on the blue plastic-coated metal picnic tables with their reticulated pattern of slats.

No one else could see him, and I had a reputation for talking alone. A few people thought I was some form of special needs, others that it was for attention, and others bought my excuses of studying lines for plays, especially when I would quote Shakespeare to them in a passionate fury of soliloquizing excellence. There were a few ones who attempted to kick my ass for this because they were shitty people no matter what. Can't please all the people all the time, no matter how much charm and theatrical excellence you pour on.

"Wow," he exclaimed in his high voice. "Even the high schoolers who I'm sure can see me don't usually try to talk to me."

"There are other people like me?" I'd never thought to ask a ghost that before. It made sense; surely there must be others out there who could see the dearly departed if I could, but I never thought to inquire about them.

"Every now and then, one comes along. They pretend they can't see me, but I know they can't help but stare my way."

"So what's a cool kid like you doing passing the time here?" I asked him.

Some ghosts went about roaming in certain places because they had no idea they were dead. They went on trying to do the things they were so used to doing in life. Sometimes they got frustrated because they were trying to get the attention of a person who had continued living. Other ghosts only stuck to one place because they knew they were dead and wanted to feel comfortable there. Sometimes they resented people coming around and trying to change the things they remembered. And there were those ghosts who, like people, had nothing better to do.

I've seen someone who can't see ghosts walk by a spirit and just shudder. The man glanced about as if he had the craziest thought come into his brain and didn't know why, and then shook his head and walked off.

"I committed suicide a few years back," he said.

He flashed his wrists, and they opened up into gaping wounds with blood pouring out of them and then healed up just as fast. It was an alarming sight to see, but I took it in stride. Sometimes ghosts could create effects on their bodies like that. I had seen ghosts who kept their old wounds because they didn't know how to heal them. Maybe the trauma of their life was etched onto their spirit, and they couldn't shake it off until they worked it out of their minds. The angry ones created wounds on their bodies and scary faces to make a show to terrify someone. I was convinced it all depended on how strong their will was.

He was lucky he wasn't one of the ones stuck in that moment replaying that horror over and over for himself. I had seen those types, and they were not fun to deal with. Anyone stuck in a loop can be a bit of a sad case. You want them to see that there are still seasons and new loves and wonders still around under the sun, but they remain in a hell of their own making and project that horror out into the world.

"Damn, I'm sorry to hear about that," I said, sincerely. I had felt that existential crisis of an idea too, that this was it, and nothing really mattered. That I couldn't go on and take any of the pain of living and that hopelessness was too much to bear. It's hard to walk on when that haze seems to hang over everything. Pretty fucked up to know that kind of existential dread as a teenager, but I had seen some shit.

"I wish someone would have told me life goes on," he said. "Because here I am, still a teenager."

It occurred to me in that moment that sometimes people can't see past the choices they make and then keep on making the same mistakes. This poor guy, not able to get out of high school. I wondered if there was anything tying him to this place or if he simply didn't know any better.

"Why'd you commit suicide? If that's not too personal of a question for ya?" He gave me an expression that seemed to say *no shit, Sherlock*, and I hastily added, "Sorry, it probably doesn't get much more personal than that, does it?"

"It's okay," he said. "I did it because I was gay. Tired of being picked on by jock douche bags back in the day."

"So why do you hang around the school?"

"It's the one place I know. Where am I supposed to go? To my parents' home, where my dad told me he'd kick me out of the house if I didn't start 'acting like a man'? Where my mom told me to stop being such a faggot?"

"That's a bitch," I agreed.

"I never even got to kiss a boy," he sighed, dejectedly.

We sat there in silence for a moment in the hot late summer sun under no shade cover in that quad.

"Hey, why don't we go and have a fun time in the gay part of town? Fuck this place."

"I . . . don't know if I can." He stared at the ground with the most forlorn expression on Earth, and I wanted to hug him and hold him because he was so used to everyone always passing through him.

"Let's try together. Take my hand."

I held it out, and he was able to clasp onto it. The faintest impression of fingertips wrapped around my hand. Not solid, but more like an energy, like the sensation of a mild vibrating electric shock was going through my skin, and cold as ice.

And the memories flooded in. I saw friends' mothers not letting him stay the night because there were rumors. I saw watching Bruce Springsteen in a music video dance on stage with Cortney Cox and him wishing he was up there with that sexy guy in those tight jeans, feeling his heart flutter as his limbs swung about. I saw a teacher who loved him no matter what, telling a bully to get the hell out of his class until he could treat other children the way they wanted to be treated.

I still held on.

"Stick with me," I said, giving him a wink and taking him along. He followed, and we snuck out the front and past the campus security guard who was too busy letting a high school girl sit shotgun in his golf cart to notice me slipping through the gates.

We got on a city bus together, sitting in the back as I pointed out my favorite parts of the city to roller skate in, or which beaches I knew were the best to surf at.

We got off in Hillcrest, with its cute multicolored shops in all shades of pastels and the huge hospital I was born in hanging over the edge of the hills. Trees filled the streets as thick as a jungle, and people sat in cute sidewalk cafés looking extra fabulous and so chic. I led him to all the parts of the town that he had missed out on.

"I was a sheltered military brat from the Midwest," he told me. "My dad would have never let me hang out here."

We went to Gaymart, the cramped and tiny shop with all the best gay club attire and a back room through beaded curtains full of racy things like dildos and porn. We went to the thrift stores, and I tried on all the clothes he picked out. We went into the used bookstores and checked out books on queer identity and politics. I ordered a gelato and let him savor the scent of it before it melted too much. Ghosts love good smelling things for a reason I don't quite understand yet. I mean, who doesn't, right? But ghosts in particular love these things.

As the afternoon sun slid down in the sky, we snuck into a French film at the indie theater. Gary and I sat in that movie theater, and I leaned over to kiss him, to see if I could. I wasn't attracted to him at first, with his freckles and his spiky hair, but he had dreamy eyes and a line to his jaw that seemed so straight and angular, like it was drawn with sharp lines by an artist with a pencil, and I loved that for some reason.

And I really liked *him*, and thought, why not? Sometimes ghosts can draw strength from certain things, and every now and then even people without my abilities can see them if the ghost is strong enough to pull a form together. I wanted to see if I could empower him through something exciting, a feeling that would get someone's blood running if they were alive.

I put my lips to his and felt him come together, solid and quivering. I had kissed one person in a romantic way, a girl named Danielle Murphy, at the playground near her apartment when I was there to play with her before school. This was different. She was soft and smooth, and those kisses were ones between chaste little children.

This was something more sensual, from two young men who had the drives and desires of adolescence and who were trying to get all the pleasure they could out of each other while delicately darting their tongues back and forth in each other's mouths. I ran my hand across his firm chest underneath the actual fabric of his shirt and playfully pinched a nipple. I could feel him and he was warm and vibrant, no longer cold and crackling. An older woman in the seats glanced at him and did a double take, wondering where the other boy came from.

We forgot about following the plot and the subtitles to the Jean Cocteau classic on the screen and locked lips there for the rest of the film, running our hands over each other's bodies.

I felt quite simply great knowing he had probably never found someone in high school that he could relate to and be his real self with, let alone make out with in an almost empty theater. Here he was getting a joy he never got in life because the world never gave him a chance to ask. He had the bad chance to be gay in the middle of a huge spur of homophobia from the AIDS epidemic, and so we were making up for all that lost time.

We left the theater together, and he always waited for me in the quad at school after that. We got along from the get-go, but after that, we were thick as thieves and I saw him every day I was at school.

Sometimes I would play music for him. He could become entranced by it, swaying to the rhythm like a young child in awkward motions. I'd play all the eighties hits that I figured he would appreciate. We would dance on the roof of the gym that we snuck onto to "Modern Love" by David Bowie and "Hungry Heart" by Bruce Springsteen. I had a copy of the soundtrack to *The Wedding Singer*, and we often sang those songs played on my janky-ass CD player hooked up to a pair of tiny speakers as we tried to moonwalk like Michael Jackson.

I never tried to coerce Gary into doing anything for me. Instead, I worked things out with him and did favors for him. Ghosts don't need much, but sometimes I would bring little gifts of good smelling things for him. He loved when I would burn incense; he swore he could feel the heat from it burning and could take in the scent of it.

I never tried to use him in any way that he wasn't comfortable with. I asked him to do things, and he would because he was my friend and we had an understanding between the two of us.

There were a few instances where I was tempted to get him to try and make the books fly out of some asshole's locker at him. But this seemed petty. I felt that it wasn't a good use of his energy or mine. And it felt tantamount to slavery. I figured that if I would never do something so inhumane to a living person, it would be even worse to brow-beat a deceased person into submission whenever I wanted them to do some errand or other.

Imagine how terrifying a prospect that would be, being fucked around from person to person for possible centuries. I shuddered to think I had any kind of power like that and resolved never to use another entity, living or dead, in a cruel way.

7.

I MET JENNY CIENFUEGOS on a spring day that was setting me on a date with destiny I couldn't see winding into paths leading to pain and heartbreak at the time, but the writing should have been all over the walls of the beautiful bedroom I glimpsed her wandering out of as she strolled onto her balcony.

The crisp air that day smelled the way soft blossoms feel when they brush against your skin as they're blown in on a breeze.

That ancient king of Israel must have felt the same thing when he looked upon Bathsheba as she bathed in the spring, only he had the agency to do something about his desires. I could only stare and wish I belonged among those old money, trust fund fat cat motherfuckers in the neighborhood, all acting as puffed up as if they were the next heir to the throne of who knows what kingdom, but determined to win it through privilege and call it their own sweat and blood.

Jenny had the saddest look on her face, of a young woman who was troubled by cares that no one the age of teen years tearing around this earth should have been subject to. Her trip to her balcony must have been less for fresh air and more an attempt at escaping something that was working on her soul.

Stumbling onto her was the unlucky or maybe very lucky blessing of one of my misadventures from my early days of thieving. I was sixteen and too wild to be a sensible child, too impulsive not to have a compulsion for trouble.

I still have trouble figuring out exactly how it occurred, but teenagerdom made me resent A.J. in ways that may or may not have been fair to him. He had tried so hard to keep me on the straight and narrow, but the more he tried, the more hypocritical I found him to be.

I fell in with Vanessa, and she was exactly the kind of free spirit I wanted to embody. She was a girl from my side of the tracks who was brave and fearless in ways I only dreamed of. She taught me how to steal wallets, and we would go out in the streets and practice, pretending to be so lost in conversation that we bumped into our target and stole their pocketbook in the transaction.

We would try to one-up each other, see how many we could steal from people on a bus until they got wise and we had to get the fuck off. We almost got nicked a time or two and had to run through yards and hop over fences to escape a cop once.

I discovered catered events were full of a whole team of people hired on who hardly knew each other. And their uniforms could be purchased at a certain shop in town, no questions asked, happy to take your money.

My target was a gigantic mansion in La Jolla, Fin de la Terre—oh gosh, I loved saying it and having every syllable roll off of my tongue smooth as butter. It overlooked the cliffs down to Black's

Beach as if it was too stable to feel the vertigo of staring at that drop. The place had all the style and open space of a columned and glistening Roman villa, with gardens full of roses around it on every side, connected by tiers of brightly tiled walkways. Fountains shot jets of water that caught the rays of the sun, and palm trees reached out to touch the sky between ornate hedges twisting around its grounds.

I had seen this place so often while surfing with A.J. at La Jolla Shores, always admiring how it commanded those gorgeous jutting escarpments and took up the whole area like it was a fortress, keeping the views of that diamond blue sea to itself and not letting anyone in the community dare to intrude on its reveries.

"I want to live in a place like that," I said to A.J. once when I was a kid. "I bet you never have to worry about anything if you live in a house as big as that."

"Don't ever go near that house," A.J. warned me.

"Why not?"

"Because I said so!" he snapped.

I drooped in consternation at his tone and splashed the water alongside my board absentmindedly.

He realized I was taken aback by his tone and said in a softer voice, "Sometimes there might be funny reasons why grown-ups ask ya to do things. But we've got good reasons thatcha wouldn't understand."

"I'm smart, you can tell me. I'm a great secret keeper."

"It's not about how smart ya are." He put a reassuring hand on my shoulder. "It's about keeping youse safe."

Since he was my father, I wanted to believe he knew what was best. But he'd sparked a curiosity in me, and sparks have a habit of making blazes.

That house was my Mount Everest, my white whale, and my source of the Nile River all in one. I was out to pierce the mysterious heart of it and open it up. No longer would it sit up on the hill, foreboding and closed up, but with some gentle coaxing, it would spill out its secrets and let me in.

I might not have even ever wanted to go in, if it wasn't for the word "no." Give me a lever long enough to move the world, and I'll set it aside for an emergency. Tell me not to use it, and I'll take us to the Andromeda Galaxy.

I don't know what drew me to it, but I learned all I could about it. I checked public records and looked for news stories. It was one of those estates so fancy they give it that bougie French name, Fin de la Terre. It had stories of bootlegging and murders, intrigue that made it seem more of a fascinating person than a home, that amazing sentinel on the coast.

When I heard there was a fundraising gala at the place, my ears perked up and my spidey sense went a-tingling. I had to get in.

On the afternoon of the event, I went up to the entrance of the property on the side where I had seen several of the staff coming in. I had a white T-shirt with my black slacks and shoes on, and a baggy, formless blue jacket of their uniform variety draped over one arm. I had a backpack on and could have passed for a student from the nearby University of California on the way to a part-time job.

Vanessa wasn't with me on this one. I wanted to one-up her in a way that would make her head spin. I did have help from my friend of the deceased variety, Gary. He was my point man on expeditions that required a bit of invisible reconnaissance. He was good at getting the lay of the land since he was undetectable to most mortal senses.

In this instance, I had him check the names on the caterer's list of employees showing up for the day. He found one and told me as I hopped up to the man behind the podium. He wore a suit and Ray Ban sunglasses and looked like he didn't have a semblance of a sense of humor. "Name and ID?" he asked flatly.

"Name's Matt Lackey, should be on there. As for ID . . ." I pretended to fish around for it in my pockets. "Shit. Oh darn, I can't find it. I think I left it in my apartment, dammit! Long night studying, I'm so sorry. I can run back home and get it, but I'll have to take a bus and . . ."

"Bring it next time."

"No prob. Thanks a million!"

And just like that, I was in. The ace was in the house as I strolled into a high-profile gala at this mansion in La Jolla, all without making a fuss.

I recalled from seeing it back in the day and that I thought it was a damn shame no one ever roamed about the grounds of it. It was a crime beautiful places like that are always owned by the wrong people. That work of art was such a wonder of columns and mosaics that caught the magic of the early afternoon sun or rose above the ocean to meet the sunset-lit sky, and if it was mine, it would be a place of art and learning and love.

Instead, those sights were under lock and key. People bought and stole all the land they could and decided to gaze upon it only every once in a while, but not with an appreciative eye. I had a huge chip on my shoulder, not going to deny it for one hot minute. So on the day they opened it up, I was going to clean it out, in the most brazen and crazy way imaginable. I ran into a bathroom and quickly changed into a cream-colored sport coat and crisp white dress shirt, with a pair of khaki pants from my backpack. The shirt was a little wrinkled from being folded up in there, but it would do. I slapped on a pair of shades and was ready to mingle.

I was swimming in that sea of decadence, a dashing pirate prince ready to raid the strongholds. The people at this gathering were merely fancy savages who draped their bodies in scarlets and silk and acted like they were civilization itself, but they were really only fat on the gains of their own privilege, and I was so happy to be a thief in their midst, taking what I knew they didn't deserve.

"What do you do?" one older lady asked me before I helped myself to the contents of her leather handbag while she reached for her third glass of wine in three quarters of an hour. She had been regaling me about how the solution to homelessness problems was to not let undocumented immigrants into the country. Human migration hadn't been happening ever since our ancestors all wandered out of Africa in her mind, and that need to relocate was all the cause of our current society's ills.

"Oh, I'm on the lacrosse team for my Catholic school," I told her. I did not have the foggiest idea how to play lacrosse. I only knew all the preppy jocks dug that shit.

Don't mind if I help myself to your cash and your credit card for later.

"There's a guy over here with a fat wad of cash that he keeps telling the cute boy bartenders he'll tip more with, but then he stiffs them," Gary told me.

"Perfect. Why are the rich ones always the cheapest?"

"I'm going to go to Empire State University after my senior year," I said as I schmoozed that older man. "My father went there, he manages a bank. I'm not sure where he got off to. He's also called Warren Worthington, and he's got a little pull with the admissions people. I'd be the sixth generation to attend, very proud family tradition." And other such lies.

He kept telling me he thought I looked like a young Robert Redford and asked me if I wanted to do a few lines of cocaine with him in the bathroom. Nice praise, but I got the vibe from his stares at my ass as I grabbed him another drink that he had other motives than complimenting a captivating young man.

I went with him and faked doing a couple of bumps of the stuff. He told me he got the ultimate hall pass by having a wife who was sick with cancer and asked me if I wanted to go to Puerto Vallarta with him for spring break, the two of us alone. I made out with him for two whole minutes, wanting to wash my tongue off with steel wool afterwards. And then left him with a hard dick and blue balls when I told him I needed to go because my girlfriend would wonder where I was.

"Call me," he pleaded.

"You betcha, stud."

He was down a watch and wallet after that little tryst—parting is such sweet sorrow.

All these people showed me was that the rich didn't deserve this cash and they didn't deserve this kind of power. This was a charity event, and one man admitted to me, as I pretended to suck down champagne but secretly dumped it in the plants (I never drank on the job) that he was setting up a 501c3 only to sell a painting, tax-free, for his daughter's inheritance. I was gonna love buying all kinds of shit with his Visa.

They were all there, the best of society, crossed every T and dotted every I they could to make sure their trust funds were airtight so they could keep that money machine fattening the next greedy generation of little assholes.

They prayed every Sunday to their White Anglo-Saxon Protestant idea of the divine, who, ironically enough, said it would be easier than a camel to get through the eye of a needle than it would be for them to get into Heaven. But not to worry, they were making fine bequests in their wills to make up for the fact that they were shitty people while they lived, and were probably betting Jesus was as forgiving in the salvation department as the IRS was in the tax deductions department.

I was on cloud nine and actually believed I was doing the world a favor.

That monster house stared at me as I raided its guests. No, not a house, because a home had a family to it—this place had servants. This edifice had no soul that a family provides, just a deep hole that threatened to suck me into it. If I wasn't careful, it could strip me down to composite molecules with its imposing stature and huge glass windows that reflected the afternoon light as it muttered "You don't belong."

"Oh, I do," I told it right back. "I'm right here, and this is where I was always gonna slip in."

No house can really stare, I knew it, but I still couldn't shake the penetrating feeling that it had its gaze on me, no matter how I eluded the security cameras and checked the eyes on me.

I was good. Shake it off.

My back story stayed the same for all so as not to arouse suspicion. It was all one big game, and I loved playing it. My performance deserved a bow and a standing ovation. This was an art, what I was doing. And the best part of it was I almost believed it myself.

As I robbed them, I felt for a brief moment the power of these wealthy and influential people and that bloated sense of self-importance with all the privileges thereof. All those gilded souls wobbling about, playing with others as they saw fit, moving pieces around on gameboards so they could get the highest score, ready to kick over the board for everyone else when they worried there was danger of losing. A whole legion of boys and girls who never learned to share their toys all strutting their stuff and acting important.

I could deny, deny, deny all day long, but I secretly wanted a taste of what they had, and I was probably only slightly less amoral than they were. I was a perfect fox in the henhouse, clever and able to get into places everyone thought safe.

All the fancy excuses I could make up meant nothing, because when all was said and done, there I was, cozying up to their power and loving the taste of it. Stealing their jewels and loving the feel of it. Lying to their faces and loving the thrill of it.

It was there in the back of my mind, that power—snake-coiled around a branch with two apples, saying taste of the one or taste of the other. One gives you knowledge and the other life, those two different, deep human desires, symbols of overcoming limitations. I was leaning away from the apple that provided wisdom and wanting a big bite of the one that provided a moment of thrilling existence so pure that it would make me so extra glad to be alive and override all the things that were drab and depressing and gray. A glaring moment that would live on in my heart and keep me satisfied when all the world was over and all would be ghosts, but that thrill would still be there in space, in a blessed memory.

I wanted to sin and sin again if this was wrong, because I was loving it!

Those others called their thievery more respectable names. They profited off of the sweat of people and stole the fruits of their labor and called it capitalism. They had their garden party joys supplied by wealth that they compounded off of their parents' wealth, all culled from a system that was keeping people everywhere down, while their overstuffed faces dripped canapés and crudité onto the well-manicured lawn.

They spoke of the world as if they had the perfect solution for all its problems. They had to know it because only smart people are rich. And that solution was that everyone else simply needed to work harder, because clearly they themselves did, and look what it got them. No fucking idea how scarcity worked, or how lucky they were, thinking to themselves that they deserved what they got because they were so industrious.

There was a roped-off section of the grounds where the eroding cliffs had given way and were in the process of being reinforced. I walked towards it to get a better look because I was always fond of staring into the occasional abyss.

That was when I caught sight of her.

She walked out on that balcony of her room like it was the only refuge in a sea of frustration and sadness. If she could have flown off of it right there, she would have sprouted wings or fashioned them from whatever was at hand.

She had olive skin and long dark hair that went down her back. She had wide dark eyes, open and inviting, and a look of concern in them as if she lived in sorrow instead of a palace.

I guessed she was my age, but something about her had the stamp of profound maturity of someone who had to grow up from day one and walk before she was allowed to crawl. She wore a black top and immaculate white pants that glowed brighter than if they were made of new snow reflecting the light on a sunny afternoon.

She would always be fashionable. Even if she had on rags she pulled out of a bin, they would wrap themselves around her in the form of a gown like Cinderella, and off she would go to dance the night away. And even after twelve, they would still not poof into something from the dust bin. But I got the sense that everything was a display with her.

Her every gesture told me she was here—not only here at this house but here in this rich world—to prop up someone's conception of what their life should be, and she did not thrive in the confines of the cage she was kept in. She moved like she was meant for this wealthy life, but she shuddered at the claustrophobia of it all and only wanted a chance to breathe.

At least that's how she was in my mind.

Her glance was stately, the way a queen's should be, and it happened to shine my way for the briefest, most precious second, before she quickly turned around and marched back into the house. I imagined her afterimage remained on that balcony, the way a spot still remains on the retina after a light has flashed on and off in the darkness.

All I could do was sigh at losing sight of her, when I wanted to climb up there after her. I went around the side of the building to sneak a clove cigarette that I thought made me look dashing. There was a bench in front of a fountain. I sat down on it and laid one leg over the armrest to complete a look of louche carelessness.

Where would I go next? Who knew. The sky was the limit. I always wanted to go to Paris. New York was right around the corner, maybe a cool Southern city like New Orleans or Miami. *The storm is coming, and I want to catch it on the horizon and ride it out to the next side of the world,* I thought, and I had every intention of doing that. I wanted to keep it all going and steal everything I could from the people who didn't deserve it in this town and then ride off into the sunset.

I tossed the butt into a hedge with practiced careless ease when the girl came out.

"You got another one of those?" she asked.

"Of course," I said, pulling one out and lighting it for her. I tried a fancy lighter trick to put it back into my pocket and wound up almost dropping it onto the ground, but I caught it at the last minute. She stared at me with a bemused look on her face.

"It's still cool if I saved it at the last moment, right?"

"Too cool," she replied, then took a drag of the spicy scented toxic stick after I lit it. "It's especially cool if you gotta ask."

"Validation is important. Gotta make sure I'm keeping my audience riveted."

"All these people here are trying to impress everyone. They're so boring. Don't look for validation, just own it."

"I'm not looking to impress anyone," I said, lighting up another cigarette.

"Really? Then what are you doing here?"

"Enjoying the party."

"How'd you get here?" she asked, sizing me up. "I know every one of the boys on my father's guest list, and you're not on it."

"Well, I'm the Count of Monte Cristo." I made a theatrical gesture like I was holding a cape over my face.

"Right," she sneered. "And why shouldn't I call security on you?"

"Okay, I'm actually Edmund Dantès." I smiled. "I found a treasure after escaping prison, and I've come back to claim what's mine." I held a palm out at her to show it was empty, and then I reached out towards her hair. "I think here's some of that treasure." I had one of the hundreds I had swiped between my fingers and made it fall like it was in her hair.

"Fine, whatever," she said as it fell onto her lap. She clearly had seen one of these before. "Be mysterious. I'm not impressed."

Whether she actually wanted me to or not, I took that bait. "So, if I were to impress a girl like you, what would I have to do?"

"Hmmmmm," she mused. "Get me something no one else here can get."

Glancing around the grounds, I thought about what that could be that was on hand. "On it," I said, again tossing my cigarette off.

"Wait, what are you doing?"

"You'll see."

There was a big magnolia tree nestled there on the grounds about fifty paces away, all unappreciated in its blooming glory. It had a pale trunk that complimented its snowy blooms and dark green leaves that took the heat away from the day under its fractalated shadow. It was thought of as simply an ornament in a garden, when it was really doing so much more, doing amazing things like making air from carbon, sucking in sunlight to make food, and spreading its immaculate white petals open wide in a big gesture of love to the universe, saying, *It's so fucking beautiful to be me!*

We were sympatico; I was vibing with that tree. We both knew what it was to grow up from the dirt and make something pretty.

I jumped up and grabbed its lowest branch. It was a skinny tree and shook a little bit, but it held my weight. Clamping my feet together, I shimmied up its length, loving the feel of ascent, thankful for its wonderful rough texture and the sunlight breaking through its leaves.

Bit by bit, I scampered up the trunk until I finally reached one of the branches with the fist-sized white starbursts of a bloom growing on them at the end of it and was able to break off a stalk with three gorgeous white flowers blossoming off of it. I dismounted by letting go of the branch and landed with a soft thud on the grass. I bowed to her as graceful as if I'd finished a performance and then ran back to her and gave her the flowers.

"For you, my dear!" I announced, putting them in her hand and then kissing it. "You said something no one else here could get."

Her eyes were wide in what I mistook for admiration but then realized were looking nervously past me. Two very broad-shouldered gentlemen were coming my way, and I knew I was the one they were zeroing in on.

"Look at the time," I said, puckering my lips for a kiss. "No?" She shook her head in consternation, so I blew her one. "Maybe on our second date, then!" I hollered as I exited stage left, down the side of the house, only to find two more men of the heavily built variety coming down the way. I was trapped between them all, with nowhere to go.

"I get it guys, I'm ssssorry," I slurred. "Shometimes my old man letsh me have a little of that champagne, and tha' stuff hits quick!"

"Come with us," one of the men said.

"I got it, I got it." I held my hands out. "I fucked up! Bad boy! Bad! I'll be on my way."

But instead of letting me go, they grabbed me by the arm and hustled me towards the big wooden doors of the house, and that was when I knew I was in over my head.

"I never got your name!" I called out to her as they led me off.

8.

I HADN'T SEEN THE INSIDE of the building yet, and it was massive, like nothing I was used to.

The floor was polished marble so smooth you could slide off of it. I kind of wanted to see if I could do a *Risky Business*-style slip across it all, but the men were holding me tight.

Every space seemed curated with entrancing objects designed to make people gaze in amazement, and I was being rushed past them all. The halls were filled with tropical plants in ornate pots. I whistled as I gazed at Impressionists and other famous masters I knew from art history class. Here a Monet, there a Matisse or a Chagall. Mirrors lined the ceiling, giving it an added extra look of expansiveness.

"Can I just use the bathroom before we get where we're going?" I asked.

"Nope," the guy holding my arms behind my back said. He had an accent from somewhere—sounded European, but not any place I could name.

They were all somewhat normal looking, as far as guys with way too many biceps and not enough of a neck were concerned. But they all had faces that were wiped clean of any note of feeling or trace of sympathy.

"All right, but if I pee my pants, that's on you," I warned.

"So pee them," he said, calling my bluff.

"I can hold it." I continued being shuffled down a long corridor.

I really did have to go at first, that fight or flight response that is your body saying *Drop all this weight, we gotta get the fuck outta Dodge*, but the sensation of having to pee went away.

One thing I hadn't bothered with in my reconnaissance work, and in hindsight, this is the worst mistake you can ever make, was not knowing who was pulling the strings, who the man behind the curtain was.

These people could have been Serbian war criminals or Latter-day Saints for all I knew. Either way, I didn't want to have to fuck with them and find out, but there I was, dragged down to be dealt with.

They might have done anything from call the cops on me to going to work on my fingers and toes with whatever they had at hand on the grounds and then chop me into teeny pieces for the fish. I was imagining my bones being picked clean until they were smooth bits that washed up on the shore and someone picked them up to make a necklace. I was about to become the jewelry at one of these galas, and then the circle of consumer culture would be complete.

We came to a service elevator, and I was taken aback by the fact that the building was so big it needed elevators for people to get around. I also had a wave of panic pass over me. I knew that getting into it was how I would disappear. I imagined some sadistic fuck with a torture room with soundproof walls, and started breathing heavily and glancing from side to side, looking for any way I could use to escape.

"I think I'll take the stairs," I said.

"Quit fucking around."

My Eurotrash companion gave me a quick smack to the temple, and I saw stars long enough to be pushed into the elevator without any further need for hassle on their part.

The doors quickly opened when we reached our floor, and I was led down another long hall. This one had beautiful Persian rugs on the floors with their intricate twining vines and colorful beasts prancing all about. I looked to the floor and saw lions stalking deer and singing birds calling out in full-throated exaltation songs captured in thread that would never be heard by the ears of anyone besides their creator.

Statues lined the hall, busts of Grecian-looking men with stern looks set in their eyes in stone, and naked women holding up vases of water to bathe in.

A suit of armor stood ready to do battle against "heathens" in the Holy Land, the shimmering hands over a long sword, as if ready to take it up again at a moment's notice should the need arise.

I was shuffled through a doorway with a carved battle scene on the big creaking wooden doors. Scores of knights in rows, carved in relief, were raising their swords against other knights. A man in armor was on horseback, slamming a lance into another man, who fell back off his steed, suspended in a pose of agony by a masterful artist's whim.

One sympathizes, friend.

I was not wanting to walk on and looked about for a way to squirm away and jump out of a window. Something with a balcony, a drainpipe, a long curtain, anything to try out my best Zorro impression and leap out—stylishly, of course. I'd adjust my tie and say that they don't fuck around with cheap tippers in this joint.

My captor must have been sensing my thoughts, because he gave my arm a twist that made me wince, as muscles were moved in ways they were not meant to be bent.

"Aaaaah!" I shuddered. "Careful with that arm! I've gotta pitch tomorrow, and they've been awful mad at me since they found out I threw that no-hitter on LSD."

"Shut the fuck up," he said. "That was Dock Ellis, anyways."

"Ooh, a man of culture. I like it."

We entered a dimly lit room, compared to the daylit grandeur of rest. The curtains only let a faint bit of sunlight in. A man was sitting in a leather-backed chair with huge armrests that looked as if it was made for someone to receive heads of state. Snarling wolf heads popped out of either side, lending an imposing air to the scene. As if being hustled in wasn't imposing enough.

He had ashen-blonde hair and big, bright, and alert eyes that calmly took in every detail of me in one glance. His face looked young, but there were touches of crow's feet at the edges of his blue eyes that said he could have been in his forties or early fifties. However old he was, he must have been gorgeous when he was a young man, and he was still a stunner. His jaw was strong and his lips were full, almost pouting like mine, but not quite as big. His outfit was a gorgeous seersucker suit, perfect for the warm weather but still elegant. It was in light gray pinstripes, with a light blue shirt.

"Sit down," he said, motioning to a chair similar to his but less ornate in front of his wide, marble-topped desk. My desk at home was all full of papers and my big clunky computer monitor. It was used for all kinds of schoolwork and covered in layers of various messes. His was a desk that you use to conduct affairs in. Documents of great importance were probably signed over it and hands shaken to seal important deals.

"I think I'll . . ." I began, and he merely snapped his fingers in my direction and one of his men pushed me down into the seat. ". . . take a glass of water if you're offering. I prefer Perrier, if you have any." I peeked back at my Euro bouncer friend with a hopeful smile. He gave me a look that screamed *Watch your fucking mouth, kid*, and I sighed and turned my attention back to my host.

"Leave us," my host said. "And get him a Perrier."

"Uh, with ice, please?" I winked at him, glad to get him to follow my orders for a second. He shot me the evil eye and walked out of the room. When the door was good and shut and I knew they were out of earshot, I finally spoke up.

"Your guys are leaving us alone? That's brave of you."

"That's brave of you to run your mouth after what you just did," he said. "My men are waiting outside the door. One signal from me, through a means of which I certainly won't tell you, and they'll rush in in five seconds flat and incapacitate you." He gestured to the wall behind him. It had swords of various makes and periods hanging on it. I recognized katanas and sai, and even a morningstar flail. "I'm also not helpless myself in the slightest."

I could feel Gary there beside me, ready to rattle objects in the room and cause a stir. I shook my head no to him and gave his hand a quick squeeze.

"So, Mister . . . Worthington, was it?"

"Correct. Worthington the Third, don't forget the suffix. Of the Long Island Worthingtons. We were here trying to escape the dreadful rain for the season and simply had to stop on by. They said your weather is perfect here in America's Finest City, and they ain't lyin'."

"When are you going to drop the act and tell me who you really are? Or do I have to get my men and their powers of persuasion to get you to sing for me the songs I want to hear?" he asked, and then he formed his hands into a steeple and calmly appraised me once again. "Your suit is good, not quite on par with the people who come to my affairs, but you could have pulled it off if it weren't for your shoes. They look a bit seventies, hand-me-downs from your . . . father?"

"Pop's been betting on the ponies a tad bit too much, drives Mom mad. He can't wait for the Del Mar Racetracks to open up again. She's taken to drinking, that's why she couldn't make it here today." I mimed chugging a bottle and made a glug, glug sound.

"And as for the college you plan on attending in the year after next? Empire State University? There is no such school."

"Aaaww, fuck!" I said, truly pissed at myself on that one. "They said that one on *Spider-Man*, and I thought if it takes place in New York, they'd name an actual New York City school. I should have gone with Columbia, where Jack Kerouac went. I knew I should have trusted Kerouac!"

"Or actually did your homework before the assignment was due, kiddo."

He seemed at ease, relaxed. I wasn't sure what to make of all this. I knew somehow this wasn't a matter he was going to call the authorities on. And I knew he liked me. Don't ask me how, but I could feel it. I just didn't know how he would handle the whole thing. I had to play it right, but I didn't even know what the rules were.

"So what gave you the audacity to think you could steal from *my* guests?"

There it was. Emphasis on the fact that they were his guests. He didn't want anything coming close to affecting his personal business. What that business was, I could hardly guess.

"Well, if I would have known they were your guests, I would have tried down the block at the next house," I offered. He smiled at this.

"You remind me of someone . . . well, me, when I was your age," he confided to me.

I've never liked people who see too much of themselves in others. They usually have singularly annoying egos, and they tend to want the world to be like them. It's not that people remind them of themselves all that much; it's that they want people to follow their ways, because to them, nothing else is important.

"I won't hold that against you," I replied.

"But that little mouth of yours always running will get you into big trouble." He sighed. "So why did you risk it all to pick flowers for my baby girl?"

His baby girl. Interesting. She did not look like him in the slightest, but sometimes things are funny like that.

"Sometimes you can take one look at a person and you simply figure that they're worth a risk," I said, smiling my most cocky smile. But that wasn't a lie. She was a girl I would have gambled it all on, betting high on a chance with her, just to see her smile.

"That girl was born to break hearts," he warned.

"Born to, or taught to? There's a pretty big difference."

"Find out for yourself."

"Pardon?"

"I might have need of your services from time to time. You'll need to learn how to lie. Your aliases are about as see-through as a ghost in front of a screen door." Funny choice of words.

I stared at him skeptically for a good long moment. I glanced around the room again, taking in all the opulence, all the trappings of power, from the portraits to the bronze statues of pagan deities dancing about in pastoral bliss, and wondered why the hell did he want me.

"What's in it for me?"

"Other than me not calling the authorities on your impertinent, brazen little self?" he said, laughing again at my audacity. "You'll be compensated handsomely for any jobs I require you to pull off. And I can help you improve upon your methods. You could use a bit of polish and refinement. I can definitely give that to you. No more diamond in the rough, you'll have enough polish to gleam when you must shine. You'll be able to fit in among any type of society. You don't fit in with high society. But I can teach you how to fit in. Teach you how to be sophisticated. Teach you how to steal and actually get away with it."

He was singing the song of every word I had ever wanted to hear. A rich patron who could give me access to resources I had never dreamed of. This was the big time, I thought. My pop had given up on any kind of a wild life, and strangely enough, I had picked up on all his bad habits.

Sure, A.J. was reformed. He had finished a college degree when I was a kid and now was working an honest life as an accountant. But I saw him as a man who was working only to sweat and save for himself until he keeled over at a desk in someone's office building.

I wanted that good life, to see how green the grass really was on the other side, to see the world and how much of it I could fit into the palm of my hand.

I knew I was possibly shaking hands with the devil, but there were always ways to wriggle out of these kinds of deals. Didn't Faust go to Heaven in some versions of the story? There had to be due process in the courts of final judgment, didn't there?

What more could I say, because without knowing me hardly at all, he sized me up and found my heart's one true desire and put it on a hook to dangle in front of me.

The devil doesn't really have a contract that he makes you sign with a gold pen when he makes his terms. He simply shows you your heart's desire on a silver tray right in front of you and then puts the lid back on it when you've had a glimpse of it, knowing you'll do whatever it takes to get the whole taste of it. He sang my song to me, and I was humming the tune right along with him.

What more could I say except "Okay, I'm in."

"Keep the money you swiped off my guests," he said. "Throw out the credit cards, you'll get caught using those things sooner rather than later."

"Hasn't happened yet."

"Yet."

"Who are you?" I asked. "What do you do?"

"Who I am is David Moreau. What I do . . . is complicated. And personal. I'll tell you as needed."

"Be oblique, then," I said, holding out a hand, which he shook with a firm grip. "My name's Alex. Alex Rose. Look forward to working with you. When do I start?"

"Tomorrow."

"But that's a school day."

"That's going to be a problem for someone like you?" He raised an eyebrow. "I might have overestimated your capabilities if a truant officer is enough to deter you."

"I just wanted you to know it better be worth my time."

He laughed at that. "It will. You can be sure of that."

He stood up and gestured towards the big doors. "Leave out the side door. I don't want the guests seeing you on the way out."

"Thanks for letting me know you care, makes a guy feel wanted."

"Oleg will escort you out."

"Don't want me swiping the silver on the way out."

"Precisely."

I winked and waved, and then I walked out without so much as a backward glance. But I could feel his stare, watching me, calculating and appraising my moves on the way out.

Gary was at my side, and I nodded reassuringly to him. Moreau went down the hall with us, silently shadowing me and my unwitting escort.

His man was there, bottle of water in hand. I popped the cap off and took a big swig. "Cheers, my good man," I said, winking at Oleg and then walking down the hall. "You were showing me the door, n'est-ce pas?"

"With pleasure," he muttered.

"I'll see you around!" I chirped as I walked along with him. As we strode down the hall, I glanced down a corner and saw the girl there.

"Come to see me on my way?" I asked her.

"Something like that."

"I never did get your name!"

"Huh." She smiled. "That's too bad for you."

She leaned in close, and I thought she was going to kiss me, but instead she hugged me close and whispered into my ear, "Take care with that spirit of yours, keep him out of trouble if you can't stay out of it yourself."

"Wait, how do you know about him?" I stuttered.

With that, she kissed me on one cheek, smacked the other, and pushed me off to wander my way out of that labyrinth of a building with my Nordic chaperone.

9.

THAT NEXT DAY, AFTER MEETING MOREAU, I dialed it in sick to school. Used my same old excuse, in A.J.'s voice, telling them I had diarrhea real bad, and they always tended to not ask too many questions after that. After that, I slept in for another hour; he didn't specify any time, so I was gonna enjoy this.

This time at that palace overlooking the crashing Pacific, there was no sneaking in through those big gates. I simply rang the buzzer and they opened right up.

On this occasion, I took my time wandering about the grounds. The sea air felt delicious on my skin, even though I could feel it drying out from the salt. I had always hated getting sticky things on me when I was a small child. Anything. Ice cream, if it dribbled down my chin or my arm, was something I had to wash off immediately, otherwise it would feel as uncomfortable as if I was sticky all day and everything I touched was all gluey too. Same with sand from the beach. I could never wipe it off enough.

So it felt good to not care. To have salty sweat on my skin and not worry that it was contaminated but merely something to feel and let me know that sometimes things were simply dirty and you could live with them. Sometimes life was a mess and that was okay. And what a beautiful mess it was, indeed!

I danced around a light post, spinning around on it like I was Gene Kelly, singin' in the . . . well, sunlight.

Gary was moping a little. He was not on board for this experiment with these people.

"Look, Gloomy Gus," I teased, "I'll get out of any hot spots that come up with this, it's what I do."

"And you've been doing this for how long?" he asked, not impressed.

"Long enough to know how to get out of trouble like a champ. I mean, stealing wallets since I was twelve, so what, three years?"

"And then on your big debut, you fuck it up and get pinched."

"Geez, you make it all seem so amateur hour when you put it like that."

"You mean in perspective?"

"Oh, piss off."

That was probably a bit too harshly dismissive, and I felt bad about saying that to a friend. I picked a rose from the bushes along the driveway, in case she should be there. I held it out for him to have a sniff.

"Look," Gary sighed, eyes darting from side to side. "This guy caught you and then offers you a job. Sounds suspicious."

"I'll take care."

"Have you ever seen someone die?" Gary finally asked, in a last-ditch effort to keep me from this place. Do or die time, and he was already dead, so it was all do for him.

"Um, actually, no," I said after thinking about it for a second.

I didn't know if that was a good or a bad thing. I had seen a ghost at his own funeral. He was standing among the crowd, sobbing along with everyone in attendance. I wasn't sure if he was shedding tears at the general situation of dying or because he expected the whole ceremony to be different than what it was. Who plans for a funeral though? I hoped people would get drunk as hell at mine and make it a real mother of a blowout. A real send-off, Irish as hell, in honor of my ancestors on my pop's side, and Oscar Wilde, whom I shared a birthday with, may he rest in peace.

"I have seen a person die since I've been dead," he said, his voice taking on a note of sorrow that was heartbreaking to hear. He had the shimmering quality in the midday sun of a mirage. His tears dripped down his cheeks and then disappeared as they fell. "It's a different view when you're on the other side. They don't always stick around as ghosts like me. Some simply disappear. They might go somewhere else, but I just don't know! They aren't always blissful when they go. They can be in shock, complete terror, like the joy is sucked out of them and they're scared as hell and not wanting to let go. But they go away to something, even if it's nothing. Don't risk yourself with these people. It's not too late."

I stared into his brown eyes, not fully bright as they could have been if he was a flesh and blood person again. "Look," I told him, holding my hand out, "I love that you're worried. But I need to see this one through."

"But why?"

"I need to see what this man can promise. He could have turned me in, but he didn't. And I want to know why."

That wasn't all of it. I was holding out on him, and I didn't want to tell him all of it. I had something special with Gary and didn't want to drive any wedges between us.

"What else?" he asked, pointedly. "It's her, isn't it?"

There it was, and I couldn't even put on a good poker face despite all the lies I had ever uttered. I sighed a deep sigh and tried to stare off, but glanced back into his sad spirit eyes and couldn't resist my ghostly companion.

"Okay," I admitted. "Maybe a little."

That wasn't the half of it. She was the majority of why I was fascinated with this whole ordeal. I wanted to get to the heart of the enigma that was her. I never had someone like me I could confide in. I was overjoyed to find I wasn't alone in this world and that someone could maybe dig into the mysteries of people like myself as we revealed to each other our dreams and desires.

It was a touch naïve. I knew it, even then.

But I was holding out hope and thinking I could maybe find a companion who could help me endure the mysteries of life and death I was forced to catch glimpses of since I was old enough to walk. Maybe the world wasn't such a scary place if there were people who I could band together with, people who I could count on to dispel all the uncertainty as we rallied together under a common cause.

Maybe she and I could create a nation of two odd kids, a strange citadel against all the cruel people who would shun us. The people who had always called us crazy, or thought we were liars because we saw things differently than the rest of the run of humanity.

For that, I was willing to risk big and bet high.

The stakes were as great as my life, or so I believed, but I didn't think I would be complete in this life if I didn't try. I never wanted to regret things I didn't do, and if I piled on a few things I did regret doing, that was better than the uncertainty of the wouldas, couldas, and shouldas.

I wanted to live hard, always did, and this place was one of the big mysteries in life, where living happened on a grand scale. Sure, it was filled with people I didn't understand, but I found them insanely compelling. I wanted to penetrate the heart of their mystery, find their secrets, and take them and give them back to the people. Those hoarded fires they guard might be able to light so many ways for the rest of the world, and I wasn't willing to let them only burn in one person's house.

"Look, if things get too intense and they are up to anything I'm not down with, I'll skedaddle. Scram. Sayonara, hasta la vista, baby. I'll find a way. Cut the ties with them and slip on off into the sunset. I'm a white knight, I've got this. St. George fighting the dragon."

"There's something else," Gary whispered, almost as if he was afraid, as though there might be someone listening. "There's a reason why we ghosts are all about people like you, Alex. It's not only that you can see us. It's that we see you. From miles off. There's something about you, like a diamond, or a pearl. You have this radiance about you, and we can sense it. It draws us to you, makes you compelling and hard to resist. You're a magnet for people who have passed on."

"Just my natural charm and good looks, I'm sure," I said, flashing him a smile.

"It's more than that. It's like an aura. You've got it. She's got it. Moreau has something else. It's like there's something at work inside his soul, an energy that's trying to play tricks with the light instead of magnifying it. Like his soul is hiding something and it covers itself up as it radiates, but there's great strength to it, I can feel it. It's something powerful, and it's old and it's hungry."

This made me pause to reflect for a second.

"What about Mrs. Beakley?" I asked. "That's not her real name. Shit, I'm not sure what it really was, that's what I called her. She was this ghost always crying in front of my church. She saw me, but sometimes she ignored me."

"I dunno." Gary shrugged. "Some ghosts are like people, they're so sad that even diamonds don't shine for them."

Gary was unshakably loyal to me, and I knew he wouldn't lie to me like a petty trickster ghost that throws about dishes off of shelves because it wants people out of its house. He was scared of this man, and he could sense something I couldn't.

But the sad part was this didn't deter me. This fascination with darkness I had wouldn't be satisfied unless I touched the heart of it and saw if it was going to try and stick to the tips of my fingers.

"I'll be careful!" I promised him. "I gotta get in, I told him I'd come on over. He'll wonder why I'm wasting my time out here."

"I'll be around if you need me," he said, and I could feel him slipping into the fringes, where he wasn't a visible presence to me anymore, but a feeling, the way you know there's someone in a room.

And with that, I walked through that sunshiney expanse of a driveway and up to the big front doors of Fin de la Terre. They towered impossibly tall, made for titans to enter, not for ordinary people. I was here stepping across the threshold of this house of giants, hoping to find the goose that lays the golden eggs, and a harp of gold, all the things my greedy little picking and stealing fingers could take back to my village.

"Hello!" I called out into the huge foyer. This was an *actual* foyer, with a huge crystal chandelier above that sparkled in a nova burst of glittering glass. The floors were an even more gleaming marble than the other ones I'd seen in the halls, like they were imported from a kingdom I'd only read about in books in their rosy-pink hues and golden molding where they met the walls.

And there was David Moreau at the head of the stairs looking regal in a blue suit with a nicely fitting vest and pocket square. His black leather shoes gleamed like they were carved out of a solid chunk of obsidian, quarried from the same magical place where he got the marble floors and fitted to him perfectly by a master craftsperson.

"We'll have to do something about your attire," he said. "I insist my people be presentable."

"I didn't get the semiformal part of the invite," I said, frowning as I looked at my white turtleneck and black jeans, checking for what was so imperfect about my wardrobe choices.

"We'll find something to make you look the part," he said as he came down the stairs.

"And what is that part?"

"Someone who can blend in anywhere." There was the gleam in his eye of a hidden passion was behind every word he said. "Someone who can play whatever role is required to get the job done."

"And what jobs do you have in mind?"

"Those come later," he said, then finally descended to the lobby with me. "Walk with me."

We wandered through spacious halls, every one of them filled with amazing things. One room had taxidermy stuffed animals, mouths stuck wide growling in a menagerie of musty smelling things that were once fierce creatures to be reckoned with.

Another had musical instruments in it, enough to start a small orchestra. Another had an actual movie theater.

Every room was wonderful, designed to impress and convey the power that the inhabitants wanted to portray to anyone who dared to come in from the ordinary world to this little paradise of theirs. I stared longingly in each room, trying not to seem overly impressed but wondering what it would be to enjoy this kind of grandeur on a daily basis.

"Where were you born?" he asked me. "I think people carry the stamp of where they come from with them all their lives. It molds them and they can't shake it, try as they might, even when they try to pick up the pieces in someplace new."

He had such an odd way of speaking to me. Most adults tend to talk down to young people, as if they have deep secrets that are too precious to give up and it will lessen them if they should ever let anyone else be on a level with them. This man spoke to me like I was on a level with him, and it drew me in to him.

I found him so compelling, and I wanted to be as elegant and as confident as he appeared. He had an aura that seemed to command respect, whereas I always assumed I was the underdog and the outcast in any room I entered. Ill at ease with people even though I loved them and desperately needed their company, even though I would have been too cool to admit it.

"I was born right here in San Diego. Mercy Hospital, or so my pop says. The Catholic hospital in the gay part of town."

"Ah." He nodded. "America's finest city is your Bethlehem. That makes sense. You have that laid back air of a true Californian. Nothing will ever cause you to have the slightest care in the world, if you can ever help it. After you." He motioned for me to go before him through a narrow doorway into another long hallway.

I shrugged. "Well, they say life's too short to worry."

"For the lucky ones, it is," he sighed.

I had no idea what he meant by that. He said some very peculiar things, and I had the impression he was talking in riddles, like a modern sphinx. He had that hint of danger to him that the Theban monster must have had too, as if he was something composed of all ordinary parts individually, but on the whole, they were simply all too bizarre a combination.

That's what it must have been like for the travelers on the road to Thebes. Seeing something made of normal parts, a woman's head, a lion's body, an eagle's wings. You'd think, *I know all these things, but what are they doing all together like that?* And so you couldn't help but try to answer that riddle when she proposed it to you. Because she herself was the riddle.

That was how I felt about him. All was seemingly normal, but something was wrong in the way it was put together.

"My Bethlehem was in Clairvaux," he confided. "This was … a long while ago, in Europe. Things were very different then. It was a savage place, where old superstitions ruled our way of life. You should be grateful we're in the era we live in. It's a time where we can make great changes for ourselves for the better. Where people don't think that the past has to repeat itself simply because we abide by that age-old excuse of doing the things we do because that is the way they have always been done."

My world history wasn't as good as I would have liked, and so I wondered what was so savage about Europe for him. I knew a world war had taken place around the time he must have been born, but I didn't see how they could still be feeling its effects. I wanted to know more from him, maybe see into a fraction of that mystery, answer one of his riddles.

"I don't let anything from the past make my choices for me," I said. "I'm always looking for what's on that next horizon."

He paused in thought, gazing off out through a big window we were walking by, to the Pacific, with its crashing waves and salty sea air coming in so strong I could almost feel it, a bit of the ocean intruding on the land.

"Sometimes the past is harder to shake off than you think," he sighed. "But still, we persist. We carry on and on."

"So when is my training gonna start?"

"It's already begun," he informed me. "We're getting to know each other, I'm sounding you out. I'm learning where you need to improve on your methods. Your wallet, for instance. You need to pay closer attention to what's going on around you."

I felt about in my pockets for it. Did I even bring it? I had to have brought it with me. He then held out his hand, displaying it for me to see.

"Nice," I said. "Didn't even feel that. But look inside."

He opened it up, and it had only a bunch of photos and a five-dollar bill, as well as some twenty-one-year-old's ID that I used to buy booze. "You want my cash, that's right here," I said, pulling the stolen wad of cash out of my front pocket.

"All of it?"

I checked it out. I had counted it the night before, there was three grand. I had only a grand. "Now, how did you do that?"

"Sized you up, figured where you were carrying something."

"Right, I do that one all the time. But how'd you get one past me?"

"You really need to watch your surroundings, especially when someone is letting you by in a tight space."

"Ah, when you let me by in that doorway."

"You have a lot to learn," he said, smiling a broad Cheshire cat smile.

The rest of Wonderland felt differently in his presence, but I felt like a victim being the recipient of that grin, like the teeth could change from happy to something that could gnaw on the world if they were given too much room to flash so brightly in it.

I could feel Gary comforting me. A gentle nudge saying "I'm here."

"But what do you want to learn? What do you want to do?" he asked. "Surely you don't want to spend your days going about and stealing money from marks at garden parties? There's more out there than that."

David led me to a side room with a huge safe. It took up an entire wall, as large and imposing as a huge relic that belonged on a barren field that people would excavate. It could probably prop up a corner of the pyramids and still hold more weight.

"What is this for?" I asked.

"You're going to crack it one day," he said, smiling proudly. "How's that for a challenge?"

I stared up at this monster of a lock box, full of secrets and passages to great new heights, and I knew that would be the grail I sought here, in dark tons of steel. Well, one grail, at least.

I didn't know where to begin, but I knew this mechanical contraption would be the secrets to life on the edge itself, and I would be the one to master every trick this smooth black beauty was willing to show me in all her cold, locked-up mystery.

"I—" I began, when all of a sudden, the phone on the wall rang. He went on over to pick it up.

"Yes? Already . . ? When do you need me . . ? No, not too busy, I'll be on my way in a minute."

He hung up the phone. "I have business to attend to. Affairs that require a personal touch. Come back here this weekend. I won't arouse anyone's suspicions by making you miss any more school. Enjoy the house for the rest of the day in the meantime. Any of the open rooms are yours to explore. Make yourself familiar with the grounds while I am gone, but don't try anything ... that would violate the rules of hospitable conduct. I take these matters very seriously, and I have ways of knowing what is amiss in my house that you don't want to test the limits of."

"Jawohl!" I said in a German accent and saluted him as he rushed off.

The afternoon was spent wandering into room after room. Every one of them led off into some other warren of rooms. After a while, I was pretty sure I was quite lost and might have to work hard to get out. I sat down at a beautiful Bösendorfer and began to play "Can't Help Falling in Love," the only song I was confident enough to play without assistance from sheet music, and even then, it was only the melody parts with my right hand. I didn't know any of the left. I should have since I'm left-handed, but sometimes you surprise yourself with how you learn.

I paused after messing up a note and listened for a noise I believed at first that I might have been playing on the keys, but then realized it was someone sobbing.

It was the guttural sound of choking noises coming out of a mouth, combined with moans and lowing sounds. It sounded like a cow mooing with sad, soulful tones, as if it wanted to speak words to save its life but couldn't. I thought of Io turned to a cow, with a giant with unsleeping eyes set upon her and how horrible it must have been to be trapped like she was, moaning and unable to get those staring eyes off of you. This place felt as watchful as if there were eyes all over it like Argus. Unsleeping and set over by vengeful powers, making the powerless understand how helpless they are and in need of a divine intervention to charm those eyes into sleep.

I slowly searched the hallways for the noise, walking past works of art and tropical plants twining towards windows for light. I had absolutely no idea where in the house I was, but I needed to find the source of that moaning.

Something grabbed ahold of me, and I was so tense and focused on the noise I almost jumped. It was Gary. He was so determined to warn me that he had manifested into solid form and was trying to keep me from going any farther. He shook his head, and his eyes were full of so much worry he might as well have been facing a second death all over again. He bit his lip in his anxiety and was the picture image of dismay.

I squeezed his hand. "I've gotta see what this is."

He followed cautiously, in that hover of a walk he had. We rounded a corner and discovered a woman in a black dress, looking elegant like she was attending a cocktail party. She had short, curly hair in a mess of beautiful tangles. She was a ghost, I realized. It took me a minute to figure out what she was, she was such a solid image of pain and suffering as she stood there, cradling herself as if she was cold. She moaned again, and I tried to approach her to see if there was anything that could be done for her.

She turned about to face me, and I nearly screamed. She moaned again, and I realized why her moans were so full of bubbling sounds like she had something in her throat. She had no tongue and blood was coming out of her perfect *O* of a distorted and tortured mouth.

Her eyes were rimmed in awful, seeping red. They were so dark I couldn't make out what color they were over the blood. It was because she had no eyes! Only dark holes where they should have been and puckered, blood smeared skin around the edges.

She reached out and grabbed the collar of my turtleneck shirt, and I made a startled noise. This made her moan even louder.

There were slashes all over her neck, along with great big ones on her arms and shoulders, like she used them to defend herself from an attack with a knife. They glowed sore and red.

I was in a panic. I knew she could do precious little to harm me physically, but I was so frightened I wanted to turn away and run. I couldn't handle those moans coming out of her voiceless mouth. Blood flew out in drops and flecked out of it as she cried, only to disappear as it hit my shirt. I would have ripped it clean off if it had left a stain on it.

She still clutched onto my shirt with a physical force I could not get to desist. I had felt ghosts make their presence solid, but this one was amplifying her pain into an iron grip. I crouched down with her on top of me, sputtering and crying tears of horrible dark gore.

"Molly!" a voice shouted. "You're okay. You're okay. Shush, shush girl. It's okay. Shush, I'm here."

It was the girl from my first encounter in this place. She held the poor and tormented spirit to her, hugging her and making cooing noises to calm her. "You scared her!" she said to me.

"Well, shit, sorry to have startled her!" I exclaimed sarcastically. "My bad!"

"She's in pain, I need to help her."

"No shit, she's got no fucking eyes and tongue."

The spirit moaned louder at that and I instantly felt bad. She still had ears to hear, after all.

"Shhhhhhh! It's okay, Molly. You're still a gorgeous gal. We love you."

The girl glared at me as if I was the one who caused this poor ghost's distress. She motioned with her eyes as if I needed to make things right with her. I took a deep breath and swallowed a lump in my throat. I reached out a hand and placed it gently on the ghost's shoulder the way I would if I was trying to comfort a child. "I'm sorry, Molly. I didn't mean to come into your house and startle you. I'm sorry."

She moaned again, but it wasn't so pained and full of grief.

"I'm going to calm her, give me a sec," the girl told me. I hesitated, staring at the two of them until she shot me an annoyed look. "Wait outside, near the cliffs. Don't worry. I'll be out in a minute."

"Okay," I agreed. I didn't want to be in this house a moment longer. For all its immense size and grandeur, it seemed that the walls were closing in and threatening to choke out all light.

I attempted to go out one way, and she grabbed my sleeve. "This way," she said, motioning down to a different hallway. "Take that one all the way to the back exit."

As I walked away, I heard her singing softly to the ghost. It was an old timey song about a place called St. James Infirmary or something like that. A woman who was sweet and cold and fair. It seemed like it was meant for funerals. It was strangely beautiful and haunting.

10.

ALL THE GLEAM AND GOLD seemed cheap as I stumbled out of the house, like they were a brittle facade for the horrors that threatened to leak out from the seams. No matter how much you tried to silver-gilt the outside, blood was determined to spill out and threaten to fill the streets if it could, finding ways even after we died to tear open the wounds and make us realize death is a heartbeat away and all our efforts to avoid it were only running from the inevitable.

God, I wanted to curl up and scream as long and guttural as that ghost.

When I got outside, the fog was rolling in, creeping towards us in a wall of mist straight from the ocean, threatening to make the day's sun a memory. I watched the surf pound against the sand and thought of how easy it would be to slip down there, see if I could get carried far enough before the fish began to feed on me and dissolve me into algae in that wide and turbulent sea.

My horror at everything conjured up sirens in my imagination. Foamy dream apparitions singing their songs that seemed so enticing but were really only lures to being bleached bones scattered among the coral as the fish reduced the rest to dispersed elemental compounds that salted the waves of that wide and dark sea.

When she finally came out, I was sitting on a bench, with my arms curled up around my knees like a sad elf in a fairy story. She placed her hand on my shoulder with a graceful, comforting ease.

"My name is Jenny Cienfuegos," she said. "That was Molly."

Jenny. She was no longer the mysterious femme fatale when I looked up at her, calling to me from the balcony of a party I crashed, or the frustrated spoiled debutante I was trying to impress while simultaneously annoying the pants off of her. She was a person about my age, with a bigger heart than I imagined. For all our efforts at maturity, we were still kids, and we sat there together as if we didn't have anyone else in the world besides each other and gazed at the sunset as it streaked the horizon red.

"I'm Alex," I finally managed to say.

We watched that sunset like it was commemorating a momentous occasion, and I can still picture that glow on the sky in my mind and that feeling of her nearby, comforting me the way she must have made that ghost feel. She made me remember that the chaos was not so all-encompassing. She was there, and that gave a touch of joy back into a scary and shocking world, and even if the light was going away, I realized it was never away for long. I'd see it again tomorrow.

She gave me a big hug so full of warmth that the best, brightest sensations that the sunlight left behind from the day must've been in that sweet embrace.

"So how do you know her name if she can't speak?" I asked her.

"I gave her a pen and she wrote it down."

"Huh." I was amazed at how obvious and easy an idea that was. "That's a great idea."

"Some ghosts are nonverbal," she explained. "Tongue or no tongue. The secret is trying to find a way to communicate with them. To get through to them."

I realized I had gravitated towards the more verbal spirits in my relationships with those who were among the non-living. The thought of anyone not being able to communicate through words was disturbing to me even though I knew people could do just fine without them. I wrapped everything in words. I used words to light the way out of confusion, fashioned my fears into them so they could be rational things I could comprehend and then overcome. I used words when I was nervous to ease the tension and disarm people emotionally.

I probably talked too much.

And here was someone who could look for ways to communicate with people that were meaningful and able to get through to those who needed it most. I wanted to learn from her.

"So how did it happen?" I asked her, a hint of desperation in my voice.

I wanted to find out what it was that could have done such a terrible desecration to her. But I was also deeply afraid of whatever it was.

"She doesn't know who it was, but it was a man," Jenny said.

"Jeez! Fuck," I muttered. "Do we know who it could have been? They could still be around. Fucking hell, was it someone here?"

I glanced around, feeling the windows of the house watching

again with eyes of shining glass that concealed on one side and took in our words and movements on the other.

"She died in the 1930s. It's tough trying to figure it out, because she really has no idea what decade it is. She can only write out scared ramblings. It's not much of any value. In her mind, she's probably reliving the things that happened to her all over again."

My heart unrestrainedly went out to that poor ghost, reliving a hell for years that no creature on Earth ever deserved to have to cope with. I wanted to take her ethereal spirit form in my arms and cradle her like a helpless baby. Hug her and rock her until all the tears were gone and she was whole again and able to breathe freely instead of gobs of blood and tears of pain. I wanted her to know that she was loved, that another person was caring for her and about her, even if it had been decades since she had touched the world with human fingertips.

"Oh," I said. I clutched the sides of my head, reeling from the implications of that. "Oh, oh, ohhhh." I was going to start moaning like Molly and never stop until we were both dead and wailing throughout this house. "To hang on like that for so long . . . How can anything ever stand that?"

A horrible vision of Hell filled the limits of my comprehension, and it was one prolonged note of agony, stuck in a track on repeat and forcing someone to blindly grope about in gloomy halls for eternity. I wanted to scream at a universe that could come up with a punishment that unfair.

"That's why I try and comfort her," she said. She placed a hand on my shoulder to do the same for me, but I could feel her frustration with every bit of pressure her fingers put on me. "No one should have to put up with what she has had to endure. I'll find a way to discover who the bastards who did this to her were and make them pay. In this life or the next."

She said this with such conviction that I absolutely believed she would make them pay in the worst way possible and didn't want to be the people who provoked her anger.

"I've looked her up in newspapers from back in the day. There was a girl from around then who went missing. An Irish maid named Molly, and she fits the description. Nobody found her body though."

"Well, you're a saint for doing that," I said. I was still shuddering at the thought of it all. Jenny patted me on the shoulder and rubbed my back. Usually I would find those gestures to be condescending, but they were perfect and soothing. "I don't know if I could deal with that, being the only one around who can hear her and deal with her."

"She terrified me when I was a kid," she said.

"Since you were a kid? Damn."

The spirits I remembered seeing as a little boy had me frightened they were going to crowd out my thoughts if I focused on them. They were always around the corner, waiting to surprise me when I least expected. I had never seen one who was murdered in such a horrible way. I took Jenny's hand and held onto it, and we stared out into that gray sea.

"One day I tried to see what I could do to help her. No one else would. I couldn't leave another woman in pain like that without trying to do something to ease her suffering. I started playing music for her and it would calm her down."

Her hand was smooth and soft, where mine was rough and dry. I wanted to twine my fingertips in hers and leave them there for as long as I could.

"So if you're David's kid, how come your last name is Cienfuegos and his is Moreau?" I asked.

"I was adopted." I thought as much, but was glad to hear it confirmed. "I never wanted to give up my mother's last name."

"I never knew my mother," I said. "It's just me and my father. And Windsong. She's sort of a trippy hippy aunt."

"My mother died when I was a kid. I remember it, it happened all of a sudden. David came along and let me know I was coming to live with him after that, and he arranged for it all, adopting me and me coming here from Mexico. He got me U.S. citizenship and everything."

"Very nice of him."

"He . . . can be kind," she said, and stared off in the distance. It seemed there was more to tell on the tip of her tongue that she was trying to figure out if she should say or not. "What do you want from him?"

"I can't resist a challenge."

"Sounds reckless."

"Maybe. But maybe people aren't reckless enough," I said. "I want to live a really authentic life, and not say I waited in the wings while the action was going on." She stared at me quizzically, like a disapproving parent, and I decided I had to make my case to her. "I want people to say that I fought fiercely, was a friend to those who needed one for all eternity, and . . . fucked frequently!" I declared to her with all the enthusiasm and zeal of a Marxist reciting communist propaganda. "Is that so much to ask for?"

"Hmmmm. . . And have you ever had sex? It's hardly frequent if you haven't even done it yet."

"Bases one through three!" I countered, still trying to maintain a degree of coolness and enthusiasm. "Wait, what is second base anyway? Pretty sure third is oral stuff."

"Sounds like you're off to a great start. Tell me how all those others work out."

"I've got all the time in the world to get it right," I said, trying on my best smarmy grin.

"Well, be careful how you use that time around here. This place has a way of sucking people in, living and dead."

"We'll see who sucks who," I said, then paused. "Dammit, I can come up with a better line than that, gimme a second . . ."

We laughed for a little while and stared at the approaching darkness and stars together.

I knew I should be getting back home—Pop and Windsong would be starting to worry—but I finally knew I had found an accomplice in all things strange. Someone who got me. That was worth more to me than any lessons I could ever learn from any master of any skills. I wanted to savor every second with her, because I didn't know when I would ever know the calm in the soul of having someone like me be so close again.

When I had told adults about the spirits I saw, it was just to have them tell me it was only my imagination and that I would grow out of my childish preoccupations. This hardened me from a young age, made me worry it was me against the world, because I was alone and fighting against it at all times. An army of one boy, determined to defend his cause, of which he never had the chance to form a manifesto for, because he didn't even know what the aims and goals he should strive for were. Just a drive to survive and make it without giving himself up for anyone ever.

Here was a soul who got me in some ways at least. Sure, we were from opposite sides of the tracks, but I was determined to know more about this special person and let her know me. I finally said goodbye to her for the evening, but I knew I would keep coming back to this haunted and haunting place.

11.

I HAD BEEN WORKING WITH David Moreau for over a year. I came over every day I could after school and on the weekends. Always made sure to get my homework done, so as to avoid suspicion, but the lessons with him in this trade were an obsession. I wanted nothing more than to be the best there was at what I was doing, and what I was doing was learning how to steal like my hands were made of glue.

Every day on the way in, I would pick a new flower from the grounds (even these I would steal) and crumple a piece of paper with a letter I wrote to Jenny around it and toss it onto her balcony. She didn't always respond, but every so often I'd see her and she would drop a letter of her own down from off the balcony.

The letters might have been full of the most profound statements of teenage angst and confessions of things we had never told anyone ever in our wildest dreams. Or they could have been filled with trivial things such as how much school sucked and what we had for dinner.

It was a dream to be even close to Jenny and have her to talk to. I loved having a confidante, a willing ear to blurt out all my thoughts to. Someone to hear all my crazy adolescent dreams and ambitions that I was too shy or afraid to voice to the rest of the world. But my big joy was learning the tricks of my trade, and I wanted to be the best tradesman ever in the field of tricks.

I learned how to pick pockets, pick locks, and crack safes.

I loved the art of it, using sleight of hand to distract a target and steal the contents of their wallet, or their jewelry. David would have me go out on little thieving forays in the shining streets of San Diego, careening through the neon bars of the Gaslamp District, slipping off among those fancy doll houses of buildings. There was a dark joy in it for me to dispossess wealthy people of their property before they knew that the kid who bumped into them had made off with their necklace or their watch.

The steps didn't take long for me to master and I made a fine dance of it, a real show. Carrying a camera along, taking pictures of the architecture and telling people that they loved it when I took pictures of a Victorian-style building for my photography class. "Let me get one in real quick right here." A man comes along from his liquid lunch break, a tad bit tipsy on his way back to the daily grind. Then, bam! "Sorry, sir, did not mean to bump into you! I had to take that shot, the light was perfect. And I knocked your briefcase out of your hand. Here, let me help you up!"

And while I'm doing that, one quick movement pulls the leather strap out and another slips it off. Bam again! TAG Heuer in the bag! Precision Swiss timing stolen with a precisely rehearsed dance of fingertips on a grip of a wrist.

That was the fun stuff, doing a waltz on the streets with my unsuspecting partners. We'd meet for a few seconds, have a twirl together, say our goodbyes, then it was off on my merry way with a little keepsake from one of those brief lovers and our passionate affair. They always left me breathing heavy afterwards and wanting more from the next paramour in the streets, those unsuspecting partners, always in such a hurry to get on with their lives, never knowing that our love would leave me with more to remember them by than they were taking from the romance.

Oh my!

Then there was picking locks. Cylinder locks were a puzzle I wanted to fit all the pieces into just right, working those pins so everything slid into place long enough for me to twist my way into completion on it. With my tension tool giving things the slightest nudge, I would slip my pick in, feeling for that sweet spot, that one where the pin hangs in the shearline, where the space is finagled perfectly between that inner and outer cylinder and you know you're in. Every time that lock gave way, it was open sesame! A secret door had opened that only the skills of a trickster could work out, and I was the one with the bag of magic flimflammed from the enchanted cave where wonders never ceased.

The safes were the thorniest, most tricky bramble to try and scramble through. There were the obvious blunt force ways to break into them, like an angle grinder or drilling at a certain point. But I also learned how to finesse it all and break on into them in several more subtle ways. I would sit there for hours, listening to the safes Moreau presented me with, with a stethoscope on and listening for the two clicks that let me know I was in that contact area, the space on the dial between the two clicks.

I made graphs charting out what the point on the dials were, but he insisted I should be able to do it in my brain if I had to. Ordinarily I would have been all about throwing the numbers and axis graphs to the wind and saying fuck it, but I found it was extremely hard to remember those things and focus. I had to clear my mind and have the numbers live in it and those be my only thoughts.

It pushed everything to the back of my brain and made my focus laser intense.

I was dead to the rest of the ego trips the mind usually makes, only a solid beam of precise concentration with one intent in my mind. Nature might have made me out of random combinations of elements, carbon and water and calcium swirling about in complicated dances and all one day to return to dust like the Father Sheslo says on Ash Wednesday. But I was determined that my spirit—my mind, heart, and soul—should all seek heights that no ordinary boy of my age would dare to dream of.

Spinning and listening and spinning and listening.

David would do everything he could to rattle my focus. One time, he played Beethoven's Fifth on speakers that made the floor shake when it got to a raucous part of the melody.

"I can't hear a damn thing with you doing that!" I yelled. "How the fuck am I supposed to do this!"

"How anyone does anything under pressure," he replied. "Push the distractions to the back of your mind and focus. You have a good ear, trust it, and do your work despite everything going on all around you."

"Fuck this!" I said, throwing up my hands in frustration and giving the safe a kick, which only hurt my toe and did nothing of any value to the process.

"How are you going to do this in the real world, where there could be any number of distractions?" he asked.

"Hopefully in the real world I won't have you breathing down my neck and hanging around on me like body odor."

"Hmmm, you're wasting your time venting your anger on me," he calmly observed. That was the most infuriating part. I was ready to throw the damn safe at him, and he was acting as cool as if it was a walk in the park. "Again," he ordered.

"Why don't you let up on him and let the boy have some fun instead of all this safe cracking?" a voice that was music to my ears asked before a face that was angelic to my eyes entered the room.

Jenny came in wearing her tight shorts and T-shirt. She had finished exercising and now casually drank a bottle of fancy water with cucumber flavoring in it that put my Brita filtered tap water back at Windsong's place to shame.

"Hmmmm," Moreau mused. "Maybe the boy could use a different lesson."

"Uh, excuse me," I muttered. "Boy, here! Maybe I should go out and take a smoke break while you two have your little discussion of me while you pretend I'm not even here? Might make it easier if I giddy-up on out and save you the trouble."

"You'll do nothing of the sort!" Moreau declared as he strode up to his stereo and changed the song to a more modern one with a haunting keyboard melody that made me want to cry while getting up and twirling around at the same time. It was Annie Lennox's cover of Procol Harum's "A Whiter Shade of Pale."

"C'mon," Jenny said as she grabbed my hand and dragged me to a clear space of floor, where a lady and a unicorn were displayed on a rug in the center. "We waltz."

The mythical creature beneath our feet allowed the woman in her medieval gown with its dagged sleeves and yards of flowing ribbons to place her hand gently upon him, in a display of submission and magical interaction that I was certain was a virginity metaphor of some kind that men weren't meant to fully understand.

"I'm glad you arrived, my darling," Moreau said as she placed my one hand on the small of her back and the other in her hand. "I've been teaching him the antisocial graces for long enough, it's time to polish our diamond up and show him the social ones."

"Again with the diminutive references," I muttered. "'Our diamond!'"

"Ignore him," Jenny said in her calming voice. "Nobody waltzes anymore anyways, so just enjoy the ride and have a little fun for a change."

"Cultured people waltz!" Moreau protested as he pretended to attend the safe while he watched over us.

I was extremely uncomfortable having him watch his daughter as my mind went to places that involved us doing this with less clothing.

"Look more at your partner's eyes, less at her feet," Jenny said. I fought the urge to shy away from her bright eyes that could light up an entire cathedral and smile that could charm a kingdom. "It's a simple box step, one-two-three, back-two-three."

My footwork kept getting mixed up on the backwards steps, but she led us both back into that square formation and set the pace. I soon stopped stepping on her toes and smiled as I sank into the rhythm. "I think I'm getting the hang of it!" I exclaimed, maybe a bit too pleased with myself, because I mixed up a step as soon as I said it, but then quickly got back into the groove.

"You're good at improvising when you're in the heat of things," Jenny said to me as we twirled around on that rug.

It felt light and dreamy to be in her arms, like I belonged there, and could stay there forever. It was hard to concentrate on what she was saying because I was so happy to simply be there in that make-believe moment. But why did I think it was make-believe, even when I was in it? Was it my fear that nothing good lasts, or was it that the whole experience was beyond my wildest imaginings of happiness? I prayed it was the latter, because I was tired of all the cynicism, which was all the former could ever bring about.

"But when you are focused on the job at hand," she continued on, "you're rigid. You need to let life enter into the equation and go with the flow of it." She then did something that made me almost lose my footing and had us veer to the left as we stepped, same box pattern with our feet, but moving in an arch instead of that tight square we'd been confined to in our steps.

I yelped out an ungraceful that sounded like "Uh, waaaah-hhh!" but still followed her lead and kept on with that fantastic and enthralling dance. The music was a rain of smooth silver bells all magically falling on the ground and producing a beautiful cascade of sound.

"Well, it's easy for you to talk about going with the flow," I said sourly, "when your life is easy and everything you need is at your feet. Some of us have to work to get where we want in life."

She frowned at that comment, and then the emotion went out of her face. I worried that she would stop the dance, but she went on and on with each step, one-two-three, back-two-three. The nonsensical lyrics about vestal virgins and ghostly faces were a dull roar in the background. She took a deep breath and said, "You know, all you need are four walls to make a prison if you can't get out of them. Doesn't matter if the inside is lined in silk and enameled in gold."

"I'm sorry. That was a shitty thing to say to you. I don't know what it's like to be you or what kinds of struggles you deal with every day. And I don't think you don't work for what you get in life. I'm sorry."

"Hmmmm, let me think about whether to accept your apology while you see if you can spin me without dropping me on the ground."

"Okay, but promise not to step on my two left feet. One of which is in my mouth at the moment, so no worries with that one."

I lifted my arm up, holding her delicate hand in it, so smooth and full of little bones I worried I might hurt if I squeezed too hard. She spun about, and I gave her an extra twirl for good measure, to show her I was capable. I had the whole world in my hands with her there.

She came out of it and slipped her foot around the back of mine and fell into me, knocking me over, with her on top. "You dropped me!" she exclaimed.

"Sure. Or you dropped yourself onto me. So, I guess all is forgiven?"

"Only if you kiss better than you talk to girls," she said.

"Well, I'm well known for being gifted with my tongue, they say, which probably translates well to either . . ."

She pressed a finger to my lips and whispered, "Shhhhhh." Then she locked her lips to mine, and it was more refreshing than if I was a flower taking in that first drink of raindrops after months without any precipitation. I wanted to spread apart and burst into bright colors in every direction.

I slipped my tongue in between those lips, and she danced along with mine with her own. Our legs were no longer a part of this waltz; the steps had moved about to the rest of us.

She pulled back slowly, with my arms still pinned to the ground. I remained locked to her lips as long as I could until finally she sat on top of me and stared at the safe contemplatively. "Looks like you've got your work cut out for you," she said. I couldn't tell if she was talking about the safe or herself. "And I don't want to keep you from it, so let's play around later."

And with that, she daintily hopped up and slowly walked out of the room in a deliberately seductive saunter. I checked to make sure Moreau wasn't still present because that would have been awkward as hell, but luckily, he left while my attention was elsewhere.

"Great," I muttered. "Now how am I ever gonna focus?"

12.

MOREAU SENT ME OUT ON ASSIGNMENT several times for fieldwork. I was roaming about downtown La Jolla one of those days, following a girl about my age down Prospect Street, with all its shop windows and ocean views, not knowing I was about to have a run in with Destiny in her most lovely and caring form. She had on a striped crop top with the kind of spaghetti straps that they were always sending girls out of classes for wearing, which I thought was pretty ludicrous. Young boys could get horny over anything, and the teachers acted like it was the girl's fault that we were all hormonal and not taught proper boundaries.

She had cute jeans on that were baggy in the legs but showed off her butt in a way that made it hard to concentrate on the job at hand. It was one of the rules I learned from Moreau—or from another experience, I forget which—never get thrown off by your quarry, always throw them off. But maybe I didn't care if I got thrown about on this day.

She strutted along on the sidewalk as the light coming through the branches of a rubber tree poured down and decorated her tan skin, and played about in her chestnut-brown hair. Leaning up against a streetlight, I waited for the right moment and strolled after her when she passed me by. I bumped into her as she waited at a crosswalk, taking her wallet right out of her bag while she was distracted, as I steadied her and apologized.

"I am so sorry!" I profusely apologized. "I was daydreaming and should have seen a cute girl like you from a mile away instead of running into you. Are you okay?"

She had a look of horror in her eyes as she stared into mine, and I tried to figure out what it was from. She couldn't have seen me take her wallet out or she would have called for help. There was something alluring about her that kept making me appraise her over and over. Her dark brown eyes remained wide open in a gorgeous deer-in-a-headlight stare as she tried to mouth words but found herself unable to.

That's when it hit me what it was—I knew her. But not her. I knew her from school as a him. "Kostya?" I asked.

"Oh my gosh," she gasped. She put her hands over her lips in the cutest way imaginable. "Please don't tell anyone!"

She stared down at my hands, and I realized I had been holding onto her shoulders the whole time after steadying her and I let her go. "No problem. Your secret is safe with me."

"I gotta go . . ." she whispered nervously and started to take off.

"Wait!" I hollered after her. I couldn't steal from a girl I sat next to in theater class. "You dropped this." I held out her wallet, and she turned around and stared at it cautiously. "It fell out as you were taking off. Sorry, didn't want you to lose it."

She slowly sauntered up, her beautiful brown eyes staring at my green ones the entire time. She tentatively held out her hand, and I placed the wallet in it. "Thank you. And again, please don't tell anyone at school." She turned around and began to walk off again.

"Hey," I called out. "Can I buy a girl an ice cream?"

She turned around in surprise and demurely twirled a finger around a strand of hair. I found it extremely hot that she would single out just one, and I smiled my most charming smile, which was pretty darn charming if I do say so myself. "Okay."

We walked in silence for a while and I had butterflies like I was in middle school again, all first realizing that girls existed and that they could be talked to but not knowing the words. I was good at talking to guys, and would have been able to go up and talk to the Kostya I knew from class, but she wasn't really him.

After a couple of blocks, we arrived at a cozy shop in the middle of a hill. The gorgeous hotels towering around it with their columns and the bougainvillea blooming everywhere made the village a gorgeous color-splashed Impressionist painting of a locale. I held the glass door open for her, waiting for her to go in. She stopped at the doorway like there was a forcefield keeping her from entering. "You know, you don't have to do this for me if you don't want to."

"No, I insist. As payment for bumping into you."

"That's not an ice cream buyable offense!" She laughed.

"Okay, well, ice cream buyable excuse, then."

"You're not afraid to be seen with me?"

"Afraid I'll say something stupid and you'll get bored, maybe."

"I'm sure you'll say something stupid, but I don't think you could ever be boring."

"Oh, I can talk your ear off about art history and why Dean Moriarity is my idol, like I do when I want to make any other girl in school run and hide. That's always a crowd pleaser."

"I think more girls pay attention to you in school than you think, Alex Rose."

"Oh, you *do* know my name, then!" I laughed. "I was gonna ask you if I needed to give you a hint. Because I remembered yours, Kostya."

"Please, call me Korey."

"Korey," I repeated, savoring it, as if it was a little slice of pineapple on the edge of a mixed drink. "I like it."

A man stopped and stared at us like something was wrong, and I was about to ask him if he had a problem with the two of us, before I realized we were standing in front of the open door and blocking people from entering. "My bad!" I said.

We let him in first and then ordered two cones. She had strawberry cheesecake, and I had bubble gum. "You actually like that flavor?" she asked.

"Not really. But my pop used to buy it for me every time I passed a spelling test, so I kind of wanted to reward myself."

"For what?"

"For getting a chance to talk to you. You're always really shy in class."

"You would be too if you never felt like you belong," she said, hanging her head.

"I might surprise you."

I thought about all the ghosts and the things I'd seen, but that might be too much to tell and not expect someone to think I was anything but crazy. But also, I didn't want any of the madness that was a part of my life to touch her. I wanted to keep her as safe as possible from it all.

"What's your excuse?" she asked. "All the girls think you're drop-dead gorgeous, but you don't talk to anyone. Except maybe Vanessa. What's the deal with her anyways? Are you two going out? Lovers? Secretly brother and sister?"

She laughed and snorted and then put her hand over her mouth again, her face going red with embarrassment. We took our ice cream and walked outside, down towards the cove, with its endless blue waters.

"We might as well be siblings," I said. "She is my partner in crime."

That might have been a bit too much information. I didn't want to give too much away, but maybe I really did. And she felt safe to spill it all out to. But I was afraid that if I told her about the real me, she would turn tail and run.

We walked along on a grassy lawn and down to the sharp cliffs. The ocean waves lazily lapped against the rocky cliffs, which was in strong contrast to my rapidly beating heart and butterflies in my stomach.

"So what's your deal?" she asked.

"I don't know? What's your deal?" I probably said that one more harshly than intended and backtracked to smooth it over. "Sorry, but what do you mean?"

"What do you want out of life?" she asked with an honesty I found compelling.

And such a strange question to ask another high schooler. Who knows what I wanted back then. But no one ever really asked me that. They tried to tell me what I should want in life, but they rarely ever asked what I wanted. It was rain from Heaven on high when I was just about to die from thirst to hear someone concerned for me.

"To travel the world and get into trouble," I said, a big grin on my face. "But only the kind I can get out of. You?"

That was mostly true. I wanted everything to be spicy enough to taste the flavor of it, but not enough to burn.

"Hmmmm ..." she mused. "To get out of my father's house. He always thinks I'm a sissy, or a faggot. Even though I'm only being the real me when I'm like this. If he knew I was out here wearing this, he'd kill me."

"I don't see a sissy," I assured her. I'd finished my cone and put both hands on her shoulders, and stared into her deep dark brown eyes. "I see a very strong woman."

"I don't want to always have to be strong."

"Then just be you. The strength will come when you need it. Or when you work at it. I'm not sure. But I'm sure you've got it when it really counts."

She fell into my arms, and I held her there like that, both of us alone on that Impressionist painting of a beautiful day park, with the cool breeze flowing around us, the light making every colorful surface dance, and the warm sun on our skin. I wanted to keep on holding her in that embrace, propping up someone like her when she didn't think she had the strength of her own to do so, and enjoy that supportive glow shared energy and compassion, but I peeked up at the sky, with its sinking afternoon sun, and remembered I needed to complete my assignment and bring back a dozen more wallets to Moreau before sunset.

"I would love to stay here, but I have to go," I whispered to her. "My boss is expecting me, and he's a real monster when I'm late."

"You're not leaving because it's me, are you?" she asked, a look of sadness in her eyes.

"Not at all," I promised her. "I'd love to see you, the real you, that is, again."

"Maybe I will do something strong," she said and fished about in her purse, pulling out a pen and a scrap of paper. She scribbled something down quick on it and took my hand and pressed it into it. "I've always wanted to give a boy my number, but never had the courage to. Call me. If anyone else picks up, ask for Kostya, but Korey will answer."

"Count on it," I said.

And then I did something brave myself and kissed her right on her lips. She yielded right into it, closing her eyes and opening up her mouth a tiny bit, enough to let me feel her sweet breath slip into my mouth, and it was like I was touching a special hidden piece of her heart and soul in that kiss. The real heart and soul that she hid from the world, and only I was able to feel it on that day.

I ran off and kissed the paper she had handed me as she waved goodbye, and stuck it in my pocket. And then it was off to take what wasn't so carefully hidden in other people's pockets.

13.

BY MY SENIOR YEAR IN HIGH SCHOOL, I was picking up new tricks and adding ones of my own. David smiled on me, the pupil who made his teacher oh, so proud. I still had not cracked his big safe with its electronic locks and cameras.

He was a very odd man, and I attributed it to the rich and the things that make them the way they are, but the things I discovered were rather unsettling. He never stayed around after sunset. It was always this meeting coming up, or hours to be put in at the office, the location of which I was never to discover.

"Best not let certain business interests overlap," he said, and I had to accept that at face value.

He never ate or drank, as far as I saw, even if food was right out in front of him, and always insisted that he had already dined or that he didn't feel hungry today. His people might bring over food for us, but he would push the food around and hardly touch it, or dump a glass out into a sink or planter when he thought I wasn't looking.

Sometimes he would say a very random fact that I wasn't sure how he could have known, and when I'd check around on this bit of information, I'd find that he was probably right. It'd be something so obscure that no one would think to look for it, but he'd talk about it as if it was general knowledge.

We were talking about religion one day, and he explained how the Crusades were what really led to all the unrest in the Middle East.

"Colonialism might have played its part in the modern era," he said, "but the seeds of it were sown when Christians took up the sword and the cross and decided to take back the Holy Land. People knew this back in the day. The Jew who was accused of blood libel, and the captured knight sold into slavery for a pair of sandals."

"You think they would have fetched a higher price for a man, maybe a camel or something," I said.

"Camels would have been too precious for a price for that commodity."

"Duh," I said. "What was I thinking? They left out camel bartering in my AP Euro history class."

I found out later that he was right. I read up on it in a book on the Crusades by Karen Armstrong, a brilliant work about religious conflicts, that I came across by mistake while doing a paper. I hadn't thought twice about what he said until I came to that bit of information and stopped in midpage with my jaw agape.

The rest of the time, I was still trying to crack his safe but couldn't get it right. I kept hearing clicks in the parking position, and I was sure it was because his had anticracking technology.

"You can still do this," he said with the gleam in his eye of a man who has important hopes riding on an outcome. That laser focus was too much for me, that glare of his was as intense a magnifying glass.

It could intensely examine all the fine details, but it also amplified the light as it got too close and made me wilt under its focus.

"Look," I sighed, sitting back and clenching my fists in frustration, "why do you care so much? What am I to you that you won't let up and have such a vested interest in how I perform?"

He stared at me blankly for a second, and I was afraid I had crossed some sort of a line. I searched his face for signs of emotion, anything that could indicate whether this was the calm before a storm and he was going to go into a rage or if he was collecting his thoughts in a measured way.

"Have you ever felt that the world was so wrong that it would undo itself and you are the only one seeing it slowly fall apart all around you?" He stared off as if he was looking beyond the room, like the walls couldn't contain the intensity of his concentration, and he was listening instead to the deep voices of an intense passion.

"Yes," I responded without hesitation.

I might not have been on this earth too long, but I had seen enough of senseless struggle, people acting on greed instead of helping each other, and blind hatred for people who are different from each other that seemed like it couldn't be avoided no matter how far along we progressed as a species.

"Then wouldn't you do what it takes to set it right?" he asked with an earnest look to his eyes that said he wanted nothing more. He had the air of a man possessed, given words from above, and they formed the substance of his vocation, a promise that he would bind to himself with chains stronger than anything made in this world or any other.

"What are you going to do? Run for some kind of office? Use your money to start an initiative?" I asked him.

I still didn't have the foggiest idea what he really did. I checked into him in all the ways that I could and found a man who was hidden behind impossible jargon in foundations and offshore accounts. He was like a ghost, but living vibrantly and visibly in public, surrounded by a mansion that would never fall into disrepair, but still haunted by his desires and strange yearnings that he could never quite fulfill.

"An initiative?" He laughed. "You might say so. But all this around me is a facade. This home is the petals you see flashing vibrant and red that cover a thorn ready to prick your fingers. This lifestyle is those brilliant colors of a poisonous amphibian you glimpse in a jungle that draw you in when they should be warning you. My wealth is a dram of poison in a beautiful golden goblet that promises to satisfy as it burns you inside. It means nothing, simply a means to move about without people questioning my true intentions."

I looked around the great big room as he gestured about, with all its curtains with patterns that looked like they were woven by angels and gold that caught the light and made even the dull things around it have a gleam that could catch your eye and keep it there in endless fascination.

"And what are your intentions?"

"To change the world!"

"Like a revolution?"

"The world has seen too many of those! You know what happens in a revolution? The wheel goes from down to up for one point, but others are still ground far down. Crushed in the great big momentum of forces moving that they can't even comprehend as they are run under in a rush towards progress in a direction they have no control over."

"Kind of like Fortune's Wheel in Shakespeare's plays."

"Precisely!" He smiled at me, his kindred spirit in a captive audience, and I did find him so very appealing, like his hidden depths might be precisely what I needed to guide me up into the light. "I want to move people away from that constant upheaval of upward and downward trajectory. I want to place them at the center of the wheel, where they can spin above the dusty roads and never worry about being crushed under by anyone's rise to power again."

"How are you going to do it?"

"All in good time, my dear Alex, all in good time."

"But what do you need me for in it all?"

"I want you by my side!" he said, placing a hand on my shoulder and looking me in the eyes with a penetrating gaze that seemed impossible to turn away from even though it was uncomfortable being under the power of a will that was so intense it blotted out all views that differed from its own. "I need people such as you, talented and driven, with a desire to set all wrongs of the world right. I need someone with an appreciation for a vision that no one else can fathom, and a will to do the great and terrible things that will need to be done to bring about a better tomorrow. Can I count on you?"

"I don't know," I admitted. "I want those things you want. You make it all seem like an offer I can't refuse. But I need to know more. I won't ever blindly follow anyone."

"When I am done, no one will refuse me," he said. "But I can accept your answer. For now. In the meantime, I have a test for you. You've been holed up in here for days working on this, let's get you something to do in the field."

He pulled me up from the floor and led me out of that room.

14.

"**CONSIDER THIS A TEST,**" David said to me. We were in his Lamborghini, and he was taking it around the corners at speeds that crushed me back into the seat like I was flying on a jet and not on the solid ground beneath us. "An opportunity to see how you can work in the field and if you are ready to take on bigger challenges."

I loved being in this car. It cut like a dagger of impossibly sharp metal as it hummed through the streets, fired up by some primal energy, like it had lightning coursing through it.

"Haven't I done things 'out in the field'?" I asked. "Isn't stealing a necklace off of a woman while her husband is watching me field-work enough?"

He whipped around a slower moving car as we shot onto the 5 and towards downtown. The dusty canyons with their dry and golden grass gave way to the palm trees and beaches of Mission Bay and people riding bikes and skating along on the winding paths. We spilled out onto that gleaming sunny highway as brazen as a secret divulged to the world, screaming down in a rumor, trying to be subtle but audaciously shocking in our affronts to decency as we tore along.

It was almost June, technically not summer yet, but there were people out all about, enjoying the warmth and soaking in the sun as they lazed about or exercised in this city where there wasn't ever a cloud in the sky that could turn everything cold for too long before it would revert to mild and sea-breezy again.

"Those were merely practice," he said. "This is a rite of passage. If you help me with this, I'll know you're ready to throw your lot in with a cause that is worthy of my training."

"Fine, be oblique." I laughed. "I like a challenge anyways."

"I know you do, but you need to be smart about how you pursue them. You take on more than you can handle sometimes. Don't let a challenge become an obsession."

"I'll only obsess over the things I know I can get a handle on."

"Well let's show you a puzzle I've been obsessing over. I want a fresh pair of eyes on it. Someone with a perspective that might be a little more . . . outside the box than mine."

We parked the car on the street in Old Town. He hopped out of it as if he didn't have a care in the world and left it without a backward glance. He left it out on the street, windows open as people watched us slide out.

We walked through the shops and restaurants. The place was pretty, with an old world style to it of saloons and hotels with walkways that wrapped around them and courtyards full of fountains, like it was from the wild west, but redone in tourist trap hues designed to make the people walking through stop and buy a clever shirt with a character or a slogan on it. We strode past those folks and towards the cemetery on the other side of the short stretch of buildings.

I could see the spirits of people wandering around the houses in various modes of concentration on their activities. Some were so old they had clothing on from earlier eras, when everyone dressed like a doll and even the poor shined their shoes to an immaculate hue to attend church.

The Whaley House Museum offered chances to see ghosts wandering around its rooms, but the real ones were out in the avenues, milling about. If I focused, I could see spirits in different levels than the confused and wandering dead of the streets. Some were on higher levels, not like directions above or up in the sky, but in a different state than the confused and muddled ones of the streets. Even other ghosts passed through them, unable to see them for all the confidence and serenity they possessed. Others were locked into struggles, same as humans, fighting and cursing at each other until they were blue in the face, and all for nothing.

"Where are we going?" I asked my mentor as we hastily strolled along.

"To get a glimpse at your assignment," he said.

We had reached the cemetery, a tiny open park wedged between restaurants and shops with clay tile roofs that looked like stacks of ochre macaroni. It was a dusty affair, with olive trees and a massive date palm that kept the space covered with random bits of shade over the miniature shrines and dripping candle wax. The candles huddled in miniature towers of tiny frozen solid stalagmites of remembrance in reds and whites that reached up towards Heaven in attempts at monumental endurance of long-gone souls.

"Behold our man, Leonard Moore, in all his glory. We're in luck, he usually comes out around this time to buy a pack of cigarettes and sell a gram or two of cocaine here and there in the bars in the afternoons, but I didn't think we'd catch him quite yet. Follow me."

The man was a heavyset white guy in his early thirties, wearing a FUBU sweatshirt and baggy pants. He had frosted tips to his spiked-up hair, in a style that was way too common then. His vibe screamed he was trying very hard to be hip and in with the younger crowd.

"So what's so special about this guy?"

"Lenny here has got a few million squirreled away in a location that he has no idea of the exact whereabouts of."

"Sounds like a half-assed pirate."

"Something like that. He and his partner ripped off a bunch of very angry drug dealers with ties to Mexican cartels. They hid their cash out in a secluded place in the East County when things were too hot, but he was so piss drunk when that took place he doesn't recall exactly where. He let his partner face their wrath, and they put two bullets in his back. He forgot to find out from his partner where that drug money was hidden before he let him take the fall though. We're not dealing with the brightest bulb in the marquee, as they say."

David had a way of saying English language euphemisms and idioms as if they were hilarious and new to him. I took it that it was due to his continental European naissance and just one of those little foreign quirks of his.

We ambled along behind him. His gait was the shambling series of shuffles of someone who was very obviously intoxicated in the middle of the day.

"He spends his days in a paranoid cocaine-induced haze of extreme anxiety and fear that the drug dealers will connect him to it all and he will have to admit under torture that he doesn't know where their money is. The rest of the time he spends frantically wracking his brains for any location he and his partner could have possibly been to and then searching about it for any signs of disturbed earth."

"He must be enjoying retirement."

"Right. Take a good look. This is what happens when you don't stay in school and say no to drugs."

The man was feverishly glancing about as if he was worried death might come from any side. I had seen people who had come back from wars and were so rattled by the terrible things they had seen that they lived in that hellish state of high alert, where everything was a danger and even familiar sights were something to snap at if they moved too quickly. I felt a tinge of pity for this poor creature. Sure, he did it to himself, but no one should suffer like that.

He lit a cigarette, and I instantly decided I wanted to change my one-every-so-often cigarette habit into a not-gonna-fuck-with-those-cancer-sticks-again habit.

Everything about this man screamed a shabby sense of style and self-awareness trying to shout out that they were important, and I cringed at my wanting to steal shiny things from people and make off with money. I needed to have a better reason for it all, otherwise I was only trying to impress and keep my ego fed. I saw the ravages of desire run rampant in that man, as he struggled to splash about through currents that the rest of the world swam through with instinctual ease.

"I have interrogated him, so to speak, been through his possessions, kept him under surveillance," David said as we ducked into a shop and examined the cheap merchandise for a second as our quarry scanned about nervously behind him. "Maybe there is an angle I'm missing. A hint that is screaming out at me but I'm not listening for it properly."

"Hmm," I reflected. "Nothing screams out to me. I'll watch him though. Gimme a little time to see what I can see."

We followed him for a bit longer, and I couldn't help but be disturbed by this man. He was so hateful to me, a base creature full of lizard brain impulses and unexamined emotions. I wanted to despise him, but I pitied him. I saw someone who I could be under the right circumstances in all the wrong ways possible that a life could take you. And I wanted to take his pain away, show him that he could have it better if he only tried and stopped treading down these horrible rounds that were getting him nowhere.

We followed him into a bar, at the foot of a crumbling cliff, some tucked-away hole in the wall where people liked to go to avoid the light of day and drink their pain away, where he talked with a friend at the counter as he drank beer after beer. We watched him as he went out into an alley with a man he was speaking with for a minute. Saw him exchange a baggie of blow for a handful of cash. Broad daylight and no subtlety to it, no class. Just a needy transaction prompted by survival instincts fueled by addiction and greed.

We followed him back to his ramshackle bungalow near the cemetery. It should have been a cute little number, nestled away among other pretty cabin-sized buildings with roses crowding in vines that strangled wooden trellises and tropical plants growing rampant around it in a wild garden that threatened to spill onto the paving stones. But it seemed cheap and tawdry. A hideaway for a man at the end of his rope, and I was supposed to find where his rope had been hitched to in the past.

"Observe him," David told me. "See what you can see about our friend here."

"I really don't know what I'll be able to figure out that you weren't able to," I protested. "This sort of thing isn't really my . . ."

"There comes a point where a person is asked to go that extra mile for those they care for," he said. He placed a hand on my shoulder like he was bestowing an honor on me like knighthood. "I'm asking that of you. Prove to me that my hopes are rightly placed when I hold you high in them."

And with that, he patted me on the back and left me there to watch our friend as he played *Tomb Raider* on PlayStation and racked out lines of cocaine. I sighed a deep sigh and thought about how I was going to go about this.

15.

I BUSIED MYSELF THAT MONTH with finding out about my newfound prey. He wasn't the most graceful of big game to hunt, but I learned a lot from him, specifically how the other side of the other side of the tracks lives. I'd thought I knew privation growing up in somewhat fancy neighborhoods but still struggling, but watching this man was a lesson in how privileged I was to not have my mind twisted by drugs. Simply seeing him operate made me wonder how he scrounged up enough common sense in life to make it this far.

I used my usual cover of a college student out with a camera to take pictures of the cemetery to hang around his place. I broke into his bungalow when he was gone. He went through the trouble of padlocking his door but then left the bathroom window wide open. Gary was with me, taking point and making sure I wasn't liable to be caught by surprise.

While there, I went through his belongings. His bathroom was a complete mess and hadn't seen anything resembling a cleaning product touching its surfaces since Kennedy trounced Nixon in the first televised debates, probably.

He had a PlayStation hooked up to his TV that was the focal point in his living room and a few scattered VHS tapes among articles of clothing randomly dropped wherever they were probably taken off. Dishes were stacked up in the sink, next to, surprise, surprise, an empty bottle of dish soap that was filled with water to try and have it go the extra mile. No papers in the house to help me out, only a random pink slip for a 1980s Oldsmobile that was older than I was.

I reached out with everything I had in that living room. I tapped into my other senses, taking in a deep breath and clearing my mind, letting my consciousness expand into the spaces that ordinary perception didn't reach. Those quiet spaces that would dart about on the periphery, but were invisible head-on. I fixed my special sight on a center that if I stared at long enough would come into sharp focus like a Magic Eye artwork.

I received a jolt in return. At first, I thought it was Gary, come to warn me about something, but I peeked up and saw that he was already right there, glancing around nervously.

"What is it?" I asked him.

"Something is here," he said. "Something that isn't *here*, but I can feel it in the air."

"That makes zero sense," I said dismissively, but I could feel what he was perceiving. It was like a presence that wouldn't show itself but was powerful enough to leave waves in its wake.

"Who are you?" I asked.

A voiceless scream was the response, along with a push that actually had some solid force behind it. I fell back onto the floor and didn't know what to do at first but stay there. I didn't want to get back up and antagonize the thing. It was just beyond my perception, hiding from me but making its strength known, telling me to fuck around and see if it was to be tested.

A glass crashed as if to prove that it meant business, and even though I probably should have picked up the pieces, I decided to sneak back out to avoid any further damage of objects and suspicion on the part of my quarry. I went home that night full of questions. My pop had a lot of questions too, it seemed.

"Where have you been going all this time?" he asked.

"I've got a side gig goin' on," I responded, probably a little harshly.

"Your school called." He looked the picture of sadness. That whole "I'm not mad at you, just disappointed" look that only parents can do and lets you feel the guilt of fucking up in their eyes. "Your grades are still stellar, but your teachers say your behavior is a problem and you're always absent."

"If I'm getting good grades, then what's the problem?"

"You can't keep skipping out on school."

"So what? You mad because I don't fit in with the other army ants and march where they tell me to?"

"I'm not mad," he said. "I'm worried. Where are you going?"

"Working."

"Working for who?"

"A side gig. It's under the table. It makes good money."

"I know. I see the clothes you've been buying. I know I couldn't buy those for you."

"Yeah, and that's why I wanted to take the initiative on my own. I'm tired of depending on you."

That was cold. I loved him, but I saw him as having given up on the dream and fallen in with the rest of the crowd. It wasn't fair, but I wanted more than the ordinary world he was trying to integrate with.

"You're right," he sighed. I wasn't quite expecting that. "I haven't always been the best provider for you. But I'll make up for my mistakes. I swear to you I will. But be careful. Someday maybe you'll have kids and you'll see what it's like."

"If I ever do, I won't raise them like you," I muttered before I could stop myself. That was a bit too far. He looked crestfallen, as if I had both taken the breath out of him and kicked him while he was down at the same time. "I'm sorry, that was shitty."

He sighed deeply and walked out. I wanted to run after him—I should have run after him—but I felt I would be giving up on an important matter of honor. I don't know what, some silly shred of ego that couldn't admit I was wrong. I was a dumb little kid still for all the smarts I had and the things I could do.

After that, he stopped asking where I was going. I kind of wished he would, and let me know he cared.

My guilt was buried in work the next few days. I began to love that little section of the town. It was so decked out for tourists, but it had an appeal to it that said the world might go towards all kinds of strange and terrifying ways, but everyday things of beauty will survive the test of time. Old Town's big church tower rose up over the single-story buildings, its bell tower probably a massive sight to behold at one time, and now just a pretty adornment on a wedding cake of a neighborhood, all showiness and sweetness, like the past in this part of the world wasn't full of native bloodshed and conquest.

I tried to imagine the vibrant scenes from when this area was all wild and pirates might have roamed through streets with princesses as they participated in the commerce of a dream of a town where anything was possible. I wanted to live in interesting times even though it wasn't exactly a blessing to wish that upon someone in certain cultures. But those people of the past probably never grew up in an era where folks worked in the crowded beeswax cells of good little drones as they made honey and money for the queen. I was determined to at least appreciate this path I had chosen, because even though there was striving to it like you wouldn't believe, I loved the action of it all, loved that I was reaching my hands down deep and getting them dirty.

Lenny was on the move again, and I was determined to get as close as possible to him to see if I could charm some detail out of him that my mentor was unable to. I wanted to fight the monsters, answer the riddles, find my way through the maze, and bring back bounty for the whole tribe to share.

But more importantly, I was deeply drawn to the challenge. I wanted to succeed where no one else had done so before. I wanted the thrill of knowing that I could do the impossible things, the taste of that victory on my tongue, the rush of adrenaline that let me know I was deeply and vibrantly alive.

And so I followed this shambling man, this wannabe gangsta who was in over his head and feeling the walls closing in on him. He didn't even know that the one who was after him was a sixteen-year-old kid with fake identification and lock picks and enough pluck to track him to the ends of the earth.

I followed him down the street and slightly out of the neighborhood, away from the tourist traps, crafted to be the replicas of a marketplace of a bygone era. He went back to the divey bar on the cliffside. That seemed to be the extent of his radius, like a mental tether was keeping him bound to an area. Kind of like a ghost.

I entered the bar after him and pulled up a stool next to him. The bartender asked for my ID and I gave them my fake, which was convincing enough that he stared a long time and then asked me the standard questions about when I was born and all that. I rehearsed the whole bit so much with David that the proper responses flowed out seamlessly. When he was duly convinced, he handed it back to me.

"Sorry," he said. "I gotta ask."

"Naw, man, you're doing your job," I replied coolly. "I've got a baby face, I get it all the time."

I ordered a Sierra Nevada pale ale. My hopefully soon-to-be friend Lenny downed his shot. "I'll have another," he hollered at the bartender.

"Fuckin' A," I said to him. "Long day at work? I'm done with this bitch for the day and can't wait for the weekend. Is it Friday yet?"

"What day is it?" he asked.

I paused for a second, wondering if he was serious. "It's Wednesday."

"Oh. Yeah, fuckin' tough to keep track, they all kinda blur together."

"I've always gotta remember to set my alarm," I said. "Otherwise I forget what day blurred where, and my hangover makes me late for work."

"What do you do?"

"I do aggressive appropriations and acquisitions for high-end clientele," I said. "They want a product, and it's my job to make sure they get it in the most cost-efficient way."

"You seem kinda young. What are you? Twenty-one? Eighteen with a great fake ID?"

"Just your average prodigy. I'm Scott Gatsby."

"Nice to meetcha, Scotty. I'm Lenny."

"Just Scott. Pleasure to meet ya."

I shook his hand. His grip felt cold and clammy, wet from a beer he was nursing along with his shots.

"I got this guy's next drink," I told the bartender. "I'll have a shot of whatever he's having too."

"Hey, thanks," he said. "To our wives and girlfriends! May they never meet!"

That was about the most douchey toast I had ever heard. And also, I knew he had neither. I went with his motif and took it a step further. "Here's to honor! Hitting honor, getting honor, and if you can't come in her, cum honor!"

We clinked our glasses and downed a shot of Wild Turkey that I almost coughed back up. I quickly sucked down a sip of beer so I wouldn't show myself up for a kid.

By the end of the night with him, I was sufficiently shitfaced. That was definitely the drunkest I had ever been, and I was concentrating on not giving up the game while doing shot after shot with the man. We were on dirty jokes, which was a good way to not reveal too much that he might catch me up with while keeping him sufficiently amused.

"So this blind man walks into a bar," I said to him, "seeing-eye dog on a leash and everythin'. An' he comes inta the middle 'a tha room, 'n he starts swingin' 'is dog around by the chain. Everyone is obviously stunned. Finally, someone says ta him, 'Buddy! Tha fuck ya doin'?' 'Just havin' a look around,' the blind man replies."

"Haha!" he chortled. "Yer not a bad guy, Scotty!"

"Scott," I corrected him. Don't know why that was the hill I was willing to die on, it seemed in character. "And watch out! I'm one 'a the worst! True reprobate!"

"Ain't we all though?" he said. "Here's ta us reprobates!" He raised his glass again, and I raised mine. I had started to spit my shots out into a beer bottle like in that movie about coyotes and chicks dancing on bar tops in New York.

"Here's ta lying, cheatin', and stealin'!" I said, holding a glass up high. "If you're gonna lie, lie for a friend. If you're gonna cheat, cheat death. If you're gonna steal, steal a heart. And if you're gonna drink, drink with me."

"Damn straight!" he said, and we clinked glasses again. He turned suddenly morose after we settled back down and sat for a minute. "That was really beautiful. Really, beautiful."

"Aaaawwww, you learn these things when yer Irish," I replied. It was cheesy as hell in my opinion, but some people are easy to please.

He put an arm around me all of a sudden, almost knocking me off of my bar stool. I felt bad about this authentic outpouring of affection, because I definitely saw him as a means to an end. This man had nothing about him that I found essentially compelling. He got in bed with murderous drug dealers knowing exactly what they were all about, and he didn't care. He only wanted their money, to hell with where it came from. He set up his friend and let him get taken out by those killers.

And yet that simple gesture was enough to melt my heart. Somehow, an understanding had passed between us. I saw him as a guy who was full of hopes and dreams, even if they were twisted. He was someone capable of love even if he found ways to use those he loved. He was a man with the capacity for kindness even though the world had probably not always been kind to him. I saw someone who had similar options like I'd had in my life placed before him, and he went in different ways. Ways that were selfish and thoughtless of others. I saw ways in him that I could go if I wasn't careful. I saw a person who was kind of like me even though I didn't want to admit it, even if I was actively resolving never to be like him.

Those thoughts were pushed to the back of my mind as I remembered the job. He was still my adversary. He was still my prey, and I needed to be more liberal about sinking my teeth in when the right chance should occur.

"I've lost people," he confided to me. "Guy who was like a brother. And I treated him like shit. Let him down when he needed it most." He gazed off and tears welled up in his eyes. He wiped them off real quick and glanced away, embarrassed. "He was my friend, that Papa Decky. I wasn't there for him when I shoulda been. And you know the crazy thing? I swear he's still around. I feel him over my shoulder sometimes."

Bingo.

"Papa Decky? Funny name. But he sounds like a helluva guy."

I could feel the spirit from before. He had been hiding out wherever he was in the ether, but he bristled at his name being mentioned. Names were an almost irresistible currency with the deceased. If you knew a spirit's name, you could have power over them. Papa Decky. *Gotcha, baby!* That was him!

"He was," he said, fighting back tears. I put my arm over his shoulder. "And I wasn't there for him. I left him ta go on 'n ..." He trailed off, realizing he was starting to say too much, but I knew the secret already. *Yeah, you done fucked up, Len. Ya done fucked up.*

"You were probably there for him more than you know," I said, giving him a pat on the back. Here was where my empathy for him dropped out of the soles of my shoes. I couldn't stand the idea of someone abandoning their friend to die while they slipped off. *Good, feel that guilt, bro. You should feel bad about that.*

And still, I did feel for the guy.

"Closing time!" the bartender belted out, followed by the ringing of an annoying bell. "You don't gotta go home, but get the fuck outta here! Drink 'em up, let's go."

They turned the lights on, and I saw why they were dim in the first place. The place became a scene of caricatures of drunkenness. Various tableaus of inebriation were all around, with men downing beer that spilled down their chins and onto their shirts. A couple was making out, and the man had an obvious hard-on as they went at it and the woman wrapped her arms around him as he grabbed her ass.

Good for them.

The barback was collecting glasses and telling people to leave. Tattoos jumped out of pale skin that appeared a shade more colorful in the dark. Bags under eyes and veins around the cheeks were revealed on faces that appeared a bit more without blemish. Contortions of discomfort appeared in postures that were a bit more confident.

Our tab was settled up—I covered all his drinks. I tipped the bartender profusely, because my friend here had been looking for every chance he could get to complain about the service and feel good about not tipping properly.

I waited for the taxi I had called, and Lenny thanked me copiously as he headed off. "Are ya sure ya don't want to chill at my place?" he asked. "I got a couch ya can sleep on and we can watch *American Beauty*. Ya ever see that one? Sucha great movie!"

"Naw," I demurred and slurred. "Thanks, but I gotta work in tha morning, 'n it's alrrrrready way late."

"Les' do this a'gain sometime!" he slurred in return.

"Count on it!"

And with a big awkward bro hug he man-handled on me, he went on his way. I watched him stumbling off and tried to shake off the sympathy for him. Because deep down he was one of the dangerous people. I was one of the dangerous people too, but mainly to myself. I was reckless and needed a new thrill whenever the feeling of excitement was gone away.

This man was a danger to others, because he would do what it would take to get what he wanted. I was willing to do things that most wouldn't, but the ends had to justify the means. I wasn't going to become a killer, even if by neglect like Lenny.

I was beginning to see all kinds of places in the sand where I was going to draw the line and realized I was making a maze in that sand with all those lines that could be hard to find my way out from. But I was determined to keep to my own path, no matter how twisted.

16.

MOST HOUSES ARE A WAY OF KEEPING others out when we tell ourselves they are places where we keep the love in. In the suburbs, it's all a little fiefdom, where people pretend they are lords over their own silly patch of turf and ranch-style architecture. Their picket fences are painted white to keep them pretty but still have spikes to remind us that they would place our heads upon them should we ever believe we could simply waltz on in without permission.

I was learning the steps of dancing around all the false flares of confidence that we call suburban dwellings, and seeing their nuances in a different light.

The rich are even more blatant about keeping people out. Those high fences are made to let you know that they worked hard to profit from others working so very hard, and they will keep you out with extreme prejudice. They could have anything in the world there to kick your ass to the curb, and the less you could see of their pleasure gardens, the better. Their towering gates are there to let you know that Heaven is open on an invite-only basis, and the poor cherubs of color that rise at first light to do celestial chores can take the side entrance when they are needed to clean up the mess.

My cab took me to David's sprawling expanse of luxury that was really a fortress with a glamorous veneer and skipped around all the defenses. I'd already figured out the blind spots with his security cameras and climbed up from the back from a hiking trail that surfers used to get down to the beach. I was as drunk as a lord, as inebriated as I had ever been, and damn near fell off a cliff, but I certainly wasn't about to sleep it off on a weeknight at my pop and Windsong's place.

The lampposts out in the yard were accomplices to my breaking and entering as I danced around them, keeping to the shadows until I made it up to Jenny's balcony. I took one of the many rocks from my pocket I'd gathered on the way and aimed for her window. It flew out of my hand and made a crashing sound as it bounced around in her room. I was counting on a window being closed and it making a little thunk and realized that that whole deal probably worked better in movies.

"Pssst!" I shouted out in a terrible stage whisper. "Jenny, I forgot your number! I wanna make you my-ee-ine! 8-6-7-5!" I threw another rock in for good measure, and she turned the light on. "Sorry, Jen-nay! My momma always said girls like a box of chocolates and rocks!"

She popped out of the window, a look of extreme annoyance coloring her features that I could feel even though she was in silhouette. "What *are* you doing here right now?" she hissed.

"Just happ'nd to be in yer neighborhood." I smiled with my head downcast and my hands behind my back with my foot tracing back and forth in a semicircle on the ground in a caricature of sheepishness. "I took a cab ta get here, but thass neither here nor there."

"You're drunk!" she said, exasperation in every syllable.

"No, naw . . . Maybe a lil' . . . Okay, yeah, I'm shitfaced."

"I'm coming down."

"Perfect!" I declared, sticking a finger up in the air. "My plans are pru-ceeding apace!"

"You won't be thinking that when I get down there to chew your ass out!" She sighed and went back out of sight.

I passed the time doing my Gene Kelly thing, swinging around the light post in her courtyard but with half his coordination.

She rushed out and pulled me off the pole. "Hey, careful! You messed up the big song and dance number I had prepared for you. It was gonna go somethin' like, 'Yer a rich girl, and you're all up at night, but you know that don't matter anyway . . .'"

"Get in here!" she said, glancing about nervously from side to side.

"Ladies first," I said, waiting for her to come in and almost falling over while trying to lean on a doorpost.

"Get in!" She shoved me in.

As I shambled through the halls, I tracked dirt on the immaculate marble floors. Every few steps, I had to lean against a wall or an object for balance, and she had to make sure that it wasn't a priceless work of art or artefact that might be damaged. "I need a minute here, thass all."

"Come on, let's get you up where you can rest," she said.

"Okay, but I gotta piss."

"Don't you dare piss anywhere around here! C'mon!"

She took me up the stairs, posthaste, dragging me heavily by the arm, a bunch of dead weight going in all kinds of other directions than the ones she intended. As we rounded a landing in the stairway and made it halfway up the next flight, I fell back and rolled down the steps we had made it up.

"Ha, hah! He he ha!" I giggled as I lay there on the floor staring at the ceiling and feeling mightily amused at Lord knows what. "Okay, I'm pissing here," I said, fishing around in my pants.

"Don't you fucking dare!" she said, pulling my hand out and me up. "You're cleaning that entire fucking floor with every scrap of clothing you have on if you do!"

"Does that mean you wanna see me naked?" I tried to wink at her but probably only ended up shutting one eye for a long time.

"Maybe." She smiled. "Not right now, when you're being a complete asshole."

"So later when I'm kind of an asshole. Slight asshole."

"Or factory setting, as I like to call it."

"Ouch! Ouch, dang girl! As long as I'm your asshole. Wait, thass not right . . ."

"Hurry up and get to the bathroom before you piss your pants!"

She pushed me into one of those fancy bathroom affairs of theirs, with scallop shaped sinks and baths on clawed feet that flashed in colors as bright as the sun, all of it a gleaming distraction to my double vision. I barely made it without pissing myself, which was classy as fuck. My dick tried to go into action before it was even released, and I had to pinch it and fumble about to make it just in time to pee on the back of the toilet lid, which was better than in their halls. I finished up and made sure to shake profusely, even if it was mostly on the floor.

I made it out, leaning heavily on the doorway for support but trying to have the air of a carefree slouch. Jenny saw right through it. She had already laid out a few blankets on a sofa and dragged me to it.

"Where are you sleeping?" I asked.

"Away from your drunk ass in my own bed," she said, smiling.

"Well if you need company, give a little whistle an' I'll be there."

She laughed. "Don't worry, if I wake up in desperate need of someone puking in my bed, you'll be the first person that comes to mind." She bundled me up in the comfy blankets and kissed me on the cheek, making it quick before I could try and expand the gesture. "You really shouldn't come here at night." She looked around the room nervously as if it was listening in on our words. My drunken giddiness had worn off for a second, and a sense of impending doom in that labyrinth of a building was creeping back in.

"I know, I know," I quipped. "There's a room up in the attic you can't go to, and if you leave the key around with blood on it, he'll know you've seen his dead wives."

"Something like that." She smiled at me, and I wanted to kiss her, but figured it wouldn't be the most gallant of gestures.

"Izzit alla the ghosts here?" I asked her. "Izzat why nighttime is not right time?"

"Confucius once said 'Respect ghosts and gods, but keep away from them,'" she warned.

"Well, Confucius also say . . ."

"Shush, shush, shoosh, we've all heard that . . ." she cooed. "What were you doing coming around at this hour dead drunk, anyways? You aren't really a party animal unless there's something for you to steal at the party."

"I's jus' doing important research."

"Researching a bottle."

"No, iss fieldwork. I've got a lead on somethin' big. 'S gonna be bitchin'."

"What do you want?"

"To always be a little boy and have fun, duh. Next question!"

"No, what do you really want? Why do you do what you do? Stealing with my father. You don't really care about the items you snag. You steal thousands of dollars and jewels to fill a treasure chest and they mean nothing to you. You might buy a new outfit here and there, some music or a book. But who knows what you do with the rest? So why stealing?"

I'd told myself every cute little lie in the book to make the things I did seem right. But the truth of it was, I didn't think what I did was wrong. I stared deep into her enchanting eyes for a moment and thought about how I could best open up the secrets of my heart to her in a way that she would understand.

"I's a big fan 'a *The Odyssey* when I was a kid," I confessed. "I loved how Odysseus was clever enough ta win th' war for th' Greeks by sneaking inta Troy. He got out of every scrape imaginable! Every one. And he saw ghosts too! Anyway, there's this whole part where he falls asleep at the wheel of 'is boat, and the men go about 'is stuff while he's passed out. An' so they open up 'is bag with all the winds in it. They were almost home, but it blew them back ta sea! An' it's supposed to show you that thas whatcha get for bein' greedy, right? But I was rereadin' it the other day. 'N ya know what I was thinkin'? Mebbe Homer was tryin' to jus' scare people outta questionin' what the people 'n charge are all about.

"We live in a world where the people in charge wanna keep us down 'n not question why they got it so good. We have all these industries run by a buncha fuckin' white-ass bros. We have advertisers that tell us we're too fuckin' fat, or too fuckin' broke, or too fuckin' lame to have all the fun that the folks up on the TV are havin', but we can fix it all by buyin' a buncha shit no one ever really needed in all the history of the entire world. Soda, 'n cigarettes, 'n slot machines . . . Fuck 'em! No one needs that shit. We have everything stacked against us, tryna make it so we don't know which way's up, unless they tell us! Unless we can buy our way out. An' ya know what?"

Jenny was listening intently, with eyes focused on me because I was on a roll and saying something of great importance. I soaked that in and enjoyed the extra special way it made my heart glow like fireflies on a summer night to know she cared. "I don't know, what?" she prompted.

"Stealin' is the only thing that makes sense in a world like that! Everything's stolen from someone in this country! The land from the Indigenous People, the labor from the slaves, the time we have to live by some fat cats who want us to make other cats fat. Didja know the statue that represents the goddess Liberty on the Capitol Building's made by a slave? 'S true!"

She nodded in approval of my enthusiasm.

"It'sall a system of bullies. The ones they taught us weren't okay in school, but somehow when we grow up, we're supposed to become jus' as bad as them. Fuck that! The only way to really be good in this world is to stop that system, any way you can. Otherwise you're justa bully yourself. Or, 'n this is just's bad, you're someone who sees the bullies pickin' on someone weaker and doesn't stand up and help."

"So, by being bad, you're actually being good?" Jenny asked.

"You betcha. As long as I stay the right kind of bad to the worst kind of people."

"So why did you come here tonight?"

I thought about making up an excuse, some way to massage it over and act as if I had a bit of business to attend to, but I was a kid with a crush. She was the one I wanted to confide in, wanted to tell all those hopes and dreams, my fears and my desires to. She was my other soul, my kindred spirit in this crazy world where I talked with spirits and living people seemed alien to my temperament.

"Well, I couldn't go back to my pop's place all smashed," I said. But that wasn't enough. I wanted to tell her more, and it was do or die time. "And I wanted to see you. I love you."

"That's sweet," she said. And then she kissed me on the lips all of a sudden in a gesture that made me melt right there in the unexpected pleasure of it.

This was everything I had ever wanted, coursing through me with an amplified intensity, all in one spectacular sensation of delight that seemed to travel from my lips to every part of my body until I sighed and forgot everything around me.

I opened my eyes a peek and saw her perfect cheek and serenely closed eyes. I closed my eyes again and savored her mouth opening up and connecting to mine. Her tongue teasingly darted between my lips and then retreated as my own entered her mouth. She sucked on it, so hard it almost felt uncomfortable, but I wasn't opposed, in fact, I was a fan. I reached out an arm and held her closer to me and she yielded, her body melting into mine as she ran her hands along my chest.

Her mouth tasted like the feeling of summer vacation starting as I used to run home from the last day of school. Her lips felt like the glow of Christmas lights dazzling my eyes as a child. Her skin smelled the way Jim Morrison's growling voice and the notes of that piano struck my ear the first time I heard The Doors, wild and uncontrolled, full of seductive chords that made me want to go deeper into a new darkness that was beckoning me with its beautiful promises of savage joy.

She pushed me away with a playful shove and lay above me smiling, her hips crushing against mine not quite comfortably, but I didn't mind it in the slightest.

"Don't fall in love with me," she warned. "I'll only hurt you."

"I can handle pain," I said.

"I know you can. But nobody can for too long, and that's all you'll ever get with me."

"It doesn't have to be that way," I protested. "You make me feel good just by being around."

"It never lasts."

"It can if we work at it."

"All work and no play . . ."

I pictured some crazy world-ending event, where all people everywhere suddenly disappeared. Everyone just pop! Vanished, except her and me, and we were alone together in the ruins walking hand in hand. We would climb up to the tops of the buildings and see everything stretched out before us in limitless possibility because we knew that it could all be whatever we wanted to make it, and it would be only us.

I pushed the thought to the back of my mind, because it was a shameful fantasy.

But I thought about all the directions I could take things. About how I wanted to see the world, and I wanted a companion like her with me. I could do anything on Earth if she was on my side. Fight off an army, found a country of our own, find a lost civilization, make it to Mars. Our imaginations would be the limit of what we could do together. We'd make a sorry little pair, but we would have each other and that would be enough.

But what did she really want? She was a mystery to me, never quite giving up her secrets. A glimpse here and there, and then she darted away, lightning quick.

She was about to go when I pulled her in closer to me and kissed her again. I thought for sure this would be taken as a huge overstep of my bounds, but she returned the kiss with a burning intensity so shocking I wanted to jump, but instead returned to her that same fire.

She slid her hands under my shirt, caressing every muscle as she ran her fingers up and along my chest. She playfully pinched a nipple and then pulled my shirt off, stopping before it came off of over my eyes. She held the shirt over and kissed all along my stomach, each kiss wet and making my skin quiver in anticipation of not knowing where they would go or where her tongue would linger next.

She unzipped my pants and took my cock into her mouth, running her tongue along the length of it and then wrapping her lips around it and letting them travel down it until it was almost all inside her mouth, then back to the tip, up and down in a rhythm that made me want to go mad.

I finally pulled the shirt off and pulled her off, lightly grabbing her face and bringing her in close to me so I could kiss those tender lips of hers.

I kicked off my pants, clumsily getting them stuck around my ankles. I had expected pants to come off in a more fluid motion after watching every love scene ever. She was taking off her blouse, and I unzipped her pants and started to bring them down. I stared at her hips, thinking they were too good to be true and this couldn't be happening. I knew I was going to be taking in every secret they had, this was no longer going to be an unexplored territory for me, a place I felt about in a dark theater anymore, or something tantalizingly rubbed against through wet clothes.

She lay back on the couch, and I slowly peeled her cute pink underwear off, kissing her soft thighs all along the way. I spread her legs apart and put my tongue between them, loving the taste. It was hot and wet, like a new spice from food I'd read about in a book and never had on the tip of my tongue before. It was almost salty, but it made my mouth water instead of drying it up and making me thirst.

I licked it up and down, pushing my tongue deep in and letting it explore, surprised by the variations in texture and the sweet explorable depth. I don't know what I was expecting, but this was infinitely better and all so new that it was almost confusing. I ran my tongue slowly along until I reached a hard little mound that made her sigh when I explored it. I decided to keep repeating this until she finally pulled me up and kissed my lips.

There was something special about kissing her mouth after my tongue had been inside a part of her that intimate. It was an offering to her of all the delight I had taken in while pleasing her, letting her lips taste what mine had savored.

She pulled me over her and grabbed my backside, crushing our hips together. I held onto my cock, slipping it inside her and feeling right at home once it had found its perfect fit. Once I was inside her, instinct took over and I began thrusting, loving the feel of her, not knowing what it was I was doing but trying to play off of her reactions and making every second of it pure Heaven.

I was lost in kissing her and running my hands all over her as she gripped my thighs and then raked her hands all over my chest. She moaned and held tighter, her breathing reaching a point where I thought she wouldn't be able to take another gasp of air in until she finally let it all out and shouted out, "Oh, God!"

I had been on the verge of release and took that as a sign that I could finally let go of everything, spilling it inside her. I sighed, not anything as loud as her, but with the intensity of the air being knocked out of me, only it was without any pain accompanying it.

Her muscles were still throbbing down there, like they were still trying to hold on, beating in a tap, tap, tap to try to get one last embrace on me before I slid out.

I lay on top of her, lightly, not sprawled, kissing her lips and then making my way down her neck, stopping to pay attention to the spot where it met her shoulders, then making my way back up to her lips again.

She slid out from under me, got up, and gathered her clothes.

"Sleep," she said simply. She kissed me again, briefly, a sweet reminder of pleasure I wanted to stretch on and on. And then she got up and went slowly to the lights and turned them off. I stared at her every step, wishing she would turn around and come back.

And then I drifted into a dreamless sleep. I woke up with the worst hangover imaginable and a pitcher of icy cold water by my side. I searched the house for her, taking care not to disturb Molly as I treaded lightly around the room I felt her presence in, but Jenny was nowhere to be seen.

I put on my shirt and went back to work.

17.

THE SUMMER WAS UNDER WAY, and I was determined to see if I could make good on my assignment. I decided to do something drastic one day to get everything rolling. I waited for Lenny to go off on one of his trips to the bar, which were a pretty regular occurrence, leaving him occupied until closing time and the wee hours of the night. He left earlier in the day on the weekends so he could grab brunch and then extend that into a Saturday of epically inebriated proportions.

I sat outside a café, drinking a cup of chai tea and enjoying the spicy taste as the sun danced in the leaves of an olive tree that swayed in a refreshingly cool breeze.

Gary was next to me, glancing nervously about. "Are you sure you want to do this?" he asked for the millionth time.

"Unless you have a better way of getting this ghost's attention, go right ahead with it," I replied. "I could use some more insider perspective on the topic anyways."

Gary and I had practiced what I was attempting to do on the ghost that lingered around the house together, and it seemed like it was a sound way to go about and summon this spirit.

"There's more things unknown out there than there are things known," he warned me. Gary sounded a tad bit older than his appearance suggested, and I thought about how often we really base our impressions and opinions of people on how they appear, when there is so much going on underneath that is working in all kinds of amazing ways. "Be careful."

"Aren't I always?" I said, winking and smiling before taking another sip of my creamy drink.

"No, you're not. You're the opposite of careful. The anti-careful. Careful's evil twin. If careful had a clone from the bizarro mirror dimension, where good is bad and bad is good, that would be you. Listed under the heading of antonyms of careful in the dictionary."

"Okay, I get it. Shush, he's on his way out."

I watched our guy make his way on off, ambling along at a brisk pace as he went down the street past the cemetery, finishing off an early morning beverage of most likely the alcoholic sort in a red plastic cup as he walked along. He traveled down the busy street for a while and I waited until he was a tiny blip in the distance, gave him a few minutes longer, and then made my way on over to his house.

He'd wised up and locked the windows after the glass fell to the ground during my last break-in, but I made my way around the back and got my lock picks out from their handy-dandy fold-up black leather carry case. After a minute of finessing, I was able to pop the lock and make my way into his place from the back door.

"Just stick to the sidelines," I told Gary as I tried to enter without making the door scrape too much on its off-hinged path while I opened it.

Entering his kitchen, I was immediately hit by the smell of rotting produce and spoiled milk. The fridge had broken down, judging from its wide-open door, and instead of throwing the contents out and getting it fixed, he tossed them in the trash can and left them there to do their thing in the heat. I took a deep breath and sucked it in, then walked straight into the adjacent living room, where it was thankfully less overpowering but still present.

Vines obstructed the windows, and the blinds were partially drawn, letting the random rays of sunshine that snuck through cast an eerie haze to it all. The whole place was dark and reminded me of the bars he loved to frequent. Dark wood, dark furniture, dark aura to it all.

The cramped and crowded house could only slide into a bigger mess with him in it. I would have thought a person who spent his time at home so much would be more inclined to keep his space tidy, but apparently, Lenny was in a world of his own, and the cares of domesticity did not apply.

I reached out with my special senses that I had been practicing throwing out, instead of hiding from, casting them out in an invisible net, filling up all the spaces in the house. I felt that psychic pushback from my friend, a tiny warning shot that went up my spine in a jolt that made the hair on the back of my neck rise up. The temperature felt suddenly colder even though it was the middle of a summer day.

I took out a large pocket knife I had brought along especially for this purpose.

When I asked Moreau what he knew about ghosts one day, he was surprisingly helpful. Most people thought it was too dreary of a topic at best to speak often of the dead. Moreau showed me books and books on the topic. Old ones I was sure were not on anyone's list in the libraries. Ones on vellum or scrolls laid out, with special tools to roll through. He had many that weren't only informative, they were cultural treasures and works of art.

Anything I could on the occult I greedily read—summonings, spirituality, possession, all of it. Most of it was absolute tripe and fit for new-agey religious rituals. Some of it seemed practical, and I would try out methods in books I read to do half-assed seances, using trial and error to make efforts at better communicating with the spirits I saw around. One of them, which I believe was titled *The Underworld*, said that the Greeks would frequently offer up blood sacrifices to the dead because they needed the essence of life to communicate and be conscious again.

That seemed like a theory I could test out, and I had seen it have an effect on Gary when we tried it together, drawing him into a deer in headlights trance and allowing him to come to more vibrant colors and fleshing out.

I held out my palm, knife poised above it like Abraham about to turn his own blade on his son, Isaac, my own flesh being the substitute for a proper sacrifice to the spirit I was trying to speak with.

I glanced about the room, sucked in a breath, and prepared myself for the pain I knew was about to come, but more importantly, the fear of the unknown of monkeying around with forces I had no idea about. I could be summoning anything! Some disembodied entity, maybe, a formless creature that was going to rip me to shreds for having disturbed its activities.

Ghosts could be scary if they were not in their right mind. They could be stuck in a loop of agony and willing to lash out at anything that was in their way. I could be bringing about the concerted attentions of a complete psychopath, unleashed from his reason in the state of anxiety and dread he probably would be in from realizing he is indeed dead and gone.

I dug the blade in deep, wincing as I did it, trying to cut deep enough to get a good trickle of blood flowing, but not so bad that I would have to seek medical assistance or have a crazy scar.

I looked at my palm and saw a rosy-red gash along the width of it, right along its lines. Blood pooled up in it and formed tiny drops that all collected into bigger pools. I clenched my fist and felt it hot and sticky. I help it up high.

"Papa Decky!" I called out, reaching out with my extra senses as well. "I, Alexander Lawrence Rose the Third, summon you. I come in peace, bearing you no ill will. I merely wish to speak with you."

It sounded melodramatic as hell, but I figured that was how you were supposed to address ghosts. Maybe you weren't supposed to tell them your name though. I was a little rusty on my Book of Samuel, and I had no Witch of Endor to assist.

One hot drop of blood slipped out, leaving a line down the side of my fist until it dripped down where it met the wrist. It detached itself, and gravity brought it down towards the floor like usual, until a funny thing happened. It started to slow its descent. I thought for a second that time was altered in some way and I was watching it fall in slow motion.

The drop reversed its trajectory and made its way back up until it hovered in front of me. It floated there like a small red balloon, playfully suspending itself and begging me to reach out for it. I was almost tempted to, but then it pulled in more blood from my hand, making the drop grow in size. At first it was a fine, dark red mist, but then a form started to coalesce around it, appearing like a shape coming out of the foggy blood cloud.

He was a young man in his early thirties, with a ruddy, round face and the eyes of a sleepy bear. He had a new beard of copper-colored stubble and close-cropped hair slicked off to one side. He was tall and barrel-chested, with arms that were probably capable in life of lifting me off the ground with minimal effort. He wore a tie-dyed T-shirt and jeans and flip flops.

"Only my friends call me Papa Decky," he said in a deep voice with an accent from somewhere I couldn't quite place, but knew it had to be a television character. "It's Herbert Decklin. Or Herbie if you wanna be brief. Until I get ta know ya. And I don't know who you are there, Danger Stranger."

"My apologies to you, sir, I meant no offense. I'm Alex Rose."

"Why are you talking like that, Allie?" he asked.

"It's Alex, not Allie. And like what?"

"Like you're trying to be Thor in the comics or somethin'? Why ya tryin' ta sound all stick up yer ass?"

I knew where the accent was from. He sounded like Bobby's mom from the cartoon *Bobby's World*. He was from the Midwest somewhere.

"...I don't know. I thought you were supposed to address unseen entities like that." I blushed from head to toe in embarrassment. I already felt stupid about this and didn't want to make a hash of this whole chance.

"Wait, what?" he asked, a look of shock on his features, panic creeping into his eyes as he glanced all around. "I can't be a ghost! What's going on?" He curled into himself, his hands up to his face as muffled sobs came out of him.

"Hey, hey! You're okay," I said, keeping my voice calm in an attempt to sooth him. "I can help you get through this, you're gonna be fine . . ." I tried to reach out and pat his shoulder to comfort him, and then backed up, realizing he was a ghost and the gesture probably didn't have the same meaning if it went straight through him.

"Boo!" he shouted, turning around and twisting his face into a contortion of wide-open mouth and red eyes with the lids peeled back. I jumped back and realized it was only a funny face like a kid would make. "Ah, hah hah huh, hawwwww!" he bellowed. "I can't believe you fell for that shit! Whaaaah, ha hah!"

"You asshole!" I said, and then I started laughing too. "Okay, that was a good one, ya got me."

"I gotta liven things up a little bit here'n there," he said, a broad grinning running wide from ear to ear. "I know I'm dead. And it can get fuckin' boring not being able to do anything sometimes. I've been saving up that idea for quite a while now."

"It's a good one," I said.

"All righty," he shot back at me, all business all of a sudden. "Enough of this chit-chat and fartin' around. You called me up. I wasn't really lookin' ta talk to anybody, and I certainly don'wanna be in here in this crappy place my former 'friend' crashes in. So what's the story, morning glory?"

I thought about it for a second. I didn't know anything about this guy, only a name for an insane attempt at summoning him that actually somehow worked. I was like a cat stuck up in a tree—once I got up to the top, I had no idea what to do there. I had spent all this time wondering if bringing him around would actually work, and I didn't stop to think what would happen if I actually brought him about.

Honesty being the best policy and all, I simply leveled with him.

"Look, I heard all about what your buddy Lenny did to you. That was shitty."

"And you were all chummy with him drinking it up!" he almost spat at me. He was getting worked up, and I didn't want that.

"That was only to do a little homework, sound him out a bit," I calmly told him. I took a seat on the ratty leather couch, brushing aside some McDonald's wrappers and kicking my feet up on the litter strewn coffee table to appear relaxed and maybe get him to relax too. "I'm not looking to do any business with him, he's kind of a loose cannon, as I'm sure you know."

"So what are you lookin' ta do?"

"Practice," I said. "I wanted a challenge, and what could be more challenging than buried treasure?"

"How old are you?" he asked. He seemed a bit more relaxed, a bit loosened up. "You sound like a dumb kid."

"Sixteen, almost seventeen. And I only act dumb. Nine times out of ten, anyway. That way when I do dumb shit, you're not surprised, and when I do really smart shit, it blows your mind."

"And I'm gonna help you get my loot?" He laughed again, that big hearty laugh of his. "No, you might have a little high of an opinion of yerself there, kiddo, but I think you're dumb." I let him laugh it out and merely sat there cool as a cucumber with a little smile on my face. I crossed my arms behind my head and leaned back. "Sorry, but I worked hard for it. And I don't know if anyone will ever use it like I wanna, but I ain't gonna let some little punk-ass kid swipe it from me. And fuck Lenny, he can sit around not knowin' where it is and worryin' if the cartels are gonna catch up with him until his dyin' day. It's the least he deserves."

"Fair enough," I said. "But what did you want to do with that money? Buy a big bong and tickets to go see Phish? A VW van? What?"

"Naw, nothin' like that! I was tryin' ta help someone."

"Who?"

"What's he ta you?" he asked, warily.

"I don't know." I shrugged. "Maybe I could help them for you …"

"Now why wouldja wanna go 'n do that?"

I thought about it for a second. I thought about this grubby little hole we were both stuck in at the moment, him because he was haunting it, me because I was trying to get what I wanted from it. I thought about what I really wanted to do. I didn't want to spend my days ripping off the landed gentry, or swiping Rolexes on the streets. I wanted to reach big and dare until I died trying. Because the world was truly too big and it was calling to me. It was telling me to get out there and take a bite out of it, see where the roads out of this one-horse town went to. And I thought about our mutual friend, drinking himself into a paranoid and drug-addled early grave with his gangster ambitions. I thought about what he would do and decided I was going to do the exact opposite of it.

"Because it's the right thing to do. If I were in your shoes, I would want someone to do the same thing for me."

It was easy as that. But most people can't see something that easy. They make up all kinds of complex schemes and reasons for why they want to fit the world into a mold of their making instead of letting it work out into its own beautiful thing. They tell themselves lies to help them get away with not lifting a damned finger to help their fellow human beings out, dead or alive, really there with them or only remembered.

Sometimes the easiest answer was simply don't do to someone what you wouldn't have them do to you.

"I was raised up on the Golden Rule," I said, sitting closer and motioning for him to take a seat, so to speak. He crossed his legs and was hovering in place. "The emphasis is on the 'do unto others' bit, but maybe doing unto others makes us meddle too much into the world and try to make it what only we want it to be and not what anyone else wants it to be. Maybe what we need to do is just step out of the way. Sometimes the harder thing is to do nothing. And in this case, that doing nothing means not hurting someone with my greed. Doing nothing is not keeping a bunch of money that someone could do better with than I could ever think to spend it on."

"You'd do that?" he said, looking cautious, but maybe relieved that someone could possibly be thinking of him.

"Who is it for?"

He sighed. "My brother. He's gotta rare disease, and there's a treatment out there for 'im, but the insurance won't cover it because they don't cover new treatments, but it's out there and it works! I didn't wanna get involved in this cartel shit, but I was gonna use my half of the money to pay for his treatments."

My mom lay on her bed in that bright room in my mind's eye, the curtains being moved to separate us. I thought of this poor big lug of a ghost feeling that same way for his brother and decided I was going to help him. No questions asked, didn't care what he needed, I was going to do this for him.

"My mom died when I was barely old enough to remember it," I said. "I remember her being in a hospital bed and crying because I didn't know what to do for her. Of course I'd use your money to save your poor sick brother. Let's make a deal. You tell me where you hid that cash, I'll use my half of the money to do whatever it takes to make your brother better again."

"Let me think about it," he said. "I need a minute to see if I can trust you. I'm gonna go off and do some reflecting. You can call on yer ol' pal Papa Decky if you need anything."

"Take your time. I'll be around. I'll give a little whistle."

He disappeared, fading out again as if he was back to being one with the air.

For a minute, I sat in that room, thinking on how good it felt to be doing something for someone. I wasn't directionless when I did things like this, I had a purpose, and that shined a light on my paths. I thought about how many more people were out there and how I could do good by them too. Sure, I was stealing, but I was only going to steal from people who had more than everyone else and were selfishly refusing to give it up for those who needed it the most. There were people calling, and I had work to do for them.

I made my way back through the horrible-smelling kitchen, and attempted to make sure nothing was out of place. That was when the whole world went dark.

18.

I OPENED UP MY EYES and had no idea where I was or really any idea of what was happening at all, other than the back of my head was an explosion of pain. It was centered around a spot in the back that hurt even more every time I bumped it up on whatever I was leaning up against. Then the overpowering smell of rotting food and spoiled milk filled the air, and I almost heaved and realized my mouth was filled with something dry.

My mind was filled with panic for a second, because I couldn't reach with my hands to tend to it, they were simply not there as far as I could feel. Something was keeping me from moving and a harsh light was beating down on me, burning me like an ant under a magnifying glass.

I screamed, but no sound came out.

"There you are," a voice called out. I couldn't make out where it was coming from, but I could tell whoever it belonged to was pleased, loving that I was helpless and unable to move.

Again, the overpowering stench of food came across in a wave, and I almost puked inside my own mouth. I sat there, gagging, tears streaming down my cheeks, drooling out of the corners of my mouth.

"I'm gonna take the gag out, but if you scream, I'll cut your lying little fucking tongue out with yer own knife, capeesh?" the voice said.

I couldn't think how to respond and only opened my eyes wide in fear.

"Hey!" he said, smacking my face with a big meaty hand. "Did I beat ya fuckin' stupid? Nod if you understand!"

I nodded vigorously. My vision stopped blurring and was only a little hazy around the edges. My captor came into my full view, and I realized it was the face of Lenny. He had a crazed look to him, his eyes looked like they were a size too big in a subtle way. But they were very full of manic energy and had a bloodshot-red hue to them.

"Gaaahhh!" I gasped, taking in deep breath after deep breath, glad I didn't have to breathe in that sour smell.

"Take it all in," he said. "If you have to puke, now's the time." On the kitchen table right behind him was a huge pile of cocaine. He did a bit off of the tip of my knife from the ritual before, blood still on it, and then proceeded to cut up lines of it.

I did puke, bile taste coming out along with an acidic burn in the back of my throat. I wished I hadn't drank that chai tea earlier.

"Help!" I shouted at the top of my lungs. My voice came out scratchy and sounded like it was someone else's.

He immediately rushed over and punched me in the side of my head. I saw stars for a second and laughed, despite the gravity of the situation. I had always thought that image was some kind of joke from cartoons.

"Oh, you think that's fuckin' funny!" he said, spit flying into my face. He waved the knife in front of my eyes like he was charming a snake, and I instinctively backed away from it. He grabbed onto my face, pinching both cheeks. I tried to squirm out of his tight grip, but he had hands like iron. He pressed the blade against my lips. "One more time and I fucking stick this in yer mouth, pop it out the side of your face. *Got it?*"

I nodded.

I peeked up and realized my hands were tied together to a big metal support pole in his kitchen that went through the countertop. I was hanging off of his counter like a slab of beef in a Rembrandt painting. My arms had gone numb hanging up above me. I could feel my fingers, but they were all pins and needles. They felt like someone had put ones made of plastic and two sizes too big on.

My dress shirt was still on, but it was unbuttoned down the middle.

He went back to his cocaine and started snorting up huge lines of it. He pretty much looked a perfect caricature of a gangster from those films like *Scarface*, where they are doing so much it's all over their nose and upper lip. It was like there was nothing else in the world for him as he went to town on that drug, sniffling a bloodhound snort and then leaning back and sniffing again to make sure it all got sucked back into his nostril.

"Now what's your story, ya little cocksucker?" he asked. He was not going to be easily persuaded by any answers I could come up with, so I decided I had better choose every word carefully. "The fuck are you? Really? Ya ain't a businessman or whatever ya said back at the bar. I don't think you're a fed, ya don't have the look aboutcha. You workin' for the fuckin' cartels?"

I took a deep breath and thought about it for a second. I stared off and noticed Gary was in the room. He had a look of sorrowful resignation, like he was expecting me to join his ranks at any minute and there was nothing I could do about it. I nodded to him in a wordless assent that he was right. I fucked up. And here we were, facing the consequences of that.

It gave me an idea though.

"I was Papa Decky's confidante," I said.

"Bullshit."

He had an irate look on his face like he knew he was being fucked with. I scrambled to massage over what I said, to make it believable. "It's true. He'd been trusting me for a while, and he said to me he would cut me in on his half of the profits. He was thinking that you were gonna turn on him, and he might have been right . . ."

"The fuck do you know!" He came up and backhanded me with enough force to whip my neck back. He then began crazily pacing about the room, a whirlwind of energy, as manic as the Tasmanian devil from *Looney Tunes*, spinning one way and then another.

"Go ahead," I said to him. "Papa Decky let me know about all kinds of things about you and your operation. Ask me anything, he told me everything."

I bit into my lip as hard as I could and then bit harder. It felt like my teeth couldn't get any deeper until finally that hot copper taste filled my mouth. I had no idea if this would work but had to give it a shot. "Papa Decky, c'mon if you're out there . . ." I whispered and spit blood onto the floor.

"What was that you said?" he asked, his voice sharp. He was on alert for anything I was trying to pull on him. He geared up to smack me again.

"It was meditation! My mantra, I needed to calm down for a second!"

He probably didn't know what a mantra was, but this seemed to satisfy him. "Fuckin' watch yourself," he warned.

The room began to chill again, and the ghost of that big cuddly man appeared like he was coming out of a haze, but not solid in any way that Lenny could perceive. "Awwww, no, Allie Boy, whadja do?" He was about to cry.

I shook my head and gave him a wink. I wanted him to play along and hoped he got the message. He took a deep breath, or at least appeared to. I didn't think respiration was a necessity for him, but lots of ghosts repeated habitual actions of the living. He shook his head and leaned back, on alert, but waiting for me to tell him what to do.

"So like I said," I said to Lenny, "Papa Decky confided all kinds of secrets to me." I glanced at the ghost of his friend, hoping for an answer. He took the hint and whispered something in my ear. "He told me all about the time . . . you were at summer camp and you, uh, you kissed a guy. It was your first kiss."

"That fucking . . . He wasn't supposed to tell anyone!"

"Well, people might let all kinds of other information slip when they think you're gonna turn on them. He also said . . . that you have a birthmark on your penis. Looks like a cow's spots on the skin."

"All right," he said. "So you know stuff. Too bad that stuff is all gonna go away when you're dead and tossed out into the desert offa I8 in Imperial County. I should kill you! I trusted you, ya little fuckin' ratfink!"

"If you kill me, you won't know where the money is. Then you'll be stuck here, running from the people who're after you. And they will get you. If I did, they could. You ain't exactly low-key, are you?" I nodded all about him to his messy house and with its dishes and trash everywhere.

"Why did you come around here?" he asked. "Why didn't you just take the money and run?"

I thought about it for a second. My head was spinning and it was hard to concentrate. I was fighting waves of nausea and extreme discomfort. My jaw hurt where he hit me, and I wanted to make sure I could buy as much time as I could to figure out what to do next.

"I wanted to see if you got to it first," I said. That was flimsy as hell, but it seemed to do the trick for him, and he nodded sagely, as if he would have done the same thing.

"So where is it?" he asked again, bringing the knife about threateningly and staring intensely.

"He said it's hidden in two places. He thought he could have leverage on them if they only found one. And he didn't trust anyone. He thought you were being followed."

"Okay, so where is it?"

"The first spot is the public storage space off of Morena. Grant Street. Unit 202."

"And the other?"

"Nope, you get the one, then we'll talk."

"I can make you talk."

"It's right down the street. You get the one, and then I'll take you to the other."

He snorted more cocaine, weighing his options while feeding his addiction. He took out a beer from a box in the fridge, one of the only things in there besides a carton of Chinese food that was probably going to go the way of his milk. He opened it up and chugged it down. He then grabbed another. "One for the road," he said, smiling. I smiled back. "When I get back, we're gonna have a loooong talk . . ."

"I quiver in anticipation," I said.

He grabbed a chain and tightly bound it around my hands and picked up a combination lock from the other room and put it on them. I was gonna need some Houdini-level shit to get out of that mess. He then put the gag back in my mouth and wrapped more tape over it. I sucked in a deep breath and tried not to notice the smell.

He stopped at the door for a second, said, "See ya 'round, kid," and left.

I waited until I heard his car start up and was sure he was well on the way.

"You got a plan?" Papa Decky asked. "He's gonna be pissed when he finds out that's not where I hid the money."

I shrugged. I had no plan whatsoever. I only wanted to buy a bit of time.

I'd hoped he'd have left me an implement to get out, but my lock picks were nowhere to be seen and therefore out of the question. My arms felt like they were going to come off. I had just enough slack to slide the rope and chains shackling me to the post, but couldn't see anything to break the lock with. And even if there was something, I couldn't have wielded it in the right way to break it. Anything strong enough to cut the chain would have been a miracle, and things that could have given me leverage to try and snap the links were out of reach. He was smarter than I gave him credit for.

I kicked at the kitchen drawers beneath his countertops, all grease covered from food spills and they opened a crack before slamming back shut. I was going to need a little dexterity, so I kicked off my shoes and clumsily shoved up my slacks and hooked my toes under the material around my ankles to slip my socks off.

The floor felt sticky to the touch, and I shuddered even though I had been lying in it for a good long while. The afternoon sun was slanting through the dirty windows and it glared down, making droplets of sweat bead on my upper lip and my hands feel incredibly slick.

There was a row of drawers to the side of me, and I went about opening them one by one with my toes, finding nothing in them to use to help me out. I wanted to scream and kick, but I took a breath and tried to think what to do next.

To my other side was the fridge, which appeared to be empty of anything useful. Across from me was the table with its pile of cocaine. The knife was gone; he had taken it, so no way to use that for anything creative. For someone hardly able to string coherent sentences together, the man had all his bases covered.

I sank to the floor in frustration and cried until I worried I would actually dehydrate and stopped my sobs. I sniffled, wiped my nose on the sleeve of my dress shirt, and wondered what was going to happen to me. Would I become a gloomy spirit haunting this dreary place like Papa Decky was? I hoped he wasn't stuck here, because I couldn't imagine living in this place as a living person, let alone hanging about here until the angels blew the trumpets of Judgment Day and called all the wandering and lost souls to their final resting places.

Would they have an open casket funeral, or would I be stuck here to rot like the contents of his fridge? Or would he make good on his promises to drop me off somewhere along the 8.

Maybe Jenny would come by and put a bouquet of flowers on my grave, swing around once a year on my birthday. I imagined her, dressed up like Wednesday Addams, and thought that she did look gorgeous like Christina Ricci in a way, something about her dark hair and the shape of her face. I hoped she would put red roses on my grave. Red for the feelings I hoped she had burning within her heart for me.

I was getting too romantic and in love with the idea of an easy death. I needed to think.

I pulled the cabinet door underneath the sink open with my toes. It slipped out of my sweaty grip between them the first few times, and I tried to mutter curses in frustration and only mumbled and tasted my gag.

I gave a sigh of relief when I saw what was in there and began to form a plan.

19.

IT WAS SUNDOWN WHEN he returned. The room was straightened up by the time he came back, to the best of my abilities with only two feet to work with and my arms painfully losing circulation, anyway. The drawers were put back right, the fridge was shut, and the cabinet was closed up, mostly as everything had been. My shoes were off, but he probably wouldn't have thought anything of me kicking them off in this heat. And he probably didn't think I was dexterous enough to pick anything up with them. The room looked picture perfect for one where a man had a teenaged boy bound and gagged.

Just in time for him to come in and start tearing things apart in a rage.

"You fucked me!" he shouted, cuffing me on the side of the head, throttling me by grabbing me by the shirt collar, and then bashing my head against the cabinets for good measure.

I expected a rage but wasn't exactly prepared for this, with my mouth still stopped up. My breath came out hot on my upper lip from my nostrils. His breath came out in steaming waves of stale beer and cigarette miasma, bad in its own right as the rotted fridge contents.

"You little cocksucker, why'd you go on and fuck me!"

My crew of familiar spirits was hanging in the wings, wanting to act but unable to affect things, and so they stood helpless and distressed.

He went over to the table, racked out a line of his cocaine, and snorted deeply. Then he cut another up and snorted it. I watched eagerly, making sure to see if he was taking it all in.

"Now you're gonna tell me where the fuck it is, or I'll . . . I'll fuckin' peel your fingernails off!"

"MMMMMMMMM!" I mumbled at him. He came over and undid the gag. "Thank you!" I gasped.

"Fuck you!" he said and smacked me. "Where's the money? There isn't even a unit 202!"

"Hey, it's a little hard to think when some gorilla is smacking you all about!"

"You're about to find out how hard it is to think without a head on your shoulders."

"Okay, okay!" I said. "Jeez, do another line of blow, why dontcha?"

"Start talking!" He went over and grabbed the last beer from his fridge and began to chug it.

"Okay, maybe I had it mixed up with something else, but I remember," I said. "It's up on Cowles Mountain. Up past the towers on the summit. If you take me there with you, I can show you. It's kind of tricky."

He went back to his beloved cocaine and did another massive line of it. Three so far. He was on a roll.

"Bullshit," he said. "Tell me why I shouldn't fucking kill your ass right now?"

"Well, how 'bout the fact that you're gonna die if you don't get ahold of a poison control center as soon as fucking possible?" I smiled broadly and narrowed my eyes like the cat that ate the canary.

"What'd you say?" He finally stopped moving and twitching about and had a look of shock on him and his face was pale.

"Did I not speak in plain fucking English?" I was suspended still in the chains and ropes but was enjoying the view. "You've just inhaled a heroic amount of strychnine. You shoulda cleaned out underneath your sink a bit better before you invited company over."

He raced to the cabinet and flung it open. In it was sitting a brown plastic bottle of gopher bait, the toothy little rodent blazoned on it in an unflattering photo, meant to show people that this was a dangerous pest indeed, a vicious creature to be wiped out.

He picked it up and frantically tried to see what the label said. "What'd you do?" he shouted.

"Now, I know you're not much of a reader there, Len," I said, feeling like I was holding all the cards even though I couldn't even see my own hands, "but that's strychnine in those, and while you were gone, I crushed it up and put it into your cocaine. I'll spare you the effort of reading stuff about chemistry and tell you that you've probably got ten minutes or so before you start having muscle spasms, and then you're really fucked."

He gripped the bottle in frustration with an agitated look on his face as he twisted it about. He was the perfect picture of panic, a man who had no idea how to react to the present circumstances. He kept on squeezing the bottle as hard as if he could pop the antidote out of it if he tried hard enough. "You're lying. No way you could have opened this bottle with your hands tied."

"Am I?" I coolly asked him. "Or did you just so happen to fuck with a kid who spent his days climbing trees and trying to lift things up with his toes like a monkey?"

"You little . . ." He dropped the bottle and began punching me repeatedly. Once in the gut, completely knocking the wind out of me, and then several to the head. I tried to defend myself by kicking him off, but he was too big, and I was barely able to hold him back.

"Oooowww, *fuck!*" I gasped. "It's not too late! Go get help! You can save yourself, why don't you call the poison control?"

He ceased his fit of rage for a moment.

I hung there moaning and worried I was going to pass out. My right eye was swelling shut, and I was seeing double all around. I spat out blood on the ground. My already cut upper lip had a few new friends to be kept company with, I figured from the way the taste of copper filled my mouth. I could feel where I had been hit so hard I bit into my own cheek.

He was breathing deeply, clutching his fists in frustration. Whatever he was doing was probably only increasing the likelihood that the poison was coursing through his system much faster.

"Call them up, and then they find you here?" he asked.

"Better that than the alternative!"

"And then you get off scot-free, and I go ta jail for this?"

"Call the poison control," I begged him. "It's not too late, they can help you!"

"Nuh-uh," he said, his face lighting up with the most wicked smile.

It was a smile of desperation and perverse joy, a hateful contortion of what true happiness should be all about, and I still see it in my nightmares. He stared at me with a look in his eyes that said the soul dropped out of him and he was already dead and willing to make everything he could in the world that way before he went out of it.

"If I'm gonna go, I'm taking you with me," he said, in a calm and matter-of-fact voice, that seemed all the more frightening for the actions accompanying it. He picked up the bottle and poured a handful of the pellets into the palm of his hand, the excess spilling out over the sides and through his fingers as they sprinkled to the ground. He slowly made his way over towards me, his eyes fixed on mine the whole time.

Papa Decky and Gary were trying to grab ahold of him, but they lacked the concentration to properly affect anything in the material world, and so they wrung their hands like the epically sad and hair-pulling angels in Giotto's *Lamentation*.

"What are you doing?" I pleaded. "You've still got time! Go! Save yourself!" I had thought for sure his self-preservation instincts would have kicked in, and he would have rushed to the doctor's to try and take care of it. He had other ideas, apparently.

"Open wide ..." he said, in that frightening sotto voce drawl of his. He reminded me of a parent feeding their unruly kid, only he had lost his fucking mind. He pinched my cheeks, opening them up. I squirmed and thrashed my head from side to side and was met with another painful backhand slap. I still resisted, knowing that if I gave up the fight, it would be lights out for good.

He clenched his fist, more of the nasty little pellets slipping through his fingertips, death overflowing from his dirty, calloused hand. I pushed back with my legs this time, kicking him in the groin, thrashing them about, and received another blow that knocked the wind right out again.

He gripped my cheeks again, and I sighed, hoping to be able to spit them back out but preparing myself to die on the floor there with him. I still kept tense, refusing to go quietly, hoping to bite a finger off if I was going to swallow poison. He forced my mouth open, and that was when a loud crash sounded.

A million points of light exploded all around us as the darkness reached out and swallowed Lenny, tearing him off of me. Another loud crash sounded in the living room, followed by a wet slapping sound, like meat being tenderized. It went on for a few seconds, which may as well have lasted years, and then they were punctuated by a dull thud.

I realized the light was from the glass on his French door shattering. The shards lay there on the floor in a million dangerous starlights glittering on the ground. I remained there sprawled out, my legs refusing to work but knowing I should be ready to use them to defend myself against I had no idea what.

The dark shape came back into the room, too big to make anything out other than that it was in the form of a tall man. There was a loud clack, followed by a jangling noise as the chains slipped off and fell to the ground. Then there was a shuffling sound and my hands were free. I slumped down to the floor, my muscles burning like they had everything they could ever take and finally gave up on the whole keeping-it-together thing.

I didn't care who this person was. They could have been cartel hitmen and they were after me next, I only wanted to take one minute and breathe. I was so tired of fighting.

An arm reached out to help me up, and I frantically tried to shrug it off. "No. No. NO!" I shouted at it as I almost fell into broken glass trying to scooch away.

"You're okay," a voice whispered, and I was overjoyed to discover it belonged to David. He had his collar up and it was hard to see his face—he seemed to be avoiding the light. But I recognized those cold, steely-blue eyes of his. They were penetratingly intense, with a frosty look that burned brightly in the porchlight that shone in from outdoors. "I've got you, and you're going to be all right."

"Oh God," I whispered and hugged onto him, happy to feel a person I knew, any person really. Because I was so sure I would never hold another human being tight again. I was afraid I would be a chittering ghost in some gloomy underworld, or orbiting around the confines of a haunted house, calling out to the inhabitants but never hearing a response. I hugged him tight as he lifted me up in his arms. "I'm so glad to see you."

"I'm so sorry," he said. "I should never have sent you to do this. You are too young, only a boy. In my time, where I am from, boys your age were considered men, and we sent them off to war. We sent children to die, and I almost sent you off to that occluded destination too."

"S'okay . . ." I muttered. "Because I got it."

"You what?" he asked in disbelief.

"I got it. I know where the treasure is." I smiled and cried tears of joy that felt so good to be able to feel on my cheeks. "I know, it's not treasure, juss money. But I found it. I found the treasure. Guess I'm still a little kid at heart, huh?"

"Rest," he said. "Shut your eyes, and when you wake up, this will all simply be a memory."

I tried to stay awake, because I was worried I might have a concussion, and I knew it wasn't a good idea to sleep with one of those. But I soon entered a deep slumber and didn't bother trying to fight anything at all anymore.

20.

"**AND THE MONEY WAS WHERE** I said it would be?" I asked David later that week.

"Yes," he affirmed. "End of Mussey Grade Road in Ramona. Over the concrete bridge, north side of the old horse corrals, twenty paces, with a rock on top."

I was healing nicely, no concussion. A few ribs were bruised, not broken like I feared. It hurt like hell when I took in too deep a breath. I convalesced at David's mansion, where he had his private doctors seeing to me. And Jenny was there to help me through it all. She never left my side at first, but when it seemed I was up to my old self again, she went off and attended to her own affairs.

She and David were not really that close for people who were related, even if not by blood, I noticed. She was silent for the most part when he came in, even to an uncomfortable extent, and it was almost like he spoke around her, with me trying to bridge the gap between the two in conversation.

Most of my time training was spent with him alone and with only glimpses of her. As much as I wanted to stay and try to catch any time I could with her, I knew I needed to get back to my pop and Windsong. They were frantic worrying where I had got off to. I made a half-assed excuse about having to take a trip for my job, but this wasn't going to cut it for much longer.

Mostly, I didn't want to come home looking like I had started an underground fighting club among all my friends in academic league. They already had their doubts about my "job," with its odd hours and the fact that I was cagey about the details of it. I didn't spend lavishly, worrying that it would attract too much of their attention, but I had around fifty thousand dollars squirreled away and was about to have a whole lot more.

I intended to keep my promise to Papa Decky, and I was already in the process of setting up an anonymous donation for his little brother's needs. As for the rest? I had no idea what to do with it. I wanted to go to college. And definitely invest it. No sense letting it sit around and do nothing. The only problem was I was still a minor and needed to wait another year to be able to really do anything useful with it.

"So what happened to Lenny?" I finally asked David. "What did you do to him?"

We were in his office. I was in one of the ornate chairs across from his massive desk. I had my feet up on it, which I'm sure annoyed him, but he tolerated it. I loved the idea of putting my feet up disdainfully on a flamboyantly expensive object.

The sun was low in the late afternoon sky, and I was sure that Moreau would come up with one of his classic excuses for why he had to leave at night. I really wanted to know what his deal was and swore I would find this secret out about him.

"It needn't concern you," he said, as if it was a trivial topic, but I had to know that one, and I had to know it immediately. I figured mysteries were the stock in trade for a man like Moreau, but I was an accomplice to murder.

Whatever happened to Lenny was my responsibility, even though he probably would have stuffed me full of poison and left me to rot in that kitchen of his. "I cleaned up after we left. No one will ever know you were there," he added.

I couldn't stand the thought of having someone's blood on my hands. I believed there was nothing a person could do that can't be undone. I had to, because if I didn't, I might be one day held to account for all the things I'd done. Stealing was already tricky enough to justify; I didn't need stealing someone's life to be the one layer of grime on my soul I couldn't wash off.

It's never too late to turn your life around and do something good with it, A.J. had told me, and I believed him. But it would be hard to find strength to spin around to the right way with the fact that I was a killer weighing me down.

"It does concern me though," I said. "I didn't intend to kill him. I wanted him to run and get help. I counted on him wanting to save himself."

"People won't always do exactly what you want. You need to make plans for that contingency and adjust accordingly."

"I think we need to have faith in people too." I had seen the horror of a man bent on killing me over saving himself, and that was enough to drive a person mad. I needed to believe that this wasn't the case with everyone, otherwise the world was full of horrors and a sun that shone for no reason at all. I needed to believe that people could always make better choices than we expected.

"Some people are beyond saving," he said. "You did what you had to, and that's good enough to get through the day."

"It shouldn't be though," I said, taking my feet off of the table and staring him down. "Good enough should never be the most you can do to help out a person, to keep them safe from harm."

"Alex," he sighed, putting his hands into a steeple as he contemplated his words. "A great many people aren't worth the effort to save. They need to want to help themselves first. Most lack the moral conviction and the intelligence to introspectively peer deep down and realize that they are, in fact, the problem."

"No person is a problem. They *have* problems, but they aren't problems."

"Ah, they all have those problems though! You can't make their problems yours. You can't spend all your life trying to rehabilitate one soul, when there are masses at your doors screaming to be let in from the cold. They need help too, and you need to think of the bigger picture."

"It's easy for you to talk about people screaming at a door when yours are so far from the street people couldn't possibly shout loud enough for you to hear."

I didn't know if I really felt this way or if it was a chip on my shoulder from having nothing for so many years. But I resolved in my heart then and there to never take more than I need. And if I did, then I would give it to those whose needs amounted for more. That's all there was to it.

"This is all a facade, remember?" he said, smiling broadly. He looked around the room, breathing it all in and staring at the layers of color and class wistfully, like they were all doomed to mean nothing to him, when there was so much to see. "We need to be able to say that we have a goal with it all, otherwise our actions are meaningless. And we need to be able to do anything in the world to achieve that goal."

"Well, that's a lesson you'll never be able to teach me," I told him. "I need to hang onto my innocence, even if it's been tarnished, blemished, and dragged through the dirt. Because if I don't, I could go on and on killing to get what I want. I didn't see what you did to Lenny in that room, but I have a pretty good idea. And I'll never kill another human being for you, or for any cause you can name. It wouldn't be worth the cost to my soul."

He sighed and seemed like he was about to speak, but he held his breath. It could have been my words, but I think it was the intensity with which I stared at him as I said them. My hard and unyielding gaze adding a steely emphasis to those utterances. No words could put it more succinctly, just the force of my will, focused in the set of my jaw and my stare, letting him feel the unblinking determination that I wouldn't tone down.

I received a hard stare of his own. It was cold and full of frustration, and somehow I knew he was scheming on how to make me see things his way. He was a man who never took no for an answer, and the life he built around him showed it. The gorgeously columned mansion he lived in was a testament to it all.

"You want to know what happened to Lenny?" he asked, a hint of playfulness in his voice that sounded so out of tune with the gravity of the matter. "Let's ask him ourselves, shall we?"

"What are you talking about?"

"Come, walk with me," he beckoned, motioning with his finger. He got up from behind his desk and wandered to the door. He stood at the doorway, his hand out as if for me to take, with a dramatic flair that seemed urgent, but poised. "Come."

I drew in a breath and got up from the chair. I was dreading what he would show me. The secrets he promised to reveal threatened to add weights that would try and pin down my soul, I was sure of it, keeping me scrabbling about on the ground instead of free to soar. But I followed him.

The halls were unusually darkened as we wandered through them. For such a large house, his servants usually kept out of sight. But someone at least turned the lights on all over the place every night, keeping the gold gleaming and the art on display. There was only dying daylight all about, as I caught the sun sinking down through an open window, the breeze blowing the curtains as eerily as shrouds on a spirit.

We went down a winding flight of stairs instead of the elevator, silent as the grave the whole time. I desired to blurt out the question that was on my lips, that important *What the fuck are we doing???* but it didn't feel right. The quiet house was an echo of the sense of trepidation I felt, as if the whole building was holding its breath.

The cool breeze greeted us as we walked out of a pair of doors that were enormous even for a side entrance. Our wandering took us though the winding garden paths, through hedges that wound about into a maze, something winding and organic, but cultivated when it wanted to be growing wild. A dim orange glow came from around the corner and a smell of smoke drifted our way, mixing with the sea air scent and carried in on the fog that drifted in.

In the courtyard, a great fire was burning. It was in a massive fire pit, a tower of flames, with the logs that overflowed from the bounds, dropping hot embers onto the stones surrounding them and giving everything the glow of an erupting volcano. The sun was peeking out from a gap in the clouds and making its final descent in the darkening sky, that last ray of light dropping to a pinpoint that vanished and left the horizon around it a deep velvety purple.

Moreau was no longer at my side. I frantically looked all about for him. "David?" I called out.

"Up here," his voice boomed back in the darkness away from the firelight. I saw him on the upper level of a porch that wrapped around that side of the house, next to a fluted column.

"Nice trick," I shouted up to him. No answer. This had the taste of another one of his lessons. Maybe he would teach me how to teleport. It was after dark and he was still about, refraining from his usual excuses and exits. "You're up awfully later than your usual bedtime."

"You wanted to see where your would-be murderer was." A dark object crashed down on the paving stones near me with a sickening slap. "Let's bring him to us, shall we?"

A small package, wrapped up in butcher paper, was lying on the ground. It wasn't near enough to the fire to be in danger of being consumed by the flames, but I picked it up to make sure it was out of their reach and examined it. It was somewhat cylindrical, but skinny and about a foot long, with a heavy end. It felt like it was wooden club, or maybe a branch of a tree.

I glanced up at him and couldn't make out much of his features. His eyes glowed incredibly bright in the light, as if they were the only thing distinct about him. They said *Do it, see for yourself,* only he wasn't saying a word.

I slowly unraveled the paper and tried to make sense of what was in it. It felt firm, but with a soft coating on it. It was hard as a piece of wood, maybe with soft bark all over it. I almost dropped it when I pulled it out and realized what it was. My stomach curled like it was going to involuntarily squirm away from me and maybe release the contents of my lunch on its way out.

A hand, with the arm up to the elbow still attached to it. The flesh at the hacked-away end had bits of it that hung out in shreds, darker and flapping about like lunch meat. A bit of bone protruded. I didn't know what to do with it; dropping it seemed out of the question, but holding it in my own two hands felt so wrong that I couldn't help but squirm and try not to stare at it.

"What the fuck is this?" I demanded.

"That right there is Lenny," Moreau declared. "He put himself in a position where he would take a life, so now this is all that is left of his remains."

"Why would you show this to me? Is this some kind of sick fucking trophy?" I wanted to throw it at him in disgust. It was obscene to have this even after everything the man did.

"It is a connection to him," Moreau explained. "He isn't on this plane anymore, but he can be called back with the right coaxing. And ghosts are often drawn to their mortal remains."

"And what makes you think I could do that?"

"Don't lie. For a thief, you're not very good at it, whether it's to yourself or others. I know you've been able to speak with the dead. That you can summon and control them. Make them do things for you. Jenny can, and so can you."

Hearing this brought up a great sense of betrayal, knowing that Jenny was telling him things I had revealed to her in confidence. Things I had never told another human being, not even A.J. It was like she had laid me bare, naked in front of the world for everyone to poke and prod, even if it was only one man she spilled everything to.

"And what should I do?"

"Feel for his presence. See if you can summon him."

I tried to protest, but the temptation was too strong not to try. Even if I thought the man was utterly pathetic and a horrible human being, I never wanted to have anything to do with his ghost. But I wanted to test the limits of my abilities. I reached out with my senses and immediately felt him nearby. He was waiting in the wings, ready to take his cue, but not in a form of any sort to do it. He was a void where a person should be, waiting to collect itself together. "Come," I called to him.

And he did. He began to take a form that could be seen, not a shade that only I was glimpsing, but a shimmering dewy vapor pulling itself into the form of a man.

"Yes!" Moreau beamed. "Yes!"

The poor beleaguered spirit glanced up at the man with a look of abject fear and a sorrow that made a beaten dog look fortunate. He knew this was the one who killed him, and here he was in his power again.

I was so moved to pity I wanted to cry. This poor man had suffered so much and had done so much to make people suffer. I wanted so badly to hate him, but I couldn't bring myself to do it. He was the poor son of someone, he had made people laugh and made people smile at one point, he had hopes and he had dreams once. And here he was, reduced to a cowering shade, summoned to this audience to suffer after he should have been released from this mortal coil.

"Have him pick up that chair," Moreau said. "Do it."

I had never really tried to test the limits of the ghosts I had interacted with to affect the physical world. It seemed a violation of trust to do it. They were my friends. But this man had tried to kill me, and I had to find out.

I nodded to him. "Go. Do as he says and pick up the chair."

He silently trodded over and did as he was told. His head hung low the entire time, like he was phenomenally sad and expecting to get beaten for doing it. And to my surprise, he picked it up.

"Yes, good! Good!" Moreau cheered. I still couldn't make out Moreau's features, but his eyes were the wide-open portals to an incredibly excited mind. "Now, go and have him put his arm in the fire, tell him to feel the heat."

"No," I said. "That's too cruel."

"It doesn't matter. He won't feel anything, he hasn't got any nerves left, besides the remains of the ones you're holding in your hand. Imagine how effective a thief you can be with an invisible army to do whatever it is you want them to."

I knew I should resist what Moreau was asking me to do, but something about his words had a force behind them that made them too strong to resist. They had a magnetic pull to them that made me forget my reason for a second.

The fire was glowing bright and casting a light on everything that made it seem like raw emotion was spilling all over the scene. The poor ghost was quivering and about to sob.

"Go," I told him, against my usual better judgment and sense of compassion. He hesitated and shook his head. "Go! Do it, encase yourself in flesh, feel the heat!"

He slowly walked over to the fire with the gait of someone approaching his own death sentence. Something he probably never had the chance to do because it no doubt came on so suddenly for him. In his face was dread and remembered pain.

I noticed Gary and Papa Decky, both watching the scene like two sorrowful angels. Their eyes had something in them I had never seen before—fear.

They were right to be afraid. What was to stop me from doing it to them? Once I went down that path of making any one ghost do something against their own will, how could it not spread to the way I treated others?

They might no longer be living humans, but that didn't mean that they lost their humanity. I wasn't about to make any afterlife a torture chamber for the deceased. I wasn't about to make anyone a slave to me, even if he had done terrible things. No one deserved that. I didn't believe in Hell, so why would I try to go about making one for anyone at all on Earth?

"Stop," I told him. He looked up at me, no doubt expecting fresh tortures or some violent act against him. "I don't care what you did in your life, but I'll be damned if I'm gonna fuck you over for the rest of what's after it. I don't know where you go after this, but leave, do it now!"

I held the hand up and threw it into the fire. I didn't know if he would be freed or if he would still wander. All I knew was I would not have the temptation around to try to use him by anything that might tie him down to this world or any other. The paper lit up and the flesh began to bubble and melt as it curled and turned to ash and smoke.

The ghost slowly faded and went back to somewhere, I really didn't know where, and I truly didn't care. I was just glad that he was out of harm's way.

Moreau stood on the balcony, clenching his fists. He whirled around and stormed back into the house with a great show of anger and frustration, but I was surprisingly glad.

I was proud of myself, feeling a bright and warm glow from having resisted that strong temptation to cause harm. I had no idea what came over me. All I knew was it had the power of an addiction and an urge, calling on me with promises of my wildest desires but expecting me to perform horrors, and it wasn't me, and I resisted it.

I didn't realize how much tension I had been holding in and finally let it all out, dropping to my knees and letting tears spill down my face. The heat from the fire quickly turned them into sticky tracks down my cheeks, but I was glad for the feel of them. I wanted those tears of release to be there to remind me of how good it felt to let it all go.

Jenny came up, sat down with me, and wrapped her arms around me. "C'mon," she said. "Let's go."

21.

"I'LL GIVE YOU A RIDE BACK," Jenny said to me away from the fire.

"Thanks," I replied. "You know, you can come with me. I have no idea what we'll do, but we'll do it together."

"Shhhhh," she warned. "Not here. Don't say things like that."

We wandered to a bench underneath her balcony and sat down on it. I wanted it to be Romeo and Juliet. I didn't care if we died together, so long as we had those intense moments of love before it all went entirely lights out for the both of us in that tomb. I wanted a story of a love that would live on, not a parting of ways with her, because I found nothing to be sweet about the sorrow I was experiencing at leaving her.

We sat there in that courtyard, with its tropical plants and immaculately trimmed rose bushes and hedges, and I wanted to prolong our moments with each other, didn't want them to end.

"You know I can't leave with you," she said, eyes downcast instead of gazing out at the beautiful starlight reflecting into the flat expanse of the Pacific. "I'll never get away from David. He'll never give me up without a fight."

"I didn't know there was fighting involved."

"Let's not talk here," she said, glancing around nervously again. She walked me around to the front.

I left that house, taking nothing from it but memories. Memories and the satisfaction of knowing that in David's "uncrackable" safe that I'd spent hours working on with him was a single slip of paper there that no one but I could have possibly put there. It read "Dear David, Good times. Peace out."

We hopped into her Ford Mustang, an old antique model like the one in The Doors video for "L.A. Woman," and she took it around the corners at breakneck speeds. It growled like a wild jungle animal.

She was going a different direction than my place, but I didn't care, so long as it was with her. We were teasing down the little bit of coast highway that spilled onto Torrey Pines Beach, with its huge cliffs that towered up like golden gates and big salty lagoon that stretched out and back around the other side of the cliffs. I played there all the time as a kid and wanted so badly to have someone to explore with. I was tired of my lonely wanderings already, even at a young age, and wanted her to stay so I would never be lonely again, even though I feared this was her way of prolonging the moment before we had to part.

I glanced from time to time to her intense focused stare as she whipped around one curve and then the next. She looked the picture of concentration on everything in the job at hand so as not to think about anything else.

We kept moving north and went through all those beach towns, with their perfect white houses perched in various configurations on the cliffs. That sense of inadequacy threatened me again, worrying that she was from a world like this that I would never understand. All those houses, for all their bright color, seemed dark places where power was displayed and wealth was amassed, like the horde of a dragon, shimmering and forbidden, dangerous and alluring.

We made it to Del Mar, creeping through the stop signs and lights, the beige grandstand of the racetrack with its Spanish terracotta rooftops towering up in the background. She parked the car and hopped out, *Dukes of Hazzard* style, and I tried to do something equally as cool and almost fell out the side. I was still entirely sore from being battered around and tied up. Sometimes I would close my eyes and see that soulless gaze of a man intent on ending everything that was me, Alex Rose, and I shuddered to think that I could have been a "was" instead of a more present tense.

It was going to take a while to shake this whole affair, but I wasn't going to let it slow me down.

We roamed about along that beach, listening to the waves come roaring to the shore and then washing back out in their perpetual cycle of forces of motion and change. I felt as kinetic as those waves were, constantly crashing against immovable objects and trying to get out into the wider expanse where I could disappear if I wanted to and show up anywhere else around the world.

I held her hand, and she let me do it. We walked like that for a half hour, not saying anything, only taking in the sounds together.

She finally spoke. "I used to come here as a kid. I loved the dog beach." She nodded up ahead to the other side of the river. "David would never let me have a dog as a kid. He thought dogs were too much of a mess, and he didn't want one running around the house."

"What kind of maniac doesn't love dogs?" I asked in mock shock, but also wanting to know what the real reason was.

"The kind who always has an agenda," she replied. "You might think David is this titan of industry, with a mysterious past and tricks up his sleeve, but you don't know him like I do. He doesn't stop at getting what he wants. You're lucky to be getting out when you can. Don't let him keep you the way he's keeping me."

"Is he hurting you?" I gripped her hand and clutched it tight with the other in a protective gesture. "Because if he is, I don't care, money or not, I'm gonna come after him."

"I'm all right," she said. "Really, I'm fine."

"Really? Because all you gotta do is tell me and I won't stop until you're safe as can be."

"Shhh . . ." she whispered, although I had no idea why. There wasn't a soul on this beach. "I bet you would too."

"Fuckin' A, you'd better believe it."

"Let's just enjoy the beach, okay?"

We walked along the river and away from the shore. Back among the houses and the fairgrounds. The late summer air was perfect, the way it can only be in Southern California, not too hot. Cool enough to take away the edge of the day. You could sleep outside anywhere and feel comfy enough to lie there all night. We shuffled along in the sand a bit more, as it made vibrating tingly washboard quiverings on our feet as we slowly strolled across it.

"You're going to see and do amazing things, Alex," she said. "I wish I could be there with you, but I can't."

"Why not?"

"When I was a little kid here, I imagined Prince Charming would take me away," she said. Her dark eyes glinted in the light from the nearby houses. Her dark lips were a perfectly kissable shape, but I knew now wouldn't be the proper time to try and get that gesture of affection from her. Her dark hair softly whipped about in the breeze. "I know you're probably the closest thing I'll get to Prince Charming. But you're more of a snake charmer, aren't you?"

"Maybe I'm a leopard trying to change my spots," I said. And I did lean in and kiss her. She kissed me back, and I could tell it was filled with longing and desire but also like she would pull away at any minute. Something about her was always guarded and secret. Something in her wanted to open up but was afraid of being hurt.

She finally pulled apart from me, and we started to walk back.

"You're off to go see the world and take what you can from it, Alex Rose." She grabbed my hand and twined her fingers around mine. "I know you're going to do something spectacular, something big. But you're going to have to do it on your own, you don't want me holding you back."

"Maybe that's something you should let me decide on my own."

We crossed under the railroad tracks and back to the noisy shore with its chaotic, primordial energy and its deep becoming waters, places of dark creation.

"No, I'm pretty sure the world is what you want," she said. "One person wouldn't be enough. You'd get the notion at any time and have to pick up things and go."

"I'd pick them up with you. We could go together."

"My place is here. For now. I'll think of you all the time, wondering what you're up to, but I can't come with."

I tried to think of the right words to say, a magical formulation of words that would act as a love spell, the perfect abracadabra to get her to understand that she was the only one for me. Something pure and poetic to show her I would go to the ends of the earth for her, and take her to the ends of the earth with me.

But before I could even stammer out a coherent thought, she simply said, "Let's get you home."

And off we went.

The drive back to my place was simultaneously the shortest and longest of my meager existence. It was quiet and somber, but I wanted every minute with her to last just one longer.

She pulled into the street on the hill, and I stared at that white house with poisonous oleanders all alongside its borders. With its ice plant in the front and overgrown jungle in the back. I was happy to see it, but dreading being alone without her in it.

I kissed her and she kissed me back, until, finally, she said, "I have to go. Love you, Alex." And she left me there, knees feeling weak even though I wanted to use them to run after her, heart hurting in my chest because it was beating for nothing but her.

I tried to sneak into the house, but all my skills were for nothing since I was so exhausted. A.J. was waiting right there at the foot of the stairs, arms crossed and a look of concern in his features.

"I know where you've been," he told me. His voice was a mixture of hurt feelings and disappointment. All I wanted was a moment to collect my thoughts, and I knew I was not going to get it. I tried to think about what he meant by that. Had he somehow found out about my business in Lenny's house?

"That mansion you've been hanging out in," he went on. "I told you to stay away."

"Oh, that," I said, sighing a minor sigh of relief that he didn't seem to be onto anything I'd recently done.

"What do you mean, 'Oh that'?" he almost shouted. I was

completely taken by surprise on this one and wondered where this hostility was coming from.

"That's where I've been working. I've been a personal assistant to the owner."

"I've seen you going there."

"Wait, what?" I hadn't thought he'd have been so concerned. I also wondered how I had no idea that he was tailing me.

"You think you're the only one who can sneak about?"

"Ooookay," I said. "So you followed me. Good for you. Can I go to bed now?"

"No, you can't!" he said, pushing me down onto a couch. I saw red at this gesture. I did not like being touched without my permission and definitely didn't condone being handled roughly after what I'd just been through. "You're gone out at all hours, you have bruises and cuts, you miss school! You're up to something. You need to fucking shape up and fly right!"

"Or what?" I told him, standing back up. "What are you gonna do? Fly right? Why, so I can be a little worker drone like you? I'm not gonna always struggle and get nowhere like you."

He raised his hand as if he was going to smack me and then looked down at it as if shocked that he had it in him to do so.

"I want you to stay away from that place," he said. "And stay away from that girl you've been with over there."

"Excuse me? You don't get to tell me what to do!"

She might have already done the job that night for him, but I wasn't going to let him make decisions for me about who I could and could not see. I went up the stairs, right past him.

"Get back here!" he commanded, and he grabbed my shoulder.

"You let go of me right fucking now," I whispered to him, gazing like hot iron at his hand on me, smoldering and sparking. I stared fixedly at him and was met with the same look of stubborn resistance.

I tried to force him off of me, but he held on tight.

"Don't you even think of walking away from me," he said.

"You can't hold me back," I told him, still trying to get out of his grasp. "Ya know, all my life you've been doing that, ever since you had them keep me from Mom when she was dying. I don't need you anymore."

"You don't know what you're saying."

"I! Don't! Need! *You!* Anymore!"

He let go of me, and I almost fell back, I had been pulling away so fiercely.

He had a look in his eyes like the thread connecting to me had snapped and he was looking around frantically for where it was so he could tie it all back together.

Tears were starting to come out of my eyes as I stared at my father. He seemed simultaneously an oppressor and my first and best friend. I felt sorry that I had grown apart from him, and that this was all my fault, but I wanted nothing more than to get away from him.

A huge wave of dread came over me, like the world was blacked out for a second and things had lost their luster. I was so confident before, and now I realized that the world wasn't how I remembered it. I might have been a little full of teenage angst before, but this was different; this was a dread like everything was fucked and it would take a miracle to unfuck it. I wanted to lie down in the earth and dig deep enough for it to swallow me whole. I wanted to get away because I couldn't bear to be near him at the moment, my pop, a man I had admired and looked up to for so long.

I took the opportunity and ran back out of the house. I ran down that road, moon shining on it all same as that one night so long ago. Back to that canyon, where I had seen that mysterious Haunted Woman and woke up later on. It had a shining glow to it that made it appear like the surface of an alien planet. I ran out there and just screamed as loud as I could at the sky.

I was alone in the world, and that great expanse was going to be my only companion on many an occasion, I knew it then. So I opened up my arms to it and shouted out a savage greeting of adolescent rage, one that was going to echo throughout my years.

I'd like to say that that raging voice has calmed down since then, but it never really has.

22.

I MET KOREY AGAIN MANY YEARS LATER at that big festival that they don't really call a festival out in the desert in Nevada. It was back in . . . not sure which year, honestly. They blend together. I was with my good friends in a theme camp by the name of Funky Monkey. I was helping them with one of our events, as any good camp puts on, at the very least, one of. This year, we were doing body painting.

There was a big bike ride where all the women went topless, and we offered to paint people up with an airbrush gun and body paints. It sounds a little like we were all looking for an excuse to touch some knockers, but a guy asked me to paint little eyeballs on his sack, and I didn't turn him down. I Purelled the fuck out of my hands afterwards, but that's neither here nor there.

There I was getting into a good rhythm and working on my skills as an artist. I was wearing a silver and gold dress that I had bought at a thrift store, a cute garment that a girl had maybe worn once to prom. My friend and fellow campmate, Sarah, was out there in the streets, hollering at people to come in in her sweet high-pitched Wisconsin accent. "C'mon in, hee-yah, getcha boobs painted!"

Our friend Jimmy Neighbors, not to be confused with Jim Nabors, was also out in the chalky dust street, yelling on a megaphone for people to come in, in his gravelly voice that sounded like Beetlejuice's. He was wearing cut-off Daisy Dukes, with one testicle hanging out of the pants leg.

"You need to maybe just have a woman to get people in here," I hinted to Sarah.

"Why, what's wrong with Jimmy Neighbors out there?" she asked. We always called him by his entire name for some reason, it flowed better with him.

"If we're trying to get ladies to feel comfortable with getting their bodies painted, maybe it should be with someone who isn't yelling at them in the streets with a bullhorn and hanging his balls out of shorts with his belly hanging over them," I mused. "Dunno, not being a woman myself, I could hardly say, but could be an idea."

"Yeah, lemme handle this," Sarah said, winking.

She went out on the street. "Here, cupcake," she said to Jimmy Neighbors. "Lemme take over for ya, while you get a bee-yah to drink."

"Sounds good," Jimmy Neighbors said, and he wandered off to get his hops 'n barley on.

So we replaced a man with the voice of a hobo who'd been smoking a pack a day since he was tall enough to reach over a countertop for a gal with a thick Wisconsin accent, and it turned out to get a better line coming around the block, who'd have guessed?

"Come on oh-ver!" she yelled as people came up the street. "We'll paint-cher tits!"

The line was humming, and our music was on point with one of our friends DJing. I was doing my best to paint a unicorn on one of my friends. I was trying to make it smile back at you as it reared up on its hind legs, and for whatever reason, it was coyly staring back at its ass, which was all poppin' out like it wanted to have a bite taken out of it. A very thirsty unicorn. Which sounded like the title of an amazing children's book.

"Hey, you!" Sarah shouted out to a gorgeous girl in a bikini walking on by with a colorful umbrella. "We'll paint yer tits for ya, and maybe yer vag too if ya want!"

"I would let you if I had one!" she said, and pulled down her red bathing suit bottoms she was wearing.

"You get to go to tha front of the line with that!" Sarah declared, and took her by the hand and dragged her on to my spot for painting. I smiled at her, and she flashed me the prettiest little grin with two beyond captivating dark eyes staring back brighter than the sun on the horizon.

I smiled back even harder and blushed for a second, forgetting my task at hand of fucking up a unicorn.

"I think it looks pretty good," my friend said, smiling at me as I tried touching up a smear of purple on its tail.

"Sorry, Ashley," I said sheepishly. "You caught me off guard, didn't know it wasn't a twerking unicorn you wanted."

"No worries." She could tell my attention was elsewhere. She gave me a quick kiss on the cheek and hopped off.

My new canvas sauntered on up and plopped down right in front, all at home and comfy. "Nice dress," she said.

"This old thing?" I said in a Southern accent. "Why, ah only wear this when mah good one is at the clean-ahs."

She laughed, and I wanted to do whatever it took to hear that sweet noise again.

"I'm ready for my close-up." She giggled. There it was again. Magic.

"Much better than 'paint me like one of your French girls,' heard that one all day," I said, eyeing her up and down, figuring out which would be the best spot to adorn her stunning form with my best work. "Please don't judge based on that last one. All unicorns have a dump-truck ass, not very many people know that."

"I know," she quipped. "Most people pay attention to the magical abilities of the horn, but the ass has the power to make you wanna get up and dance when shaken."

"Ooh! An expert in mythical lore, I see!"

"I'm a witch."

"As in, the religion, or someone who's good at enchanting people?" My gosh, I felt that was laying it on thick, but she was too cute. She was funny, with a quick wit, and a voice as melodic as soft silver bells ringing.

"You'll have to find out and see."

"Well, I can't wait to."

We stared at each other for a second, and I wanted to gaze into those eyes for as long as I could, but awkward human interactions demand some kind of verbal response, so I said . . .

"Ummm . . . what do you want to have on you? Painted on you! Sorry."

"Um . . ." she said and giggled again, "you're not a painter of unicorns, but can you paint flowers?"

"I think I can manage. Any ones in particular?"

"Hyacinths," she said in a voice sweeter than the words she uttered. "Those are my favorite."

"Get the fuck out!"

"What?"

"You're gonna think I'm bullshitting you, but my Aunt Windsong had a bunch of those flowers growing in the yard outside. We planted them because I loved the Doors song."

"Aah!" she screamed. "Yay! They're my absolute favorites!"

"Well, prepare to be astonished as I try to paint them from memory!"

I proceeded to paint a halfway decent rendering of a few many-colored hyacinths, looking like columns of beautiful stars in purples and pinks. I drew a house around them, because those were the lyrics of the song. And maybe I wanted to have people wonder what we were doing in a house somewhere someday.

Her skin felt joyfully loud, as if there was a song under the surface of it, waiting to be belted out.

"You have no idea who I am," she finally ventured. "Do you?"

"You're Korey," I told her, matter-of-factly.

"I thought you'd forgotten about me!"

"I've got your old phone number on that scrap of paper in my wallet," I admitted, glancing nervously at the ground for a second. "It got me out of a bit of Russian jail time."

I decided I was telling way too much about the dangerous personal stuff, and maybe it was time to let up on that, so I nervously laughed like it was a joke. She blushed.

We paused for a second again, awkward but smiling.

"I absolutely love getting flowers done all over me. They make me feel like a nature goddess!"

"Like Demeter," I said, smiling again as I stared into her dark eyes. They looked like they were full of deep secrets that she was waiting to tell to the absolute right person.

"Another woman who got the raw end of a deal from some man," she sneered.

"Yeah. That's kind of cruel what they did to her daughter. But there's more sides to that story, different ways to look at it."

"Different ways to look at raping her daughter?"

"Not even gonna defend that aspect of the myth. Things were fucked up back then."

"So what is so different about the story as you tell it?"

"Ooh, then I'll have to tell it as best I can." I laughed. "Okay, so the story goes, Demeter was wandering around the world looking for her daughter Persephone after she was kidnapped. Couldn't find her anywhere. And something like only the sun knew about her whereabouts, and maybe . . . Hecate, goddess of witchcraft . . ." Her eyes perked up at that mention. I smiled. "You like her, huh? Although I forget why she was there. Fuck, I'm kinda messing it up already. How'm I doin'?"

"Great by me," she said, smiling and batting her eyelashes.

My hands wandered up her thigh as I painted a crawling vine that wrapped around to her knee. Hyacinths didn't have vines, but I was seeing where artistic license could take things. Her skin was as soft as the pink, purple, and white petals I was covering it with were supposed to be, and smooth as a ceramic vase. Like something exquisite to the touch, meant to amplify beauty in every direction.

"So, anyways, Demeter decides that she's going to go about roaming the earth, not stopping until she finds her lost daughter and brings her back home. And in the meantime, nothing is growing, she's neglecting her duties as a goddess of things that grow and provide sustenance for the whole world. And you would think that this would only be a human problem, but this affects the gods too.

Because they need those sacrifices that humans make for them. Without 'em, the world gets into chaos. Which kind of makes you wonder how much we depend on the gods and how much they depend on us."

"Oh, they do depend on us too. Everything is in a big cycle and all connected. One thing leads to another and it all has consequences. Karma is real."

"Right." I smiled and continued while making a circle of vines and flowers around her stomach, twirling into her navel.

Her gorgeous midsection could have been the navel of the world at that moment to me, because everything else besides her was out of focus. She was the only thing real to me at that moment in time.

"So Zeus pleads to Demeter to go back to doing her duties again, and that all leads to how she gets Persephone back. There's the whole famous part about eating the pomegranate seeds, and that's why we have the seasons, all that. But the real amazing thing about this story is that we see that one part where a woman had power over all the most powerful men, even at her most powerless moment. It's one of those things you have to read between the lines to see, but it's there, and once you realize that that power is there in her, it's hard to forget."

"So what kind of hidden power do I have?" she asked, not coyly, but very seriously.

I thought for a second, considering my words, wanting to say the exact right thing to this captivating person. The people in that big tent were a din I barely registered, all having fun drinking and making merry, but she was my focus at the moment, beautiful Korey, with her springtime air of excitement and renewal.

"You have the power . . . to make people appreciate the simple things in life. I don't worry that I'm missing out on anything exciting out there. And that's how I usually feel, like I might miss out on something more when I'm here doing something like this, but with you, it feels right to be present. I'm here with you, and I'm enjoying this moment, talking to a smart and beautiful woman, and it seems like the best thing in the world to be taking up my time."

She smiled. "Hmmmm and you have the power to make a girl feel comfortable in her own skin. Look at this paint job! It's perfect!" She lifted up her arms and gave her stomach a little shake that I found utterly impossible not to stare at. "How do you know so much about myths and flowers and unicorns with booties that pop?"

"Lots of time with nothing to do but either make trouble or read a book," I said.

"Do you wanna get out of here and walk around with me when you're done with this?" she asked.

"Thought you'd never ask," I said, putting my brushes away and wiping the dust off of my dress.

23.

KOREY AND I WANDERED AROUND that once-in-a-year city that day, and although that wasn't my first time being out there, everything seemed exciting and new.

"So what do you do, when you're not out here?" she asked. "Perfecting your still life art on willing women?" She put the nozzle of her CamelBak in her mouth and made a sucking noise as she gulped down water.

"I'm …" I began, choosing my words carefully, even though this line had been carefully rehearsed many a time, "in art and jewels. I deal in rare gems and find the right buyers for them." That wasn't exactly a lie, but I wasn't about to tell her what I really did. I had been stealing jewels and really anything of value from rich pricks for the longest time. So I hoped fencing things counted.

I had my same partner, Vanessa, who I had known since I was a kid, and our specialty together was finding aggro alpha male types at bars who liked to take advantage of women. I posed as her gay friend, she posed as a drunken party girl, and they would then go to town, trying to get her overly intoxicated, roofie her drinks, take her to dark places. The works, as far as the department of evil things that make men the worst is concerned.

We would then turn their tricks around on them and take everything we could get off of them. Wallets, watches, phones, nothing was off limits. Bonus points if they invited her over and we could incapacitate one of those dickheads and run fucking wild in their house. Those people didn't deserve to have all that power and privilege, so we made sure it went to the right hands.

"I'm looking to get out of the business though," I told her. "I want to do something good for people, and I have the money saved up to do it."

"What is that?" she asked. "Here, have some water."

She gave me the nozzle of her CamelBak, and I took a long drink out of it. I used the opportunity to lean into her, and she leaned forward. I was always terrible at figuring out those moments when a first kiss is appropriate. I never wanted to be all handsy and gropey, especially after all the terrible people on my jobs I had seen doing what they did. So I wanted to make sure everything was consensual and welcome.

"May I?" I asked, leaning in towards her lips.

"Please do. You don't even have to ask."

"I always do."

We kissed, and I felt the cooling contrast of her wet lips as we stood there under that hot sun in the middle of the day, and I was locked to that pleasurable exchange and not wanting to let go.

She exhaled sharply through her nose in a little sigh of enjoyment as I traced the smooth curve of her face along her cheek with my fingers and then held my hand to that silky skin. As we let go, we stared into each other's eyes. Hers were a dark expanse, a twinkling tiny self-contained universe filled with new and amazing sights, something to discover and explore.

"So what do you want to do to give back to the world now?" she asked.

"Nothing but kisses back to you at the moment," I said, and drew her in again, tasting her lips, loving the way they fit perfectly onto mine. This time, my hands went lower, caressing the small of her back and up and down her waist and midsection. Her hands locked around my neck, drawing me into her and holding me tight.

"Not a bad vocation," she said when we finally released each other and walked on, hand in hand.

We were in the center of the esplanade, wandering among huge works of art, ribbons of dust dancing along on the streets like perfectly white sails in the wind. Huge pagodas made to be burned one night towered high on white dirt, and cars in the shape of insanely complex moving beasts cruised along at slow speeds like huge sea creatures, playing music in their wake as people scrambled on and off. People jumped onto a set of swings hanging from the back of one of them, laughing like they didn't have a care in the world.

We wandered on together in our newly found happiness.

"No, I do have a plan for something special," I confided to her. "I've always wanted to be an actor, but life is a little crazy, and I've had to do what I gotta do to get by. I've saved enough money, though, and I want to start up an acting school."

"Oh yeah?"

"Yeah, a special place that gives kids a chance to have all the things I never had. A free tuition to a graduate-level acting program, that the revenue from the school's theater pays for. And it'll be for

LGBTQ kids and all the rest who need to catch a break. Let them be what they want."

I wiped a tear from my eye, hoping she wouldn't notice, but she probably heard the break in my voice betraying my emotions.

"That's really sweet," she said. She stared into my eyes, and I usually shied away from people who did that too directly, but with her I wanted to hold that dreamy gaze until the sun came down and I needed a light to see it. "Speaking of LGBT, you remember what kind of equipment I've got, right?"

"I saw your little show in line."

"And that doesn't bother you?"

"Bother me? No, not in the slightest." I slipped an arm around her to affirm what I said. "If anything, it makes you more fascinating."

"How is that?"

"You've got stories to you, and experiences that few other people do."

"I probably do. But you just might too."

"You know yourself in ways I've never had to consider in my own life. I was born into what I am, but you've worked for it and come out all the more amazing for it. I hope that came out all right."

"Hmmm, I'll take it." She kissed me on the cheek, and we wandered off again in the dust as the wind picked up and lashed pieces of it into our eyes. We ran under the cover of a building that looked like a big church about to be blown over by a tornado. It had a huge piano in the middle on the one end, and a row of pews lining up to it.

A man was sitting at the piano, playing an utterly beautiful tune, an opera aria of some sort. He swayed to the music as he played along, as enraptured as if he was in a trance.

"I've always wanted to really learn to play the piano," I whispered to her. "Like, play it good. But I've never had the patience to sit down and practice."

"Let's go check him out."

We tiptoed up to him as if we were disturbing a sacred rite and sat down behind him in a pew. He opened up his eyes all of a sudden and shot a long look in our direction, while still playing.

"Hey there!" he exclaimed.

"Sorry, didn't mean to disturb you!" I said, holding my hands out as if to show him I meant no harm.

"No worries!"

"You play so beautifully," Korey said, smiling that bright smile of hers at him. That kind of attention made me want to play an entire orchestra for her.

"Oh yeah," he responded, leaning into it as he emphasized a note.

"You're so good I bet you could play with your feet," I said, utterly in awe of how the music poured out of him like he was born to make it.

"I could probably play it with my dick!" he said.

"Do it!" I dared him. I thought he was bullshitting, but then he whipped it out and proceeded to mash it on the keys, pounding out Chopsticks. I sneaked a look over at Korey, and she shrugged and laughed. I shrugged back, whipped mine out, and joined him in an impromptu concert.

A woman in goggles and khaki pants came in with a frantic expression on her face.

"What! The fuck! Are you doing?" she screamed.

"Playing Chopsticks?" I shrugged.

"Did you bring any wipes to clean this up?" she yelled.

"No, but let me see if there are any back at my camp!" I said and grabbed Korey by the hand and ran out the building.

"Wow, she was pissed," Korey declared, out of breath.

"Well, she should expect penises to touch things if they're out here!" I exclaimed. We slowed down when we were far enough away. "I totally don't usually do stuff like that. I got caught up in the moment."

"Nice piece of equipment you play with, there," she said.

"Thanks," I said, blushing. "Perfect for those moments when I try to practice like a serious pianist."

"It's okay to get a bit caught up in the moment," she said and kissed me long and hard. "Do you want to do acid with me?" she asked once we were finally lips apart and walking about again. "I've got a whole vial of it."

"So ..." I began, wondering how much to tell her. I didn't want to scare her off, but I was tired of being the only one who knew certain things, and sometimes it feels so liberating to be honest. I wanted to lay my cards on the table with her. Certain cards anyways. "Hallucinogens can be a little crazy for me."

"I think they're crazy for everyone," she said as we stepped aside for a lit up person on a bike to fly past us.

"I ... How do I say this and not sound like a crazy person?"

"By admitting it sounds crazy and carrying on calmly," she said, squeezing my arm gently for support.

"Ever since I was a kid, I've been able to see ghosts," I confessed to her flatly. I stared into her face, expecting the reactions I had whenever I had said confessed this to anyone. Laughter, saying "yeah right" like they thought I was teasing. Confusion, like they thought I was making some sort of overarching metaphor that they didn't quite get. Arguments coming up in their minds for why they didn't believe in them and what I probably was really seeing.

Instead she stared peacefully as if taking it all in, and then she politely said, "Okay."

"I'm not crazy, I swear this isn't talking to myself on a street corner kind of a thing."

"No, I doubt you're that type, you seem pretty sane to me," she said. "I believe you. I had a grandmother once who used to talk to people who weren't there. She said she could see two children playing in our street. And then we found out that two children were killed on that street while playing in traffic."

"Oh God," I sighed. "Thank you so much, I'm just glad you don't wanna turn tail and run or whatever."

"No." She gave a flash of that mischievous smile again. "If anything, it makes you more fascinating."

I couldn't help but slip out a loud, spontaneous laugh at that. The sun was setting over the hills beyond the Black Rock Desert. People were all crowded onto high structures or stopping in their tracks and gazing towards it. We stopped in our tracks, and I wrapped my arms around her from behind. The sun was a bright circle of orange that lent an otherworldly hue to that already otherworldly place.

"How long have you seen them?"

"The ghosts? As long as I can remember."

"Are they good or bad, these ghosts?"

"They're neither. Or they're both. Like people can be, I suppose. They do things even though they're dead people, and sometimes they are helpful, sometimes they're full of selfish or harmful intentions."

The sun was casting its last flashes of light on the surroundings as it winked itself out. People immediately started to howling as long and echoing as a wolf pack, "Ow, ow! Ah-whooooo, whooooo!" We howled along with them, and it was such a simple pleasure, but it felt roller coaster exhilarating.

"If you don't want to do acid, you totally don't have to," Korey said. "No pressure."

"You know, let's do it. My poppa always told me to try new things."

"Only if you want to."

"I want to do it with you. You'll be my guide?"

"Best guide there is!"

"I believe it!"

And with that, she took off her backpack and rummaged around inside of it for a second. She reached all the way to the bottom and then found what she was looking for. A dark brown glass container for medicine to be applied in drops. It was covered in a plastic bag that was all crinkled around it.

"I'm gonna do drops on the tongue, you down with that?" she asked.

"Whatever you're doing," I cheerfully assented.

"Hmmm, better not do all that I'm doing. I did this last night too, so I'll probably take two, maybe three. You should do one. This is some good stuff."

She took the cap with the dropper off, dipped it back into the vial, and squeezed the little plastic bulb at the end. She then held it up over my head. "Peep, peep!" I exclaimed in a baby bird chirp, opening my mouth. I felt the drop of liquid on my tongue. It almost tingled like mouthwash. She then held it up and placed a few on her outstretched tongue.

"All right, enjoy the ride!" she said.

We roamed about as the darkness set in and the lights of the city turned on and became the dominant scenery of the land. The place became a wonder, more vibrant than a coral reef or a botanical garden, and filled with about as much activity.

Our acid kicked in in a series of waves. At first, I didn't know if what I was seeing was simply the craziness of such a wild place around me or if I was feeling the effects. When it came on, I knew it was there from the energy I felt in the air and all throughout myself. One second before, I didn't know for sure if it was working, and the next, I stared at the ground and saw the dust was all moving about in fractal forms that shifted as if combining into a whole but then splitting apart into their own glorious and gorgeous shapes.

I wanted to dance and move about, that was the overriding impulse, and Korey seemed to feel it too. We wandered over to a crowded enclave gathered around a facade of a building that looked part carnival funhouse, part jungle gym for Olympic athletes. Around it were parked several vehicles shooting fire out into the air.

"Let's get in there!" Korey said, taking me by the hand and dragging me deeper into the mix.

People were about everywhere in suggestive and wild outfits, and I swore I was staring at the pantheon of every religion in the world. I saw Baron Samedi in his top hat and skeletal face, but maybe it was just a man in a costume. I saw angels and devils dancing together, or they could have been people with wings on meant to glow about in the night.

I couldn't tell who was among those of this world and those of the Otherworld, the domains where we glimpse strange things in our dreams and imaginations that leave strong impressions that haunt our memories and tempt our psyches to seek for things beyond the ordinariness of daylight and life.

The ghosts were there, though, I could tell. In the background, agitated and awestruck, but still there as quiet as actors waiting in the wings of a play, all ready to take their cue when they wanted to raise the curtains. I brushed them off with a dismissive gesture, and they went quiet for a time.

"Closer" by Nine Inch Nails blasted on a speaker system that created sounds of echoes of thunder resounding down a large valley, booming and shaking the foundations of our minds as it filled our bodies with vibrations that made us shudder. The whole time, I held Korey close, and we swung each other about.

I was a flurry of arms flowing in all directions, like a Hindu deity, and I felt as if a strange presence within me that was beyond myself had taken over, a vessel for a tremendous energy that was seeking to escape out into the universe. I accidentally bumped into a guy in leather pants, with the look of someone who was about to start trouble. I had no intention of seeing that happen.

"Hey!" he yelled. "The fuck you doing!"

"Sorry, man, my bad!"

"You gotta be more careful than that, watch out!"

"Hey," I said, holding out a hand, calmly. "Hey!"

"Yeah, what?"

"Have you ever heard of Nine Inch Nails?"

"Huh?" he said. And then, "HA, HA, hah hah ha!"

And we all laughed like mad children, wonderfully pleased with ourselves and our inside jokes and semiverbal humor.

"Let's get out of here," Korey said after that calmed down. "Go somewhere a little more private."

"You betcha."

We wandered back towards my camp, but not before we stopped in front of a giant, gorgeous female goddess. She was leaning forward in the strained pose of bracing to hold the weight of heavens on her shoulders, but with arms open wide in a gesture showing that she was willing to accept us all into her embrace.

"Whoa," I declared.

"Pretty, huh?" she said, and we both stared for a long time.

Bright beacons touched the dome of Heaven above her, and I could see seraphs made entirely of a sourceless light in meditative contemplation, and they smiled down. They were as shiningly invisibly operating as the ones steering the ship from *The Rhyme of the Ancient Mariner*, all working about and interweaving with everything, fluttering in busy work behind the scenes in the world.

I was speechless in a flood of divine energy pouring down on me and threatening to inundate my mind. I didn't know if I would ever speak again, until I simply muttered, "It sure is."

We went back into my camp, kissing each other the entire way.

"Where's your tent?" she asked.

"Right here," I said, leading her into my big luxurious number of a dwelling. I held the flap open and didn't bother to give her the tour because we were busy tearing each other's clothes off, fierce as horny werewolves. I pulled her top off first, trying not to snap the elastic on her but wanting to see what was underneath. Her nipples had been poking through the fabric, and her chest seemed to swell in the warm night with her breathing.

She reached under my dress and began stroking my hard cock, pulling it out with her hand out to lick it with feline grace before putting it back under my dress and resuming her lovely rhythm with her hands as we locked lips.

I pulled her down onto my air mattress and began removing her bottoms.

"Do you have any protection?" she asked. "Never mind, I've got some."

She went into her bag again and pulled a condom out, slid it onto me, and then guided me into her.

I felt that I had connected to a lost part of myself that I had been seeking all my life without really knowing it. She moaned and I thrust harder, loving the feel of her hips as they slid up and down, loving the press against her butt as it smacked against my pelvis. I reached around to the front of her and held on as I went farther into her.

"Oh, that's right! Just like that!" she gasped.

I knew at that moment that she was everything wonderful about the opposite sex, every woman who had ever lived, and I was loving every aspect of her as she opened up to me.

She was Cleopatra, brilliant and resourceful, backed by the love of her people who she loved in return. She played a man's game and would have won if it had been only her there commanding at Actium and not relying on some man to lead in her place.

She was Helen of Troy, trapped between two clashing worlds and used by men to justify their own wicked ends, when they really would have started a war for another cause all by themselves if she hadn't come along. Still, she was so compelling that no man could dare to harm her in the end, even in their greatest fits of rage.

She was Joan of Arc, being burnt at the stake for daring to challenge their norms and show them that a woman could take on the ones in power, all while playing within their rules and worshiping the way they did. They were jealous that they weren't called to something great like she was.

She was all of those, but none of them. She was Korey. She was there with me, and I wanted to make sure she felt so good that she wanted to stay forever.

24.

"YOU'LL NEVER BELIEVE WHAT I do for a living," Korey said. We were lazing about in my tent.

It was hot as all hell inside, but I'd grabbed a cup full of ice from my cooler and was slowly rubbing it in circles on her chest.

"Doctor?" I put an ice cube in my mouth and kissed her open lips with it. We passed the ice cube back and forth from one mouth to the other with our tongues for a bit, the interplay of hot and cold the right measure of numbness and vividly responsive sensation.

"Nope," she finally whispered when we had swallowed the last bit of ice and let our lips have a brief rest. Her lips anyways. Mine were wandering down her neck and on her shoulder with the same energetic intensity I have whenever I need something to occupy my hands or whatever part of my body it is that feels all wiggly. I swear I can't sit still for a minute.

"Hhhhhmmmm, secret agent."

"Guess again."

"Okay, last guess ... private dancer. A dancer for money."

"Nope."

"Well you do have the legs," I said, reaching under her thigh and spreading it apart from the other.

"Cam girl."

"As in porn?" I said, staring at her with one eyebrow raised.

"Yup."

"Huh."

"They call it shemale porn, which is kind of not the preferred designation among the community, but I don't mind because it pays the bills."

"So you jerk it for guys to watch?" I said, nodding. "Cool."

"It's good money!" she said, a defensive edge in her voice that seemed vulnerable in a way I found endearing.

"I'll bet it is!" I laughed.

"You're not mad?" She sat up and stared me directly in the eyes, searching for that flush of jealousy she was expecting, or the hiding of a barely repressed emotion.

"No, why would I be?" I replied genuinely, shrugging the suggestion off.

"Most guys would be."

"Good thing I'm not most guys."

I don't know if jealousy enters into my equation too often. Sure, I see things and think they would be nice to have. That's kind of why someone like me steals, right? I covet things like the little sinner of a Catholic boy that I was raised as. Well, not raised as, they probably tried everything in their power to get me not to do it, but I needed that experience of being alive.

But that hatred of another that is so often part of jealousy isn't on my radar. Where you believe you deserve something more than somebody else and you are blindingly mad at them for it. I might definitely feel that most rich assholes don't deserve half of the things that they have, and I have no problem prying them out of their grubby little fingers, but I don't think I deserve those things any more than they do either. So I take only what I need and see that the rest gets to those who need it more.

"Let's get out of here, roam about for a bit," I said, taking her in my arms and kissing her all over again.

"I've hardly got a thing on!" she said. "And I need to do my makeup!"

"You look great!"

"Besides, people in your camp will see me come out. I don't want to do the walk of shame."

"We only do the stride of pride around these parts. Besides, they'll love you. And I think you always look great. Anyone has a problem, campmate or otherwise, can fuck right off."

"So, you wouldn't be embarrassed to be with me?" she said, gazing into my eyes with a sense of urgency that demanded the proper response.

"I feel embarrassed for anyone who doesn't want to be with you!" I assured her, hugging her tight. We were sweating profusely, and I didn't care, as long as it was her.

"Would you introduce me to your family?" she asked.

I paused at this one. I thought of my, at that point, strained relationship with my father, and wondered what A.J. was doing. Windsong had passed away, and I still felt guilty for not doing more for her even though I did everything I had it in me to do.

"Would that I could," I said, embracing her and planting a kiss on either cheek and then a long slow one on her forehead. "I don't see my family anymore. These people in my camp are kind of all the family I've got. So, definitely, you're in with them."

"I'm sorry to hear about that."

"Don't be sorry," I said, lying back on the pillow on the bouncy mattress and staring up at the ceiling of the tent as it billowed up and flapped about. "People talk about your blood relations and how that is supposed to mean a whole hell of a lot, but they can hurt you worse than anyone else in the world and keep on doing it. When you choose your own family, that can be twice as special as anyone in your blood. You're a bunch of lost souls that found each other."

"That's beautiful."

"You're beautiful."

"You wouldn't be ashamed to go to a nude beach with me?"

"I'd tear off all my clothes on the beach with you as soon as we hit the sand! Let everyone get insanely jealous of how great we look out there. Fuck 'em! All anyone would see is the most drop-dead stunner those sand dunes had ever witnessed! Then I'd carry you out into the water like a mermaid, and if we don't like anyone there, we can swim on until we find another world of our own, where we can just be us, no excuses, no apologies. Ha! Something like that ..."

"That sounds sweet!" She laughed. I wanted to keep making that laugh come about whenever I could simply to hear it. Every time I brought one out, I felt as loved as a king at his coronation must have felt, reeling in the glory, and hoping to not let his admirers down.

I went in to kiss her one more time, not wanting to stop planting them all over her. I went from her mouth, down to her neck, and all over her breasts, paying special attention to every inch my lips grazed.

"So what drew you to me?" she asked. "You could probably have any girl out here, but you chose little ol' me."

"Oh, now you're just buttering me up!" I teased, giving her a little smack on the butt and getting up to grab another drink of water with a few ice cubes in it from my cooler. I always loved walking around naked, but with her it felt perfectly right. We were as innocent as antediluvian primal beings wandering in a garden, no worries about the knowledge of the world corrupting us, because we had each other, and that was all it took to keep us happy.

"No, it's true. You're like a rock star, all muscles and cheekbones."

"And you're too hot to be a groupie," I said, kissing her. "You're the queen of the stage, with only one name: Korey. You're iconic, and all the guys would love to be with you, but somehow I got so lucky!"

"Now who's doing the buttering?" she said as she pulled me tight to her and kissed me up and down my chest.

"Maybe because you're someone who goes on being you, no regrets and no apologies. And you're still kind. I can tell you've got a good heart that loves the world and everything in it, even when everything in it can scare the hell out of anyone else. But you swallow that fear and cast all the bad things out with love. You are all full of joy, and that joy's contagious. I've seen everyone around you smile for what they think is no reason, but I can tell it's from how you look at them like you love them even though you have no idea who they are or what they're all about. I wish I could bring a fraction of that light into the world. I love you for it."

She looked like she was about to cry, and finally one perfect tear rolled down her cheek. I touched it with my finger and licked that fingertip clean, savoring her gift of moisture in a place so dry. She leaped onto me and kissed me deeply.

"How long you gonna put up with my ass?" I asked her, half serious, but worried for a half second once it came out, really wondering why she loved me.

"Hmmmm, until the sun crashes into the moon," she said, smiling dreamily, but with a conviction to her words I truly believed.

"And how long you gonna love me?"

"Even longer after that."

And then there were no more words needed, and we abandoned our plans to get out of the hot tent.

25.

IT WAS SEVERAL YEARS AFTER I had said goodbye to her on that beach when I heard back from Jenny. Two decades, to be precise. Plenty of time to try and forget about the past and let it echo about in my mind like those specters I saw since I was a child echoed about in the world.

I had closed up that chapter of my life and moved on.

Korey and I were living in a cute apartment in South Park in San Diego, an entire floor of an old Victorian mansion to ourselves that had surprisingly no ghosts scampering about in it. The outside was a bright pink with purple trim that would have looked gauche on any other type of home but was the perfect fit for that doll's house of a building. We had a whole botanical garden's worth of plants about the place that Korey took care of because I was remarkably adept at killing them when I was left to tend to them. Perils of living on a thief's schedule, I had all kinds of time to learn ways to commit crime, no time to commit to learn the art of horticulture.

"Are you trying to break your neck out there?" she asked me as I sat two stories high up in the branches of the rubber tree in the backyard.

"Well, all little boys grow up but one," I replied and hopped down onto the porch with a thud.

"How did you wind up killing poor little Spike Lee?" she asked, regarding a dwarf saguaro cactus we had in the living room. We gave them names of Hollywood celebrities that we figured suited them. There was Fran Drescher, the orchid, and Patrick Swayze, our rubber tree in the backyard, because he was always swaying about and dirty dancing in the wind.

"I don't know. I watered him once a week and everything."

"You watered a desert plant once a week?" she asked, one eyebrow raised.

"Yeah, why?"

"A cactus. One that's made to collect moisture from about one rain a year."

"Oooohhhh . . ."

"What did you think that would do to poor Spike Lee?" she asked, smacking my butt.

"I thought they could collect rain when they wanted to and, you know, not collect it when there's an abundance of it," I said, shrugging.

"You're never feeding *my* cat when I'm away," she told me. We had a little orange tabby cat named Garfield that she brought into our place from her previous apartment. He took a minute to get used to me stealing the attention away from his girl, but I think we bonded over our mutual distaste for Mondays and our mutual enjoyment of petting sessions.

"Sure, he's your cat when he's in imminent danger of me killing him through overfeeding," I said, "but as soon as he needs a ride in the car where he freaks the fuck out the entire way, he's *our* cat all of a sudden."

"Don't you boys gang up on me!" she warned, a mischievous smile on her face.

"I don't need him when I can take you by myself," I shouted, picking her up and carrying her over my shoulder into the bedroom, where I gently tossed her onto the bed and then hopped on top, covering her with kisses and pulling one of the straps of her spaghetti top down with my teeth.

Such were the scenes of our newly engaged bliss.

The one thing that troubled me about our relationship was that I led a double life. I hadn't really told her what it was I did, and I didn't know if I ever should. I figured it wouldn't be fair to turn her into an accomplice, so the less she knew, the better. But mostly I was afraid of what it would do to us as a couple. I didn't want to lose her, and I figured a surefire way to do that was to go, "Oh, by the way, honey, I steal what I can from rich shitheads. It's all good, though, I plan on going clean from the life any one of these days now, so don't sweat it, babe!"

So I pretended that when I was casing a place, I was checking out estate sales. When I was out late eyeing a potential mark, I was meeting a client for drinks. And when I was actually pulling off a job, I was away on business.

All easy enough to tell her with a straight face, but I didn't like lying to a person who meant so much to me.

I was counting down the days when I was finally set enough to go legit. I had investments enough to keep it all going, but I wanted to be really set, not simply comfortable. I wanted a sure thing. And life was never really full of those, but I was going to try, dammit.

I had a plan and I was sticking to it though. Get in, get out.

I had my partner, Vanessa, to consider, but she was no stranger to making wise decisions with her money. I wouldn't have gone into it with her if she actually was an unhinged partying maniac like she pretended to be. She would be okay, and she had to realize that we could only do this for so long. Oh, but I wanted to do it for as long as I could!

As for what I would do for a rush afterwards, I wasn't sure. I didn't know what would equal the thrill of coming out of a heist and not getting caught, of outsmarting wicked men who pretend their money and power makes them somehow better than other people. They were the truly evil ones, not people like me who stole possessions. They stole peace from people's souls to slake their awful desires.

There was nothing as thrilling as catching them with their pants down, literally on more than one occasion, and making them finally feel what it was like to be at the mercy of someone else. To find that we had photo evidence of them that we would release to the police or their partners, and then let them sit about, impotently fuming as we helped ourselves to their safes.

It was a big game hunt, and I loved the thrill of chasing down a man that was dangerous and cunning, someone you had to outfox to find their lair, and then rob the nest before they returned home.

All this was a joy that was second to none, but I told myself I had love and the real joy was finding the new moments with her, the ones that made our love grow stronger and more intimate, where we shared things no other could imagine. If only I didn't have such a restless soul.

I was on one of what I thought would be my last jobs. This one was a real piece of work, and I was looking forward to robbing him blind. It would have been exactly what he deserved. He dealt in jewels and had been arrested years before for trafficking in stolen merchandise. We might have been birds of a feather at one point, and I knew it, right? Look who's calling the kettle black . . .

Here's where he and I had our irreconcilable differences: He had a bogus charity that was supposed to be sending promising athletic kids who had need for money in their families to camps with basketball scholarships. These "camps" were subpar, to say the least, and this was all a tax dodge of heinous proportions. He was small enough potatoes that the IRS wasn't onto him, and with all the politicians trying to "drain the swamp," the tax men weren't exactly well funded enough to follow all the leads that they should. They still had time to audit middle class individuals, though, surprise, surprise.

And to top this off, he was seducing and plying young men who came to work for him with alcohol and then taking advantage of them in all his homes around the U.S. He was a good LDS congregant, though, never drank himself, and of course his wife and daughters knew nothing at all about this.

I was going to see to it that those kids actually got some money to shoot hoops. I was going to enjoy this.

I had been working on this one for months, learning from him, meeting with him at trade shows, touring his showrooms. Doing my due diligence, which is what anyone working with these terrible people should do and do it well. They were only interested in money and the power it provides them, and they would do whatever they could to protect that. But they get sloppy and like to brag about things. They think they can't be touched, and those are the types I love to get tactile with.

So when I figured out his passwords for his security system from a gabby new hire, it was on. I observed the camera layout of his storeroom in Carlsbad, California, and worked out how he scheduled his drop offs of jewels and art to other locations. And finally, after I found out where he parked the vans full of items overnight, I decided to pay him a late-night visit.

I could have tried the blunt approach to his little operation and done a simple smash and grab, but there was no finesse to that. I found the keypads in his security system used old cell phone technology, because like all greedy bastards, he was cheap. His distress calls in the system communicated through a cellular network. You can buy a small cell tower for about a grand.

I have a specialty one I modified from an idea from some wise kids at Champlain College, using a Raspberry Pi, an LCD touchscreen, and some SIM cards. I used it to connect his keypads to my base station, making sure that any alerts it sent out didn't go where intended. I then connected to the keypad's modem and disabled the sensors the system was connected to in the building. Free rein of the whole shebang and I was feeling like a kid in a candy shop, if that kid was a kleptomaniac who loved taking chances, which I was.

I waltzed through all the rooms, passing one hallway of his showroom filled with enough trinkets and reproductions of famous paintings to fill it wall to wall. They were all shit and wouldn't fetch me anything. He sold them to other rich idiots in this part of town, letting them think they were authentic. While I normally had no problem with making people who didn't deserve to have that kind of money to spend part with it, I thought it was pretty fucked to shake hands with someone and pretend you were their friend as you robbed them blind.

Hypocrite much, I know. I just didn't like the little fucker, and I especially hated grimy salespeople types. It might have had something to do with imagining him ripping off an old lady. Windsong had Alzheimer's in her last years, and people calling her with scams aplenty took her to the fucking cleaners. I was gonna enjoy this one, and what's that they say about enjoying your job and never having to work a day in your life?

I strolled past a big lion statue baptismal font, meowing at it. I then hallelujahed when I saw the room with that safe. That was the big time. I was pretty sure he would even have a hoard of silver bars stashed about there that night.

I crept into the safe room and was about to get to work on that great big beauty, when I heard a noise and noticed I wasn't alone in the room. I put my hands up so as not to get shot by some security guard or overzealous employee with too much loyalty to his company and not enough brain cells, wanting to chance a life and death situation over an asshole employer that probably didn't pay for their healthcare.

"What's a nice guy like you doing in a bad place like this?" a woman asked. "Still trying to make your way up from the wrong side of the tracks by playing with all the suits and ties?"

I knew that voice. I'd heard it in my dreams and thought about it at least once a week after having tapered down from at least twice a day. "Jenny!" I hissed. "What are you doing here?"

"Well, I know they say curiosity killed the cat, but I wanted to see how you worked."

She leaned against the wall like she'd melted out of the shadows, wearing a black pantsuit that was belted at the waist. That and her heels gave a feminine flair to an otherwise androgynous outfit. She was to die for in any garment, but this one made her seem like she could deal that death out with a professional's skill.

"The phrase was originally 'Care killed the cat,'" I told her. "And I'm not really in the mood to get any more cares, worries, or causes for concern from you."

I didn't know why I was so bitter. I wasn't the type to hold grudges. There was something so raw about seeing her again though.

"Aaaaawww, not even a little reunion for old time's sake?"

"You could have dropped me a line."

"You're surprisingly off the grid," she said, as she walked over to the safe and smilingly tapped on it with an air of pointedly relaxed sangfroid. "But your work screams your usual motives. That same little boy with a chip on his shoulder, grown into a maladjusted young man with a still boyish face plus a few new chips. It wasn't too hard to find the type you'd be looking for and get to them first."

"Ooorrrrrr, maybe I'm a well-adjusted young man working in a malfunctioning world," I replied. ". . . With a few new chips," I conceded after a second's reflection. "Again, what are you doing here?"

"Oh, simply trying to see how the master works. You weren't trying to get into this safe?" she asked, leaning up against the side of it coquettishly before grabbing onto the handle. "Because I may have beat you to it . . ."

She opened the heavy door up to an empty safe. I sighed audibly, and she smiled playfully.

"That was months of work right there," I muttered.

I turned on my heel and left. I went out into the storefront and smashed a random jewelry case, for the fuck of it. I pulled a few random pieces from the case, trying to look for the good ones, but it was hard to tell in the dim street light from outside. I felt like such an amateur, doing a job that any thug with a blunt object and pair of legs to run could pull, but I wasn't going to say the whole night was a waste.

I scampered out into the street, the proverbial thief in the night instead of the smooth exit I had in mind and headed for my car around the block. It was an old van that was going to be junked, one I was able to buy for a few hundred off of someone without going through the proper registration channels. I had already loaded up the items I stole from his van on the street into it, so at least I had that. I hopped in, and she followed, jumping into the passenger seat. "Oh, now you need a ride?" I asked.

"Aren't you gonna wanna buy me a drink?" she asked.

"Right after I throw you out of this moving vehicle." I did consider doing it at a low speed once we got the hell out of Dodge, and far enough away. It would serve her right to let her land on her ass for once.

Truth to tell, I wondered why she sought me out, and I wanted to hear what she had to say. And also, truth to tell, old flames sometimes don't really burn out quite the way you think they do.

26.

WE SHOT BACK TO TOWN, tearing down the coast, the wind whipping our hair with the windows down because that hooptie van had no AC.

"They usually have fancier getaway cars in the movies," Jenny said.

"They also would probably be blasting a cooler soundtrack from the speakers instead of NPR."

We went to a noisy little speakeasy bar called Polite Provisions and sat down at a table under elaborate streetlamps that seemed organic, as if they'd grown out of the glowing white mosaic tiles in the ground in a beautiful profusion of old-fashioned splendor.

When I parked, I took off my black Henley shirt in the back of the van and replaced it with a Garfield T-shirt I had in there so I didn't look so *To Catch a Thief* anymore. It was brown and in seventies style and said "To know me is to love me." I had one like that when I was a kid, and I guess I still am a kid at heart, eh?

I ordered a mocktail, saying, "Keep them coming, drinks are on her."

Jenny ordered an old-fashioned. We sat in silence for a moment, me still fuming for her intruding on my affairs and messing up a job I had put a lot of time and effort into. She sat there staring with a bemused smile on her gorgeous face that made it all the more infuriating. The privileged friend of mine with everything in the world going for her, all grown up and still doing her thing as she decided to play games with people who were struggling to get by.

We sat at a table outside on their narrow patio, a nice dose of almost European elegance that made me think of crazy writers in the 1920s arguing together and escaping the ennui of America in their grander adventures that they actually lived out instead of sitting by and dreaming of them.

"You want my attention," I said. "You've got it."

"On the wagon these days?" she asked.

"I had about twenty good years of drinking. I don't like to be a slave to my bad habits and compulsions."

"And so what you were doing tonight was ...?"

"Putting food and drink on the table."

"Seems like you've got a big family to feed."

"Gotta keep enough in the pantry for winter."

"How would you like to never worry about going hungry again?" she asked, then smiled and took a sip of the drink the waitress brought over.

"Thank you," I told the waitress and motioned for her to bring another. She smiled at me as she walked off. I turned back to Jenny. "So what's the catch? You trying to see if my soul is for sale after all these years?"

"How 'bout saving lives instead of selling your soul?" she said as she placed the drink on the table and leaned forward, staring into my eyes, trying to peer into the depths of me. I tried to remain impassive, but she had already perked my ears, and I definitely wanted to hear her out.

"My particular skill set doesn't usually save lives," I observed. "You might want to try a doctor."

"Funny you should mention doctors, because a particular few are the issue ..."

I waited for her to go on. She smiled and took another sip of her drink, leaning back and relaxing. I tried not to get distracted by the shade of her red lipstick. She crossed one leg over the other, and I turned my attention back to her words so I wouldn't think of her body.

"The coronavirus pandemic, darling," she began. I noted the "darling" in there, how she loved using pet names to seem intimate with people, but she also used them with everyone. She always seemed to want people to know that she could be anyone's if they were lucky, but no one's because she didn't want it that way. "We've practically all had it, or are going to get it in some way, but remember before the vaccines, when we were all struggling to understand where it came from and the conspiracies were everywhere?"

"I'm still having trouble picking up a Wi-Fi signal with my vaccine," I quipped. "I thought for sure I could at least have a 5G mobile hotspot every time I got hard."

"And how often is that?" she asked, eyebrow raised.

I was trying to be mad at her and not sit around flirting. I had Korey and wouldn't have traded anything in the world for her, but I was finding it hard to resist the paths that my mind went down when thinking about one of my first loves.

"Every morning when I wake up, like clockwork." I motioned for her to continue about her other topic. I was going to have to watch what I said, and that was hardly ever my strong suit when I felt like I had just the right thing to say. Just the right thing to say usually being just the wrong joke that I just couldn't write off.

"Oh yeah. Where was I before you distracted me? Everyone was wondering if there was cause for concern with the virus being made on some Wuhan lab. Easy enough to chalk that up to the fearmongering of racists and authoritarians in charge looking to demonize a foreign enemy, right? Except there was a legitimate reason why people thought it could have been there . . ."

"Right. There were people in the National Institute of Health who even believed it might have come from a lab, not just the alt-right shitheads and the tin hat crowd."

"So one of the things that was making people question if COVID-19 was part of a lab accident was that people had been tinkering around with gain-of-function in virus experiments."

"What's gain-of-function?" I interjected. "Pretend I was out picking pockets and breaking and entering when I should have been in biology class."

"It's when they give a virus new functions it doesn't have naturally. Maybe they tweak it so it can spread easier among, say, ferrets, which are closer to humans, genetically, than lab mice. It lets them determine if a virus will be risky to people. They do it all the time. People use it to try and prevent pandemics by spotting where the threats are. But there's always a chance things can get out of hand. If you create a disease that doesn't exist in nature, what happens if it gets out?"

I took a slow sip of my drink and glanced around the room. It was hard to tell that there even was a pandemic that could have killed us all in social situations the way people were crammed from the halls to the walls in that place.

It the roaring twenties in there, everyone breathing free even though the air was probably filled with a deadly disease or another that we'd gotten used to. But we were all vaccinated, or had the disease, or were going to get it, so we all went back to life even though we all knew it wasn't really the same. Best to drink it all away under bright lights and take a breath of fresh air outside so we could all take a hit of a vape.

Our roaring twenties are pretty strange. I wondered if the people back a hundred years ago during Spanish flu had been afraid of the way things were headed when it was all so crazy for them too with people dying from diseases and fascism on the rise, or if they would have rolled up their androgynous sleeves and sucked back a gin and danced. Maybe they should have been afraid instead of dancing. Maybe they should have danced harder to keep the cares away, who knows?

The nightclub across the street, the Air Conditioned Lounge, which never truly felt like they had an air conditioner in there ever, was overflowing with people loving the noise and sounding as joyful as if they were proudly awake after a long sleep.

People spilled out onto the street. They laughed and stumbled about to their Ubers and kissed their friends goodbye.

And so it all goes on, we stumble and we get back on our feet again. And some people were more somber and vowed to try to do better after the world shut down, tried to do the things they never did before, see amazing new sights, learn the skills they never got around to mastering. And some only wanted to spend their money as if it was burning holes in every pocket, wallet, and money market. Some simply wanted the thrill to go on and on, everyone else in the world be damned.

Well, we all deserve a little fun; maybe they needed an outlet.

I wanted to be among the helpers though. I was trying to make sure that if we all had a second shot at doing things right, I wouldn't waste mine on cheap thrills. Or expensive thrills, and that was easier said than done. I wanted more than ever to go clean. But I wanted to hear more of what Jenny had to say. I wanted a challenge.

"So are you saying COVID was a man-made event?" I asked in almost a whisper, staring at her and leaning in to look into her eyes. "I don't believe it."

"Oh, COVID was not," she replied, batting her hand as if to banish the thought. "Not as far as I know. But there was suspicion that the Wuhan Institute of Virology was working with Chinese military scientists sinister purposes. And people didn't think it was squeaky clean on the American side in the whole affair as well. Talk was in the air of an American institute that was planning on experimenting with furin cleavage sites."

"So, a bat at the market in Wuhan with hairy tits caused it?"

She rolled her eyes at my joke but couldn't suppress a giggle. "Furin cleavage sites are spots on the surface protein of a virus that can increase its chances of entry into human cells. An organization was looking into bat coronaviruses for furin cleavage sites and adding new ones to make them infect human cells more easily." She leaned in close and brought her voice down low. "Someone has been taking up this work, with a deadlier virus. And someone is trying to steal that deadlier virus. You ever hear of MERS?"

"That's not that infection you get from hospital beds, is it?" I asked.

"That's MRSA, and no. This one is far worse. Middle East Respiratory Syndrome, transmitted to humans through dromedary camels. It kills something like four out of ten people it infects. This one has previously only been transmissible through close contact, but, well, looks like someone tweaked it. Made it so it has ten times more growth than previous strains. It's got a name denoting its MERS-CoV origin, but people have been taking to calling it Dracula because it can be airborne, like Dracula turning into a mist and sliding under doors and through the air."

"Cute. Why wouldn't you want to do that?" I sighed, shaking my head. I took another sip and observed the lovely, lively scene in the crowded bar again. The waitress came by with another drink. I smiled and thanked her. But I also thought about the odds, what number she would be out of ten if that virus getting out were to happen. "Jeez, maybe we should stop fucking with animals so much after all this."

"The strain is in a lab in Manhattan, but someone has been trying to get the samples." She took a piece of paper and a photo out of her shining black leather purse. She placed them on the table.

I picked them up, unfolded them, and glanced at the picture. It was a pencil drawing of a woman with dark hair, accompanied by an image of a woman from a security photo that was too far away to see any striking details. She wore glasses and had fashionable clothing on, dark pants and heels, a white, shoulderless blouse that made her form seem athletic and powerful.

"We've checked into it," Jenny said. "She calls herself Rachel Sedghi, but that's fake. She had billed herself as a top virologist, but we think she has ties to Iran. All we know is that she wants these germs for whatever it is she has in mind, and she wants them bad."

"So what do you want me to do about this? I'm not a virologist. Shouldn't you go to the FBI with this?"

As soon as I said it I realized that might not be the best move. The federal government was being run by fascists who were enabling a wanna-be tyrant. The Department of Health and Human services was in the hands of a conspiracy theorist who swims in polluted water and straps whale carcasses on his car while driving on the highway. They would be absolutely no help in any way whatsoever.

I thought about how inept the administration was during the COVID pandemic and about just how fucked we were having them in their time back already. The last time around the president spread conspiracy theories like wildfire, told people not to take proper safety precautions, and had everyone who mistakenly put their trust in them drinking bleach.

If this plague got out, we would see more of the same but on a tragic scale. They would expect people to work in public and die at their desks. The rich would take a dip in their profits for a second and then recoup their losses while the people in the thick of the world who had to scrape by just to live would be the ones who suffer. There would be riots in the streets, bodies filling up morgues, and people tearing their friends and neighbors apart.

Our lives and safety were in the hands of insane, selfish people.

"Apparently they're not concerned. The government is trying to cut waste, and safety of citizens is not a priority in light of that mandate. But we are convinced she will make an attempt to do something with the virus, and we don't want to chance that."

"Who's this 'we,' by the way? Your father?"

"No. I was rescued from him by . . . others. They were my savior, they helped me when I thought I would be in a prison of his making until the day I died. You can trust me when I say you can trust them."

"Hmmmm. So where do I come in on this?"

"We want you to steal it before she can."

27.

WE TOOK A TRAIN TOGETHER out to New York City. A big, rumbling beast of an Amtrak that crawled through the Southern California deserts and hills, a huge gorgeous relic of an American leviathan, the favorite mode of transportation from an era when people used to have all the time in the world because the world didn't change as fast with touches of buttons to deliver and screens that booked flights anywhere in the world. Not my favorite means of travel as far as expediency measures went, but I loved watching the thunderheads well up on the horizon.

They seemed to be mirroring the energy I was feeling, like there was electric and kinetic turbulence in the air and rains that could pour down and sweep away a landscape if they all came out at once. I felt the promise of release and the thrill of change, because a storm means something gets destroyed, sure, whether it's a poor creature in the path of the flood or the house that gets hit by lightning.

But it also means new life as all the seeds that were lying dormant so long in the desert sands get a chance to reach out with their new shoots and widen their petals in a dance with the sun before they burn up and wither in their wars against the army of the day with its spears of sunlight and its marauding waves of heat. They don't care what kind of casualties they inflict as they pillage across these impossibly huge waves of sand, and so the plants and creatures have to fight on until the water comes by with its reinforcements, providing assistance against the other elements, in their big dance of life and death.

A cycle was playing out before me, being a part of this plan of Jenny's as she dragged me back into a heist, together like we seemed meant to be. I was surprisingly relieved to be in the thick of it all, because that thrill of it all was life in all its high-octane fury.

I had been trying to live simply and fly straight. I knew somewhere deep down that it was all an act and sooner or later, I would thirst to break free, like those plants in the desert. The right rain would come around, and I would spread on out of my shell and reach for new atmospheres, trading the dormant life for a chance to reach for that sky.

As if reading my mind, Jenny leaned over with a look of concern on her face. "I'm sorry for dragging you further into this life. I know you're trying to get out of this and do right. And here I am asking you along on an undertaking that sounds crazy to pull off."

I wanted to rage and tell her that I wasn't going to be her errand boy. But she knew me too well, knew I couldn't resist a challenge, and knew I always wanted to be the hero. I wanted to rage, and instead I sighed and saved the righteous indignation for the money changers in the temple, and stared out the window at the turbulent southwest vista that flashed by alongside us. I let the clouds storm for me instead and looked her in the eyes.

"I . . ." I leaned back. "I worry that once I go down this track, I'll want to stay in the game and won't be able to stop."

"I'll make this so worth it, it will be your last one," she said. "Our last one if you want it."

"One last score," I muttered. I took my gaze from the window and leaned in closer to her, as if it was confidential, even though we had the entire car to ourselves. "You know what I worry about?"

"Huh?"

"I worry that I want to keep everything all hectic and fucked up, like I'm an action junkie who needs that adrenaline fix to get through the day, otherwise everything else is meaningless."

She was about to interrupt, but I continued on.

"Like, what if I had it within my power to make the world a better place? Right all the wrongs, feed every starving mouth, and clothe every person shivering in an alley, but I decided not to? All because I think it's too interesting to see things a little shaken up. Because I need the thrill of when things go all turbo and everything is chaos. I'm scared because I think that I can't run away from the danger. Like a moth can't resist a flame. What if I get in fucked-up situations because I like to fuck it all up?"

"You don't fuck anything up. You've got hidden strengths that even you probably don't know about. And talents that make people wonder at you. I can't command ghosts the way you do. I can see them, I can talk to them. Maybe make them throw books across the room or cause you to have a chill as they pass through you. You can make them solid like they are alive again. You can command them with the force of your will if you wanted to."

I cocked my head, perplexed by what she told me. I figured my abilities were the standard, as far as seeing the dead go. I had no idea I was somehow better at it than anyone. "That's not much of a consolation to me. I don't want to make an army of the dead or keep them as slaves. I'll never use a ghost in a way that hurts it or makes it feel like less than a living person."

"And that's because you're a good person, even when you're a bad one. What did you tell me you were doing with that money you swiped?"

"Giving most of it away. But even then, I'm doing wrong. Yeah, those rich motherfuckers don't deserve it, but if those organizations get found out that they took money from a career criminal who committed multiple acts of fraud, they could be the ones whose reputation takes a dive. I want to do things right. I want to give something back to the world. I'm worried that I give that money away only to assuage my own troubled conscience. Not because I know what it really means to do something good for someone else."

"You give it because you're a good person," she said. "You're just caught up in a world that doesn't want to let anyone be good."

I knew she meant that as a consolation, but I was immensely depressed about the thought of a sad spinning world where everything was mad and crazy and important decisions hung on a knife's edge. I wanted the beautiful world that was out there to be something that could inspire and teach us lessons we could use to pick everyone up along with us.

I didn't want it to be that savage desert we sped through, where everything was competing against each other and the only thing that won was whatever took the most from the rest. I wanted it to be as inspirational as the sunset that shone down on us with its blazing reds that made you feel comfort in your soul and dark purples that brought you to tears with their beauty.

But I was worried that comfort it brought me was only because I was on the other side of the window. If I was out there, I might be as greedy for my own satisfaction as any wild thing from that harsh environment. Maybe the thought of being trapped inside boxes like this room on this train with my own thoughts was what drove me to these extremes. What if I needed to get away from my own self, and being wound up in some other chaos was better than the one that my own mind produced?

I prayed I could keep my eyes towards the beauty and order of it all and not get drawn too close to the allure of the storming danger of the great and crazy expanse that held the promise of constant and brutal action.

I got up and went through my belongings. I put away my black coat that was hanging up over a seat.

"That's a pretty coat," Jenny said.

"Thanks. It's a gift from my father. Pop got it sometime in the late sixties, or early seventies, back when he was probably trying to pimp out his threads on the dance floor."

I ran my hand over the smooth purple lining of my frock coat. I loved the way it whipped about like a cape. It was perfect for me, something that drew the eyes of others but wasn't so ostentatious to be mistaken for Elton John's wardrobe. Not that I had anything against him, just probably shouldn't be too flashy as a thief. Even though purple was tempting fate.

"I carry it around when I travel. It always brings me luck."

"Well, by all means, bring that mojo," she said.

We got off the train in Penn Station when we arrived in Manhattan. That hub was always a labyrinth of randomness that managed to turn me around each time, so when I got out, it was always between a forest of skyscrapers that left me dazzled and shocked by the material splendor if it all, and with no sense of what direction I was making my way about in. Metal construction scaffolding was set up around the exit, adding to the confusion, shining poles crossing each other and making me feel claustrophobic and confined.

All of a sudden, they gave way and I was staring at the Empire State Building, iconic and stately, giving off a sense of a symbol of power of a city that has always managed to tower over all others. The Empire State told you that you could build bigger than this one, sure, but in the imagination, this bad boy will always soar above the clouds that others are stuck under.

We Ubered our way downtown to our hotel in the Meatpacking District, close to the river and with a pool on the roof. The inside was a vibrant palace of an interior, all marble and warm lights, a sharp contrast to the seemingly always gritty streets of the outside.

We had a day until showtime. We'd reviewed our plans and rehearsed what we could on the train. Now we waited. I took a shower and paced around the room for a few minutes.

I was wearing my frock coat, a Byronic wanderer. I had on tight-fitting black jeans and a white dress shirt.

"I'm going to go and check out the building," I told her after I'd had enough of the room.

"Not much you'll find out about it on the outside that we don't know," Jenny said. "But you never were one to sit still in one place for long, huh?"

"I need to get out, I don't like to be caged up."

"I think that could be a good epitaph for you." She smiled.

"Bad boys like me don't die in the end, we just ride off into the sunset," I said and winked at her on my way out.

I hit the street, interested in the hum of the world flowing around me, that great susurrus of human activity that this city produced like the buzz of bees in a hive. The streets under my feet made me feel at home. A path in motion was all I craved, a destination to travel to, even if there was nothing to do there, just something to direct my energy towards.

I wandered along the tracks of the High Line, a beautiful garden bursting through old architecture and structures, imagining what it would be like if that virus were to get out and get to everyone. Would nature come up through the cracks of civilization, where it had been patiently waiting? Would she no longer choke on our exhaust and be ready to repair the world like she always did, cracking rocks with a root or a flood to shift landscapes in ways we'd always envied?

I went by the building on 8th Avenue, to keep my word, but I didn't actually need to see it. An ordinary building for that part of town, a facade of pilasters with a frieze on top that resembled Greek columns flattened to the side of the building. It had a big entrance with the street address blazing above it on a metal grate sign of very industrial looking architectural addition.

I only needed to see the neighborhood, orient myself around the area and know where I could run to if things went south. That being done, I headed north. Uptown and on into that green heart of the city, Central Park. I wandered down its winding paths. It was early summer, and some of the trees were still sprouting new leaves, and the roller skaters were over by Bethesda Fountain, grooving since they probably had done since the days when Studio 54 was the most happening place in the world and they were the queens and kings of those streets and clubs.

I gazed out from the parapet at Belvedere Castle after seeing

Cleopatra's Needle. The park was so full of amazing things like that, which almost seemed anachronistic or at the very least idiosyncratic. Glimpses of the past in that fascinating city of technology and constant progress.

From there, I roamed due west and meandered along those streets full of claustrophobic mansions squeezed next to each other in between giant luxurious apartment buildings with towers on top of them that reached up towards the sun with their parapets like palaces in the sky.

Everywhere, the city seemed so vibrant and full of life. I was loving wandering about in it all, enjoying breathing that glorious city air, even if I caught a whiff of something strong here and there.

Sure, the city was full of the scents of garbage and puddles filled with things best left unexamined, but it was also full of smells of food and the leaves from the trees as they fell, and just life. That was the smell of activity and the feeling of people in a constant mundane battle against entropy, as they tried to maintain their hectic lives.

Lives that you could be forgiven for maybe thinking weren't really much when you looked at any one, but when you saw that they were a part of this great big civic organism, you stopped and appreciated each one as they hurried by you. I wandered into a bar off of Amsterdam Avenue that I went to back in the day, Jake's Dilemma.

Ten years previous, I was traveling to Saint Petersburg, Russia, which seemed like another world to me at the time, and it might as well have been. I wondered if I would ever see America again due to getting arrested and thrown into the gulag if I got caught over there, so I decided to unwind for one last night in a city that exemplified America in all its better or worse glory. I wound up playing beer pong with a group of teachers who had gotten off work fifteen minutes before and were enjoying happy hour on a payday, so a very happy hour indeed.

"We work at a Jewish day school," they told me. They were so much fun. Every one of them really loved making a difference; I could see it in their eyes, even when they were kvetching. "It's a real chore to deal with rich parents who don't appreciate us for all the amazing things we do for their children," they said.

That morning, they had finished up a March for Fairness, as they called it, and they all showed me pictures on their phones of kids holding up adorable signs they made, with handwritten messages of tolerance and acceptance that they taught them. They showed me a video of kids marching and chanting "What do we want? Fairness! When do we want it? Now!"

I was moved to tears seeing a vocation that inspiring. It gave me hope that the next generation was onto something that maybe I was unable to find growing up, and I didn't resent them for it. I wanted to do what I could to foster that kind of wide-eyed zeal for life that those kids had, to cherish it and let it grow into something beautiful that could take your breath away.

It was right then and there that I decided to eventually get out of the game. If such a thing can be done anyway. But I wanted to try, dammit! Do the impossible, bring something good out of something bad, and maybe save my soul in the process.

That old bar, ten years ago. And that was where I ran into A.J. again. Or I should say he ran into me, because it wasn't by chance and I sure as shit wasn't seeking him out.

I went into that cozy establishment maybe only a hundred feet long by twenty foot wide in total, with its wooden countertops and foosball table in the corner, and sat down to order a drink. I didn't drink booze anymore, but I decided to order a Shirley Temple for old time's sake. I stared out the window at the busy Manhattan street and felt like I was in a dream. The bartender brought the drink over, and when I reached into my pocket for cash, he held up a tattoo-sleeved hand and shook his head. "Already been paid for," he said. "Guy said to give you this."

He handed me a white business card with a king of hearts on one side. The other said, in a fancy red script, "*Cheers, bitch.*"

"Mother*fucker*," I muttered, shaking my head and searching for him.

When I was a kid, I went to a winery up in the hills of San Diego's East County with him. I was sixteen and used a fake ID and drove him home after even though I probably shouldn't have been behind the wheel either. We were roaming around the winery's garden, and they had these fantastic bronze sculptures all around. A.J. held a glass up to one of them, a beautiful gleaming woman with outstretched arms that a bunch of people were posing for pictures around, and said in his most outdoors voice of all, "Cheers, *BITCH!*" Everyone stared, and we nearly fell over laughing.

It was our go-to toast for a good while. "Cheers, bitch!" After scanning the narrow interior space, I found him sitting at a table by himself, nursing a beer. I picked up my drink and walked on over to him. I held in my breath, not quite knowing what to say.

"Take a seat, sonny-boy," he said, motioning towards a bar stool right next to his. "I got some chips and guac."

"You hate guacamole," I said. "Said you always liked the taste of it, but your stomach didn't."

"But you always loved it."

I shook my head and smiled. For a second, I was a happy

precocious kid again and thought of times long past. I pulled up a chair and sat down. I sat there and waited for him to speak. He patiently enjoyed the bar crowd fluttering on about as we sat there, sipping our drinks. I caved in and grabbed a chip and dipped it in that sickly green deliciousness. The chips were garden variety tortilla chips, but the guacamole was homemade and surprisingly not bad for a place so far north of the border, where the Mexican food tends to go south should you be brave enough to order.

"I've been low-key following your exploits," A.J. said.

"Really?" I scoffed. "I thought I was pretty good about covering my tracks. Law enforcement doesn't even know who I am."

"Yet," he said. "But I've gotten wise. Not everything, but enough to figure it was my baby boy pulling these jobs. And if I did, you can be sure that others aren't far behind."

I paused for a second and gazed at him with narrowed eyes. I thought about every track I might have left uncovered. I thought I had done a baller job of it all—even Korey didn't know what I did— but I needed to do better, it seemed. Jenny found me too.

I was leaving too many loose ends for someone who wanted the game to end.

"All right," I conceded, putting my hands up like I was being taken in by the cops. "Ya got me. Guilty as charged. So what are you gonna do, take me away?"

He made a derisive snort, as if the thought were ludicrous to him, because I'm sure it was. "Yeah right, with all the things that I've done, I've got no room to judge." We sat there staring each other down, and then finally he reached across the table and grabbed my hand. I almost darted back but gave in and allowed it. "When was the last time we talked? Really talked together? I miss my baby boy." He looked so sincere and earnest, his eyes big and full of fatherly care, and I wanted to stay mad at him for past spats, but I didn't have the energy to be mean. I took his hands and patted them with my free one.

"Nine years ago?" I ventured. "Windsong's funeral. You were about six sheets to the wind on Jameson, and I was about twelve. I . . . might have been an asshole to you."

"I mighta been mean, when maybe I should have been more understanding."

"All water under the bridge."

"No, I was tough on you, when I shoulda been there for you. I've always been tough on you and I'm sorry. It's only that . . ." He trailed off, searching for the words to say. I waited for him to go on.

"It's okay," I told him and nodded to him reassuringly, and he went on.

"I always worried about you becoming too much like me, and I never wanted that for you. I made mistakes in life, made lotsa bad choices, and every time I saw you and saw how you reminded me of myself, it made me want to do everything I could to stop that, but I think I only wound up pushing you away."

"You did what you had to, and I made my own choices and didn't always make the best ones either . . ."

"Naw," he said, putting his hands up, gesturing for me to let him continue. I paused midsentence and motioned for him to continue on. "Remember when you were a kid, one time when you were maybe five and you came ta me?" I had a feeling I knew where this was going, and I took a deep breath, dreading it. "You said ta me, 'Pop, what if you saw someone who is there but they aren't? What if you can see people all the time and you know everyone else can't, but you see them and you know that they're there?'"

I did remember that conversation vividly. I was being dropped off at school, at Hanson Lane Elementary. I didn't want to go to school that day. I had been seeing a woman across the street who kept searching for something, and every time I glanced in her direction during recess, she stared at me with her intense and penetrating eyes and hollered a bunch of questions at me, which I did not have the answers to. It made me cry. And the worst part was no one would believe me. I figured for sure my pop would. "You told me it was my imagination running away on me."

He nodded slowly. I stared at him in nervous anticipation. I was already fighting back tears and didn't want to spill them in this crowded place.

"What I didn't tell you was I've seen 'em too. I've always seen 'em. I didn't know what to tell ya, and I was afraid you'd grow up to be as crazy as I thought I was."

At his confession, I let my tears spill. I didn't give a damn who saw. That was the one time in my life when I needed help the most. The one time when I wanted someone to say I'm there for you and I understand, and he did understand but he was not there.

"Why are you telling me this?" I asked as I wiped my eyes. I wanted to get out of there. Even though no one around seemed to notice, I felt like every eye in the building was on me. I should have found it comforting knowing I wasn't alone, but I had been alone all those years, and he could have made that better with a few words.

"I wanted to tell you I'm sorry," he said. "I want to tell you why I did what I did. It wasn't the right choice, and I'm sorry for it. I want to make it right before you go and do something that might go wrong in a bad way. I know about the job you're on."

"What do you know?" I asked, shooting a wary eye at him.

"Maybe a bit more than you ..."

"So tell me."

"The people who you're doing this for aren't who they seem. There's a whole big picture that you're not comprehending."

"Someone is stealing a virus," I whispered to him. "I'm going to steal it before they can and make sure it stays out of harm's way."

"Who told you that?" A.J. asked.

I paused for a second and took a breath. I had been working under assumptions from my relationship with Jenny, but what did I really know about her? I knew she was kind when she had been through so much, but I didn't know who we were working for. There was something about her I trusted, a magnetism that made her hard to resist, even when I wasn't sure what to make of her, something that made me act without questioning too fiercely when I should have been a bit more suspicious.

Did I want to be a hero that bad? I was so in need of redemption that I wanted to risk everything, and what was I expecting? A parade? They don't do that for thieves; they get you a long ride to the inside, bars and stripes. I was always impulsive, but this was too big of stakes to hope that my usual combination of dumb luck and sharp-witted quickness on my feet would save the day.

"So what do you know that I don't?" I asked again.

"David Moreau is somehow involved with this. You deal with David Moreau, you're dealing with the devil."

"Jenny said she wasn't working for him. And devils haven't scared me since catechism." I scoffed. "They're just an excuse for all the real evils in this world that people carry out on their own. Saying 'the devil made me do it' is what you do when you don't want to face up to your own mistakes. You're gonna have to do a bit better than that."

That might have been more than a little defensive snapping back at him like that, but the truth was, I was in a panic mode and didn't want to show it. Jenny said she was free from Moreau, and I took that one at face value, no questions asked. I wanted so badly to believe that people were good, but she in particular I wanted to believe in. Maybe it was because we had shared so much in that house together, or that I felt she was a kindred spirit, and I needed that. But I was wrapped up too deeply to call the whole thing off.

"I've had dealings with him too," he said. "Here." He took a couple of photos from his pockets and laid them on the table. I picked them up and glanced at them and then paused and held them closely, doubting what I was seeing.

They were pictures from the 1970s maybe, with that sort of washed-out look that color photographs from that time had, bright and full of different tones and shades, but not quite as vibrant as you'd expect to see on the streets. The clothes and styles of the figures in them were definitely from that era.

There they were in the pictures, my pop, long sideburns and a mop of wavy brown hair that was so unlike the short length he used to trim it to as long as I'd known him, with his arm around what looked like my mother from pictures I'd seen of her and what little I remembered. And to their left in the shot was David Moreau, same as he'd always been. Those bright blue eyes were twinkling like they were full of secrets he was too proud to share, but willing to let you know that he had them all to himself.

They were all on some rugged ruins, it looked like Machu Picchu, and they were all posing together as if they were the best of friends.

One picture of the two men had them exhaustedly leaning on each other at a summit with their arms around their shoulders like brothers in battle or long-time companions. Another had them gazing out over a sun-spilled view on a mountaintop that seemed to pour out into nothing it was so high up. And another had them examining dirt covered artifacts together, small stone figurines in hand.

"Is this his relative or something?" I asked, but I knew no person could be that much of a look-alike without being a twin. "Okay, that's just weird."

I thought of all the plausible outcomes for how I could be seeing what I was seeing. Was it a trick of the light, something that caused him to look like Moreau from an angle? I had once seen a picture of Alain Delon wearing a gray suit like I owned and thought it was a photo of me until I saw it was merely an odd angle where he might have passed for me. Was he some sort of spy with plastic surgery jobs done on him?

"It's him," A.J. said, with definitive authority. "You've felt it in 'im. Something about him isn't right. Like a cold shudder goes through your soul while someone walks over your grave when you look closely enough at 'im. He's always mysteriously gone or outta sight right when it's nighttime. He's had his eye on me and the ones I love for years. I tried to keep you from alla the bad things I've done, but that didn't happen."

He paused for a second and a tear welled up in his eye, which he did his best to fight back. I scooched closer to him and gave him a big hug.

I thought about all the things I had done. I never wanted to be bad, I only ever wanted to be the best at what I did, and what I did just so happened to be bad. I knew from a young age that the world was full of cruel people who broke the rules to get what they wanted from it.

Maybe if I had been born into a different life, I could have used my family's wealth to run for office. Maybe if I had the patience to tie shoes and teach the ABCs I could have been a kindergarten teacher and shaped minds. Maybe if I taught myself how to paint, I could have made murals around the town to beautify the neighborhoods, like those gorgeous ones in Chicano Park by the place I lived in with Korey. Maybe all the maybes were simply empty possibilities and best to be not distracting me.

"You did the best by me, and enough of the fault is my own when I made the mistakes I made," I said, consoling him as best I could. We were not very emotional with each other, but sometimes it would all come out in a torrent. "Sometimes people are just drawn to trouble as sure as waves are gonna crash on the shore. You can't get mad at the waves when they knock you around, it's the way the currents take them."

"You know, my last score was the night you had your accident as a kid," A.J. told me. "It went south and some bad shit happened. Blackboard didn't make it out of there, and that's why you never heard from him again."

I'd surmised as much. I thought about Blackboard Tommy one day and why he mysteriously disappeared without a trace and looked into him in the papers. There was a story about a heist gone wrong and one Thomas Steinhoff, aka Blackboard Tommy, being fatally shot by police in the aftermath.

"Go on," I encouraged him.

"I felt guilty about it," he continued. "I blamed myself as a rotten father for letting that happen to you. I thought it was all God's judgment on me for being a shitty dad, getting involved with things I shoulda never gotten involved with in the first place."

"I did wonder why you would still carry out a job when your only son was in the hospital. Kinda fucked."

"Not how it happened. I didn't know you were hurt when it happened. We left early in the mornin', 'n I assumed you was still asleep."

"Natch. Well, good to know."

We both stared off for a bit. Painful memories flooded my mind, things I tried so often to forget, and they were threatening to blot out the nicer parts of the day. I watched a few college kids drinking beer, the amber liquid sloshing around in their glasses.

"You know alla those jobs I pulled back in the day? Probably not, I didn't say much about it to you. But I was doing them for you. For a better chance for you. I had all that money saved up so you could go to college. I wanted you to have the things I couldn't have. You had all the brains I never had, and I wanted to make sure they went to good use."

"I'm sorry I never stuck around long enough to take you up on the offer," I said.

He signed. "Well, the money is yours. I have it for you, and you can do what you want with it to make a better world. I know you can still do it."

"Thanks" was all I could muster up without choking on a sob. I wanted to do something good, I did. I thought of all the big dreams I had as a kid, all the wonderful dreams I had in mind before life decided to try and shake me awake. I wanted to be that kid again. To be that wide-eyed and optimistic, thinking that everything could be okay if we all worked hard at it enough.

He gave me a big hug, and we sat there like that, two men, not caring what the rest of the world did as we let emotions out that had been building up for an age. He was my pop again and I was his baby boy.

"So what are you gonna do?" he asked.

"I'm gonna see this through. But I'm gonna do it my way. Maybe it's time I stopped going with the flow and made my own waves."

"Please, don't do it," he said with an urgency that scared me as he tugged on my arm. "Just don't!"

His pleading eyes froze me in place, so bright and welling up with tears, like he'd been holding them in ever since I was a kid, because I sure as shit didn't remember seeing them flow ever. I gazed into those familiar fatherly eyes and said the second worst thing I ever said to him. I lied and said, "Okay."

And then relief flooded his face, and the tears turned to ones of joy.

I smiled and said it again. "Okay. For you."

I sat with him a little while longer. We talked about old times, caught up. I told him about Korey, and that was tricky explaining her to someone from his generation.

"So, she's born a dude?" he asked.

"No, she's a woman. She was assigned male at birth. There's a difference between sex and gender."

"So how do you two . . .?"

"That's none of your fucking business," I said with a very serious face. And then I broke character and laughed. "Every chance we get!"

"And she's the one for you? You love her?"

"More than any other girl I've ever known."

"Then I'm sure I'll love her too if she's good enough to get ahold of my baby boy." He paused thoughtfully on that one and then he raised his glass. I clinked mine to his, lovingly watching him as he downed his beer.

We had a few more drinks after that. He had his hefeweizens and I had my bubbly waters. I kept glancing at the time, wanting to turn the hands back, or get caught in a pocket of special relativity that let everyone else pass on by while I savored these moments.

I didn't want to leave him, but I knew I had other obligations that were calling and things to do. Jenny was probably already wondering about my absence, and I wondered if there were others who were noting what I was all about. Time to get conspicuous.

"I love you, Pop!" I told him as I embraced him one last time. I didn't want to turn around, I just wanted to see his twinkling eyes with his bushy eyebrows above them and his big smile across his stubbly face. "Peace!" I shouted out to him, our usual sign off to each other.

To which he replied, "Out!" A great big smile crossed his face and made me shine one right back at him that was so big my eyes squinted.

I exited, stage front door, through the gift shop and out into the chilly almost evening. The humid air of New York had its usual steamy kiss of teasing recognition the summer brought in that reminded me that I'm a Southern California kid no matter what and my blood is tempered to different climates where the weather doesn't really change into something so sticky. And we stay exactly like our weather⊠always cool except when we're hot. I took off my coat.

I wanted to give Korey a call, but I didn't have my phone for her on me. I never carried it about when I had business. Never mix that stuff with pleasure. And never let them see you bleed. And never let the evil you bring about touch the ones you love. They need to be kept at home and in bed all snuggled away, safe and sound from that in dreamland.

At least, that's what I thought as I hailed a passing cab and shot back downtown to the job I intended to work to my own angle. If Jenny was really working with Moreau, I had to take precautions against that. Make a plan to take what I needed from her if I had to. Lives were depending on me, lives like Korey's, which I held to be more precious than my own.

Time to stop taking things on faith and take an active hand in destiny. Chance was what ruled my days. Time to stop relying on luck and make some of my own.

28.

THE GALA EVENT WAS THAT NEXT afternoon. I was dressed in an ink-black tux that looked like it could have been fashioned from a block of obsidian, with lapels like the ears of a housecat and a white pocket square.

Jenny cut a stunning figure in a black evening dress with a plunge neck and long sleeves, cinched at the waist. It pooled around her feet like a fountain of sea foam that billowed in waves of night flowing around her as she walked. She had on a gold collar that made her look especially enticing, her neck stretching out above it like it was inviting lips to kiss it and her chest down below it capturing the eyes of anyone who glanced her way.

We got out of the limousine, one of those dark and luxurious chariots that roll down the streets in that town, inviting guesses as to what was happening inside and what manner of powerful person is orchestrating world affairs by phone as they wind their way down streets that are absolutely crowded and humming with every form of activity.

We weren't the type of powerful people the passersby would think were in that limousine. Not the type of powerful who could hire and fire swathes of people with the push of a button and the call of the right number. Not the titans of industry who make the markets tremble and have ridiculous followers on their Twitter feeds fawning over their every decision. Not the powerful who need to show it off because we want to make people in awe of us.

We were the type of powerful who could sneak into their world and take what we wanted. We were powerful because they had no idea what kind of X factor we represented, and by the time they figured it out, we were well on our way to a warmer clime with their cold hard cash or whatever it is we took from right under their noses.

A thief in the night is powerful because they make the powerful fear that the wealth they greedily clutch to could be taken away if they forget where it is for long enough. So that thief has the full force of an elemental nightmare backing them up. We make them remember why they cried in their cribs at night and their mothers had to come and console them, only Momma isn't around to help them anymore and they have to tough it out by their lonesome and face the dark.

Jenny handed the security our invitations and we slipped through the front, unnoticed for the threat we were as they noticed us for the glamour that we represented.

I felt the old familiar thrill as we walked up the stairs to the bank of elevators in the lobby. The rush of sneaking in without an objection as I passed through layer after layer of security into the heart of it all, knowing that's where I could get cornered, and having to keep my guard up all around as I got deeper and deeper into the lion's den. Here, there be no clear maps because you're at the edge of the world, matey. Just a wilderness thick as a jungle and your wits to get you through it.

Jenny caught my smile from the corner of her eye and returned one back to me. She kissed me on the cheek when we stopped, waiting for our elevator to take us up into that gathering in the sky.

"You never look more at home and at ease than when you're doing this kind of thing, you know that?" she said, as I smiled on, on top of the world. "What makes you love this so much?"

"Most people think they have a station in life," I replied, leaning in as if I was going to kiss her so I wasn't blaring things out. "They think they can afford the things that they do and make the money they make because that's what they earn and that's what's fair. I learned a long time ago that that's all bullshit."

I marveled at all the spectacular trappings of capitalism around us. This polished lobby that led to important people, all milling about, wheeling and dealing. Telling themselves they were saving the world while they hounded out every tax break they could squeeze out of the system as they posed for photo ops to smooth over their scandals and make it seem like feeding the people was a beautiful side effect of their unbridled greed and struggles for power.

"The people above are making it harder for everyone underneath them. Even their charity is a means of control. They're all a bunch of arrogant, privileged pricks who think that the world should be saved based on what they decide to fund. And they're the ones fucking it up to begin with. They pay starvation wages and then fund programs to end homelessness. They pay politicians to bow to them and then train the next generation of leaders. They produce all the trash in the world and then try to save the whales from it. They take what they can and give out the bare minimum back in return. If the world were a pearl, they'd hide it away in a dark safe and take it out where only they could admire it with their friends in private.

"I'm the wild card out there. I throw a wrench in the works and stop everyone long enough to realize there's flaws in the machine that wants to grind us all down. I pretend to play their game, and before they know what's going on, I'm on my way with what should never have been theirs to begin with and onto the next big score."

I paused for a second as the elevator door opened up and three people came out, walking in that hurried New York fashion. I held the door and gestured for her to enter, then I slid in after her.

"That's a nice speech," she said as we made our way up. "Been rehearsing that one?"

"Every time I'm about to go into confession."

"Oh, it's a good pep talk."

"I thought so."

"You don't go to confession."

"I've been good lately. Ish."

She smiled and kissed me on the cheek. She tried to plant another one on the neck, and I slipped out of those sweet tingles across the surface of my skin before I wound up getting lost in it. The door opened, and we soon found ourselves weaving in and out of that huge sea of people.

The crowd glittered like jewels and their jewels crowded their bodies.

I wanted to snatch some of them off of them. I was itching to steal the jewel encrusted watch of one man in particular I spoke with, who was droning on about an ayahuasca retreat he had in the Andes and how he had a revelation about a new idea he was going to implement in whatever tech venture he thought was going to make him the next Steve Jobs.

I'm sure that's what the powers that be are aligning the universe towards, douche. You hit the metaphysical goldmine there.

But no, we had a job to do, one mission, and that took precedence, taking the right things.

"There you are, darling," Jenny exclaimed, bumping my tech bro friend out of the way and handing me a drink.

"Oh my gosh, thank you," I whispered.

"Champagne for me, ginger ale for you," she said as I sipped from my glass. And in a lower whisper, "You got your magic ready?"

"What am I, an amateur?" I said, feigning shock. I felt for the tiny glass bottle full of liquid that I had in my pocket, and yes, it was still there. "No serious replies, please."

"Wouldn't dream of taking you seriously, darling."

I felt out there with my other senses and knew the friend I had summoned was hovering nearby. It was like seeing a person out of your peripherals and knowing a room was occupied. "Thanks, buddy," I whispered and felt pleasantly reassured.

"If I can have a moment of your time," a person working as a default MC said into the crowd. The music, random hits by Bruno Mars and Lady Gaga from a band hired for the occasion, died down. "Here's a man who needs no introduction, he does so much for our organization. Our founder, executive director, and man who wears many hats, Mr. John King, everyone!"

Our man came shuffling up to the podium on the stage. He was an older gentleman with sunken eyes and a long neck, perched on a body with a slightly protruding stomach. Everything about him suggested proportions that were mostly normal, but slightly off in an almost comical way, a child's spinning toy of a body that could fall at any moment because of his imbalances.

He had a drink in hand. I was briefed on this and paid attention to how he downed a sip of liquid courage before he pulled out his speech and awkwardly tested the mic.

"Testing, check, one, two," he said. "I know you all think I probably spend all my time on the golf course as executive director, and sometimes I do. But my real handicap is gin."

The crowd got a good laugh about that one as they all sucked down their cocktails. Nice dad joke to open up with. A little offensive to people recovering from substance abuse issues such as myself, but I wasn't going to get all huffy about it. I didn't need to get on a tear these days, and it suited me fine. I felt kind of bad for him that he needed that buzz to get by.

"But seriously, partners. May I call you partners? My grandfather used to call people that all the time, and I feel like that's what we are. Partners. We here at EnviroHealth Alliance are all in this together for a common goal, and what is an alliance if not a partnership?"

Good at reading the thesaurus, I'll give him that.

"We've been working so hard, and it's paid off because we have won so much in grant dollars this year that our revenue is through the roof! And that's not where we're going to stop. We will one day be the name recognized for ending the threats of viruses around the world. COVID-19 will be a memory relegated to a distant past as we are credited for achieving the wellness and complete safety of the future. A future where no one will worry about the threat of a global pandemic ever again. Thanks to us! Thanks to EnviroHealth Alliance! Thank you all for being a part of it!"

The crowd went wild, and glasses were raised as he hoisted his up and downed the contents. He made his way into the crowd and grabbed another drink from a passing tray as he went. He definitely took advantage of the free booze of these shindigs. We let him mingle for a bit.

His words might have sounded good and rang the right chords with his crowd, but I knew him for what he was. Someone trying to be a savior through his work but not caring about the cost of achieving his ends. He used connections as a screener at preprint services for papers that weren't yet public to take down any research that was detrimental to his work. He was involved in shady grant agreements. And he was responsible for the lax oversight of his organization. He didn't care what it took to gain him glory as long as the results were right for him.

"Shall we get into character?" Jenny asked.

"Showtime!" I whispered.

"John, darling," Jenny called out. "I have someone here you simply must meet!"

"Another investor, trying to donate some grant money to get his taxes taken care of for the next fiscal year?" he asked.

Meow, he was saucy on the sauce.

"Guilty as charged," I said, offering a hand. "I'm Jake Gates, as in 'I get you running right out the gate.' I run a venture capital firm, and we're always on the lookout for innovative organizations like yours to ... Oh shit!"

I found a spot to catch my shoe on, and did the trick of almost falling over on him, catching myself before I could knock into him. I grabbed his drink to pretend to steady it so it wouldn't spill, tipping the contents of my glass container I had palmed in my hand into his drink. It was a little concoction of Rohypnol and ketamine I had perfected for just such occasions.

"Sorry, these carpets!" I exclaimed. "Are you okay?"

"No broken bones," he said. "I think we'll live."

He took a big sip of his drink. Good. Down the hatch, past the gums, watch out belly, here it comes.

"Anyways, geez, I'm really sorry about that."

"No worries."

"Right. So I'd be insanely happy to see what we can do together. How'd you like to meet up for lunch?"

"I'm busy, but I'd love to set something up with my assistant."

"Sure, sounds good."

"If you'll excuse me, I've got to go," he said, shaking his head. He took another sip, finishing the drink off. As if more alcohol was going to do the trick for feeling a little off, good call. He stumbled off, loosening up his collar.

That's when my ace in the hole came into play.

Papa Decky entered him and took the wheel. I had experimented with it myself to get it right. I needed to make sure I could say what was going on at the time. Ghosts can possess people, but usually not for long. Eventually a person will fight back and regain control. Most of the time, it happens in a flash, and that person doesn't even know the ghost did it and wonders why they dozed off or spaced out in midday while running errands at a supermarket.

Ghosts can possess a person longer if that person isn't in control of their own faculties. When I'd experimented with it with Papa Decky and Gary, it involved a lot of getting blackout drunk and letting them take the wheel for a night out on the town. Gary took me on a wild night of dancing more than once at a San Diego gay bar called Rich's, and Papa Decky used me to smoke some of that good herb he missed smoking so bad as a ghost. So it was win-win.

I got to see how it was on the other side of the con, and they got to enjoy the simple pleasures of life that they couldn't enjoy anymore being on the other side of life.

Alcohol was a great way to put someone in that state, but it took making sure they consumed so many drinks that they got to that point. So, although I was firmly opposed to the date rape types, I wasn't going to pass up the tricks of their trade for the right job.

King snapped bolt upright after nearly falling down. Someone nearby was startled, thinking he was about to topple over. "Are you okay?" he asked, grabbing onto his arm to steady him.

"Never better, Daddy-o!" King/Decky said, shaking his hand and patting him on the back. "You're a real pal, thanks. Now where's the shitter? I've gotta piss like a thoroughbred!" The man pointed down some double doors. "Aaaawww, thanks, my guy! You're a lifesaver."

We walked in stride with him. "Easy there, don't draw too much attention to us," I whispered into his ear.

"Hey, it's been a while since I've felt any of this. Let me get a handle on the controls."

"Get a handle when we're out of a crowd," Jenny whispered. We wandered out of the doors and down a hall.

"Oh man," King/Decky moaned. "Please let our next person we try this on not be a sixty-three-year-old alky. I was hoping for someone with a better working dick than this guy if we're pulling a job with a babe like you." He winked at Jenny. She gave his ear a tug like you would on a disobedient animal if you were in the mood to be mean.

"You wouldn't know what to do with a 'babe like me' if you were in any body," she muttered. "Now focus."

"Hey, can't blame a guy for trying." He giggled. "But seriously,

I'm only possessing a horny eighteen-year-old our next go-round, something like that. Get a little bang for my buck."

"You having a dick again is not a burden the world needs," I said.

We made it down several levels to the labs. We took the stairs, winding down the coldly lit passages that flickered with every footfall as we scampered along the route Jenny knew from her recon work and I had memorized the basic floorplan of.

We entered a hallway that led to a secure room. Jenny already had his keycard ready. She had swiped it previously to make sure it was on hand for the party today, in case he forgot it. She handed it off to King/Decky, and he swiped it down the strip of a black door with a clear pane of glass in the middle. "Cha-ching, baby!" he said as it lit up green, and we pulled the big handle and entered the lab.

The room was more high school science classroom and less *Jurassic Park* than I had in my mind. The floor was bright blue, and steel countertops were everywhere. Various plastic bottles were lined up on shelves and cabinets. Computer equipment was placed sporadically throughout along with machines like centrifuges and microscopes. Sunlight flitted through slatted blinds.

"Strange," Jenny muttered. "Usually these rooms don't have natural light coming in."

We hadn't seen anyone yet, so we didn't need to make up our excuses for being there. Hopefully it would stay that way long enough for us to duck in and out.

It was strange to see it empty, but that party in full swing up above ensured that everyone would be schmoozing and enjoying a good time, giving us free rein to sack the cities like the barbarian hordes we were. The whole thing seemed like a hive that would be ready to hum to life at any moment. The bees were buzzing about out there, but when the sun settled down, you knew they were coming back for the night to make that honey.

We hustled through all of that and towards the end of the hall, where a big shining door was ready to be opened like the pearly gates, but with organisms that caused disease on the other side and not angels offering salvation. The angel of death was the only seraph making rounds in this paradise, stored in cold containers that people hoped to get the secrets to sustain life and combat pestilence from. The balance between life and death hung on a knife's edge in here—one slide and it could go one way or the other. One wrong slip and it was blood in the streets.

A dark pad on the side blinked enticingly.

King/Decky walked up that biometric pad and slapped a hand on it. "Jackpot!" he exclaimed.

The door clicked and we were able to swing it out. A rush of cold air hit us, and I was reminded of the walk-in freezer from the one week I spent at a fast food restaurant before I decided I would never do anything as normal as that again. The air felt like that, only colder, a wave of ice, invisible but able to seep into your bones as it washed over you. We stepped in and went to work seeking out our prize.

We opened up the storage units and were met with misty clouds flowing out of them like a volcano filled with fog. A big batch of witch's brew, hermetically sealed and kept preserved by modern means instead of sorcery. Jenny poured through their contents, looking for the viral treasure we were in the cave of wonders for.

She grew increasingly frustrated as she pulled sample after sample, not finding what she was looking for.

"Fuck. Shit. Hell, dammit . . ." she muttered.

"You left out crap and cocksucker, if you're going down the list," I said.

"Not the fucking time," she growled. I knew it wasn't, but I was getting nervous. I could never let things slide when they came to mind. "They're supposed to be here! Motherfucker! Someone must have been tipped off about us. Can you tell us anything that's happening in his brain right now?" she asked King/Decky.

"Not while he's out to lunch like this," Decky said through King's reedy voice.

"He's got to have it in here," Jenny said. "I was told it would be here!"

"So, let's cut our losses and try another time," I suggested.

"It's no use, then," she moaned. "She's probably already taken them!"

"Who, Sedghi?"

"No, the fucking Easter Bunny!" she exclaimed. "Of course Sedghi."

"Hang on a sec," I told her. "Gary, you there?"

"Loud and clear." He coalesced from a presence into his own form. Jenny nodded to him.

"Ha! Nice!" I chuckled. "Can you do a recon throughout this building, starting on this floor? See if we're missing anything?"

"I don't know if I need to look too hard," he said. "This wall already feels like it's vibrating." He flew through it and stuck his head back out. "Yup!"

I walked up to the wall and checked it out. It seemed to be all uniform, only a white wall, but the bottom was made up of random panels. I tapped them and felt about the edges. Nothing was out of the ordinary, so I kept on groping about and running my hands along the edges. I came up to a button on the corner of one of the panels and pushed it in. The panel slid out with a satisfying little whoosh. It opened up wide enough to reveal a biometric scanner.

"This has gotta be above board." I chuckled. "Seems our good friend Mr. King is keeping things from his colleagues. Decky? Wanna do the honors?"

"On it," he chirped in that man's voice. When he popped his thumb on the scanner, a green light bathed it as it crept up and down his opposable little extremity like a spectral glow. A door behind it popped open, and there it was. The Frankenstein sample with a Bram Stoker nickname, crafted for good but being grappled over by people less than such.

It was stored in small plastic tubes, which seemed so trivial a container for something that had the power to infect society and disrupt it, possibly worse than the last pandemic, to bring civilization to its knees with invisible assaults. No wonder people thought plagues were the weapons of some god, shooting invisible arrows that could strike without warning. All that in one small container of clear plastic.

A time bomb waiting to go off. Numbering our days if we let it loose. Days that we spent so much energy and resources to make sure were as free from any natural strife and sadness that we could. Tick, tick, tick.

And here I was playing with that invisible fire that could burn the world in fever sickness and choking lungs, trying to contain it myself. And I knew nothing about putting out fires, only about making things hotter in hell for the bad thieves like me trying to pretend they were the good thief. I pocketed the handful of samples.

Jenny gave a start. "Shhh . . ." she whispered. "I think I hear someone coming."

"Where?" I whispered. "I don't hear a damn—"

She put her hands up to my lips and took off out the door. I wondered if this was the plan of hers all along and I was going to be stuck in here taking a fall. I thought about taking off after her and almost started out the door when I did hear someone coming in.

"What's going on in here?" a woman with a heavy accent asked.

She walked into the lab with an authoritative stride that made me pause for a second, wondering how to handle this. She wouldn't be easily dissuaded, so I had to make sure I handled this right. She had on a black pencil skirt with a matching suit top and a white blouse.

I was about to lay my story on, but I lost track of my thoughts when I looked into her violet-blue eyes. I had been haunted by those eyes for my entire life, not a week went by that I didn't see them in the back of my mind. Those same eyes from that Haunting Woman lying out in the field. Those same imploring eyes, that were enough to drag me siren-like into a pile of bones around her.

And what I saw was recognition in them. She knew me even after all these years, even though I had picked up a scar here and there and a gray hair or two around the temples to add to the one little streak I'd had in my bangs ever since I was a kid.

"You . . ." was all I could make out. I wanted to take her up and away from here, ask her about everything she knew. This *was* her! I knew it couldn't be anyone else. I had believed she was a hallucination, a fever dream, or a phantom of a phantom that I had picked up with my senses, but here she was, so real I could reach out and touch her. That Haunting Woman who had hung over my life since that moonlit night where she left me half dead.

"What are you doing here?" she asked, recognition in her voice despite the confused expression she had.

"I was giving them a tour of the facility," King/Decky said, stepping out, seeing that something was going pear shaped and trying to save it. "Yup, just wanted to give these investors a taste of what it is that we do and ..."

Jenny cut everything short with a chloroform-soaked rag to the woman's face. I had no idea where she had been hiding out, but she was good enough to remain out of sight from the Haunting Woman. "We need to get the fuck gone, like yesterday," she said as she dragged her sleeping burden off to a corner where she could be kept out of the way until she regained consciousness.

I took a longing look at her as we hurried back out the lab and down the stairs. We didn't want to get trapped in an elevator on the way out, and we took them bounding down several at a time. We hopped into a bright yellow cab as soon as one pulled over for us and clambered into the back of it. I had the excited rush of blood thrill from pulling it off, but I couldn't shake having seen her.

"We did it!" Jenny whispered.

"Hell yeah we did!" I said in a big and audible cheer with no soul to prop up the timbre of my voice with and patted the vials in my coat to make sure they were all present and accounted for. But I kept on seeing those eyes again.

They were there in every glimpse in my direction from every single lively woman walking busily down these crowded streets. Those bright violet-blue eyes were waiting around every corner to snatch my peace of mind from me and make me fear the night like a child again. The sun was setting in the sky, and her piercing eyes were powering over the deep reds and oranges that flicked through the streets every time we passed by another crosstown intersection as we meandered downtown. Those towers of the night with office windows that twinkled like stars were all a place where she could be at any time she chose if she could pop up like she did in my life again.

I was thinking these things, lost in my own reveries as we crawled through the Manhattan traffic, when someone got into the cab from the front door passenger side. He had close-cropped jet-black hair; tight, pale skin; and a square jaw like a block of marble.

For a brief second, I thought he wasn't aware we were the cab's fare, but I realized this couldn't have been a simple coincidence. "Hey, I've already got a fare!" the driver said, and before any further protests could be made, the passenger pulled on the parking brake and just as casually snapped the driver's neck.

"Holy shit!" I exclaimed as he deftly unbuckled the dead man's seatbelt and unceremoniously shoved him out the door with one hand. Then he slipped into his seat and took the wheel. I went on instinct and started to open up the door to bail out of the car and was rewarded with a backhand so strong it made my neck snap back, and that's about all I remember before everything went black, lights out. Easy as that.

29.

ONCE OR TWICE, I CAME TO as the cab sped along the
New York City streets to a location of which I hadn't the foggiest
clue. At one point, we were crossing a bridge and I thought we could
be on the way to Queens, but we could have as easily have been going
to the Bronx, or Brooklyn.

The lights were a maddening sideways blur that trailed longer
than they should have and made my head throb. Everything would
go double and then come into focus again, and I wondered if I was
dead but felt too attached to bodily pains for this to be anything
but smack dab in the middle of the solid, throbbing, and aching
material world.

I moaned something unintelligible and felt Jenny's hand on my
cheek, cradling me on her lap. She whispered something soothing,
and I felt momentarily, dreamily safe with that simple touch, but I
realized we were in for horrors after recalling what had just happened.

"Oh fuck," I moaned and was instantly shushed by her hand
over my mouth. She shook her head and held a finger up to her lips.

Our friend Mr. King was silently crying in the other seat. I felt for the presence of my ghostly friend Papa Decky, and he was out there, giving out a warm and friendly feeling of assurance, but he was floating free and not inhabiting the body he previously was. I felt for the man beside me, with his long and sorrowful face, as he whimpered on. He must have been scared out of his wits, to put it mildly.

Our driver conveyed us onwards, not saying a word, just a pale, deathly automaton of a man, with a mission to take us wherever it was he was bound to go to.

I wondered if one of us could reach through the gap in the plastic barrier between us and the front of the vehicle and take him out, put him in a choke hold until he lost consciousness so we could pull the vehicle over, but as soon as the thought entered my brain, he shot me the darkest glare I'd ever seen, as if to say he knew what was up, and he growled like a feral animal. His eyes flashed as if they were lit with a frightening cold inner flame that peered into me and shook my soul to the core.

I glanced away from him as if blinded by a light and shut my eyes and dozed while we shot through the city. The big towers of before were replaced by warehouses and garages, big sprawling spaces where people were hard at manual work if they were there at all, while the occasional lonely soul walked along the streets.

It was one of those levitathanesque buildings we pulled up to, through an open gate in a chain link fence that was quickly pulled shut behind us after we came in. The car came to a stop, and more men and a few women came and pulled us out of the car. I tried to gauge where they were from, see if they could possibly be Russians working for the mob or even their government, or if they were some kind of American militia group or terrorist cell, the list goes on. But the people truly looked like they were a small sample from a little bit of everywhere, ethnicity-wise, no way to figure out who they worked for.

I had no idea what we were going up against, and it scared the fuck out of me. That not knowing horror of groping about blindly, where everything around you was a danger and all you could do was hope to stumble through it.

They wore black outfits that were probably military fatigues but passed well enough for civilian clothes. One had a huge knife visible out of a holster on the hip. Another had a gun on a shoulder holster, its bulk pressing against me as she picked me up and jostled me along.

King tried to resist, shouting out "No, no, please no!" as he tried to crawl off and was punched once in the stomach so hard that he crumpled in on himself and then was propped up and taken along. Jenny was dragged out by a man and did not resist. I realized each of us was being moved by only one person. Whoever was dragging King about was able to lift him up like a baby, and he was not exactly light as a feather. The woman who had me in her grip put pressure on me and propped me up in ways I didn't think someone of her size would be able to. Every one of them who wasn't a person of color was pale as bone, and the ones who were of a different background had a kind of creamy skin tone. All of them seemed almost reflectively luminescent, like icy glass in the moonlight.

The buildings of what must have been Manhattan sparkled from across the river. They shimmered and waved about in reflections on the river, and those rippling mirrorings on that waterway seemed somehow more real than what was taking place. Everything was surreal to the point that it was maddening, as if this whole scene was just off enough like a dream trying to masquerade as real life.

They directed us towards a building that seemed like the carcass of a mighty sea creature washed up on the shore, Jonah's whale, floundering motionlessly in that huge city. It had massive ribs inside that propped up its hulking metallic frame, and cables that dangled down like uvula letting us know that we were in for a wild ride, all the monsters were looking to chew us up and digest us, and our better angels could only flap their wings from afar and lament our predicament.

"Move!" my captor growled, and I had no choice but to stumble along towards an uncertain destiny that awaited in the dark corners of this massive space. I complied and saw a light in the corner office, a tiny box of a room on the far side of the space, where he must have been directing us. A group of figures were huddled around a man sitting in a leather chair at an imposing desk. They got up as we approached.

"Thank you, Camissares," a familiar voice said to a stunner of a young man in a mandarin-style suit, the high, dark collar giving him the look of a priest, but so much more stylish and tailored to his muscular form than a clergyman. He was slim with long dark hair and a face that looked somewhat feminine but with a man's hard set of a jaw. He had gorgeous cheekbones and eyes that looked like two pools of deep dark night, penetrating and full of mystery.

"Will there be anything else?" the young man asked.

"That will be all, thank you," the speaker told the man, who shut some items in a suitcase and walked off. Before he left, Camissares signaled to several of the other people and they followed him out the building. The speaker was facing the wall with his back to us, but I felt the familiar suspicion creep in.

"Not affiliated anymore, Jenny?" I whispered.

"Alex, I swear . . ." she began before we were shoved forward.

"I've had the fatted calf prepared for the prodigal children upon their return," that voice said as he clapped his hands. "I had my little difficulties with my attempts at pulling that trick off and stealing what you did from the lab. But you both did the whole thing for us perfectly. Better than expected, couldn't have carried it off quite so well myself."

"Hello, David," I said, smiling ironically. "Never called. Never wrote. I was starting to think you had blocked me on Facebook too. That's no way for friends to behave towards one another, is it?"

"I missed that cheeky attitude of yours," he said and laughed an icy laugh. "I was wondering if you still were using that sharp wit of yours to pump yourself up and not quake in your boots whenever you need bailing out of an inevitable mess you get yourself into."

"And I was wondering if you were still using material excess to make your dick feel like it swings lower," I said, glancing around at this warehouse he presumably owned.

His girl twisted my arm painfully, and I groaned as it bent backwards from a direction it was intended to go. He waved a hand for her to forbear, and she instantly obeyed. I glared at her, and she merely stared disdainfully at me. Her hair was pulled back in a severe ponytail from her face, and she looked like she hadn't the slightest bit of a sense of empathy or humor about her as she coldly admired him, awaiting his command.

Jenny bravely stood resolute in her corner. King continued to whimper. "It's me you want, Father, let them . . ."

"Shush, shush, shush," he said dismissively. "We'll get to my naughty baby girl in a second. The one who wanted to go her own way, prove she's such a badass. The bait for this trap. Here we all are again." He came up to Jenny and put his arm around her. She winced at his touch, but he still held her close. "She's always been my ace in the hole as far as it concerns getting you to do what I want, Alex, isn't that right, my little girl? That's how I arranged this reunion for us all. And here we are, one big happy family."

"Kinda like a Hallmark special," I said.

"Hmmmm, almost," he mused. He put his finger to his lips as if in deep thought as he contemplatively circled around on the expensive carpet of his office. "There's just something that doesn't fit with it all. Something glaring . . ."

He fixed his gaze on me like a shark must do when it spots its prey. He sauntered up and held my head up by the chin. I glared at him and resisted the urge to spit on him, but only because it would probably be rewarded with my arm being popped entirely out of socket. "Hmmmmm . . . checks out." He tousled my hair and nudged my cheek in a very condescending way.

"My little girl . . ." he continued, coming back to her. He held up her face and gazed into her eyes. She glared back with a look that said he could render her down into candle wax and she'd still find a way to tip over and burn his house down. He quickly kissed her on either cheek. "You're a real piece of work, but Daddy still loves you, sweet pea."

He leaned on her like a piece of scenery. "Hmmmm . . . who could it be? One of these things is not like the other . . ." he sang in an eerie imitation of the kid's song. King let out another loud whimper, and Moreau shot his head around to his direction. "*Yyyyyyoooooouuuuu* . . ." Moreau growled in a scarily low register.

Moreau leaned in towards him and slowly advanced. "You."

King whispered once more and tried to bring up his hands to shield himself, but he was held back and pulled upright. It was truly sad to see this poor man squirming and blubbering. "Please, no, please . . ." he begged in a series of moans that had the cadence of a rosary being prayed.

"You."

He slowly stalked towards him with the confidence of a predator, every step making the man more terrified than before. He knew that his life was measured in the few strides it took to reach him. Sweat dripped down the man's body and his legs were threatening to give out, but he was still being held fast with an iron grip.

"You would have sold out your own species for a chance at making your name known," Moreau declared. "You didn't care if this virus got into the wrong hands, as long as you were there to take credit for it being stopped. You wanted to break all the eggs and have the omelet to yourself too. Don't bother to deny it, it's written over every beat of your scared, weak heart, and every black thought that seeks to weave new lies to cover up for your sins."

"Puh-please . . ." he sighed.

"C'mon! E-fuckin-nuff already!" I shouted. "Let the man go!"

"And let him walk out of a court on a technicality? Please," Moreau sneered. He advanced closer and closer. Step after tiny step. He stopped about ten feet from him and eyed him appraisingly. "Besides, that would spoil what I have in mind." He shot a hand up, quicker than I could see. One second, he was standing there judging him with a sinister glare that made him shrink like a salted slug, and the next, he was holding him up by the neck with a steely grip, one arm extended and holding him high off the ground. He snapped the poor man's neck and let him crumple to the floor like a puppet with the strings cut, a tumble of limbs in a sad horrible pile.

"NO!" I shouted. "Damn you, why?" I glared at him with hatred in my eyes and then sunk down in physical exhaustion, but still being held up by the demonic girl with the intense muscles.

How did he do what he did? I wondered. He shouldn't have been able to snap a man's neck with one hand. And the way he moved simply seemed impossible. He was there one second and in a different location in another.

"There," he said, brushing his hands off on each other like he had touched something dusty and was cleaning the grime off. "Now we can hear ourselves think."

"Bastard!" Jenny shouted as she tried to lunge at him. Her captor didn't even let her move an inch, and she could only struggle in his grip.

"Shhhhh, dearest," he whispered. "You wouldn't want to spoil this moment for me, would you? Why can't we all just enjoy this time together? What does it say in Isaiah? 'I am about to do a new thing; now it springs forth, do you not perceive it?' I've got big plans for this world, we can finally make the wrong things right! Make the crooked paths straight! Unfuck the fucked-up things man has done for centuries!"

"By killing people!" I spat at him. I strained against the woman holding me back, but I might as well have tried to bend manacles with my bare hands. I was extremely confused, because it wasn't any G.I. Joe, kung-fu grip she had, no krav maga fancy shit going on. She was only a regular woman from all appearances, but there was a furnace of power burning throughout her and a body like the most tempered elements, unyielding and able to stand fast without even the slightest strain.

"Oh, when I get done, you'll understand how little these lives mean when compared to a great destiny for the world!" He rushed up to me and had a look on his face as he spoke like he was pleading a case that had the weight of the world hanging in the balance of a pair of scales. He held my shoulders so he could get a look at me with such pleading, needing eyes. "When you left me, I was hurt. I had such dreams and expectations for you. And to see you waste your talents. Idly stealing from petty people. With your gifts, we could have taken on the decadent worthless institutions that are holding mankind back. We could have been the change that the world so desperately needs."

"Yeah, well, not sorry to disappoint."

"If you would only find the hardness in your heart to act, we could do great and terrible things, young man," he said.

I sensed desperation in him, like he believed he would be able to convince everyone else he was right if he could only convince me. I was some focus of his, that laser-intense beam of his obsession was narrowed on me like a sniper's sights, and I wanted to run like mad for cover to shake it but could only stand out in the open.

He went on. "Haven't you found yourself watching the world tear itself apart and said to yourself 'If only someone *could* do something!' Haven't you found yourself wondering how much time is left to this world before the human race turns the climate into a carbon-fueled furnace, or some madman pushes a button that sends the fury of a thousand suns raining down right on us because they want to make the world pay if they can't have it their own way? Haven't you thought these terrifying thoughts and said to yourself, 'This. Must. Not. Be. So!'"

"I see someone who's just like any of those small and petty men," I replied. "Because they think their solution is the only way, nobody else's will work."

"If only you could see the things I have seen!" he implored. "I could make you see things my way . . ." he trailed off, with that grin of his. "But wait." He held out his hand by his ear like a stage actor. "Who's this I hear coming to join our reunion? Maybe a special surprise guest that my people found lurking about? Sounds like someone has a death wish! But maybe a bit of leverage will get you to snap to." He kept his eyes eerily fixed on me as he walked towards a door where his nameless servants were dragging in someone who wasn't putting up much resistance.

I couldn't stop staring at Moreau's eyes, which seemed to catch more light than they naturally should. They flashed the way a cat's eyes glowed in the dark, giving them a look like there was an inner fire that animated the man. He could capture a person with only that stare alone, and I couldn't look away even though I wanted to tear my gaze from his direction and take a moment and remember who I was and get ahold of my wits, because the more I stared at him, the more I wanted to not resist.

"You fucking bastard!" I shouted when I recognized who he was dragging in. I struggled against the grip that held me, but my captor only laughed, making me want to rip her lungs out until she couldn't breathe a sound out of them anymore. "Let him go, or I swear to God I won't rest until you die screaming!"

It was A.J. He was led in with hardly any fight against them at all, maybe an imperious glance when the one leading him bumped his shoulder. He was like a man going to an execution squad with all his sins washed away, his soul all resolute and shining and silvery bright, ready to face that firing squad.

"Here he is," Moreau declared. "The man who got the whole ball rolling. I bet you heard a bit about our past, huh, Allie Boy?" He was pulling in little things to dig in that would sting like calling me Allie, ways to get under my skin.

I needed to focus, not let him distract me, but the world was a red blur of blind rage, and I couldn't calm myself down. And even if I did, what would it matter? I looked down at my wrist and saw it was the purple and green of an over ripened piece of fruit, covered with sickly looking bruises from my struggles. How in the hell was this tiny woman doing this to me?

"Bet you have only scratched the surface about what your pop was involved in, and you want to know all the juicy details. What skeletons are in the family closet, where are all the bodies hidden? And believe you me, kiddo, there are bodies aplenty along the way."

"Stop it, David," A.J. said. "Let's leave the kids out of this and settle it our own way. Why don't you let them go?"

"Oh, they're past the point of no return," Moreau said. "They've been wound up in it all since the days they were born, and you're the one to blame."

"What are you talking about?" I asked him.

"I tried to protect you, Alex," A.J. said with a sorrow in his gaze that spoke of weight carried on shoulders for all a man's life. "I know we can never get the time back that we lost, but I can still save you." His eyes shot up at Moreau in a gaze that matched the man's otherworldly eyes with a magnetic intensity that said it wasn't to be looked away from either. "Last chance. You gonna let them go?"

"You're playing poker with no hand." Moreau laughed. "What are you going to threaten me with? The scorn of an aging man?"

"I get by with a little help from my friends," A.J. said, reminding me of songs we used to sing together. He smiled at me, then he glanced up around the huge warehouse.

In every space of every catwalk all around the building, a ghost appeared. Some edged in on the ground floor around us. They seemed to be a diverse crowd of the deceased. There were people from every era, all presumably gathered right there in New York City. There were disco cats with huge pants and shoes, Jamaican men with long and glorious dreadlocks, Irish immigrants in bowler hats, Italian Americans in their Sunday best, children in knee breeches with rosy cheeks, cute Asian American kids who looked like they just got out of school, and Native American people from back when this island was rightfully theirs, all brought together here by my old man in one big crowd he had convinced to come on his last stand.

Almost every one was carrying some kind of flammable material. Gallon containers of gasoline. Containers that looked like they were filled with what appeared to be napalm. Some other items I had no fucking idea about, but they were probably things that go boom. A few were holding grenades. He had managed to conjure them all up as solid as could be to hold their objects up and carry out his plan for him.

Spirits of long-dead people began circling the persons in the warehouse like a swarm of bees, grabbing ahold of them and getting pushed off and then grabbing back on again.

"What the fuck?" Moreau mouthed. His men were all speechless and fighting. They couldn't see the dead, but they could see the objects floating in the air as if they were hovering on a breeze. "Get him!" he roared to his men.

They flew on A.J. like a pack of dogs, beating and clawing at him. I could see bits of skin go flying and I cringed, tears streaming down my face to see him suffer like that.

"I love you, baby boy!" he mouthed. I think he did at least. I swear he did. "Now!" A.J. shouted, and before I could say or do anything, I was flown out of the room by two ghosts who whipped me out so fast I couldn't even see the ground as we flew over it. Everything was a blur.

I saw Moreau's still surprised face as I flew out of the building. And that's when the warehouse turned into a big ball of orange flame. I was out of the danger zone but close enough to feel the heat, like the full and blazing sun on a midsummer day, only so much more intense. It was enough to make all my exposed skin feel like it was burnt and raw. My black pants and jacket felt instantly hot as an oven.

I wanted to race back in there but knew it wouldn't do any good. Anything in there was being chemically reduced to its elements inside that inferno. The fire wouldn't even let me get close, and I backed up enough to get out of its searing intensity. I had blisters on my skin.

"Nooooo!" I howled, my moaning a sudden bolt of blood-torn sorrow that came from a dark place inside me I didn't know existed but was always ready and waiting. That sorrow making a mold around my soul and trying to shape me in its form. I tried to remain strong against it, but it washed over me in waves that threatened to tear me from myself and leave me drowned and defeated. I tried to think of any happy thought at all, something to make the light shine in the darkness, something that that absolute hopeless dread couldn't comprehend and would have to fly away from, but couldn't and just cried and cried.

In many ways, A.J. failed as a father. Failed miserably. But when I caught that peace-out of all peace-outs in his eyes, all was atoned for and I wanted to be a sixteen again and be able to have one more beer with him on Windsong's back porch as I snuck one of his cigarettes I swore would be the last and argued with him about something trivial.

As I was thinking these panicked thoughts, wondering exactly how the hell I should make my exit out of there and vamoose before the five-o got there, a burning form came running out of the building. It dove to the ground like a star shooting out of the sky, and rolled itself out, water sizzling in puddles as it came into contact with it. It had the form of a man and lay there for a second moaning, and that's when I decided to hustle the fuck out of there real quick.

He rolled so his body was facing my direction, his eyes lighting on me and a look of horrible recognition on his face as he registered who I was. He slowly got up, and I ran as fast as I could, but it was no use. He was already in front of me, his terribly burnt form bursting into my path and blocking my escape. I fell as I slammed into him, like I had run full force into an iron gate.

His whole body had a patchwork of burns on it that nobody should have been able to survive, let alone manage to overtake me in a full-on sprint with. The bottom right quarter of his face was charred, with his teeth sticking out of an exposed jaw where his cheek should have been. His incisors were unnaturally long. His body had clothes burnt into the skin, and a huge patch of ribs were sticking out through the charred mass of his left side. Blood oozed from the wound. He smelled like a huge log that was burning in a fire, all sappy and full of memories of the earth. The smell reminded me of burning incense.

I tried to get up and run and was immediately dealt a blow to the stomach that made me crumple to my knees. I rolled onto the ground and wheezed, coughing as I tried to get up, but could only curl up in pain. A kick sent me rolling in a mass of flopping arms and kicking feet like an ungraceful pinwheel.

"Your damned family line ends tonight for what you did to him!"

he whispered to me, his breath smelling of burnt flesh. "I don't know what he saw in you, but I only see a snack."

"Buddy, I did you a favor," I wheezed. "Now you can do what you've always wanted to do without the top brass breathing down your neck. Take up ballroom dance. Play piano. Watch enough Bob Ross to learn to paint happy little trees. Live your dreams . . ." I tried to right myself and felt a rib pop. I knew several had to be broken.

His foot came down again and merely rolled me back, and I couldn't do anything but helplessly be pushed down to the ground. He lifted up his foot again, and I held up my hands in a timeout gesture and shouted "*WAIT!*" at the top of my lungs. "Wait, please . . ." I said, stalling for time. "Is it . . . is it okay? You don't mind if I smoke in here?" I laughed, and he punched me so hard the world went dark again, and I felt like I was going to slip away for a minute. "Oh, I get it! You're trying to quit!" Again, another blow, this one making my left eye swell shut so tight I couldn't even see out of it.

He closed in on me, and I tried to hold him back, but he was too strong, there was simply no resisting him. I felt his teeth sink into my neck and thought he was going to rip my throat out with them, but instead, I went to another place and time.

I was in Windsong's house with A.J. It was all sunshine and my lunch box was heavy, but I held onto it with both hands, making sure the plastic clasps didn't come undone and make the contents spill out again. I was scared and trying to be brave, knowing that it was a step into a new chapter of life, but one that would involve a traumatic sundering from the things I'd known, the ease and comfort of my earlier childhood, and into a world of fending for myself among strangers and being challenged with puzzling new things to learn and new mysteries to solve.

"You're gonna love your first day of school, young sir, Alex!" A.J. cooed, cheering me on. "Riding inta battle on the school bus, rescuin' damsels in distress. It's gonna be great, you're gonna meet all kinds of people and make so many new friends."

And then just like that, the image was gone, like I had flown through the sky on the winds of time and crashed down to the present from a great height. My tormentor held me in his arms and sighed in relief as he drew back and took a deep breath. He made a noise of sheer pleasure as his eyes rolled back in his head and he laughed in savage glee. His skin was healing, the black and charred parts of it receding as if they were channels of a river valley drying up in the sun.

I thought I was losing my mind.

"There we go," he said in his heavily accented voice. His skin was filling out, but it was pale and reflective. His hair was thick and black, coming up around his broad forehead, and a beard on his chin was visible.

"Wh's goin' on? 'M I dyin'?" I slurred, my head lolling to one side. I remembered once when I had a flu so bad, I was weak and could barely move. I had contemplated calling for an ambulance, because I was afraid I wouldn't be able to get up of my own accord. I felt like that, only this time, I was afraid reprieve wouldn't come in a waking up without a fever like it had that other time.

I've finally done it, I thought.

Out of all the wrong turns in a short and oftentimes happy life full of crooked ways where the road ahead wasn't nearly as mapped out as it is for everyone else, those fortunate ones who had their feet set by others on the well-worn paths that so many had tread over and over before for them to clear the way into their safe and secure little existences, I'd stumbled on the one that led to the end.

I had finally hit that dead-end wall, down that dark alley where the guardian angels have given up on you.

I had to go for the glory, chase that rush, and always feel that edge. Even when the edge was a knife's blade that threatened to kill me with a thousand cuts, I walked along it, because it was the only way I had ever known. And so I chose the safety of danger at all times instead of the comfort of a slow death by being an ordinary man who could only follow the rules and do what they all told him to do.

It had finally led me here, to being held in his hands like a butterfly that some kid had picked up off the ground. Wings half smashed as it tries to flutter into the sky it used to travel so gracefully through, stuck on the ground that it had carefully avoided all this time.

"Soon . . ." he whispered.

I tried to come up with something epigrammatic and memorable for my last words but could only drool a bit of blood as I tried to breathe instead of cough and just muttered, "Uhhhhhh . . ." I'd always hoped my epitaph would be better than the first noise I made when I lost my virginity, but there you go.

"I'd love to prolong this for what you've done, but it's time we end this, huh?" he said, smiling.

I didn't even have the strength to try to bat an arm at him but tried all the same and only watched with detached interest as my hand flopped about, all pins and needles and fallen asleep. All I could do was breathe, and I gasped one last bit of air in, thinking that this would be my final act.

A great noise roared about, like a whirlwind trying to fit in through a front door, and I was back to lying on the ground. I assumed I was being laid out to receive the coup de grâce, the killing blow, like a sacrificial lamb on an altar.

But I was gently lifted in a pair of strong arms and gazed up into a woman's eyes, like a pretty pietà scene, and I thought I was already dead. It was that Haunting Woman again. Her violet-blue eyes gleamed with an icy fire, and her arms felt like a river of electric current. She had on the same outfit from the lab, where we knocked her out, but a Japanese-looking sword was slung over one shoulder.

My assailant's body lay on the ground several feet away, but his head was on the ground only inches away and staring at me.

I knew I was dying. I knew the injuries I had sustained were life ending. I felt so cold. My chest felt tight and every breath was a struggle that didn't want to come out. I had asthma as a child and knew what it was to have every bit of air coming into your lungs be a complete herculean effort, but this was different. I was coughing up blood and knew that meant something serious.

I felt strangely detached from it all though.

I had done so many crazy things, defied death so long that it was like a friend from school that you always know is gonna be around, all you have to do is look them up and they'll be up to the same old things. I had lots of things I wanted to do, sure, but they could wait for some other lifetime. Maybe one without all the trauma and fear, where everything is all that warm and rosy feeling of when you're on the edge of fighting off sleep for so long, but then you finally decide to give in and stretch out to snooze after a long and busy day.

I stared into a puddle, and the city lights that reflected in its ripples were a dancing string of snaking, sparkly diamonds, all wiggling to the music of the universe, all dancing just for me. I thought of how it would be nice if Korey could see something this beautiful and peaceful.

And then my eyes shot open, like I'd been hit with a bolt of liquid golden light.

Korey!

I was going to die here, and she would never know anything of what really happened. She would worry her all-too brilliant and spectacular brains out about it and that would eat her alive. She wouldn't know the real me, the one I tried so hard to keep from her, the one I fought to protect her from. I would die here and not be able to make it up to her. Maybe I would be one of my sad and colorless flitting ghosts, waiting around for some poor sucker who could see me, so I could latch onto them for any semblance of human warmth.

"Oh, you're not going to drink from the cup of death today, Alex Rose," the woman whispered. Her voice was so firm in her assurance that I was comforted by that sentiment, even though I swore that she was lying to me. "But you will see many stranger things in the life to come than any of those who travel to that 'undiscovered country from whose bourn no traveler returns.' There shall be plenty of time for death to come, but not for you. Not for a long time. Maybe not ever."

She took her wrist in her mouth and bit deep, splashing the blood onto my lips. It tingled where the droplets touched, like a hand that has gone numb, all pins and needles, but strangely electric, as if pinpoints of energy were trapped in each drop, releasing the chaotic potential stored up in them as they pattered into my open mouth and eager, thirsting tongue. It was delicious and sweet.

"What are you doing?" I managed to groan as the blood spilled from my mouth while I spoke.

"Repaying a kindness that was done to me years ago," she replied. "I don't know if you'll thank me for it, but it's better than bleeding out in the street. I'm giving you the choice to go on living, if you're willing to fight for it."

As she spoke, she opened up her neck with her index fingernail and stared at the blood flowing down onto her breast for a second as it spilled that crimson rose bursts of droplets in crooked rivers down her chest. I didn't know what she meant, but I knew I would do anything to hang on for Korey. She put her neck up to my mouth, and I tried to shy away, the thought of blood seemed like a contamination. And then the blood went down my throat, and I was lost in a hurricane of sensation, with everything in the whole wide world happening all at once.

Vampire! I knew that's what these beings were.

She had drained my blood that night long ago as a child! That was what the one she just killed did moments ago too, he was feeding off of me. All of them in the warehouse were vampires. Even David Moreau, this whole time!

That was why she was giving me her blood! She was making me into one like her. The thought was abhorrent to me; I hated violence, I was no killer. But her blood was the answer to every longing question I had ever dared to ask, and so delicious as it flooded my mouth and started a fire in my heart and mind.

Where everything was numb before, I now had an instant, perpetual vitality that made me want to jump up and spin in the air. I think I writhed, and she held me down. A moment before, I was resolved to accept my death, and now I was greedily drinking life in its most intense form as it opened up a new existence to me that I couldn't turn away from. Seconds before, I had given up, but now I wanted to give the world everything I had, all the time without stopping to think about a thing, because everything was so shining and golden.

I locked onto her neck with my lips, clutching onto her body like a greedy child, as if I was afraid she would pull it away. My legs wrapped tightly around her legs in a gesture that was part affection for someone who would bring such a wonderful gift, the best gift I ever had, and part need, like I was magnetically drawn to her.

It was a mobius strip of connected energy that made me feel the very insides of her veins spilling out into me as it revived and exhilarated me. I heard her cry out in pain, and I didn't want to hurt her, but I was outside myself, and I could only give in to this feeling of the greatest satiation I had ever experienced, which strangely left me wanting more.

There was only she and I at that moment, locked together in a sweet embrace that contained the warmth I had been missing from every impression of existence I had ever experienced before, like they were all just an overture to a greater symphony full of tones that would get played out more fully as the performance went on. She pulled her neck away, and I almost cried, stunned by the perceptions of the world coming flooding back in after all that, knowing that they were all pale compared to that utter delight of her warm and sticky blood filling my mouth.

But then as I looked around me, I saw that the city was not what I was expecting to see. The night was no longer a realm of uncertainty, a forest that you don't know how to get out of once you've wandered off the trail. I stared at the fire of the building and it seemed to be pouring out in a river of hot light, with tongues of flame that wanted to reach all the way up to Heaven. Every ember was a dancer in the brightness that I could follow the movements of and watch with intense interest until they disappeared into the velvety dark sky.

Rats scuttled out of the burning building, fleeing to safety, and I could see each individual one as if I was a few inches away. The pinkness of their tails was so hypnotizing, as they wiggled along behind them, scurrying away on small scratching feet.

And all the noise around me, that was coming in in ways I had never experienced before. A tornado of sound was tearing through the streets of New York, filled with every single murmuring that could be uttered, every footfall taken, every horn honking in traffic, and every lap of the East River on the banks, pouring like a funnel was spilling it into my ears.

It was dizzying, feeling that press on all sides from everything all at once. I tried to cover my ears, but everything still came on in, vibrating and thrumming as if the noises were coming through my bones. I breathed in deeply and wasn't taking shallow gasps anymore, my ribs no longer felt broken. I took in a deep breath to test it and held it in to see. My chest felt as sturdy as steel scaffolding.

I swore that the world was going to crush me on the spot. I was at the center of everything and not able to process it. Things were in my peripheral vision that seemed to be multiplied and moving about, but when I looked over at them, they were their own completely normal selves, just a building towering up into the sky or a bag blowing about on the ground. Everything seemed alive and breathing, but they still retained their original shapes and forms.

It had tinges of the strange and surreal like a hallucination, but it wasn't. There was no worry that what I was seeing was some kind of illusion that might mislead me. I knew which way was up. Looking around, dumbfounded, I was about to speak when she touched a finger to my lips and held one to hers in the sign of quiet.

"I know you've been through a lot," the Haunting Woman said

in a whisper of a voice that still echoed in my ears, "and that this is a whole lot to take in. But the night is far from over."

She pointed up at the roof of a neighboring warehouse, and I saw several people hanging off its rooftop in impossible positions. Vampires with pale skin and glowing eyes. They climbed down the side, not sticking to the wall like a lizard, but by grabbing edges and corners with incredible grip strength, leaping from point of contact to point of contact. They seemed mechanical, children's toys that could be twisted into any configurations with their flexibility and contortions. They were wearing everyday suits or dark jeans and T-shirts, and that made it all the more shocking of a sight, seeing people who could be average New Yorkers you pass on the streets that were bending and twisting themselves in inhuman poses as they scampered down a wall.

I didn't have time to take that in, though, because one by one, they jumped off of it and then bound with unbelievably large strides towards us, like they were walking on the moon, but with balletic grace in huge leaps that took them closer to us.

"Try and keep down, but fight for your life if you must," she said, and then she unsheathed her katana and jumped in to attack a tall man in a suit with a dagger drawn, who was bearing down on us.

I watched in amazement as she cut off his head and it went flying about in a comet trail of blood. She immediately shot towards another, her movements so quick it seemed she was materializing in front of them.

A man with curly long black hair punched me in the face and sent me staggering backwards. A pain that felt like my teeth were being ground together and my jaw was being clenched shut made me pause for a second. I knew it was probably broken, but as soon as the sensation occurred, I heard cracks and felt muscles throbbing and bones set themselves into place and realized the pain was gone. I opened my mouth to be sure and it was as good as new.

My attacker didn't let up and came at me with a barrage of punches to the chest that left me with broken ribs and made it impossible to breathe. The intense force of his punches should have killed me for sure from any number of them, but something kept pulling me together again after every devastating blow. I began to see where the attacks were coming from and made attempts to block them.

Finally dodging to one side, I punched him in the jaw with an uppercut with all my force behind it and watched as he cartwheeled, end over end up several feet in the air. I stared at him in astonishment—no punch of mine could be powerful enough to do that. He bounced up to his feet again and stared for a second in shock as well before his face turned into rage and he came at me again, this time with a powerful kick to my solar plexus that made me fly back. I immediately got up and into a fighting stance.

The fact that he couldn't hurt me with his fiercest attacks and I could make him fly several feet with awkward punches made me realize I was stronger than he was. He couldn't do enough damage to kill me with his attacks, any one of which could definitely have done the trick on a human being. I was durable enough to weather them and too quick to heal the wounds he could inflict. He was trying to wear me out so I could be taken down like his companion who the Haunting Woman took out, head ripped off or killed in some other horrible way.

He kicked again, but this time I saw it coming and grabbed his leg and whipped him around and threw him, surprised at how far

I sent him. He went crashing into a broken concrete pier column, with pieces of rebar sticking out and hung there, impaled on them. I couldn't believe my dumb luck.

Job well done, I thought, and I was about to join the woman again when I heard a sickening sound of bones grinding and flesh being torn as he slowly slid himself along the length of the bars. He was walking bent backwards, pulling himself along the lengthy pieces of rusted metal that were stuck clean through him. Blood dripped from the rebar in long, thick threads that reached to the ground and pooled in dark puddles.

"Stay down!" I shouted, to no avail.

He righted himself and ripped out one of the pieces of metal that had been through him seconds ago right out of the ground and swung it wildly at me. I ducked it once as it flew by and then stepped to one side as he swung it around downwards. I kicked his exposed chest and knocked him down, grabbing his weapon from him.

That's when something snapped. Maybe I'd taken enough punishment from him, maybe it was that he was aligned with the monsters who killed my father, but a feeling that was pure, blind rage took over and moved my muscles in ways that weren't my own. I smacked him hard enough with the twisted metal pole to knock him down, and didn't stop there but pounded him until I got tired of that and then threw it aside and used my fists.

I screamed as I did it, a howl that could have been heard in Hell, full of all the anger and fury that I had saved up, as I felt his bones in his skull cracking as my fists slammed into it. Roaring like a lion, I beat him as he stared up at me helplessly, with the eyes of a sacrificial animal that knows it's about to die, only he wasn't accepting, his look was pure fear.

An amazing new energy flooded my body, but I was spent in my soul, simply wanting to curl up and whimper, and so I let up and turned away from him. Every instinct told me he was dangerous, but I couldn't bring myself to kill someone who was down and helpless. Leaving him to his injuries, I turned around to find the woman but heard him laughing as he righted himself and leaped onto my back, biting into my neck with extremely sharp teeth that shredded my skin and made blood spray everywhere in front of me. His nails scratched and tore as well, digging into my flesh and ripping whole chunks of it off.

I swung him over and slammed him into the concrete. He sliced into my wrist with his fingernails as I tried to pin him down, so I slammed his head into the asphalt with enough force to feel the bones crack again, and then I grabbed his neck and twisted, hearing an awful snap. I didn't stop there and kept on twisting as his head flopped about on sinews and muscle. The head was wrenched completely backwards, mouth open, eyes staring into nothing, and I kept twisting until it was finally facing forwards again. I kicked his chest as hard as I could while still holding onto the staring head, and his body collapsed to the ground in a tangle of monstrously convulsing limbs.

In awe at what I had done, I tossed the head off to the side and wanted to fall over out of exhaustion and sheer horror, but I searched for the woman instead. She had taken on several attackers while I had been occupied with only the one. About a half dozen dismembered and decapitated bodies lay on the ground twitching and clawing, and she was finishing off her last, slicing across his chest with her katana before she whipped the shining sword around and cut his head clean off.

I was so sure I couldn't possibly move, but I was brought out of it by the touch of my savior, the Haunting Woman, pulling me along and saying, "I'm Kitane, and I'm your maker. We need to go. Now!"

I looked up and saw more were coming, led by the incredible tall man with the dark hair, Camissares. Sirens blared as emergency vehicles and fire engines pulled up to the scene. She grabbed me by the waist, and I almost cried out in surprise as I realized she was flying and carrying me off. I glanced back and saw Camissares's icy stare as he watched us disappear, coldly appraising, like a cat watching a wounded mouse crawl away.

"One thing," I said through the roar of the wind. "We need to stop by my hotel. I'm not leaving this city without my coat!"

EPILOGUE:
THE BLOOD THIEF

KITANE FLEW THROUGH THE NIGHT SKY, a shooting star draped in a black skirt, holding me in her arms like I was a baby, and maybe I was, a baby something, I wasn't sure what, but as abilities and experiences went, it wasn't human. The night roared around me, a living furnace of darkness with flashing starlight bursts of color that I tried to pick out and focus on as we raced through the skies and across the North American continent.

"New York City isn't safe for us at the moment," she'd told me. I wasn't sure what was and wasn't safe anymore, so I took her word for it.

Kitane had me feed from her again in that hotel room, and she drank some of my blood as well in the exchange. We fed like that for a long while. I took a great deal of blood from her, and then it was her turn. When it was over, I felt stronger, like my skin wasn't enough to

341

contain it all and I would tear down a wall if I simply leaned into it.

We shot along on our night journey, and even though I was up frighteningly high, I could see details on the ground that I knew I couldn't have ever seen before. I could make out drivers in cars and shapes of signs on streets. The moon wasn't even full, and I could see details on the ground that weren't illuminated by man-made lights. It was all so startling that I wanted to cry and sometimes forgot to breathe and then noticed that even my breathing was different. I could hold my breath in longer, several minutes longer when I tried it, to the point where I finally gave up and took a big gasp of air in, either for force of habit or for fear that I would never remember how to do it again.

"It's almost daylight," Kitane said with a note of concern in her voice that I'd never heard about something so commonplace as the sunrise. "We need to get to ground."

I was hearing her loud and clear over the howl of the wind. "So, what happens?" I flippantly asked. "We light on fire? We turn into pumpkins?"

"We turn human," she said, serious as a heart attack.

"Aren't we still human?" I asked, but realized it was a foolish question as soon as I said it. No human could do the things I had done, heal the wounds I healed, or see the world like I saw it then.

"We need to get somewhere where we can wait, where it's dark, away from the sun's light, and we won't be exposed."

My heart raced at the sight of a skyline I knew so very well. We were all the way to the coast as the familiar lights of San Francisco loomed ahead of us. The Oakland Bay Bridge straddled the waters like a huge fiery dragon, and the Transamerica Pyramid jutted up from the city like a monumental relic from the past in the middle of it all. We flew over the crowded hills and touched down near Golden Gate Park.

"We need to hurry," Kitane said as we hustled along the streets, which were quiet but not deserted, with people sleeping about, a few wandering around and talking out to no one or everyone.

I thought I heard one speaking, but the words didn't have the flow of an actual conversation, and I was catching images too. I rubbed my eyes, seeing if it was a trick of the light, and wondered if the images were in my brain. I focused on a man on the corner and, don't ask me how, but I knew the words and images were all flowing into and through my mind from him. His thoughts were a loop of disjointed conspiracy theories, with images of gray aliens and reptiles that wore human skin and controlled the world, along with some very unpleasant racist ideas about migrants in there to boot. He shouted audibly at me as I passed, and I couldn't help but stop and stare at him.

"Come on!" I heard right before I was dragged along by Kitane. "We can't stay here staring at people in the streets. We were being followed, and I believe I shook them somewhere over the Rockies, but they won't be far behind."

"Who are they?"

"The Firstborn of Death," she said, and I was taken back to that field from all those years ago. She had been fighting them before; that dead body lying next to her that night was one of them. "They're a rumor and a boogeyman among creatures like us. The killers of the killers."

"And what are creatures like us?"

"Vampires."

I knew as much, but it was still a shock to hear that one out loud. I should have taken that in with all the requisite wide eyes and incredulous questions that such a revelation would require, but my other senses were suddenly on alarm from an apparition I felt a powerful sensation from. It was almost as intense a migraine, enough to make my vision blur into halos and my eyes to feel like they were being squeezed out of their sockets, but it also had a tug on my heart that made it feel like it would burst out of my chest, it was pounding so hard.

Kitane sensed my distress and tried to reach out to me, but I brushed off her gesture and stared at the source of my discomfort. It was a ghost who had the build of a man, but his form was something I couldn't clearly make out. It was like he had been peeled apart inside out but was still whole.

Blood floated around him, a thick mist that circled him the way clouds do a planet. His garments were tattered rags, blackened and torn as if he had been sleeping on a hearth all night and rolled in the ashes. He had a hood that he quickly pulled up as if he didn't want to be seen by me, even though he had to have manifested just to be seen by me. He fell to his knees and raised his head up to Heaven, and even though no sound issued from his mouthless face, it seemed as if he was crying out to the stars for his frightening condition.

I tried to reach out to him, and he darted back, as if I would hurt him.

"We need to go," Kitane urged, and I grudgingly obeyed.

We had reached a seedy motel that seemed like it charged by the hour for ladies of the night and people who were not sleeping much at that hour due to their intake of uppers. Kitane hustled us in, and after a short exchange with the man behind the front desk, obtained us a room. She handed him fistfuls of cash, warning that if anyone should come around asking about us, we were never here, and then took us to a room on the second floor, where she immediately shut the door and drew the heavy drapes over the windows, blocking out any light from outside.

"*You* should get some rest," she said, a tone of warning to her voice. "You've been through quite a bit, and you'll be at your strongest if you let your body heal itself. Even creatures of the night need their rest."

"So that's what we are?" I asked, unable to resist running my tongue along my very sharp and slightly elongated canines. "Vampires are real."

"You were drained by one. You drank my blood and became one. It doesn't get much more real than that. You've got plenty of questions, I'm sure, but now is not the time. Sleep."

I wanted to protest, but I was powerfully tired, not the physical weariness I was used to as a human, but a sort of energy low that made me want to drag along, where before I could have led a parade across the continent.

"That would be the wounds you sustained. You'll heal, but it takes a little out of you. Blood helps, and mine is some of the oldest and strongest there is. You'll find that you're a stronger vampire than most for having drank it." She bit into her wrist with her fang, then slashed it deeply across the width of it and held it out. I hesitated and she said, "Hurry, before it heals," and then I took it in my mouth and felt like the sun had come into the room, only it was inside of her body, not orbiting about.

My legs went weak, and I almost fell over, but I held strong and drank on. I could see her concern in visions through the blood. She intended to stay up throughout the day and keep watch.

Her wrist healed and the blood stopped flowing. I swallowed

the last bit, savoring the taste as it slid down my throat. "Now sleep," Kitane said. And strangely enough, I did just that.

I don't remember what I dreamed about, but I am sure I did. I was awakened with about an hour to go until the sun set on that summer day by Kitane, as she shook me with enough force to make the bed move. "We need to go, now!"

"What?" I asked, unsure of where I was for a second in the unfamiliar surroundings.

"They've found us!" she yelled, just before the door burst open and three vampires, all in street clothes, with gleaming knives drawn and at the ready stormed in. Kitane grabbed me by the waist right as one made a move towards me with his knife, slashing my abdomen and opening up a huge wound that was only starting to heal when Kitane kicked the window out and dragged me out and into the light.

I crumpled in a heap and landed on my ass as we fell into an open dumpster below our room. The trash in its white plastic bags cushioned us for the most part, but some of it was hard and hurt to land on.

"Hurry!" she yelled, pulling me out. We took off and ran, as one of the now human vampires jumped down after us. His cohorts ran back into the room to take off after us, possibly to be in wait to flank us up ahead, and so I ran even faster.

We raced out into a busy street, cars almost hitting us as we darted between them. My wound wasn't healing, and instead blood seeped out that soaked into my white tuxedo shirt I still had on from the party. If I hadn't started to heal in the room, it might have been fatal.

"We need to get somewhere dark," Kitane said. "That hospital up ahead, go!" She pointed to a huge, abandoned building that loomed ahead of us.

I had always been afraid of the dark as a kid, but now I worried I would die in the light before I made it to that blessed unilluminated edifice.

I ran on.

11:59 PM
April 30th, 2024
San Diego, California

THE STORY
CONTINUES ...

From *The Blood Thief, Vol. 2: My Own Personal Bethlehem*

THE ATTACKER DID NOT EVEN FLINCH and merely just laughed until the man exhausted himself and simply grabbed at the lapels of his beautiful dark coat. Her shadowy savior quickly grabbed his wrists and held him at arm's length like a misbehaving child who struck at his parent.

He then pulled the man into him in a deadly embrace, spinning around with him like a lover, their silhouettes in the shadow twining around each other like they were sharing a stolen kiss before they bid each other good night.

He leaned back as the dead man slid down at his feet, and she recognized the look on the killer's face. It was one she had seen many a time in her profession, that exhausted but dreamily ecstatic glow of a man who had just been brought to climax, the fierce joy in his eyes of a wolf who just made a kill. He heaved a great sigh, and let a wrist go that she didn't realize he was still hanging onto.

"They taste different when they're scared," he said, matter-of-factly, as if she knew what he meant. "These men go about bringing pain and fear to others all their lives, never knowing how it feels themselves. You experience something beautiful and new when they come face to face with it. It's almost like they're virgins. Almost."

The body was crumpled like garbage. What was once a thing to be feared was discarded rubbish, littering the paving stones. That man, if that's what he was and not some vengeful demon, had played a good game with him and he was onto the last amusement. The final one of their number was trying to run off, bolting down the streets almost a block away, panting like a startled animal in breaths she could hear all the way where she crouched. The dark man popped up right behind him and crushed his skull with one blow. He then sauntered back her way, doing a brief dance in the middle of the distance and then walking dreamily on.

She was going to be next, she thought. Saved from her attackers only to have to face up to the consequences of her sins by the devil himself, this demon who danced with his victims under the street-lights until their souls left their exhausted forms and soared off to their rest from his kisses that brought death. Here in the back streets of a humid Southern town on a night that seemed a dream she just couldn't wake up from, she would finally be called to judgment and she wasn't ready to admit that she was some poor sinner.

No, she decided, she was going to go out with a fire in her heart against those who would condemn her without walking in her shoes.

"No need to fight me, sweet one," he purred. His dark hair fell over one eye and the other stared at her with a penetrating gaze that stripped her secrets from her and made her feet freeze to the ground even though she knew she should at least try to run away.

He was all of a sudden right in front of her, again seemingly before he even disappeared from the spot he was in before. She thought it was some kind of magic, like he had disappeared and reappeared like some demon manifesting itself. Later, she would realize he just moved so fast his image hadn't retreated from her field of vision. His light brown skin had a gleam to it. It reminded her of a time one of her johns took her to a candy store and she gazed at the rows of sweets. He let her pick one, and she chose a caramel that glistened like amber under the shop lights.

He swooped her up in his arms in a loving gesture, but with a grip that felt like iron bands and had her in an embrace that she couldn't squirm out of.

"Save the fight for others," he said. "We could use someone with your fire, your stamina. I could use your...passion."

He put his lips up to her neck and she felt a quick pain, like a pinch. She tried to scream out, but the breath caught in her throat and instead a whimper came out, barely a whisper, and with nobody around to hear it even if it had been loud enough to break the glass of the windows all around them.

He was locked onto her with his lips, and as she struggled, she tried to figure out what was happening to her, what in the whole wide world he could have been doing to her. She began to feel lightheaded. She could feel the pull on her neck and could tell her blood was flowing from her to him. She was surprised, thinking it should have hurt, but instead it felt pleasant, like the walls of the entire world could have come crashing down on the both of them right then and there and she would not have had the least bit of concern about it all happening.

She knew she should be resisting, but it felt so impossible, like trying to sit straight up when she was about to fall into a dreamy sleep, only if this time she fell asleep, it would be the end of her life that she drifted into.

He released her from that kiss, but still held her tight in his arms. His were like a parent's holding a child, she couldn't get out of his grip if she had a long steel bar to pry them off like the working men in the street used. They reminded her of when her father used to grip her too hard when he was using his blind and stupid strength to lord it over her that she was helpless in his power. But this man's were gentle and full of a delicate grace like some dancer who could weave and sway in perfect time to a rhythm, while her father's had been calloused and clumsy, like sacks of meat.

She felt cold, like all the blankets in the world wouldn't bring any heat to her body. Why was the night so cold all of a sudden? It had been so humid that a dog would sweat and a grown man would pant. She swore it couldn't have cooled off so quickly. Maybe she had imagined it all because this didn't feel real. It had to be a dream. None of this could really have been happening. Only she couldn't wake up. Whenever she was in a dream this scary she could always wake up.

And then, in answer to her thoughts, he caressed her and said in his soothing voice, "I'm afraid this is not a dream, my sweet one. We're here in the street and this is life itself, as crazy as it seems." This only added to her confusion, his replying to her thoughts. What was happening, and why was she struggling to stay focused on anything? The man holding her was warmth itself. If she could just curl up to him, she could get her strength back and everything would be okay.

"I drank your blood," he stated, matter of factly. He might as well have told her the sky is blue in the daytime. "Now, there's one of two ways this could turn out for you, my little fighter. Yes, you're so strong. Even now you want to fight for life, you're just what we need."

He gazed longingly into her face with a stare that the light danced in, as his inky dark irises glistened with a piercing fire that struck her slowly beating heart and made it race. It captured her attention the way a rodent must freeze up before a cobra, a Gorgon can turn a person to solid stone.

"The first option is I could finish the last drops from you. And you could find out what waits beyond the gates of mankind's ultimate common bond. You could surrender to the real eternal night and let death come on you like sleep. Just like our friends there."

He gave a nod towards her would-be attackers. They had seemed so fierce to her at some point. When was that? Was that this night? It seemed so far away, but she knew it must have been recent.

They were dolls that some giant child had carelessly discarded, playthings for a fairytale creature. Only the blood from their throats was real, the careless twists of broken necks, hanging at awkward angles that no maker of toys would ever put in something made for children.

"The second," he sighed, turning back to her, "is you could join me and drink deeply of the joy of a million nights. You can see things from a vantage where time has no meaning. You will no longer have to hide in corners or crawl in fear, because you will be the thing that men fear. All you have to do is give yourself to me."

Her eyes welled up with tears. What more could she do? She knew as soon as death was on the table that she would do anything to avoid it. Let the chips fall where they may, damn the consequences, and damn the rest of the world too if it came between her and a chance at life.

"Give yourself to me," he repeated, as he ran one of his incisors, gleaming like a little dagger made of pearl, across his wrist, "and drink."

The blood splashed into her mouth and it sent electric shivers through her. She felt warm all over, like she was having a fever, but this was full of tingling sensations that went through every particle of her body, not the chills and aches from some common flu.

It was as if every last speck of her body had come to life, only it wasn't something that had been lit up within her for the first time, more like a memory of its fullest potential for feeling that every cell in her body had, but had forgotten in the regular use of life. She thought she was in the throes of an orgasm for a second, but realized the sensation was not dependent on any physical stimulation from outside, just reacting to that warm taste that was filling her mouth and everything within.

She latched on, greedily, instinctively as an infant on its mother's breast latches on, no thinking involved, just that primal need for that hunger to be satiated. She had always done what she had to to survive, this was no exception, only this time survival had never felt so lovely to her in all her chaotic little life.

Her mind was filled with images that had to be from his mind, images of a time and place that she had never experienced. Images of the painted streets of ancient Persia. Gardens in Ecbatana and all the trees that were so full of ripe and delicious fruit that their limbs were bowed under with the weight of all that life-in-bloom.

She knew what it was like to have walked under the same sun that the Achaemenid kings had walked under, a eunuch in the court who was admired and courted by powerful men. She knew what it was like for him to fear that sun that could take away his power as a drinker of blood when he was made one himself, by another who was ancient even then.

A great convocation of blood drinkers who ruled behind the scenes of what was once the largest empire in history revealed itself to her in the vision. They shaped events until their people were routed by Macedonian Greeks, mere barbarians and savages who should not have been able to take down the most sophisticated government the world had ever seen at the point, but those shepherds and rustics rose up and defeated their armies, forced them to give up their designs of power.

It was centuries after that, that the blood drinkers of the world decided to not try to rule directly over the humans anymore, but instead broke up into factions that all swore by some sacred truce to never let any of the others rise up too high to threaten and command mortals with their designs. They would never directly interfere in the politics or religions of the people again. They went from ruling the world to fighting each other over the scraps of it.

But they were once lords of all creation!

They had believed they were ahuras, servants of Mazda the lord of wisdom and justice, in his battle against evil and that they were divinely bringing about order in the world. They were idealists and fools, and they soon realized that even immortals are like humans in their struggles for power and their squabbles.

Even immortals bleed for their foolish causes.

He had rambled on and on throughout the centuries, watching empires fall and kingdoms rise. Seeing peoples scattered to the wind and the winds cover cities with dust. He was searching for a purpose, something to give the centuries meaning, when the Firstborn of Death came along

Its influence on him was powerful, but his mind wasn't giving up the secrets about it, even though she felt its impact like an all-consuming lust. She knew that this powerful band of immortals was why he was bringing her over into this power. So she could become something fierce and strong, that would change the world into something beautiful and new instead of the smoking industrial horror that it was struggling towards.

The sublime visions of his blood communicated this to her in a rapture that seemed like it would last forever and blot out any other experience she'd ever had before. All pleasures before this seemed pale in comparison. All her dreams before seemed limited in scope. Every desire seemed fulfilled in her feeding on that intoxicating stream of pure rose red light.

He gave a soft cry of pain, and withdrew his arm, and she almost cried out for more, but it instead came out as a little moan of surprise to have the world come back into focus. She glanced around and realized the night was different from any night she had ever seen. Everything appeared alive and breathing, even the stones in the streets and the little pieces of paper whipped about in the air like birds fluttering through the night.

The sky wasn't like any night she had ever seen before. Things were in focus that she knew should have been obscured by shadowiness and that gloom was less an inky black but more a violet and indigo expanse of flowing velvety blankets of vapor that she could almost reach out and touch.

He let her down lightly, and she spun around, marveling at everything she was seeing, not believing that this was how the world could be and realizing that she was alive in a way she had never been before, nothing could compare to it. Not sex, not fine food to eat in a fancy restaurant, not the feeling of wrapping herself up in a warm blanket on a cold night. All of these things that she had thought to be the best things life had to offer were as strange as seeing the clothes you had worn as a child and wondering where your mind from that era was and what it was like to be you at that time.

Her strange savior was staring at her with sympathetic eyes and a bemused grin. "You are now one of the Firstborn of Death," he informed her. "Enjoy the hunt."

He kissed her hard on the mouth, biting her lip and there was that electricity again, that spark of togetherness in ecstatic bliss, and she knew she would follow him to the ends of the earth.

ABOUT
THE AUTHOR

CHARLES LAWRENCE CLOSE III
got this story rolling during the pandemic
when he should have been working on his
capstone project for his master's degree at
Johns Hopkins in NGO management. He
wrote enough to fill two books and still
managed to pull straight A's and graduate
with high honors. The Blood Thief, Vol. 1 is
sort of his first book. He also wrote a Jack
Kerouac style novel about his crazy times

living in Mexico and Russia, but he felt it was a little self-indulgent
and will probably revise it at some point when he gets all the fictional
characters spinning around in his brain a home on paper. Vol. 2 of
Alex Rose's adventures is well on the way!

Charlie cares deeply about giving back to the community and believes that doing unto others as you would have them do to you is the best way to live. When he isn't volunteering for a nonprofit, you can find him skating Pride parades with a synchronized dance crew, practicing jian-fa, learning the piano or turntables, and climbing cliffs and gym walls like a savagely dazzling, inappropriately velvet-wearing creature of the night.